GW00792437

Blackstone & Brenwen

The Mirror & The Meretrix

by

Andrew D. Mellusco

To Iowa.

A Story if ever there was one, & my new favourite.

x

First published in Great Britain by Lulu.com, 2006

First Edition

Lulu.com

ISBN 978–1–84753–989–2

For Hiren

1

"Mr Blackstone!" boomed Judge Hallbjorn, mindful that his voice might not reach the sixty feet to the tiny Defence lawyer standing far below. "You may now begin your closing arguments!"

Elliot Blackstone took a deep breath and then confidently approached a towering wooden staircase that stood in the centre of Hillock Court. He had requested an elevated platform be built at eye level to the Jurors, each one a comparable size to a ten-storey human building, for two reasons. The first was the necessity to always rise up to every challenge met, which was a particularly inspiring pearl of wisdom his uncle Asmodeus Blackstone, the senior partner at his law firm, had once taught him. The second reason was a much more safety conscious one, for having spent much of the first week staring up into the faces of the judge, jury members and those in the gallery Elliot feared that to continue in such a vein would be to risk a semi-permanent and undoubtedly painful injury to his neck.

Taking to the first step, the young lawyer felt slightly disgruntled that some form of lift system had not been built into the structure and that again he would have to tackle the 169 steps to the platform far above. On each preceding day of the trial the great ascent had left Elliot feeling rather breathless, with him needing to take at least a few minute-turns to compose himself, and catch his breathe, before he would allow one statement to leave his mouth. The arduous climb aside, he had gained some small satisfaction, however, in using what was akin to a siege tower in delivering each of his thunderous arguments to a court of Giants.

Today, however, would be different. Not only would it mark the conclusion of a two-week long trial, and an end to the steps, but today Elliot was offered a helping hand from a particularly attractive blonde – juror number two, Rona Arna – who had taken a liking to the young attorney since the trial had began.

Miss Arna slowly knelt and, with arm outstretched, placed an upturned palm in front of the little man. Though extremely grateful Elliot, always mindful of correct courtroom etiquette, first looked to Judge Hallbjorn for approval and was pleasantly surprised to see the adjudicator display the tiniest of grins upon his bearded face. Most Atlations felt that physical contact with Humans was a nuisance and was generally something to be avoided, unless it was in the process of eating them of course (a practice considerably curbed by virtue of the Treating Humans Humanely Act of Arbor, enacted three-hundred ring years before Elliot was born, much to his relief). Judge Hallbjorn, on the other hand, was different. He respected Humans in the same manner as Humans might have respected army ants for accomplishing great feats far beyond their size, strength notwithstanding, for on his travels Judge Hallbjorn had come face to face with colossal man-made monuments and mountaintop bastions, deep ravine-spanning dams and artificial river systems, all crafted from hands smaller than his thumbnail. At once he recognised that these tiny folk were actually quite clever and resourceful – two traits he often found lacking in some of his fellow kind. Watching Rona's outward show of kindness to Elliot the Judge was pleased that he might not be alone in his fondness for these pint-sized people.

For Elliot it was certainly a new experience as he carefully leapt onto the kindly juror's hand. A Teller had once read his palm as a child and she had gripped his wrist so tightly as she pulled his hand towards her that the experience wasn't entirely without pain, and that was even before she announced his rather grim death shortly after he would turn thirty-one. It wasn't as if the Teller Briana Ce'aul was overly frivolous with her premonitions of doom, but what Elliot remembered most was her grey beady eyes straining to study each crease and indentation of a hand that had yet to toil against the harshness of adult life.

Elliot did not have to focus too hard as he looked down at the giant hand beneath him. It was like studying one of the huge topographical maps that hung upon the walls of his old schoolhouse – each delicate line of Rona's hand looked like a county border, each vein a winding river system.

About halfway to the platform Rona rose from her knees in order to take to her feet, the movement of which caused the lawyer to tumble forward into a surprisingly controlled front-roll across her palm.

"Sorry," whispered Rona.

"With hands this soft, you shall never need to apologise," Elliot replied with all the charm he could muster. Only an outstretched hand upon Rona's wrist had prevented him from continuing down her forearm, and as he regained his balance Elliot distinctly noticed a quickening of her pulse. As he looked into Rona's kind and brilliantly blue eyes he couldn't restrain himself from raising a rather mischievous eyebrow. Whilst he did enjoy the company of tall and attractive women, with more than 94 feet between them, Elliot did realise that perhaps this time even he was aiming too high.

Elliot hopped on to the platform as it came level, bowed graciously to Rona before turning to face the rest of his now attentive audience. He straightened his tie, pulled the collar of his pinstripe robe flat against his neck and began.

"Ladies and Giantmen of the court. There is no doubt that my client is a moron. What man upon this earth would willingly trade his prize bullock for a handful of beans? The idea is clearly ludicrous. And yet Jack stands before you today precisely because he is an idiot."

Each of the six jurors looked down at the rather pathetic figure of Elliot's client, who was dressed in a hessian coat over a ruffled off-white shirt and who displayed an expression of constant bewilderment from beneath his tattered straw hat. It wasn't hard to believe that Jack was someone who failed to inspire much confidence in those he met.

"It was with the curiosity of a three ring-year old that Jack clambered through his window and began climbing his beanstalk that fateful morning. Upon reaching the top he came face to face with a beautiful young maiden who, surprise surprise, appears to have been familiar with Jack's own accuser Halvard!" the young attorney proclaimed.

Elliot then half turned, so that his back was not to the jury, tipped his head to the right and shot a piercing gaze towards a brutish looking giant sitting behind prosecution's row.

"Lest we forget that under oath Halvard has admitted being in that maiden's presence on no fewer than three occasions!" the clever lawyer continued.

As Halvard's face rapidly reddened with embarrassment, the grim looking giant, clad in a studded leather tunic and iron skullcap, quickly broke off his eye contact with the lawyer to look down at the thumbs that he was nervously twiddling.

Elliot, now in full swing, directed himself back to the jurors.

"That same mysterious maiden convinced Jack, with methods only known perhaps to the most deviant, that all that lay within Halvard's vast dwelling was in fact his own. And yes, of course he believed her. What a week Jack was having… not only to come into the possession of five magic beans, but for those beans to lead him up to a treasure-laden castle that was actually his! Only a village idiot would accept such good fortune without so much as a second thought.

"Perhaps it was due to Jack's feeble and impressionable infant-like mind that Idona, the accuser's own wife," he bellowed before spinning on his heels to point at a rather discomfited brunette in the front row of the public gallery, "managed to entice this poor man with relative ease?" Elliot turned back to the jury and composed himself before continuing in a quieter and more solemn tone.

"With open arms she welcomed Jack into her husband's home. I submit to you that Idona's gesture was no more that an act of seduction provoked by the twisted womanising her husband had committed, designed to get back at the one man who had made her feel like *the other woman*."

Idona sprang to her feet, blubbered what sounded like 'but… but…' then ran from the court with her face in her hands, sobbing rivers as she left. *Hmm, I couldn't have planned this better if I'd tried,* the young lawyer confidently thought to himself.

During the course of the trial Elliot had patiently and carefully chipped away at the credibility of all of the prosecution witnesses and now, at the end, all he needed to do to elicit the reaction he wanted was to hammer home the truth of previous assertions. As exemplified by the dramatic guilt-ridden exit of Idona it became apparent that Elliot's very hard work had not been in vain.

"Little did she know, however, that her husband had come home early from his night shift and was half-awake, readying himself for bed, while his wife was outside swiping at clouds for the morning brew. With the finely tuned nostrils of a true man-eater, Halvard sought out the hapless human that had stumbled into his home. It was in the pursuance of… what was it? Oh yes, 'grinding Jack's bones to make his bread', that the giant descended into a blind rampage, turning over every pot, pan and urn to uncover the hiding place of my cowardly client."

There was a stir amongst the jurors. Elliot knew that the Giant race's penchant for flying into uncontrollable rages was one characteristic the Atlation community considered a taboo and one of those traits not openly talked about, especially at gatherings. *Keep going, almost there,* Elliot contemplated as he took another deep breath in preparation for his next assertion.

"I submit to you that this whole sorry affair, was in fact a diversionary tactic! This orchestra of destruction was the end game of a very well constructed plan. The mysterious maiden was a pawn wooed by an enticing melody. All the players in fact were used as part of a complex plan of escape."

Elliot could see from the corner of his eyes that the gallery members, as well as the jurors, were now on tenterhooks.

"The instrument of Jack's entrapment was none other than that!" Elliot revealed as he dramatically swept his arm downward and pointed accusingly at a little golden harp below him.

Though tethered to a post the harp tilted up to look at its accuser, plucked its lowest string as if in protest then, quite surprisingly to the court members witnessing, it performed a double back flip and started playing. To the tune of 'Pop Goes the Weasel' the fifteen giants within the great courtroom quite suddenly dozed off.

The exhausted and disconsolate Defence lawyer dropped his gaze to his shoes and then, as if the sky had come crashing down on top of him, Elliot fell on to his back, placed his hands behind his head and sighed. His drive to reveal the truth to the court had made him forget that the only way the giant inhabitants of Atlatia can fall asleep is to music. By prompting the harp to react Elliot had unwittingly incapacitated all upon Hillock Court bar himself and his client.

"Well that's just great. What the hell am I doing here?" Elliot whispered to himself. He did however see the funny side of it, how the loudest court in the land that normally boomed with legal oration had suddenly fallen into an ominous silence. There he was lying quite peacefully amongst a gathering of sleeping giants, a rather nervous half-wit of a client and a dancing harp that was playing what sounded distinctly like ice cream vendor music.

"I told you so, didn't I?" yelled Jack from below. "The bloody thing is mental." He looked at the harp with an expression of one both disgusted and bemused at the sight of a sideshow freak. Defiantly the golden harp began pirouetting on the spot. "M – EN – TAL!"

Allowing the music to carry his woes away, Elliot strangely found himself recollecting his first stolen kiss with a little freckly red haired girl who had a fondness for strawberry splits. How simple it was back then, when every curiosity was another opportunity for adventure and discovery. When going fishing meant standing in a river with trousers rolled up netting Sticklebacks. Perhaps if he hadn't have put a tiny dead fish in Abigail's shoe when she wasn't looking they might still be together. He gently chuckled to himself as he remembered the soft squishing sound as she put her shoe back on, then the girly scream that came after and then the sudden and uncomfortable impact of a plimsoll thrown at his head soon after that. Though they still remained friends Abigail grumpily chose to end their 'sittin' in a tree, K-I-S-S-I-N-G' moments the following day.

"How do I shut it up?" Jack anxiously queried.

"Just throw your coat over it," Elliot called down as he got back to his feet.

Jack wrestled his coat over the hyperactive instrument, which turned out to be more of a struggle than he thought it might be, and the muffled strings of the harp finally broke off from its merry tune and with a strained off-pitch C-minor in despair it toppled over onto its side. The lawyer waited patiently, though perhaps a little apprehensively, for the court to awaken.

Three turns of an hourglass had gone by before the sleeping giants began to rouse from their unscheduled snooze. The sweltering heat of the day gave way to a cool still air as the sun receded beneath the horizon and the young attorney pulled his thick robe around him tightly to keep warm. During those three tiresome hour-turns of waiting Elliot had considered suggesting Jack and he nip to the pub for a swift half but then quickly realised that half a pint of ale in the human realm was comparable to three barrels of the same in the giant land of Atlatia. He abandoned the idea, but not before thinking whether a Human could actually polish off 864 pints in one sitting. *Porthos perhaps, but then again he always was a drunkard* Elliot pondered. So he contented himself with studying the faces of the sleeping giants around him.

Elliot enjoyed looking at people, especially when he knew they were not looking back at him. He had a curious fascination with the way faces were actually constructed and the impressions they subsequently projected. Whether beautiful was beautiful, if ugly was ugly and indeed whether beautiful could ever be ugly and vice versa? – These were the questions he inevitably found himself pondering when studying a new face. The young attorney was convinced that the more faces he examined the closer he would come to a definitive answer. 'Ah, beauty beholding eyeballs isn't it?' Bill the Blind Barman would jokingly mock over a jug of beer, always aware when the young lawyer's concentration had drifted towards another attractive customer, client or colleague. *Hmm, but have I actually seen anything ugly I thought was beautiful?* Elliot thought to himself. He hadn't.

In glass panes, pools of water and from his shaving mirror, Elliot often studied his own face. His long-suffering friend Hiren light-heartedly claimed that Elliot's vanity was a form of social masturbation – 'a self-satisfaction gleaned from any reflective surface be it in public or otherwise.' That was Hiren's textbook definition for his friend's rather unique 'affliction'. There was no denying Elliot was handsome however. A defined chin free of fat, narrow lips, a proportional nose leading up to kind brown eyes that in turn led to sharp but medium sized brows, all handsomely placed upon an oval head topped with jet black hair, the fringe of which fell half way down his forehead. His dentist noticed that he even possessed a small mole just above the right corner of his mouth. 'That's a sign of beauty you know, and inner passion,' she once whispered inches from his face while examining a slightly chipped front tooth. That visit soon turned into the most enjoyable trip to the dentist Elliot would experience for a very long time.

The trial was only the second time he had been this close to giants, and gazing up at their house-sized heads was like looking at a Human head through a magnifying glass. On the bulging cheek of juror number four Elliot noticed the beginnings of a pimple. Juror one on the other hand was displaying the first signs of crow's feet creeping from the corners of his eyes, the creases of which resembled the tops of several pitchforks. As a child he had imagined giants to be great ugly ogre types, deformed with over emphasized features like those in the bedtime stories his mother used to read to him. The discovery that Atlations were merely up scaled versions of Humans came with a pleasant and unexpected surprise…

…Elliot, then only five ring-years of age, had spent one particularly sunny day chasing Abigail through a vast expanse of barley crop, named Brewer's Field, that ended at the base of a huge grassy hill. She had stolen his homemade fishing net, fashioned from a wooden spoon, the left outer rim of Abigail's push bike and a small potato sack, and was using it to catch butterflies.

'Its not for flutterbies… give it back' he shouted after her, but she just giggled and carried on, twirling every now and again when she spotted one of the rainbow coloured insects within arms reach. Exhausted, they reached the end of the field and were startled to find a Giant using the hillside as a stool. With mouth agape and eyes wide with fear the girl shoved the fishing net back into Elliot's hands, turned round slowly and shot off like a hare back towards town. The young boy however didn't run away or yell from the bottom of his lungs but instead took a step forward lifted his head up to the giant and quite politely said 'hello'.

'And hello to you young sir' replied the mountainous stranger smiling kindly back. Elliot carried himself up the hill and neatly placed himself down beside the giant and crossed his legs. Having already heard horrifying tales of Human-consuming Atlations the young boy always thought that he might be thoroughly terrified if ever he were to encounter such a monster in real life. When he saw that the giant was not in fact a monster, Elliot soon realised that perhaps his bedtime stories were not completely true after all and soon after that he forgot about his seemingly irrational fears altogether. Elliot noticed that instead of just one eye in the middle of its forehead the giant in fact had two, just as he did, the myth-breaking revelation of which made the whole meeting much less scary.

As the young boy began knitting together daisies into a chain he learnt that the giant had been journeying back from a rather tricky mediation between a flock of crows and a group of sparrows in a land called Av-Ery far off to the west.

'Medication?' the boy asked back.

'Me – di – a – tion,' replied the Giant slowly, 'when two people, or groups of people… or birds in this case, get into an argument which they cannot reach the end of, I come in…'

'And eat them?' Elliot interrupted. The Giant let out a great chortle that gently shook the earth they sat upon.

'No, no, I help them to stop arguing by helping them to listen to one another. When people get angry sometimes they just stop listening.'

And so the legal lesson continued for an hour-turn or so before the giant stood up to leave. He extended his little finger towards the boy, who courteously shook it with both hands.

'It was a pleasure to meet you young sir.'

'Please to meet you too, ME – DI – A – TION man,' replied Elliot somewhat carefully. He then watched as the giant strolled off to the east before popping the finished daisy chain on his head and making his way back home.

The meeting had already left an impression on the boy and, after a leisurely thought-filled stroll, he walked through the front door of his house and proceeded to tell his hysterical mother (worried with fear no doubt having been told about the random encounter by a rather shell-shocked Abigail from next door) how he met a friendly two eyed giant who told him about something called the *Law*.

'Ah! You, my lad, have just met a very important man!' his father interrupted, 'very lucky to meet him indeed, for only if you have been extremely naughty would you normally find yourself in his great presence. You haven't been naughty have you?' asked Elliot's father sternly. The boy shook his head quite innocently. 'Good, because that was Judge Hallbjorn and he is an Atlation, yes, but he is also what we call a Law Bringer.'

Twenty-three ring-years later Elliot found himself studying the face of the giant man who had first introduced him to the world of Law. He had heard that this was to be the last time Judge Hallbjorn would preside over a court and he couldn't help but feel an overwhelming sense of pride that he would now be there when the great Giant bowed out from the wondrous profession they had spent most of their lives dedicated to.

Hallbjorn outwardly bore the signs of three hundred ring-years and was time warn and weathered in feature, akin perhaps to the mild frailty of a seventy-year-old human. Elliot noted however that the Judge had not actually aged a great deal from when they first met. Since then Elliot had grown from an inquisitive boy into a relatively wise and intelligent young man, markedly changed in attitudes and appearance. *Giants must age really slowly* Elliot reflected upon. As elderly as Judge Hallbjorn might look, the retiring bastion of Law and Order was still as mentally sharp as he was when his predecessor, Judge Lagmann, had indoctrinated him into the judicial sphere 275 ring-years ago.

"Mr Blackstone, the court's apologies. Please continue," yawned the rousing Law Bringer as his eyelids lifted up like a huge pair or roller blinds.

"Thank you, your honour…" Elliot was worried that the beginning of his fiery summation would now have been lost in the minds of the court members, given their sudden departure from the realm of the waking. It was with a sense of relief then that he found that each of the six jurors were sat upright and wide awake, eagerly waiting for the lawyer to slot the last pieces of his mystery into place.

"Yes… how that stringed monstrosity of a Harp conducted the whole extravagant plan in order to free itself from its life of constant servitude," Elliot continued turning back to the jury whilst simultaneously thinking *please don't start playing again, pretty please*. The harp, smothered by Jack's coat and still tethered to a post, lay quite still. Perhaps it had worn out its strings.

"Amidst the chaos Jack was free to pocket one of the many golden treasures contained within his accuser's great hall, BUT NO, he simply ran in fear for his life." Elliot had recovered his rhythm and was pacing about his raised platform delivering his argument with increased focus and fervour.

"The sorry sight of the man standing before you this day was, and indeed still is, starved to desperation. So when a panicked goose flew up into his arms as he ran, weeping, to the comfort of his own bed, he did not stop, turn around to his rabid pursuer and say 'sorry Mr Angry Atlation I think this is yours'." *Here we go,* Elliot thought as he approached his final submissions.

"I put it to you that my client is not guilty of thievery for he *believed* that what he would find in that great castle was his very own. I put it to you that *Jack* is the victim, ensnared by the complex plotting of another. And I beg you to take pity on his sorry soul for ever being brought into, what to him still remains, a daunting and overwhelming World-Tree," pleaded the young attorney with utmost sincerity.

Each juror now looked upon Jack not with the accusatory eyes of two weeks ago but with ones of compassion and sympathy.

"I leave you now with this small thought. So much did he rejoice in the prospect of having the goose bare an everlasting supply of solid gold eggs, that the first thing he did after resting himself was to pluck the bird clean and roast it," Elliot revealed. The jurors gasped, and Elliot distinctly heard juror number six whisper 'my Thor! He really must be a moron.'

"I pray you make the right decision," Elliot concluded, throwing a last reassuring nod to juror number two, Ms Arna, who looked thoroughly convinced by the Human lawyer's powerful oration. Elliot then made his slow progress back down the steps of the great wooden tower to his concerned looking client, all the while silently thinking *bloody Caelum I'm good.*

"Many thanks for the vote of confidence, you even had me convinced at one juncture," Jack eloquently greeted in a manner far removed from his idiot persona his lawyer had represented to the jury. Elliot dramatically approached Defence council's human-sized row and returned the greeting with a firm handshake.

"Well you did eat the bloody thing Jack," the young attorney jovially replied as he gently squeezed his client's shoulder in that everything-will-be-alright way sympathetic jurors like to witness. They both turned to the Judge who was beginning his summing up.

"Fellow Atlations of the jury, the question is relatively straightforward – Did Jack possess the mental pre-requisites necessary to make him guilty of theft?"…

Thus Judge Hallbjorn continued recounting the prosecution's argument that Jack had procured the beans with the foreknowledge that they were magical, swindling the butcher who possessed them, with the intent of using them to gain entrance to Halvard's castle amongst the clouds. The Judge then recapped the prosecution's evidence. Finally he moved on to Elliot's 'idiot defence' and how it was Jack who was the unwitting victim of a devious plot of escape planned by an animated instrument that yearned for freedom, again referring to the various witnesses and exhibits the clever Human attorney had relied on to support his case.

"…I now leave you to your deliberations," concluded the Judge after forty-five long minute-turns.

The jury, eager to end the matter as quickly as possible given that they risked having to attend another day in court away from their work, refrained from leaving their stalls and huddled together each adding their own contributions to the hurried debate in hushed tones.

However, to human ears the whisperings of giants are still quite audible and each moment a juror added some new comment like 'he must be an idiot he ate it,' or 'well that harp was a bit, you know, *funny*' or 'I feel so sorry for that man's mother, he's quite the burden isn't he?' Elliot's small mouth grinned ever wider. So when juror number one finally stood up after no more than five minute-turns the young lawyer, though inwardly beaming, displayed no look of surprise when he heard those two familiar and beautiful words - Not Guilty.

"Court dismissed," called Judge Hallbjorn with a final knock of his gavel. As the gallery members and jurors dispersed Miss Arna flashed a cute wink at Elliot and exited Hillock Court with one surprisingly dainty step, considering her size. The prosecution lawyer, who had been upstaged by a fellow professional significantly smaller than he, simply bowed graciously to his opponent (quite out of character for a giant, even a legal one) before shaking the hand of the now retired Judge Hallbjorn, offering a few words of respect as he promptly took his leave.

"Good luck with your retirement your honour, it was a great experience to finally put forward a case to your good self," stated Elliot with a genuine sincerity.

"Ah yes, many thanks Mr Blackstone. It was nice to see my words to you those many ring-years ago were not wasted," replied the judge courteously.

He remembered thought Elliot quite contented with himself as he watched the great Law Bringer stroll silently away.

But as Elliot extended a last congratulatory hand to his jubilant client something quite unexpected happened. Halvard, Jack's accuser, had returned to collect his golden harp, and as the grumpy looking giant flicked the ragged coat that had smothered the instrument back to Jack, the harp, which had been muffled and restrained, leapt back to life with the tune of 'Ring-a-Ring o'Rosies'.

Halvard's eyes slowly drooped and his great towering bulk swayed slightly before, quite suddenly, he came crashing down like a hewn Oak upon Jack, ending the poor unfortunate fellow's life in an instant. There the giant remained as he dozed gently off to sleep. With that the golden harp merrily bounced off into the distance, finally making good its escape.

Elliot stood there utterly astonished and for once in a long time was incapable of conjuring a coherent statement adequate enough to describe his feelings of amazement and horrification. Looking up he could still see retired Judge Hallbjorn in the distance.

"Erm, YOUR HONOUR!" yelled the extremely perplexed young attorney. It was going to be a long night.

2

The woman in the red riding hood sprinted through the forest with all the speed and grace of an antelope. As she tore past the moonlit greys of the dense foliage surrounding her stray branches seemed to lash out and a particularly sharp thorn had already sliced a deep gash into the young woman's scarlet robes. Dew-like beads of sweat slid down her arched back and mingled into the fresh wound beneath her cloak, the sting of which caused a sly grin to momentarily spread across her thin lips. There was a distinct feeling of liberation as she vaulted one tree stump and skipped over another and the girl imagined herself a free and untamed animal as her crimson cloak billowed behind her like the fiery tail of a lioness caught on the wind of a bloody chase.

The wood opened up into a small clearing where she briefly paused to catch her breath. One might have imagined her bent double grasping her knees as she snatched deep gasps of air into her lungs. She was a picture of complete calm however as her bosom softly rose then fell in controlled exhalations. What was bearing down on her could not be far now and the distant rustle of disturbed leaves warned her that it was perhaps closer than she had anticipated.

The subtle glow from a half-covered moon splashed across her face and, tossing her head back to stare into the thick vegetation she had emerged from, one could note a mischievous sparkle in her emerald green eyes. Displaying an unmistakeable air of confidence she stood there, waiting, unmoved by the apparent desperation of her situation and oblivious to the ravages an inhospitable environment such as the forest might reap upon a young maiden like her.

"Come on, where are you?" she whispered. A twig snapped in the distance and she bolted like a suddenly disturbed young deer.

Silva-Tenebrae Forest, on the borders of the Royal city of Delator, was a sprawling tangle of gnarled trees and twisted undergrowth that covered an area of several counties. Though there were those few that had sought their livelihood within its unwelcoming confines, hewing trees and gathering wild fruit from the forest floor, many considered the woodland cursed and a place not to be entered into with impunity. Tales were told of witches and other undesirables that kept dwellings deep inside the forests heart, and how once in a while an ominous green mist could be seen creeping over its thick canopies at dusk.

'They're up there brewing potions and whatnot, to send those that might enter all confuddled. And then, when your mind is all but dazed, they'd take yer they would and feed off yer till your naught but bone. Ah yes they'd have fine dining off a babbie like you.'

That's what the elders of the surrounding Delatorian villages would tell their more curious of children, tales they half believed in themselves, to scare the young into thinking twice before going exploring within that dismal place. But a small minority, such as our fleeing maiden, felt an affinity towards those older oaks that stood unshakably within, in whose knots she imagined ancient mysteries born, flanked by wild-flowers that seduced her with their hypnotic scents. She considered the forest a place of great serenity, undeserving of its less than wholesome reputation, and at every opportunity she would don her warm rouge velvet cloak to delve ever deeper into the wood's magical surroundings.

From the age of sixteen ring-years onwards her excursions had become more risqué; dancing naked before an audience of bluebells, stalking unicorns to watch them make love or wrapping herself unashamedly in the dying leaves of an autumn fall. *Is this what it means to be close to nature?* the girl would silently ponder as if some lone Eve in a garden all her own.

On numerous occasions young men of the royal court would find themselves under some strange spell, should ever their gaze have fallen upon her, for she was most enchanting. A swift slap from their disapproving chaperones would soon bring them back to their senses, however dull those might be. She once overheard the gossip of the older, wiser, courtesans referring to her as a Siren or some other magical creature unleashed to maintain the balance between the sobriety of courtly life and the wild abandon of the forest beyond. This would certainly satisfy her more than the rants of others who would silently collude that 'she would sooner steal away yer son and ravage 'is heart out than stew a good broth… the slut.'

But she never did concern herself with the prejudices of others. In Silva-Tenebrae Forest she found peace amongst the flora and friends amongst the fauna, and neither judged her.

The girl had kicked off her shoes at the beginning of the chase and now the soles of her feet were cut and bloodied. But still she ran. She might have been found gently licking her wounds clean in other circumstances, mimicking the traits of the wildlife around her, yet tonight there would be no time to tend to the bloody scratches of her wounded limbs. Her sprint would soon come to an end by a river that ran parallel to the eastern edge of the forest, the unrelenting torrent of which barred all from crossing. It was the only body of water in all of Arbor that was not affected by the World-Tree's three lunar bodies. Fighting the current at night would be foolhardy even for her. But, then again, escape was never her intention.

The sound of waves crashing against stony banks met the young maiden's ears and slowing now to a steady walk she pushed aside the last of the undergrowth and came to the river's edge.

The starlight above, free from the barriers of Silva-Tenebrae's lofty boughs, flecked the river's mirrored surface like snow flakes on a slate roof. She stood, momentarily transfixed, gazing at the miniature bursts of light dancing on the water's bobs and ebbs.

Approaching, with more curiosity than caution, she extended a pale smooth leg towards the raging waters as if to tame it, before allowing her arched foot to trace spirals upon the lapping waves. Her posture had caused her silk slip of a nightdress to ride above her thighs revealing the tiniest of goose bumps raised to her skin's surface by the river's icy touch.

She stood quite still as the crackling of broken branches sounded the arrival of her pursuer. She also restrained herself from turning around as the warmth from the stranger's towering figure cascaded onto her neck. Yet the beast did not touch her, even as the moon's soft glow highlighted her smooth skin and delicate curves.

The barrel-like chest of the Wolven heaved violently with each intake of breath as the beast recovered from the long and arduous chase, having apparently suffered more than the maiden it had been eagerly pursuing.

Though proportional in size and breadth to a fully-grown Wolven it appeared to stand awkwardly balanced upon its hind paws. If it had toes one might claim the beast was standing on their tips. The calves were noticeably under-developed, lacking the rigid tendons, protruding muscles and bulging veins. As it traced the outline of the maiden's waist with its overweight digits some would also be hard pressed to find similarity with the spindled fingers and knife-like claws of one of its more terrifying brethren. However, its fur was unmistakably Wolven, a matted dirty grey of deep plush, knotted in parts and spiked in others.

Suddenly the girl tore the cloak from her shoulders and slipped her fingers beneath the hem of her nightdress. Like a reptile discarding an aged skin she pulled it over her head and away from her hourglass shaped figure it seemed to lovingly cling to. With a flick of the wrist she tossed the silken wrapping into Restless River, where it was violently dragged away by the gushing torrent.

It would have taken a monster of much discipline to keep from ravaging the naked beauty at that moment, yet as the blood of the Wolven flooded to all its extremities it knew it had neither the self-mastery nor the inclination to deny itself such a rare prize.

Its breath became audible now, and its grunts and gasps and snapping of sharp jaws threatened to overload the maiden's senses.

She feared she might lose herself at any moment, as if her mind was being flayed by some insanity-inducing opiate.

In defiance she had thrown off her human wrappings as if to proclaim to the World-Tree that she was one with nature, to be treated no differently from any other animal that walked upon Arbor's surface. But now her heart began to pound wildly within her chest. Nervous anticipation and fear and confusion all came together now in merciless swathes. She felt herself swoon and had to firmly replant her feet to maintain her balance. Her gaze fell to her reflection cast upon the river's black surface. *Twenty-seven ring-years and it had come to this,* she thought as her eyes looked over her naked body.

She closed her eyes, whispered something that sounded like 'forgive me', then turned and pounced upon the Wolven.

*

Now, had 'Peeping' Tom been observing the scene then he may have noticed the distinct lack of tearing of flesh or splattering of blood, cries and yelps or moans that would normally be associated with a Wolven feasting upon a maiden. However, on the whole, the display was arguably more carnal than carnivorous. The sway of hips and the thrust of pelvic regions were quite telling, as were the profanities that issued from the maiden's mouth as she sat straddling the beast.

Tom may have even said, "hmm, this isn't right," or perhaps, "surely human-animal loving is still illegal in Delator?" Though given his voyeuristic disposition he may simple have continued watching whilst having a good hard think about it.

*

Thirty passion filled minute-turns later the young maiden lay spent upon the beast's body, running her moisten fingers through the Wolven's thick mane. Oddly the creature did not wince or shudder as she reached round the back of its neck and grasped suddenly at a mottled tuft of fur at its base.

With a slow pull she parted the head from its neck and, with arm outstretched towards the moon, held it aloft like a druidic trophy.

"My fair maiden Abigail, you are quite magnificent," exclaimed a particularly handsome man, relieved to be rid of his stifling Wolven mask.

There was no reply. Instead the girl tilted her head down and gazed softly into his light blue eyes, her onyx hair splashing across the man's flushed face.

"I've something to tell you Abigail, something quite important."

Eager to maintain the peace of silent post-coital reflection the maiden put a finger to his lips.

"The other night, when I came to visit you, I saw something... something," he continued, unabated yet with an air of trepidation.

"What is it sweet – "

"Don't. You know when you're with me...."

"Very well Hansel… why on Arbor you use that name still mystifies me. What's the matter? Can't we just lie here?" the maiden pined.

"I think I may have put our relationship in jeopardy," Hansel admitted.

With a furrowed brow Abigail retracted her head from his and narrowed her gaze, only to meet an equal display of concern in the eyes of her lover.

"You know my parents would never –"

"Never understand your unwholesome fascination for role-playing?" the maiden mockingly joked.

"Abigail this is serious, you're a Meretrix and –"

"I thought you said that title didn't matter."

"Not to me, but..."

"Just tell me what's wrong," Abigail worriedly queried.

Hansel breathed a heavy sigh and began to tell Abigail what was weighing so heavy on his mind and his heart, how he witnessed a murderous gang commit a daring robbery in his own home.

*

"...And that's why I don't know what to do," the young man concluded.

"But you can't! What if they escaped? They'd kill you for testifying," Abigail replied.

"What choices have I? If I don't then they'll be released anyway and they might steal from us again… or worse. But if I do…"

"If you do then you'll be questioned as to why you were wondering the corridors at night," Abigail correctly guessed.

"I fear the Magistratum will compel me to tell the truth to maintain any credibility."

"They don't know who you are do they?"

"They only know me as Hansel," the young man sighed.

Abigail gently shook her head and began kissing his cheek and nuzzling his neck. "Always playing the valiant knight Hansel."

"It's the right thing to do."

"I know… and you say that no one knows who you are yet?"

"Not by my true name… not until I've worked out how to keep you out of the picture," Hansel gallantly replied.

"My hero, always looking to protect me. Always failing to look after himself," the Meretrix bitterly added in conclusion.

"Abigail?"

There was no reply. The maiden's eyes had glazed over as if she was in some kind of trance.

"Abigail?" Hansel repeated.

"My name is Riding Hood," the maiden gently whispered into the young man's ear. "Riding Hood."

Suddenly she yanked back the head of her lover with one swift jolt and sank her teeth deep into his exposed larynx.

As she ripped out his throat a scarlet plume of warm liquid arched into the air, splashing her face like a crimson waterfall. Her left hand gripped the man's thick neck and, with rhythmic squeezes, caused fresh spouts of blood to issue from the gaping wound in his windpipe. She lapped at each jet of liquid like a child might at a drinking fountain, audibly gulping as she washed down the remnants of his torn flesh. With an air of detachment she paused briefly to stare down at his contorted face.

Hansel could only muster a gurgle as his pale eyes rolled into the back of his blood sodden head. His arms flailed up momentarily with one last reflexive twitch before he slipped quietly away.

Abigail rose to her feet with a drunken sway. She stared at the Wolven mask she had taken up in her left hand, raised it high above her shoulders and ceremoniously placed it over her head.

"We crown thee Princess Riding Hood!" she bellowed back to the forest. Then she tiptoed to the rivers edge and elegantly swan-dived into its dark abyss.

For once in two thousand ring-years Restless River dulled to a silent trickle.

3

The offices of Blackstone & Associates were not the most simple in the land to locate. Its frontage had no grandiose lobby with which to welcome its clients and it had no banner or flag boisterously displaying its company crest to all who passed by.

It was quite unlike the mirrored towers of opulence one would otherwise find in the capital city of Delator. Markedly different, one might say, from the polished pyramid of Toot & Carman (reputedly visible from space) or the labyrinthine complex of Apollodorus Dysklus & Partners, where young trainee associates might find themselves suddenly lost amongst miles of law-library shelving but for a ball of twine trace their steps back perhaps.

Elliot's office however was located in Tartarus several hundred meters below Arbor's surface; a subterranean realm hollowed out of the World-Tree's network of thick roots.

No one outside of Blackstone & Associates quite knew all there was to know about the practice, and it was this air of mystery that Asmodeus Blackstone, the firm's most senior partner, valued more than any other facet of the firm.

Maintaining the mystery was not particularly difficult given that entrance was granted to those wishing to retain the firm's services, not by revolving door or beaming receptionist but through a rather intricate ritual involving a pentagram (exactly eight feet in diameter and painted in goats blood) and a tooth (used by the five fairies who worked in accounts to identify the clients they subsequently billed). So it was that children, whose adult teeth were painfully pushing out the younger ones, were told by their parents 'best keep these safe, you never know when you'll need the Blackstone's to bail you out of trouble.'

Some considered that the ritual was overly elaborate and off-putting for those who wished to contact the firm, but those same individuals realised that a contract of representation with Blackstone & Associates was not one to be entered into lightly. In any event, anyone not working or residing in Tartarus had little choice but to engage in the arcane practice for it was the only way to lift the curse that was originally placed on that under-region by the Angelics of Caelum a thousand ring-years before. Newly appointed lawyers could come as they pleased by virtue of having their contracts of employment signed in blood – in essence their blood presence never left the offices at all.

The lawyers at Blackstone's were ruthless - capable of making grown Giants cry, intelligent - rumour has it that one senior partner separated Solomon from half his wealth in a particularly tricky divorce settlement, and they were foremost expensive.

The legal landscape had changed much in the thousand ring-years that Blackstone's had been in business and the idea of justice and the pursuit of justice had become separated only by wealth. The high demand for quality lawyers had driven up the profession's wage bracket, a cost that was inevitably passed on to the client. Given that the poverty stricken had little by way of their own teeth anyway meant that Blackstone's client base was predominantly made up of those who, whether they kept their baby teeth or not, could afford to have any removed adult ones subsequently replaced.

Elliot on the other hand believed that poor and rich alike should have the right to an equal quality of service. As such the young lawyer regularly found his shelves full with sob-story cases and pull-at-your-heart-strings-type files from penniless clients because he believed whole-heartedly that 'sometimes the really important matters are also the least expensive' or because 'justice should be affordable for all'. These noble statements could be heard issuing from his mouth whenever his moralistic attitude was put to test or, more frequently, whenever his uncle questioned why he had not met his monthly billable target.

Priding himself on not being totally devoid of all conscience, Elliot often conducted personal visits to clients, such as the recently deceased beanstalk climber Jack, rather than have them go through the ordeal of goat sacrifices and tooth extractions.

Elliot and Asmodeus were two of 150 lawyers who worked out of Blackstone & Associates. Each came from varying educational backgrounds and origin. Vincent Traum, for example, worked in the Corporate Finance Department, was educated at Bartlette's School of Weights and Measures, was the only son of two Dream-running parents and was also a chronic insomniac, often falling asleep at random moments in his office but rarely in his bed at night.

Life at the firm was a great leveller. It mattered not what lineage a person might claim, or what an individual's family fortune amounted to, or even the manner and locale in which one was educated, for at Blackstone & Associates the first step was always the bottom step – and this was the same for every new trainee. There was no favouritism as was ripe in other firms of its stature. As a matter of fact getting along at the firm was simply a case of winning or losing. By winning more cases than are lost one could then readily justify their ongoing worth to those above them, especially when the annual pay review period came around – it was basic profit or loss. The usual playground excuses of 'but my dad is head of…' or 'but I've had to toil and battle and…' meant absolutely nothing; if you couldn't prove yourself on the job then you just weren't ready.

During Vincent Traum's first week, for example, and after only two hours of sleep per day for the past five, he found himself before a particular stalwart Judge by the name of Rufus Serio for a standard application to stay a proceeding. Whilst Judge Serio granted the same, he subsequently went on to lecture Vincent on everything from correct courtroom attire to etiquette until the young lawyer's face had turned redder than the judge's robes. The experience still gave Vincent chills to this very day.

Having a trainee up in court during the first week was, what others might say, a cruel tradition, but Asmodeus always thought it best to 'test the ingredients before baking the pie', 'you know, see whether a trainee has the brass to stand up and take it before committing x-ring-years to training them'. Elaboration was often called for when his metaphors took on a culinary flavour.

Today began with relative serenity. The passageways were unusually free of the Hermes (human-sized butterflies of female form with wings of satin) who were normally found speeding correspondence from one office to another. Even the hot-headed Fire-Nymph Fury, in Insurance, was conducting herself in a calm and courteous manner.

All was quiet except for a feint grinding sound emanating from Elliot's office. A crack suddenly appeared in the stone vaulted ceiling high above his desk. With a soft rumbling the crack turned into a large fracture and broken fragments of earth fell to the floor covering Elliot's coffin-shaped desk with a light dusting of dirt that caused the snapping jaws of his staple remover to momentarily sneeze. The fissure then opened up wide enough to expel the attorney down into his chair fifteen feet below, and with a sound like tearing paper it sealed back up as suddenly as it had appeared.

"So out with it, how did it go?" called his uncle who was propped up against Elliot's doorframe waiting for his arrival.

"Hmm, well not great," sighed a rather tired looking Elliot as he leaned back into his black leather recliner.

"You didn't use the 'moron defence' did you? I told you Atlations are not the most sympathetic of Juries to sway."

"As a matter of fact I did, and we won as it happens. Not a bad little defence that one, I remember when you used it for that case with the Tweedles."

"Well they were complete idiots, not much convincing necessary there," Asmodeus replied stepping into Elliot's office.

He was never much a fan of Elliot's choice of décor and felt it looked more like a curiosity shop than the professional office the firm as a whole promoted itself as. His uncle's traditionalist opinions were not totally unjustified and scanning the room one could find pieces which wouldn't look out of place in a museum, or a fancy dress shop or indeed a church.

Elliot had a fondness for antiquity, gothica and masks, his favourite item being a four hundred year old Arabilisian fertility headdress – a fanned monstrosity of red, yellow and orange plume crowned with five gold phalluses, which Asmodeus now disapprovingly eyed through his octagonal spectacles. He was a great believer in uniformity in the office and each time he looked upon the assortment of weird and wonderful objects scattered about Elliot's generally untidy workspace he felt distinctly more uncomfortable with his nephew's arrangements and taste. Jarring and clashing would probably be two fitting descriptions Asmodeus might employ if he was ever to express the scene in prose. In all honesty Elliot's office, with is phallic headdress, bronzed candelabra, medieval tapestries (displaying erotic subjects derived from the more classically lewd), and open log-burning fireplace, looked more like Madame Payne's vampiric boudoir (which Elliot still earnestly claims never to have visited) and all that was missing from the sordid aesthetic was a satin draped four-poster bed. In comparison to Vincent's classically decorated workspace ten meters below in Corporate Finance, Elliot's office looked positively debauched.

"Yes. So… Jack must be pleased," his Uncle continued.

"Well that's the part that's not great, actually uncle… Jack will no longer be requiring our services… ever… he's pretty much… dead," Elliot depressingly stated as he ran both his hands through his sleek wavy hair.

"Right then, drink! I'll meet you in ten, just got to pick something up first," his uncle announced before he swept out of the office with the same faint air of disapproval as when he had tentatively entered.

It was no coincidence that the managing director of the firm had commissioned a bar to be cut within the firm's stony interior. It wasn't because he was a blatant alcoholic, as so many World-Tree lawyers were rumoured to be (like Bacchus, in the Trade & Customs team), but due to the fact that Asmodeus was a staunch believer in liquid therapy – that every problem shared over a glass of fine burgundy was a problem swiftly alleviated.

Elliot leaned back into his chair, puffed out his cheeks and breathed a long sigh, for it was only the second day of what would undoubtedly be a long week and already one of his clients was dead. He looked down at his lacquered desk, removed a piece of parchment, drew a crow's feather quill from its ornate bronze holder (a busty figurine of a young Valkerie), dipped it into a relatively large pot of sepia ink and began to write:

Mental note to self: the calling of a harp, as a witness, during a case involving Giants is not to be wildly encouraged, for the testimony of the former can often send the latter to sleep which, if left unchecked, can lead to exceptionally dire consequences for both Counsel and Client.

Elliot wiped the quill's nib clean before placing it in the hands of the particularly grateful quill-holder, the bronze figurine beaming with pride as it held the pen aloft like a bearer clutching at a standard.

All of Elliot's stationary was enchanted, a suggestion put forward by a stuttering clerk one slow and particularly tiresome summer's day.

'Labour saving devices – th... th... that's what y... you ne...eeed,' managed the clerk with desperate enthusiasm. So when it came to place his order Elliot opted for a snapping staple remover (which had now stopped sneezing and was purring quite peacefully on its side), a hole punch that self-emptied its tray when full, and a stapler whose regenerative capabilities meant that its staple-like teeth never needed refilling.

All the implements settled in quite well, until another long day of little work came about. Elliot was thumbing through a great dusty tome entitled 'Trial By Combat – What Not To Wear', contenting himself with the sharp and heady aromas that came from the aged manuscript, when quite suddenly each of the bored and frustrated implements maliciously turned on each other. It was a massacre - ink spilt, scraps of tiny metal everywhere and holes everywhere else. Whilst the young lawyer didn't mind so much he didn't want to risk the cleaners reporting the regularly untidy state of his office space to the building supervisor. Whilst the giant Mongolian Deathworm is extremely adept at digesting the waste from a medium sized office, it never likes to eat up more than it has to.

Vincent had once accidentally shredded an entire 25 volume set on 'Tackling Taxing Taxation' by Jack Horner. He had fallen asleep at one end of his longest bookshelf, his head knocking over volume 1, which dominoed onto volume 2 and so on until the whole shelf came off its bracket at the opposite end, causing each precious edition to slide perilously into the rotating teeth of Vincent's self-winding clockwork document shredder. He awoke 4 hour-turns later to find his precious reference material gone, and a ten-foot loong Mongolian Deathworm bent double in the middle of the office, moaning in indigestive agony. Elliot, ever the comedian, of course took the opportunity to remind Vincent that no normal person could ever stomach Horner, intimating Vincent's apparent abnormalities.

The day after the great stationary battle Elliot ordered the rather attractive quill-holder ('guaranteed to distress the most stressful of offices' – apparently), in an effort to calm the other stationary down. This succeeded and each of the feuding objects subsequently preferred impressing the two-inch high half-naked bronzette with feats of great efficiency instead of fighting amongst themselves. That same day Elliot took it upon himself to name each of his office implements. So it was that the staple remover was christened 'The Jaws of Doom', the stapler as 'The Steely Binder of Certain Destruction', the hole punch called 'Evil Punchy' and the brass figurine lovingly referred to as 'My Lady' or 'Sweet Cheeks' or whichever compliment Elliot wished to test on the proud but bashful figurette.

Like one might be comfortable with their sexuality, Elliot was totally happy with his want for a little fun and light heartedness. Each time he called over 'Evil Punchy', to nip at another document, he would allow himself a small smile of satisfaction of having not yet lost enough of his immaturity to have him deemed a *Lawyer*: a slower, more drawn out, pronunciation of the original which non-lawyers used while displaying a look of mock exhaustion bordering on boredom. It was perhaps also through a want to emulate his childhood hero, Judge Hallbjorn (who reputedly got younger as each passing decade went by), that Elliot steadfastly refused to take anything, not job-threatening, too seriously. So as he unwrapped his bespoke tailored cloak from his shoulders and made towards the door, it wasn't whilst crying tears of desperation or pulling at his hair in panic – totally the reverse in fact; he optimistically thought *what other lawyer can claim his client was crushed to death by a sleeping giant because of a psychotic harp bent on escape? None.* And with that he strolled off to the bar.

*

Elliot enjoyed walking from his office to the company watering hole as it allowed him time enough to visit a number of colleagues on the way, to compare workload, share interior design tips and partake in general non-work-related gossip. He also enjoyed the cavern as a whole and found it considerably more soothing to pace the polished tunnels and throughways than join the hustle and bustle of cobble and concrete above ground. Strategically placed lighting features bathed each corridor, curved staircase and shared communal area in a warm richness of gold and yellow and browns and the palette of autumnal colours often reminded Elliot of his conker swinging, tree-climbing youth.

Imagining the multitude of twisting tunnels that interconnected office space to office space, one might think Blackstone & Associates was constricted and, as a whole, relatively structureless. In fact it was the complete opposite. If one were to imagine a giant pinecone, the sweeping pines of which were actually hollow, each tip an office suite, each stem a passageway leading to a central column, then one would have a relatively accurate idea of what the office might look like if it was ever hoisted above ground. At the bottom centre of the structure, overhung by a conical atrium stretching from level twelve at its base to level one at its point, could be found Elliot's favourite place in all of Arbor: Brimstone Bar. However, there was one stop Elliot enjoyed making before sipping his first drink and that was to pay Vincent a visit, where he derived some slightly twisted pleasure in teasing the doting insomniac.

"Afternoon afflicted one!" jibed Elliot as he skipped into the Finance lawyer's office.

Vincent slowly pulled his forehead from its resting place at the edge of his desk, flopped back into his seat and gazed distantly towards Elliot's general direction.

"Looking good Vince, only three rings around the eyes today."

"Oh, it's you," replied the particularly pallid-faced lawyer in a monotone drawl, vaguely reminiscent of when Elliot first tried to speak after being subjected to five hour-turns of mind-numbing hand pagination. "So tell me about the case, I heard your client got squashed… shame," he continued half yawning half chuckling. Elliot threw himself into the swivel chair opposite Vincent, picked up a rather heavy volume on 'Fool's Gold – Leprechauns, A Historical Case Study' and slammed it down onto the table just as Vincent's eyelids were slowly closing.

"You know what helps me sleep?" asked Elliot as his suffering work colleague startled back to life.

"Please don't say it, I know you're going to say it, because you're always so unnecessarily crude."

"I wasn't actually. I was going to suggest a stiff drink."

"Please leave me alone."

"Nope. Come on loser, what else are you going to do? Sleep?"

"Arrrggghh…" Vincent cried out in tortured anguish.

"Okey dokey, suit yourself," Elliot said slowly edging towards the door, "but Fury's coming for a drink."

Vincent removed his cupped hands from in front of his face and raised his head in interest.

"Fury?" he bashfully questioned while nervously fixing his collar.

"That's right, she was asking about you the other day."

Vincent paused a moment and looked up at the ceiling with an expression of intense concentration on his face. It was as if he was weighing the pros and cons of Elliot's invitation in measured detail.

"Go on then, I'll come," Vincent eventually conceded with a sigh.

"Excellent," Elliot replied through a small but mischievous grin.

4

Elliot's law firm was a great promoter of equal opportunities and as a result was the most culturally diverse working environments one could find in all of Arbor. Elementals shared offices with Spirits, Demons with Dryads and Minotaurs with Harpies.

Vincent Traum was a Humaner. This was the Arbor classification for an individual who possessed more human characteristics than non-human – more specifically: 'A bi-pedal sentient lacking wings, scales, horns or tails. Not to be confused with Atlations who are considerably taller'.

Whilst Elliot enjoyed tormenting Vincent at every opportunity this was merely harmless banter and each considered the other a well-respected colleague and valuable friend. Each did keep at least one secret from the other however, and as they strolled to Brimstone Bar Elliot was unaware of the fact that Vincent was a third generation Sandman, and Vincent was ignorant to the truth that Elliot was a Half-Angelic who possessed two pearl-white wings pressed flat beneath his suit.

Every lawyer at Blackstone's brought some unique quality to the firm; this was one of the reasons why there was such a diversity of life within its walls, each species possessing its one individual trait that put it at an advantage to the rest. The Biblio-Vermiculi of Liber, for example, possessed photographic memories, an innate ability to recount ad-verbatim whatever text their eyes might have glanced upon. Fabianus, a particularly knowledge hungry Liberan in Research & Development, could often be found with a book in each of his ten pairs of stout hands leafing through anything from 'Intellectual Property Rights for the Intellectually Challenged' to 'Arbor-eat-them; World-Tree Delicacies'. His favourite subject however was history and especially the history of Caelum, which was directly related to the foundation of Blackstone & Associates…

One thousand ring-years ago a bloody war of ideologies took place in the celestial plane of Caelum, which was located in the highest boughs of the World-Tree that was Arbor.

Two brothers, Raphael and Asmodeus Blackstone, found themselves embroiled in a civil war that almost destroyed their realm. Raphael believed that Humans, free to explore every whim and fancy, were nothing but destructive termites eating through to the heart of Arbor's world of balance and natural order. Asmodeus, on the other hand believed that humanity's freewill instilled within that race a capacity for emotion and curiosity far beyond the comparable qualities of other World-Tree races. They were not alone in each of their beliefs and before long the Caelum Angelics divided themselves into two vast ranks.

Though their opinions were unshakable, when war descended, the brothers could not bring themselves to unsheathe their fiery swords upon the other.

After many had been slain, the victors – those that believed in the supremacy of the celestial and the subjugation of the Human race – banished their foes as well as those that refused to fight to a dark and foreboding pit at the base of the World-Tree known as Tartarus.

Amongst the root structures of Arbor the Fallen rallied and great discourses on the protection of Humanity took place. Eventually, after much debate, Raphael began to understand why his brother held the Humans in such high regard. All the while, however, Humans were having a hard time of life above ground and stories began to seep through to Tartarus about how Man was being seduced and taken advantage of by the other creatures of Arbor. So, while Raphael left Tartarus to live amongst and explore Humanity first hand, Asmodeus established the first law firm dedicated to the protection of Human interests. If an Angelic war could not win back Man's destiny then perhaps principles such as Justice and Rights could.

Blackstone & Associates was born and 978 ring-years later so to was Elliot.

After nearly a millennium of searching, Raphael discovered a profound beauty in the form of a Human woman called Sophia. She was fiery and mysterious and fun and loving and had all those other virtuous characteristics Raphael had heard his brother list time and time again during his great orations. They married and Sophia gave birth to a healthy boy five ring-years later. They named him Elliot.

Elliot's own uniqueness became immediately apparent. His senses were more acute than his Human friends and it was as if he could see the near invisible twitches of one feeling fear, or hear the quickening beat of a guilty heart. He rarely lost a game of poker. His Half-Angelic traits also magnified his underlying qualities of resilience and fortitude and, though it might not be immediately apparent to look at him, he possessed a physical strength far beyond his size and stature.

When a young Elliot met Judge Hallbjorn at Brewers Field, his human curiosity steered him ever towards a career in Law, his talents for detecting a lie-teller soon propelling him to a seat at the most prestigious law firm in all of Arbor, where his uncle welcomed him with open arms.

On his days away from the office Elliot could be found ridge-running the fractured valleys of Convallis, half a trunk away from Tartarus at the other side of the World-Tree. He could carve through the air with all the finesse and skill of a Swept-wing Blue Hawk, catching currents and updrafts that carried him clear above the boundaries of his office-cave deep beneath Arbor's surface. He never liked to boast about his wings and all but kept it secret from his work colleagues and friends bar two: Asmodeus and Fury.

"She's not coming is she, and she didn't really say those things about me," Vincent lamented as he shuffled himself alongside Elliot.

Elliot knew that his colleague had a fondness for Fury ever since she started at the firm two ring-years ago. What Vincent didn't know however was that Fury had the same feelings towards Elliot. There were even rumours amongst the Fairies in the accounts department that after some polishing one could find a neat imprint of Fury's buttocks, branded onto Elliot's desktop when he and the vivacious young Fire-Nymph from Insurance shared a particularly sizzling moment one memorable Hallows Eve. His stationary was still quite distraught some weeks after. Though Elliot could not bring himself to tell Vincent of that specific night, he could always bring himself to use her as an arousing enticement whenever Vincent was being boring.

"No and… no, but at least you're up and about," replied Elliot. "How did you know about my case? I only got back five minute-turns ago."

Vincent didn't respond.

"Come on Vince, she's really not that great… anyway I thought you had a date with that Harpy, what's her name? The High Court recorder from Aequitas?"

"Alauda? I fell asleep as she was talking about her pet basilisk dying of something or other, which didn't go down too well… as you can imagine," Vincent replied despondently

"You really should see a specialist about that, its not healthy," Elliot giggled. Vincent huffed and turned back towards his office. "Ok, I'm sorry. Just one quick drink then I'll leave you alone," Elliot quickly apologised.

"Quick drinks with you regularly have a knack of turning into six hour-turn feats of alcohol endurance Elliot."

Vincent's unique faculty was also his curse. He was the third in a line of Sandmen and, though it was above odds that he would turn out a Dream-Runner like his father and grandfather, his mother, being a Sandwoman also, practically guaranteed it.

All Dream-Runners are insomniacs sleeping only at sporadic and unpredictable intervals and only when the body can no longer function without shutting down and regenerating. Because a Sandperson can consciously live in the dream-worlds of others, feeding off another's serotonin levels to compensate for the lack of their own, they are often considered parasitical, maintaining deep sleep by planting desirable dreams in their hosts to prolong their feeding time.

There are those, however, that use their ability to dream-weave to the advantage of those who might suffer from bad dreams.

Nightmares often disrupt sleep enough to affect the waking performance of a sentient individual quite noticeably. A particularly powerful Sandman, known as a Somniator, can aid a sufferer to combat the malevolent manifestations of their subconscious and return calm to their sleep-time. This is a dangerous vocation, for a Dream-Runner exposes his consciousness to the terrifying and sometimes madness inducing Mare-worlds of the people they are trying to help. This was the profession of Vincent's father until he was fooled into entering the mind of a renegade witchdoctor, inside which he was trapped never to return to his own body. Upon his father's grave Vincent vowed never to dream-dip into the mind of a sufferer again. Had Elliot known the truth about his friend's sensitive past then perhaps his jibes at Vincent's constant fatigue may have been more restrained.

The young Sandman's skills did not go wasted however. Because both his parents had been Dream-runners he found that his abilities were so advanced that he could enter daydreams also. This was difficult for normal Sandmen because the waking mind is not so hospitable as to cater for another consciousness beside it. The benefit however was that they were safer. This is because the dream-realm of a Conscious rarely experiences shifts from one theme to another; in the whole a daydream is more stable and focused than a nightmare.

Vincent used his heightened ability, with great effect, to probe the waking dreams of his clients and their business partners in his work with the Corporate Finance department at Blackstone's. Every capitalist spends his or her waking minute-turns dreaming up new ways to make more money and inventive ways to reinvest it.

'Reading the dream-mind of a Corporate,' Vincent once mused, 'is like opening your morning paper at the finance section – dreary but decisive.' If he ever played poker he might have made a formidable opponent for Elliot.

"So I enjoy the odd drink. It never hurt anyone did it?" Elliot proclaimed in defence.

"Lest we forget the time you tried to commandeer The Jolly Roger after one too many drams of rum with Sparrow?" Vincent stated haughtily.

"So here we are. What do you fancy?" asked Elliot, quickly changing the subject, as they strolled down a gradually sloping passageway and into Brimstone Bar.

Elliot spotted his uncle sitting at a booth to the far right of the bar. The attorney tipped a cupped hand to his mouth and in response Asmodeus raised his goblet and nodded. There were a number of these private recesses carved into the circumference of Brimstone and were perfect for more discreet conferences with clients. Two-dozen rock crystal stalagmites that peaked at forty feet complemented the rest of the bar floor, upon which were speared millstone shaped tabletops. Each semi-transparent column was up-lit from the iridescent glow of Tartarus' main lava pool 200 feet further below which provided heat to the rest of the building and provided the inspiration for the name of the bar. The overall effect was quite magical as each table looked as if it was hovering on its own stream of warm golden air.

"Ah Bill, how have you been?" greeted Elliot jovially as Vincent lazily planted his elbows on the lacquered bar and rested his chin in his palms.

"I've been worse," Bill grinned, "as 'ave you. Heard your client got…" he winced.

"How does everybody know?" Elliot questioned, a little taken aback.

"Because its funny?" Vincent giggled. "I'll have a gin and tonic, a goblet of claret for the boss and if you've got a bottle of bourbon knocking about I'm sure he'll polish it off," he added nodding his head towards Elliot.

"You really ought to be takin' it easy, young sir… the liver is our friend," Bill advised, rather too gravely Elliot thought, as he plodded off prepare the drinks.

William Dante, or Bill to his friends, was one of the original Caelum Angelics that was banished to Tartarus along with Asmodeus and Raphael. Bill had lost his sight during the war and as a result was reluctant to take on a legalistic role within Asmodeus' new firm. He instead trained his other senses. His hearing was devoted to the harmonics of glass and other resonating substances whilst his nose turned to the hypnotising aroma's of crushed grape and hops. When Asmodeus suggested the firm install a bar Bill jumped at the chance of making himself useful and, whilst there were numerous spillages and bottles broken in the first few weeks, a thousand ring-years on Bill ran a bar better than any sighted barkeep in all of Arbor.

"Don't look now but it's Fabianus," Elliot whispered nudging Vincent, who was avidly paying attention to Bill the blind barman's handy work.

"How does he do that?" Vincent said completely ignoring his companion.

Elliot watched Fabianus pulsate himself along with his lower body. Quite rarely, all but the tenth pair of his hands were free, in the right hand of which was clutched what appeared to be a new scroll of appointment.

It wasn't that Elliot disliked him, but on occasion Fabianus was known to drone on about the most mundane of subjects, no doubt gleaned from the voluminous collection of works he kept perilously stacked in his office. Elliot had almost exhausted all plausible excuses in the past to escape Fabianus' lengthy debates and was grateful that this time he didn't have to fabricate the fact that he was due at Asmodeus' booth for a debrief. Elliot did respect all his colleagues however and if ever there was a piece of information that eluded him, he always knew he could turn to the enthusiastic Liberan to help him find it.

"'Ere we are gents," said Bill as he returned with the drinks. He placed a half bottle of 'Bad Mojo' (a special blended bourbon from the southern reaches of Arbor) together with a cup of ice in front of Elliot and grinned.

"Ahhh, perfect Bill just what the judge ordered," Elliot said gratefully as he spun the bottle round to examine the label.

"Hey guys. How's it going?" greeted Fabianus as he slithered over to the bar to join them.

"Good Fabes, considering…" Elliot stated still eyeing his bottle thirstily.

"Hmm wouldn't have something to do with a certain client getting squashed now would it?" Fabianus mockingly asked. Vincent, struggling to contain himself, swept up his and Asmodeus' drinks from the bar, thanked Bill and left for their booth, shoulders shuddering with suppressed laughter as he went.

"New appointment Fabianus?" asked Bill quickly changing the subject. "I could 'ear the rustle of yer freshly rolled vellum, if yer both wondering."

"What you working on? Anything interesting?" Elliot asked as he poured himself a generous shot of 'Bad Mojo' before turning to Fabianus with a smile.

"Quite extraordinary this one actually. A young woman was washed up on the lower bank of Restless River in Silva-Tenebrae forest. Some lumberjack found her totally starkers apart from a Wolven mask that she was wearing. She's been arrested for something or other," he said gently tapping the silk-tied scroll.

"Strange. Why was she arrested? How come R&D is involved? Sounds like my kind of criminal case."

"Because she's naked?" Bill chuckled.

"Well I best be getting on," Fabianus quickly announced.

"Not stopping for a drink?" queried Elliot probingly. He could sense that the middle-aged Liberan was squirming to get away.

"Nope. Just dropped in to say hi to Labiana," Fabianus replied looking over to a stalag-table at the opposite end of the bar, to a

Liberess in Civil Litigation who had her head bent over a number of witness statements.

"You are a smooth one Fabes. Then I shan't keep you," said Elliot as Fabianus turned and slowly squelched away with a slight blush on his face. "Oh, Fabes!" shouted Elliot. The Liberan turned back, his odd pairs of hands twiddling their thumbs impatiently. Elliot allowed his eyes to dart momentarily to Fabianus' scroll. "Nice waistcoat by the way, very trendy." The Liberan smiled back in appreciation before both lawyers turned away from each other to join their respective colleagues.

Elliot thanked Bill for the bottle and crossed the bar to where Vincent and Asmodeus were sat, pausing every now and then to say hello to an associate or two.

"Uncle," greeted Elliot as he took a seat opposite Asmodeus. "Fabianus seems a bit odd today, nervous almost, not his usual chatty self."

"Probably just worried about his new appointment. I could spare no one else to look over his new case. It's a matter outside his department but he's smart enough," his uncle replied matter-of-factly.

"I could take it on," stated Elliot fervently.

"But I heard the woman's already in a bad way, and you dropping a giant on her might not help her situation very much." Vincent sarcastically joked.

"Very funny. And how do know about Fabes' case?" Elliot questioned irritably to Vincent.

"I'm giving you a trainee," Asmodeus interrupted.

The two young lawyers slowly turned to look at the thoroughly satisfied expression on the face of their senior partner. Asmodeus had a similar wicked streak to his nephew and enjoyed dropping small surprises every once in a while.

"But… a trainee… I couldn't…" Elliot stammered.

"Nonsense. Its high time you passed on some of that invaluable criminal expertise to another eager soul," proclaimed Asmodeus.

"I'll have her, Sir… if Elliot doesn't want her," Vincent interjected.

"No," Asmodeus replied.

"She's a her?" Elliot asked with raised eyebrow.

"Thought that might get your attention. And she should be arriving through the doors of your office any minute-turn around now," his uncle added grinning at his ornate pocket watch.

Elliot quickly rose to his feet, his right hand still clutching his tumbler of bourbon, which he swiftly necked. He looked his uncle straight in the eyes for a brief moment. 'You mischievous old bugger, luring me down here so that I'm totally unprepared for the arrival of hopefully an attractive young trainee…' was what he wanted to say, but instead he reached inside his inner jacket pocket and removed two golden eggs.

"Fees and a damages award for Jack's family in the Beanstalk case," Elliot said smugly to Vincent as he placed the two shimmering orbs in front of Asmodeus.

"Good work Elliot, very well done," replied his uncle.

The young Half-Angelic straightened his tie, bid farewell to his colleagues and Bill and turned to exit Brimstone bar, breaking into a mad dash back to his office when he was sure he was out of sight.

"By the way she's a…" called Vincent. But it was too late. Elliot was already halfway to his office.

5

"He looks smaller than I thought he might," yawned Müde.

Unlike Elliot's father Raphael Blackstone and the other Angelics of Tartarus, the Caelum Angelics took their Human lovers by force. Those of the celestial planes considered the simple bi-pedals of Arbor with contempt and used members of both sexes as and when their sexual appetites desired. This 'Divine Right', as the Caelum boisterously proclaimed, was eventually abolished after many of the other sentient World-Tree races protested.

Those Angelics caught exercising this archaically abhorrent behaviour were now punishable under the joint laws of Arbor and subject to trial at Compenso; the High Court located in the World-Tree capital city of Delator. This was the first victory of justice over tyranny and it also had the backing of those races capable of enforcing the same. Though they were none too keen of Humans, the giant Atlations were always ready to swot offending Angelics, whom they liked even less.

"But there's something different about him," snapped Brummig impatiently. "Something's not right."

Five hundred ring-years of the practice of the 'Devine Right', however, had birthed a new species. A forced conception between Human and Angelic had measurable effects on the subsequent offspring and many that were born displayed physical abnormalities such as gigantism. Those unfortunates that were born malformed often died during delivery taking their mother's life with them. Those that survived grew to stand twenty feet in height and came to be known as Zwerg-Riese: Dwarf-Giants.

Though they towered over their mothers, they were shown no less love than a child a quarter their height and they lived peaceably amongst the Humans. In time the Dwarf-Giants came to learn how they came upon the World-Tree, and many vowed thereafter never to trust an Angelic. The many mothers and sons buried in Arbor's earth would serve as a poignant reminder to the Zwerg-Riese that their existence was born out of pain and sorrow and death.

"Handsome though isn't he?" Cooed Shüchter.

Dwarf-giants were still a minority within the Human realms and there were a bigoted few who made life uncomfortable for them – Human males angered that the Angelics had corrupted their gene-lines. So the Dwarf-Giants collected together and journeyed to a patch of land they could call their own where they could build a future for themselves and their children, unhindered by Man's prejudices.

They came to settle in a fertile yet untouched land on the eastern fringes of Arbor. They named their new home Stolz and they became a proud and kindly nation. They extended hands of friendship to all of the other races of Arbor and also stood firm against any aggressor that threatened the social stability of the World-Tree.

"Well there's a surprise. If it's got a butt you can bounce like a rubber ball then you're sure to want to bounce it," Fröhlich joked with a hearty chortle. Shüchter blushed and he began poking the campfire with a twig sheepishly.

Ambition, however, is a powerful driving force and a few within the settlement began to think that their size and stature and ability were destined to rule over more than just Stolz. After five generations the colony contained close to 30,000 individuals, and the young that were born within its confines were not told of the origins of their species. This was not through censorship but through the dying art of passing on history from one generation to the other.

Such was their want for independence that in finding it they lost their identity and with it their heritage.

1000 adolescent Zwerg-Riesen with adventure in their hearts and a sense of false righteousness, akin perhaps to their Caelum forefathers, marched from Stolz never to return. They formed the Zwerg-Riese Vigilantag and plundered villages and cities far from their homeland.

"I don't like him," sniffed Nieser "he looks shifty."

Though a battalion of Dwarf-Giants was sent to recover them they were too late and by the time they caught them only seven of the Vigilantag remained, the rest killed by Arborian mobs bent on administering their own brand of justice upon those that had burned their villages and stolen their chattels.

The seven, of mixed skill and ability, escaped their Stolzen brothers and went underground. They formed a rogue cell and began peddling their services to whichever unwholesome characters might benefit from them. The criminal element of Arbor began to hold them in high regard and tales of their daring heists and kidnaps and murders were sung, in the most part drunkenly, in gambling dens and lust houses the World-Tree over.

"Wings," blurted Blöd quite randomly. The others turned to look at him, huffed, shook their heads and turned back to the object that their attention had been fixed upon all morning.

The Vigilantag Seven, as they were now known, were deadly, morally devoid, and greedy and on this particular morning they were sat huddled around a warm and crackling campfire in a forest clearing two mountains away from Delator, staring up at a mirror the size of a barn door.

This was not a normal occurrence, but then again these Dwarf-Giants were not that normal. Each of them, initially awe-struck by the intricate carvings of the mirror frame (upon which appeared all the creatures of Arbor beside those of legend and myth each gilded and inset with precious crystals) was now uncharacteristically concentrating on the pane of mirrored glass at its centre.

Instead of reflecting back the exhausted figure of Müde, the stern expression of Brummig's wrinkle browed face, the flushed cheeks of a still embarrassed Shüchter, the smiling face of the always jovial Fröhlich, the ill look of the constantly suffering Nieser or even the morose picture of Blöd who had stopped picking at his ear and had started picking at his nose, it was actually displaying a scene completely detached from the reality a regular mirror would have otherwise reflected.

The mirror showed them a man tentatively stumbling through a dark forest. Every now and then the man would stop and call something out into the night sky above him, nothing audible came through the mirror though. The man held a torch straight in front of him, which he swung gently to his left and right to illuminate the thick undergrowth around him, though his face remained hidden in shadow. It was as if something or someone was stalking him from behind, the viewpoint of which was now being projected within the mirror. The man then stopped suddenly, as if something had caught his attention.

He turned sharply to the left and continued until he came upon the banks of a still stream. He stooped to gaze at his reflection cast down upon the opaque surface of the calm water, the stars above crowning his head like a shimmering halo.

Then suddenly there was another face beside his own and the man's expression twisted into one of anguish and dread.

The mirror clouded over and the image disappeared.

"Did you see the stars reflected in the water?" The six Dwarf-Giants turned to face their leader, Dok. "One can calculate that the same alignment is due to take place eight days from now," proclaimed the seventh member of the Vigilantag, who had emerged from the woods behind the rest of the band, "and the river is Restless next to Silva-Tenebrae Forest," he continued as he buttoned up his flies and retook his seat next to Blöd.

"So that's where we're moving camp?" Fröhlich queried impatiently.

“Yes Fröhlich. That is where he shall be eight nights from this day. And eight nights from this day, that is where we shall kill him,” Dok whispered.

6

"Miss Brenwen, if you could begin by telling us a little about yourself," asked Asmodeus as he peered over the top of his octagonal spectacles to the calm and conservatively clothed Law graduate sitting opposite him.

"Well, I come from a quiet village called Equus on the eastern shoreline of Equinas. During the summer I run the length of the beachfront till sunset… I love the ocean… and it keeps me fit, and during the winters I assist with the herd. Between my study semesters I spent much of my time grooming, the funds of which I committed to paying off my school fees."

"You are quite independent then?"

"I never like to rely on someone for something when it is perfectly within my means and abilities to provide for myself. So in a way I do pride myself on my self-sufficiency. I'm certainly one of the few from my graduating class to complete the course debt-free."

"The fees are extortionate. As the demand for the best lawyers soar, so does the demand for the tutors to teach them. It is a shame so many turn away from a life in law at the outset because of the cost," Asmodeus reflected. "So what made you choose a future in the legal profession?"

"Money," Epona Brenwen flatly answered. She could sense Asmodeus Blackstone was poised to engage her in some capitalist debate or perhaps query her materialistic attitudes. So, rather than wait for a torrent of predictably probing questions, she chose to clarify her short but succinct response.

"15 ring-years ago my father was arrested on suspicion of supplying various controlled substances to a number of Studdaries. It was during the Equinas Olympiad and security was at its tightest. Anyone caught peddling performance-enhancing drugs was dealt with swiftly and quietly. My Father was caught with 10 syringes of steroid supplements in his saddlebags. He was prosecuted in a closed court not even my mother or I could attend. He was even denied legal representation. He was found guilty and sentenced all in the same day, the whole process expedited so that no shadow could be cast over the Olympiad. He spent two weeks in a secure paddock before a senior Equinpare and friend of the family learned of his incarceration," Epona described. Though the whole event still scarred her to this day, her voice did not quaver and the volume with which she presented her reasoning did not rise in anger.

"He ordered a full investigation," Epona continued. "It was subsequently discovered that my father's business partner had been the one who planted the steroids. With my father out of the way his associate was free to conduct trade and negotiate deals with the many clients visiting the Olympiad free from the prospect of there being any dividing of the profits thereafter. My father had organised the meetings and the deals and his trusted colleague betrayed him just when negotiations were close to conclusion. Betrayed for money." She paused briefly to brush the fringe of her long red hair from her eyes before continuing in the same controlled manner in which she had begun. "My father was released with an apology, and the proper guilty party was tried and sentenced. During those few weeks I saw how an abuse of the law could condemn an innocent man, and how its correct utilisation could free the wronged and deliver true justice. My reason for choosing this path is ironically owed to the greed of someone who sought to destroy my family all because he wanted more money," Epona concluded.

"There are some that maintain it is the World-Tree root of all evil," Asmodeus replied.

"That I do not doubt, but perhaps there are good things that can come from it also," she replied with a hint of a smile, the effect of which lifted the mood of the interview considerably.

"What do you think makes a good lawyer," asked Asmodeus, working his way down a checklist of typical interview questions.

"There are the obvious ones such as team work and the ability to listen, which I am sure you have heard countless times.

But I think one must be suitably curious. So much of the law rests within the grey areas between legislative text and the constantly adaptive precedents that come from the courts. I think an important quality is curiosity, to read between the lines, to research adequately enough to understand the individual subtleties of case law and how they combine to form the pillars of a judicial system. Always question, never trust the obvious, those are my mottos," Epona confidently asserted.

"Ah yes… there are no stupid questions only stupid answers. That is what I have to keep telling our nervous trainees whenever they look at me quizzically," replied Asmodeus as he jovially shook his head. "Do you have any questions Fury?"

The temperamental Insurance lawyer usually sat beside Asmodeus when interviewing prospective candidates. Her fiery demeanour and intense aversion to responses of the mundane variety had customarily assisted Asmodeus in whittling out any of those interviewees that subsequently caved under Fury's avalanche of traditionally challenging queries.

"What is your greatest fear?" asked Fury quite calmly.

There was a gentle rustle from Asmodeus as the tendons in his leathery black wings momentarily contracted. As Epona was a female, and an attractive one at that, he reckoned on Fury attacking Epona with intellectually challenging questions in order to expose her as someone who was pleasing to the eye but little more. In Fury's opinion she had only known beauty and intelligence go hand in hand in one individual, and that was herself. But Asmodeus was taken aback at the subtle manner in which Fury was attempting to extort one of those few distinctly personal truths that are not generally shared with strangers, let alone one's prospective employers.

For the first time in the interview Epona took a moment of pause to consider her response. The question was easy enough to answer but was it geared in some way as to expose some other personality trait or hidden proclivities? *The dark… no, too obvious and childlike* she thought. *Death… to lose one's life perhaps… but death comes to all, fearing the inevitable… hmm.* The silence was not long enough to descend the interview into embarrassment; the moment everyone realises that the pre-prepared answers have all been expended leaving nothing but the realisation that when under pressure the candidate fails to deliver. On the contrary Asmodeus enjoyed watching Epona gently mulling thoughts over in her head. He knew, as did Epona, that the question was not as simple as Fury had intended. He even found himself willing the young graduate to *be* curious, to read between the lines.

Losing something maybe... a love... no... Epona was on the verge of something but couldn't quite verbalise it. *Damn it, I must be losing my... that's it!*

"I fear losing my mind."

If Epona wasn't mistaken she could see a small curl of a smile rise from the corner of Fury's mouth.

"Because?" Asmodeus asked.

"It is what gives me strength and gets me by. Without it I would not know love or sadness. It enables me to help others, expand my boundaries and imagine my wildest fantasies." Epona sincerely stated. The more she thought about it as she spoke the more Epona began to believe that to lose her mind would be terrifying. Fear from something momentary, like an aversion to the dark or to find oneself perched on a ledge and experience vertigo; these were instances where fear can dissipate as swiftly as they materialize. But to lose the ability for rational... even irrational thought (Epona imagined her past feelings of envy and jealousy), consciousness and self-awareness, perhaps never for them to return would leave her nothing but a collection of muscle and membrane. This is what she really did fear above all.

"But to lose one's mind would be to lose one's fear. Wouldn't you agree?" Fury pressed.

"I would agree, but then one would also lose everything else. That would be a difficult trade-off for anyone to accept. Though I might be fearless, I certainly would not be the most functional lawyer in all of Arbor if I didn't have a mind with which to think," Epona politely maintained.

Fury nodded to Asmodeus before making some indistinguishable notation in the margin of her notepad. Asmodeus turned back to Epona and asked his last question.

"Finally Miss Brenwen, why did you choose our particular firm?"

*

Epona didn't recall having any feelings of nervousness during her interview. On the contrary she thoroughly enjoyed meeting Asmodeus and found it pleasantly surprising that he wasn't brash or arrogant or unapproachable or any of those other undesirable traits one often hears a lawyer of his status being described as. It wasn't entirely disconcerting meeting Fury either, and though Epona realised that there may subsequently be some kind of competition between them she would find it no different from the rivalry she experienced amongst the beautiful bi-pedals at Archbold's school of Law; albeit Fury was a Fire-Nymph who was rumoured to turn semi-transparent at her most incensed.

As Epona galloped to her first day at work, however, she did find herself thinking back to that last question and whether her response could have been more sincere.

'Whilst Humans can't breathe underwater, fly, teleport or walk through walls, they are capable of a great many other things… their art work and literary achievements are awe inspiring, their hearts are courageous and their appetite for self-development and technological-advancement makes them one of the most important and fascinating races of this World-Tree. They are quite worthy of protection under the Joint-Arborian laws and Blackstone & Associates has long been recognised for aiding in that endeavour. I chose this firm because I value ideals such as Justice, Liberty and Equality. Humanity may be a young species but they are a sentient and intelligent species none the less and it would be an honour to shield them from the more unscrupulous races or those administrative injustices prevalent in some parts of Arbor. This is the reason I chose Blackstone & Associates to conclude my legal training and become the best lawyer I can be.'

Did I really spew out all that self-righteous nonsense? I must be losing my mind after all, Epona thought to herself as she negotiated the busy thoroughfares of Delator on her way to Tartarus.

The journey from her recently acquired stables was not a great distance from the office, which suited her very well given that she was never a great fan of the bustling morning commute. She had considered returning to Equinas prior to formally starting her new career at Blackstone's but changed her mind due to the realisation that journeying from there to Tartarus, especially on her first day to work, would have been more hassle than Epona was willing to accept. Just as well she bid farewell to her family and friends two weeks ago, shortly after discovering she had been successful in obtaining a seat at Asmodeus' law firm.

The distance from Equinas to Tartarus was certainly considerable, and one travelling on foot might take several weeks to cross from one region to the other. One might be able to utilise such modes of transport as the Pegasi, great winged Unicorn capable of transporting up to three or four passengers upon their back, though Epona always found it troublesome and relatively uncomfortable.

'It's the leg room Ma Mare, there's never enough… and you undoubtedly get stuck on a flight with complete morons who expect some form of entertainment… Humans! Never content with witnessing the beauty of the World-Tree as it rushes by', she would often complain to her mother. Even then the Pegasi only got you as far as Delator mainly due to the fact that they refused to journey underground thereafter.

The rest of the journey from Delator, on the surface, diagonally down to the root-structures of the World-Tree to Tartarus would have to be made by Ordo-Formica, a network of blind six-legged Insecti that formed a vast train linking the two cities. One could never miss an Ordo because there was rarely a gap in their retinue, the form of which imitated what might be described as a long ouroboros that looped and wrapped itself around the World-Tree's root structure. Again Epona was not fond of this transport medium either. Perhaps it was her aversion to riding upon the back of another species.

"They're going to think I'm some kind of Human obsessive… or some goody four-shoes who hasn't got the spine to dig in her hind legs and fight," she muttered to herself as she weaved in and out of horse-drawn goods carts and woodlice the size of wagons – a smooth but unreliable form of transport as they had a tendency to curl up into tight balls when ever they bumped into anything, which upon the streets of Delator was regrettably unavoidable. "I should have told them the truth, but who wants to hear you applied to a law firm because…? Oh what's the use, all these bloody places are the same!" she impatiently snapped to herself.

She had planned on a pleasant and gentle journey to the office but having roused from her sleep half an hour-turn later than she had intended, Epona was now flushed, hungry (having skipped breakfast) and running late. Whilst she may not have been the great supporter of Humans she made herself out to be to her interviewers, she wasn't a great hater of Humans either and it was most probably the dawn rush that was making her flustered self more than a little irate.

"Ah finally, cutting it fine though," she said studying the height of the sun as she arrived at her waypoint.

"Miss Brenwen, it is good to see you again. Congratulations on joining our firm," came a tiny voice just to Epona's right.

"Thank you Rex, it's good to see you too," she politely replied. Her temper had faded now that she knew she was only a short descent away from her office. "Same as before?"

"That's right, that patch of worn grass just over there should be the spot," stated Blackstone's smartly dressed porter. "Now, we haven't set it up to take you direct to your office yet, so for the moment you'll be taken to reception where they'll be able to tell you where you need to be."

Epona nodded, smiled and then made her way to where Rex had pointed out.

"Ready?"

"I hope so," replied Epona reluctantly.

"Don't worry you'll be just fine, and remember to mind the gap when you see the floor." With that Rex leapt up onto his toadstool mushroom, tucked his knees into his stomach, hunched his shoulders and inflated his neck to the width of his small body.

"Dooowwwnnn," boomed the frog in a loud and deep baritone that was quite unusual, one might think, from a creature his size.

The ground beneath Epona's feet began to vibrate before slowly opening up. The earth crumbled away and the young trainee now found herself sunken into the ground up to her shoulders. She gave out a small and nervous yelp before her head disappeared beneath the grass line. The soil continued to fall away under her shoes and then reform above her head, though not one grain of dirt spoiled her suit. It was as if she was trapped in a massive transparent capsule that was driving itself deep into the earth. Rings of glow-worms spaced at meter intervals lighted the journey so the experience was less daunting than if it had been pitch black. After two turns of a minute glass Epona saw the first pin pricks of light from below and quickly remembered to brace herself for the short but safe drop to the reception room floor. She straightened out her livery and looked up to the ceiling to witness the hole from which she had appeared promptly seal itself up again.

"I know… he's got it into his tiny head that he's going to meet the girl of his dreams who's going to turn him into a… yeah I know… well I said 'I'm not your mother'… but will he listen though… I know… he just wants to sit up there yelling 'down' in that deep stupid… Oh I'm sorry dear," said Rana, another frog who looked after reception, breaking off from her conversation with a Hermes that was hovering next to her. The messenger blinked her eyelashes 'goodbye, leave you to it' (such is their form of communication having no vocal chords) before silently drifting off down a long corridor to the left. "Do you have an appointment deary?" continued Rana turning back to Epona.

"It's my first day actually. I've been told to report to… oh I've got it here," Epona replied fishing inside her jacket for her welcoming pack.

"No rush deary, not to panic," said the receptionist comfortingly.

"Here we are…" said Epona as she opened up a neatly folded piece of paper, "ah yes… I'm to see Mr Blackstone… Mr Elliot Blackstone."

7

"That's just bloody typical of uncle. But then again I do get a trainee, which could be interesting, especially if she's..." Elliot mused as he sprinted back down the twisting tunnels to his office. "Perhaps it might work out, teaching can be quite fulfilling after all, passing on knowledge to the keen and eager... whoa!" he suddenly blurted out, sliding to a halt in front of an amused looking Fury. Elliot had skidded round a blind bend and had just managed to come to a stop before taking the brash female Fire-Nymph clean off her toes.

"You're all flustered Elliot, in a hurry?" she asked fixing Elliot's collar with her dainty but dexterous fingers, singing off the odd piece of loose fibre that looked out of place. Her warm palms then pressed his lapels flat upon his chest like an iron.

"Actually Fury, I'm in a bit of a rush."

"Not avoiding me are you? You haven't been to see me in a while," Fury playfully queried.

"Erm, best be dashing off," Elliot nervously muttered as he edged passed the seductive insurance lawyer, all the while thinking he might get pinned to the curved walls at any moment. Fury giggled in an atypically immature fashion before slowly stepping aside to give the escaping Half-Angelic some room to make good his exit.

"By the way Fury," Elliot called out as he sped off, "looking hot today!"

Whilst Fury's advances had been getting more daring since their Hallows Eve union, the truth was that Elliot really was trying to avoid her, mainly due to the fact that he didn't want to scorch anything too delicate today – such was Fury's passion known to ignite when she got over excited. Nevertheless he was an insatiable flirt who couldn't resist throwing the odd flattery or two.

"Charmer," Fury whispered under her breath when Elliot was out of earshot.

*

"And what is this supposed to be?" exclaimed Epona as she tentatively but curiously approached Elliot's four hundred ring-year old Arabilisian fertility headdress. She had slowly worked herself round Elliot's office in his absence, examining the attorney's strange looking artefacts as well as the risqué images of the finely woven but timeworn tapestries that adorned the sloping walls. In stark contrast to Asmodeus' critical sentiments toward the workspace Epona thought the collection quite delightful and was not shocked, offended or overwhelmed by the decor, which was pleasantly convenient as it would soon be her office also.

"Looks like some sort of… oh!"

Her eyes had fallen upon the protruding penises flamboyantly adorning the crown of Elliot's headdress.

"Well, well Elliot what have we here… you naughty…"

Epona carefully lifted the mask from its decorative plinth, revolved it gently over her palm before, quite cheekily, placing it upon her head.

The ambience of the office had transported her imagination to some exaggerated plane likened perhaps to a theatrical changing room, in which she felt like an inquisitive child amongst a thespian's fashion set. Rana the receptionist had told Epona that Elliot was in a meeting and might be late but to make herself at home in Elliot's office till he shows up, so Epona knew she had time to poke, prod and explore her mentor's workspace with enough time to place everything neatly back before her mentor arrived.

"Ohh hellloo," Epona seductively purred to her reflection, which was cast in a full-length mirror propped against a shelf to her left. "Why thank you… it's Baroque-cock… kind of Gothic-chic," she continued in mock conversation with herself. With the headdress slanted awkwardly upon her head she sauntered over to Elliot's desk.

"What sort of a man has a coffin for a desk I wonder?" she jokingly asked Elliot's quill holder. The tiny bronze Valkerie eyed her master's head-dress on the trainee's head, huffed, wrinkled her brow and then turned her back on Epona, perhaps in disapproval of the Equinmare's apparent disregard for other peoples possessions. The rest of the stationary had also become aware of their new visitor and the 'Jaws of Doom' was first to affectionately nip at Epona's fingers with its staple-removing fangs, whilst the nervous looking 'Evil Punchy' was desperately trying not to empty its tray all over the desk.

"How cool, animated stationary, Epona you are climbing up the World-Tree," she proudly mused to herself. "Hmmm, and what's this," she took a sleeve to what looked like two rings from a spilt mug but after some rubbing revealed what appeared to be, "buttocks?"

"Erh Erm," Elliot quietly coughed. A stunned Epona slowly raised her head to see her new tutor propped against the doorframe of his office. She could see Elliot's eyes drifting up to his favourite piece of antiquity that still rested upon his new trainee's head.

"A peni," she randomly blurted out before steadying herself, "Epona… Epona Brenwen," she introduced while gently lifting the headdress off and placing it neatly on the desk, penning in Elliot's rather confused looking stapler.

"Elliot, Elliot Blackstone, pleasure to meet you," he greeted through a friendly half grin. As he advanced, hand outstretched to shake hers, Elliot found himself momentarily distracted as Epona moved out from behind the desk.

"Oh… I… didn't."

"Yes?"

"I… didn't know you would be arriving so soon, my apologies for being late," Elliot lied. He was actually going to say that he didn't know Epona was an Equinmare. It was quite a surprise for the curious lawyer, to see a second set of legs appear behind the first as the eager young trainee trotted forward, so much so that he became rapidly conscious that he was staring at Epona's rear.

He had never met a Centaur face to face and, without any malice intended, he thought she wasn't a Mare'ess at all but a pair of twin Humans – one twin bent at the stomach grabbing the waist of the other to form the front and back halves of a pantomime horse, albeit a very attractive pantomime horse. *I'm still staring at her tail, stop it... just look up...there you go*, Elliot mentally instructed himself.

"That's okay, I was just looking around your office," Epona replied blushing. "You have some really great stuff."

"Thanks," Elliot said as they both looked down at the phallic headdress. "Have you had breakfast? We could always..." he continued breaking what would have undoubtedly become an uncomfortable silence.

"Sure, I mean *no*, I was in a rush this morning... breakfast would be great," replied Blackstone & Associate's newest addition eagerly.

*

Abigail Hood awoke to find herself in the corner of a dark and dank room. Her eyes were bloodshot and squinting from a beam of piercing light that issued from a small barred window high up to her left.

Her mind was clouded and she had trouble recalling how she had come to be in such a sinister setting. It was like waking from a drunken stupor to find oneself within an unfamiliar bed, staring up at a foreign ceiling. Abigail always had to take a moment to mentally backtrack how she had got to where she was on those occasions when she found herself next to someone she wouldn't otherwise have been next to, in a room she didn't know.

In most cases the realisation of the nights revelry and its connection to the subsequent morning after would all come together in a rush of regretful clarity, but on this occasion Abigail was genuinely devoid of all knowledge as to how she ended up in a barred room no bigger than a stable box, wrapped in a thick grey garment she never remembered owning.

Confusion quickly gave over to fear as she struggled to snatch at the missing hours-turns, days, maybe even weeks, that were locked away in her mind. A tear rolled down her soot smeared cheek, then another until she started sobbing uncontrollably into her palms. Abigail had only been this scared once before and this was when she learnt of how her family was killed when she was thirteen. Even the moment when she randomly came across the giant Atlation, Judge Hallbjorn while being chased by Elliot through Brewer's field, was more a feeling of abject shock than absolute terror.

Having lost her parents at such a young age Abigail had to find an inner strength in order to tackle the harshness of life single-handed. She would often refuse help or charity, choosing to suffer and overcome than give up and live comfortably. On numerous occasions Elliot would have to bail her out of fights when playground arguments with school bullies got Abigail into trouble far too deep for her to claw and scratch and kick her way out of.

Abigail became headstrong and determined, prepared to take on the World-Tree fighting. Elliot thought she wanted to prove something to everyone, maybe to herself, but he soon reminded himself that he had the warmth and security of an intact family unit and that perhaps in other circumstances he too might be looking for confrontations and challenges where there were none.

It was this tenacity that eventually made Abigail violently wipe away her tears, almost as if she were ashamed of them, rise to her feet and begin scanning her surroundings for any hint as to where she was and how she might escape.

Standing she was now aware that the floor was a cold stone that bit at the balls of her bare feat with an icy stab. She pushed the discomfort to the back of her consciousness and pressed on towards the vertical bars, which made up the forth wall of the cell and stretched from the ground to the ceiling. A sharp tug would confirm that the bars were solid and immovable. There were hinges at shoulder height as well as head height in the centre of the barred wall, which held up a similarly metal-framed door. Again a brisk shake of the door would show her that she was securely locked inside her cell.

The window, she thought turning quickly to her left.

Abigail had an outstanding ability to make snap decisions whenever her primary choice was taken away from her. She wasn't one to huff and panic and spend an unnecessary amount of time deliberating what to do next. On the contrary she could normally figure out an alternative route or a different solution within a few moments before she would be on her way again. It was this sense of intuition, almost as if she had the World-Tree and all its facets and eventualities predicted from the outset, which gave her an unmistakable air of confidence and World-Treeness beyond her ring-years.

She always told Elliot that she could overcome chaos but never serenity. It would be a while before Elliot worked out what she meant – that she was more comfortable fighting against the odds in an inhospitable world, pitting her intellect against nature, rather than hiding herself away amidst the mundane quiet of courtly life to ponder her loneliness.

The bars that were imbedded in the recesses of the small square window were just out of reach above her head, and she had to take two attempts to jump and grab them before she could hoist herself up adequately enough to peer out.

Outside it was morning and the myriad of perplexed thoughts crashing noisily through her mind finally succumbed to the familiar sounds of the street beyond her prison cell. Abigail could hear the clip clop of hooves on cobblestone, the sound of distant church bells and the cry of a distressed baby. Her eyes had partially adjusted to the light from outside and she could make out a courtyard and beyond that a crossroads, and then a church thereafter, which she did recognise as the Rotunda of St Vitus.

"Delator, I'm in Delator," she whispered to herself in relief, "but why am I – "

A heavy jangle of keys startled her and she quickly dropped away from the window. She could hear voices now, female voices talking in a hushed tone. Abigail couldn't make out what they were saying, but she did realise that the voices were coming closer. She decided to throw herself down to the floor from which she had awoken from and pretend to lie there still and seemingly asleep. The voices had not sounded welcoming and Abigail was still not alert enough to answer to whomever the voices belonged to.

The sound of footsteps came around the corner and stopped outside the bars of Abigail's cell. She lay on her side with her back to her visitors, curled up in a foetal position, as motionless as her nervously shaking body would allow. She screwed her eyes shut and listened.

"She has not spoken a word?" sounded a particularly eloquent and noble voice. There was an air of command about that tone and accent, one that demanded respect and obedience, which Abigail thought sounded familiar. She tried to focus on a face but another voice broke her concentration.

"No my lady, she was brought in unconscious," replied a timid and shy voice, a seemingly innocent one that was markedly different in potency than the first. "Dr – "

"Asklepia has examined her your highness," interrupted a third voice, "Restless River may have washed away most of the blood…"

Abigail's eyes flashed open in alarm.

"…but the Dr found traces under her finger nails and more staining her gums."

This third voice was more confident than the second but less regal as the first. She spoke as if addressing a superior officer, short and sharp and succinct.

Blood, whose blood? What is happening? Abigail began to frantically think to herself.

"I understand the victim has been mutilated Rose?" the first voice asked.

"Yes your majesty, what ever Abigail did Silva-Tenebrae's wildlife must have finished off. The man remains unidentifiable," replied Rose, the owner of the regimented third voice.

They know me, 'my lady', 'your majesty' they keep saying. It's the Queen, the Queen of Delator, it must be. Rose... Rose Red one of the Queen's own bodyguard, the other must be... Abigail's thoughts cascaded into her already crowded mind until suddenly they slowed. Her eyes widened in fear. *Did they say mutilated? What have I done?*

"His face has been mauled your Highness, as well as most of his body," continued the timid voice of the second visitor.

"Snow! That's quite enough detail I think," Rose snapped.

Snow... erm... Snow White, Rose and Snow. But why are they here with the Queen?

Abigail had considered rousing from her fake sleep to join in the debate, but there was something untoward about the way her three visitors were talking. There was almost something conspiratorial about their conversation.

"Hmm, and we presume he was...?" asked the Queen.

"That much appears evident my lady," replied Rose Red.

"They released them this morning, shortly before they brought in Miss Hood," concluded Snow.

"Why did you throw yourself into Restless River Miss Hood? You were supposed to return," contemplated Delator's Queen.

"Perhaps the potion was not –"

"Silence," rasped the monarch, "I brewed it myself Snow."

"Forgive me Majesty it was not my place to..." Snow quickly apologised.

"Of course. Times have been difficult of late. We must all be strong. Let us leave, we have more pressing business."

"And Hood your grace?" queried Rose.

"You shall return here when I have left. If anyone should question your presence, especially if it be Abigail's legal counsel, then you may tell them that you have been assigned to personally ensure that no harm befalls this Meretrix of the Royal Court. That will be your official role," ordered the Queen. "Unofficially however, if Abigail should mention anything at all *sensitive…*"

"I understand your Majesty. I shall take care of things. Everyone will presume she took her own life in remorse of her crime," replied Rose without the faintest hint of compassion.

Abigail thought that her heart and head might explode. She felt her eyes well up and her throat tighten. *Must keep still... but why do they want me dead?* It was as if the walls of the cell were closing in on her, squeezing the air from her lungs as they seemed to press against her helpless body. She wanted to burst into tears, to jump up and rattle the bars till the building collapsed. She wanted to yell into the face of her Queen and scream 'why?' But Abigail remained motionless, silent, dead to the World-Tree, and because of this she remained safe, for the time being.

"Not even Blackstone's can save you now my Meretrix," whispered the Queen. The malice of those words sent a cruel chill down Abigail's spine.

The Queen of Delator and her two bodyguards, Rose Red and Snow White, turned to leave, their footsteps fading as they passed from Abigail's hearing. Even when the footsteps had completely disappeared, and the sound of the World-Tree outside spilled slowly back into her tired and confused mind, Abigail kept still. She felt numb, as if she had been punched and beaten and tortured until she could no longer sense the touch of her own skin.

The Queen's malevolent talk of potions and plotting had been like the blows of a whip upon Abigail's flesh, and Rose Red's threat 'to take care of things' had been like a violent kick to the stomach that left Abigail winded and nauseous.

Finally the distraught young maiden managed to drag herself to her feet. Sobbing she stumbled back to the window in the hope of catching a sight of her visitors, but the strength to pull herself up, which she fought so hard to hold onto, escaped her and her legs buckled beneath her weak and shaking body. She slid down the wall, the rough and broken concrete grating at her shoulders, before she ended up an unconscious heap on the stone floor.

This time sleep did descend upon her but before it did, perhaps in hope, she whispered the name 'Elliot'.

8

Vincent burst into Brimstone Bar and frantically scanned the room till he spotted Elliot sat in the same booth he had occupied an hour-turn ago. The Dreamrunner hurried over to the alcove just in time to hear Elliot conclude one of his many anecdotes, no doubt chosen to impress his new tutee.

"And that is how I managed to get the prosecution to drop old Porgey's indecent assault charge," Elliot chuckled to a thoroughly engrossed looking Epona. "Hello Vince that's the fastest I've seen you move in ring-years."

"Hey Elliot, hi –"

"Vincent Traum this is Epona Brenwen," Elliot jovially introduced as he polished off his last slice of pancake with maple syrup.

"Pleasure to meet you," greeted the young trainee with a pleasant smile.

"And you," Vincent replied gently shaking Epona's small and delicate hand, " 'Epona', beautiful name – The Divine White Mare, I believe."

"That's right – The Protectress of all horses and foals. My parent's have a fondness for names with meanings."

"As do mine, 'Traum' means 'dream' I think, but then again my parents always did have a sense of humour," reflected Vincent. He caught himself thinking back to when his father was alive and suddenly became aware that no one was talking.

"So what's up Vince? You look perturbed," queried Elliot breaking the silence.

"Just bumped into Fabianus, he's just on his way out to interview this girl they found washed up."

"The found naked but for a Wolven mask. Sounds like quite an interesting case."

"Quite. I recall you once told me about a childhood sweetheart?" Vincent probed.

"I have no idea what he's talking about Epona," Elliot joked, "my heart is yet to be reserved for someone special."

"Whatever," interrupted Vincent, "was her name Hood?"

Elliot put down his knife and fork and turned to look at his colleague. As much as Vincent was not known for his playful nature on this occasion the Sandman looked more serious and less exhausted than Elliot had witnessed for some time.

"*Abigail* Hood. Why?" the Half-Angelic tentatively asked.

Vincent paused not knowing whether to continue, for he knew his next words would alter Elliot's week considerably, and most certainly for the worst. "The girl they found on the banks of Restless River," he said taking a sharp breath, "is called Abigail Hood. She's been charged with murder."

Elliot searched Vincent's eyes for any sign of mischief or practical joke, but there was none. In return Vincent opened up his mind enough to momentarily dip into the consciousness of his concerned looking colleague, only to be met with a torrent of rage and confusion which hit the Sandman with all the force of a runaway baggage train. Elliot turned back to Epona, gave her a reluctant half smile, before he swiftly gulped down the last of his tumbler of 'Bad Mojo' and rose to his feet.

"Where's Asmodeus?" Elliot calmly asked Vincent.

"I don't thi – "

"Not interested Vincent. Where is he?" Elliot replied cutting off his friend mid sentence. All patience and cheerfulness had left the Half-Angelic's demeanour.

"He's in his office," Vincent replied shooting a concerned look at Epona.

"Thank you," Elliot replied as he left the booth and briskly walked towards Brimstone's entrance. He stopped for a moment, quietly contemplated his next course of action, and then turned back to Vincent. "Vince, stop Fabes, tell him to join me in my office – however confused he gets tell him it comes from my uncle. Epona, sorry to cut short our breakfast, finish up and join us in my office," Elliot instructed the pair of them, making sure to give the new trainee a reassuring nod so as not to panic her. With that he turned on his heels and made for his uncle's office.

"You're all a too'ing and a fro'ing this morning young master Blackstone," called Bill to the rapidly exiting lawyer.

"Wish it was any other way Bill. Put the breakfasts on my account will you please," replied Elliot as he disappeared from view.

"He sounds in a bit of a fluster Mr Traum. Hope nothing's the matter?" asked Bill as he heard Vincent and Epona approach his bar.

"Just a regular day in Elliot's non-stop action-packed life," Vincent replied.

"And how is your first morning here Miss Brenwen?"

"It's very nice so far Mr Dante, thank you. Breakfast was lovely by the way."

"Oh, was my pleasure miss, and call me Bill."

"Well we best be off," said Vincent as he and Epona departed, "I think things are about to get very serious."

*

Asmodeus Blackstone was a fully-fledged Daemon of Tartarus. This was by no means a measure of his temperament or a slur against his character, and he was actually one of the most pleasant and compassionate members of the World-Root's inhabitants. The description was merely chosen in order to distinguish the root-dwellers from their over-zealous Caelum-Angelic cousins who still populated the Celestial boughs of the World-Tree high above.

Many changes befell the Fallen when they were banished from Caelum and the temperature and humidity and the dark of Tartarus each had an effect on those that lived there. Asmodeus found that his wings lost their brilliant white plumage and became black like basalt and tough like buffalo hide. He didn't mind the change at all and became quite proud of his new sleek and, he later discovered, more powerful wings. In his companions he saw other changes occur, some grew paler from light deficiency, those that frequently assembled by the warm lava pits grew darker, and others, devoid of explanation, developed horns. The Fallen had become unique, and not just from the Angelics of Caelum but also from each other. Asmodeus revelled in the fact that they were emulating the diversity of life that existed above their heads, and was resolved never to regret his banishment.

It was Asmodeus' profound appreciation for life's complexities that Elliot valued most, and he discovered there was much to learn from a mentor of such a demeanour. The young lawyer was always mindful of his uncle's wisdom and rarely did Elliot contradict his tutor, even when their opinions might have differed considerably.

This occasion was different however. Never did Elliot know of Asmodeus to withhold a case from him for reasons other than his professional ability to conduct them, after all there were more experienced litigators at Blackstone's.

Keeping this case hidden from me! What good does that do? This is a criminal matter and who knows the client better than... Elliot's thoughts trailed off.

He began to doubt whether he really did know Abigail after the decade or more they had spent away from eachother. The Half-Angelic had lost contact with Abigail a ring-year or so after her parents died, when one of her distant relatives moved her to Delator. It was a sorrowful farewell and Elliot never again opened up to anyone of the opposite sex in the same way thereafter. It was as if he had lost his soul mate. But then time has a way of erasing the woes of a lost love, and as Elliot buried his head and heart in his legal studies the memory of the strawberry split eating, red-haired, freckly, vibrant bundle of energy that once stole his fishing net soon faded from his waking thoughts.

Why didn't I contact her? Elliot sadly reflected.

Elliot entered his uncle's office to find the Daemon staring intently into the flame of a scarlet candle. Asmodeus had taken off his spectacles and was eyeing the bluish tip of the inside of the flame just above the wick. The senior partner was also muttering something under his breath that Elliot couldn't make out. Suddenly Asmodeus titled his head to the side of the candle and suspiciously eyed his nephew.

"I have to go Gabriel something has come up," Asmodeus spoke to the candle flame. Though the air was quite still the fire seemed to flicker left to right as if in response. "Okay, I shall speak to you again soon… yes, I believe the next round of drinks is on me," the Daemon attorney concluded with a sly grin before promptly blowing out the candle. His gaze returned to his nephew.

"How is Gabriel? Still coping amongst those Caelum bigots?" Elliot curtly queried.

"As best he can. Always remember that sometimes it pays to have friends amongst your enemies," Asmodeus responded sagely.

Elliot sat himself down opposite his uncle and stared round the barren room. Whilst the young lawyer was fond of his collection of assorted paraphernalia, Asmodeus preferred the subtle influence that a classically minimalist office projected. There was nothing to distract a visitor in this room, no gaudy decorations or flamboyant adornments, merely two chairs a desk and two people with infinite questions, countless answers and endless possibilities between them. This was all Asmodeus needed to conduct his affairs in a manner that befitted him most.

Asmodeus looked intently at Elliot. He had replaced his spectacles upon his face and was gently tapping his top lip with his right index finger. It become immediately apparent that neither of them needed to say anything and each of the lawyers seemed to know the purpose of the visit.

"Very well, you may take over the case from Fabianus," Asmodeus flatly instructed, "but the moment you let your feelings cloud your judgement…"

"I understand," replied Elliot sincerely, "thank you uncle."

Asmodeus watched Elliot with interest as the young lawyer respectfully left the office. He had never seen Elliot demonstrate such intensity for a case as he did in those few short minute-turns, and Elliot didn't even have to open his mouth. Asmodeus' intuition was never wrong – better to send the young lawyer on his way with the flame of justice burning brightly in his heart than to kindle a raging inferno of bitterness had Elliot been denied the case.

"I am quite sure that there is more to this matter than meets the eye Elliot. Never lose sight of the case, and your role. That is the best way to help your friend," Asmodeus concluded as Elliot moved to the doorway.

The young attorney thought the appointment might have lifted his heart but all he felt was a new weight upon his shoulders. His childhood sweetheart faced a charge of murder the punishment for which, if found guilty, was still based on the Delatorian 'Eye for an Eye' principle. Elliot knew that there was no room for error. He knew that only he could suffer the burden of her defence, and as he gently bowed his head and mournfully made his way back to his office Elliot also knew that the fate of Abigail Hood was entirely in his hands.

9

Fury impatiently threw what looked like a ledger across her room and slumped down on her ceramic desk in a huff. In the interests of health and safety every item of furniture in the Fire-Nymph's office was flame retardant, this way Fury could conduct herself with all the fierceness of spirit for which she had been originally retained without risk of combusting anything too delicate. Outside her office Fury was under strict instructions to maintain her temperature at a bear minimum for the protection of her co-workers, this is why no-one would find any physical impact of the Insurance lawyer's presence anywhere else in Blackstone's apart from her own office and Elliot's desk.

She never chose to talk much about herself and because of this little about her past was known to others.

Some of those less knowledgeable inhabitants of Arbor believed that Fire-Nymphs are born from the sparks of a lightning bolt and that it was this awe-inspiring act of Nature's violence that accounted for a Fire-Nymph's intractable disposition. Fury much preferred the mythic-birth origins of Nymphs rather than the simple and sensible biological explanation.

Every World-Tree child has at some point played parchment, shears and stone. The principle of this game – that one item possesses the ability to overcome another, as well as to be defeated by the remaining, is roughly comparable to how a Nymph is born Water, Fire or Wood.

Some Nymphs prefer to mate amongst their own kind. This is not uncommon and many consider it necessary to sustain the pureness of their breed. Thus two Water-Nymph parents will always produce a Water-Nymph baby. However it is not uncommon for a roaming Fire-Nymph to fall in love with a Wood-Nymph. In this scenario, the former does not set fire to the latter as World-Tree physics might suggest, on the contrary, they are quite capable of safely mating and their resulting offspring will always be Fire.

So, in the hereditary stakes Fire consumes Wood to produce more Fire, Wood absorbs Water to leave Wood and Water extinguishes Fire to leave Water. Thus Fury was not born from the heavens on a bolt of lightning as she would prefer, but was simply the product of a passionate Fire-Nymphet mother and a submissive Wood-Nymph father.

Each of the Nymphelementa had its own personality traits that were more dominant than other characteristics, and they were best remembered from a rhyme Fury once heard as a child:

Water-born is destined to flow, to a life in arts one might bestow.
Wood-born are most un-swerved, amongst Arbor's Nature never un-nerved.
Fire-born is full of fervour, to traverse the World-Tree one might go further.

Water-Nymphs tended to be artistic by nature, their minds constantly finding new ways to look at the World-Tree. In the ripples of a stream they can visualise anything from Cause and Effect principles to the resonance of Arbor's mystical pulse. Nymphs of this species are incredibly creative but easily distracted.

Wood-Nymphs are usually steadfast and reliable. They are predisposed to nurture and sustain. Whilst many of this species are considered set in their ways, no other Arborian race is so in tune with the changing cycles of the World-Tree and the forces of its nature. Wood-Nymphs are kind and gentle and wise.

Fire-Nymphs on the other hand have a less wholesome pedigree. They are considered impulsive, rude and unpredictable. In a small few these characteristics have produced some of the greatest Nymphonial generals Arbor has ever seen, but in others these traits can often lead to self-destruction and desolation. Fire-Nymphs are ambitious and never shy away from speaking their mind.

So, as Vincent paused outside Fury's office to check if she was all right, he did so with a distinct air of trepidation.

"Everything okay?" Vincent yawned. The morning's excitement had dissipated and the tiredness the insomniac constantly felt was once again descending upon him.

"Leave me be!" Fury growled without looking up from her desk.

"Erm, okay, sorry," Vincent quietly apologised before continuing on his way in a shuffling fashion much like a chastised child.

For once in a long time Fury felt a twinge of guilt for yelling at someone who only had her well being at heart. *Why must I always be so bloody brash*, she cursed to herself. "Wait, Vincent. I'm sorry," she called out.

The doting finance lawyer stopped in his tracks, raised his eyebrows in surprise (for he never knew Fury to apologise) and turned back to his colleague's office, picking up the abandoned ledger as he stepped inside.

"If there's any thing I can do to help," Vincent offered, "my work load is a little light at the moment."

"Thanks, it's just these bloody..." she noted her rise in temperature levels and quickly checked her anger, "...these figures don't quite add up," she desperately sighed looking down at a number of loose manuscripts fanned out before her.

"Perhaps another set of eyes might help," Vincent kindly suggested as he took a seat opposite Fury and opened up the leather bound book that the Insurance lawyer had brazenly cast aside. The Nymphet raised her head from her folded arms and looked up at the Finance lawyer's boyish features. As Vincent scanned the pages of the open ledger Fury thought how she never before had occasion, or the compulsion, to study the gentle lines and kind eyes of her colleague's face. Now that she had done so Fury found something oddly appealing about this man who was always tired but never rude.

"What you've got in your hands is a copy of a ledger within which is listed all the material possessions and assets of the royal family of Delator, every amber-piece, plot and painting," Fury stated with the slightest of smiles on her face. Notwithstanding the new flutter of attraction she had for the Finance lawyer, in a purely professional capacity she was intrigued to witness what Vincent might uncover.

"Wow, they're really thorough aren't they… but I guess that's important for inheritance tax purposes, of which even the royal family isn't exempt," replied Vincent with a chuckle. He looked up to see Fury nodding in agreement.

She must think I'm such a nerd. It's your job to be a geek... I mean a Finance lawyer... get a grip, Vincent thought embarrassingly.

"Listed against each entry in that ledger is a letter and numeric combination that denotes the current location of that specific item, 'B1' for instance stands for bedroom number one, 'K2' for kitchen number two, 'V' for vault and so on."

"They have two kitchens? A tad extravagant isn't it?" replied Vincent.

"Three actually. It is a *palace* Vince, lots of rooms for lots of guests, not to mention servant's quarters and guard houses. That's a lot of mouths to feed," replied Fury.

"Guess so," Vincent reflected, "so what doesn't add up?"

"Well, this is a list I compiled direct from that ledger of all the items that were, all but seven days ago, located within the palace vault," the Fire-Nymph said, pushing a piece of handwritten manuscript toward Vincent.

"Okay, so what happened seven days ago?"

"A robbery. A number of items were stolen by seven Zwerg-Riese."

"Not the Vigilantag Seven?" Vincent replied looking up from Fury's list of vault items with interest.

"The very same," Fury confidently stated.

"Bloody Caelum, that's a bit ambitious even for them."

"Absolutely," agreed the Fire-Nymph, "so their subsequent capture wasn't a great surprise considering what they managed to take. This is a list of the items that were recovered by the

Delatorian Magistratum when they raided what appeared to be the Vigilantag's hideout," continued Fury placing an official police record before Vincent.

"What do you mean *appeared* to be?" Vincent queried eyeing the document.

"Well the Dwarf-Giants were captured elsewhere, and they maintained that they never knew of any cavern hideout. The Magistratum admittedly found no trace of the Seven within the cave they raided or on the items that were recovered."

"So how did they know where to look for the stolen items?"

"You do ask a lot of questions," Fury joked.

"Oh, well it's part of my job. Financial disclosure is quite important when completing various paperwork so I often have to probe and fish for information a client may be unwilling to divulge," Vincent said smiling. *Now she's definitely going to think I'm a nerd*, he thought to himself.

"Interesting… well I haven't got to that part yet, that's a criminal matter, and arguably outside of my investigative remit."

"So what next?"

"Right," Fury continued, "so this is another list I compiled when I personally went to log the contents of the vault, shortly after the royal court lodged its insurance claim." Once again another list was put in front of Vincent, whose eyes were now darting between the three loose velum manuscripts as well as the ledger. "You still with me?" Fury asked

"Yep, keep going," Vincent confidently replied.

"Now this is the royal court's record of claim – a catalogue of possessions and assets the court is claiming under their insurance policy," again another official looking document passed before Vincent's eyes.

"Okay."

"Now it stands to reason that the list of claim should match my complete vault list I took from the ledger," Fury said pointing to the first document, "*minus* the list I compiled at the vault, minus the horde of items the Magistratum recovered. Right?" Fury logically asserted.

"Right," Vincent agreed. "But it doesn't," he continued, scanning the various lists of items and descriptions in front of him.

"Keep going," Fury urged, impressed with Vincent's ability to keep up with her.

"Well if I'm reading this right, item number 35 that appears in your annotated vault-ledger list, does not appear in your on-site vault list, nor does it appear in the Magistratum's record of recovered items. So –"

"So it should appear in the list of claim for insurance! But it doesn't!" yelled Fury desperately. *So I'm not going nuts – someone else sees it, through all these lists and numbers and…* she frantically thought to herself.

"What else *has* the palace claimed for?" asked Vincent as he neatly collected together all the loose pieces of parchment that Fury had passed his way.

"Item number 7 – a gold crown, inset with ruby and topaz – value 2000 amber ducats. Item number 64 – a silver sword with diamond etched scroll work and ivory hilt – value 1550 amber ducats… erm," Fury paused as she worked her way down the royal claim of insurance, "ah… Item 29 – enchanted boots, leather, ability to run at great speed – value 400 amber ducats. Item 12…"

"So high value items then?" asked Vincent.

"Pretty much, there is a suit of armour here that's valued at 23,000 amber ducats. But then again there's item 287 – shiny pebble – value ½ amber ducat," replied Fury.

"Why would someone steal a pebble, however shiny?" Vincent asked faintly bemused. "What's item 35?"

"Well that's the thing, pass over the ledger," Fury said sitting upright in her fire-resistant rubber chair.

Vincent handed back the ledger, which Fury had previously hurled across her office, and patiently waited for the description of the missing item. Fury had book-marked the specific page so she found the entry with ease. "Here we are," she said clearing her throat, "item number 35 – The Carmen Speculum, no other description. Value 250,000 amber ducats."

Fury snapped the ledger shut and looked at the astonished expression on Vincent's face. The Finance lawyer closed his gaping mouth, leaned forward and calmly asked: "What in the World-Tree costs 250,000 amber ducats to replace?"

"And why would someone not claim it back on their insurance policy?" Fury inquisitively added.

"Drink?"

"What?"

"Drink," Vincent repeated, "Asmodeus and Elliot swear by it. They say it helps them find clarity or whatever. I'm buying."

"Sounds like a plan, and I'm buying – you're helping *me* remember?" replied Fury with a grin. There was something cool and impulsive about Vincent's behaviour that gave Fury a pleasant surprise. Little did the sprightly Fire-Nymph know that the usually subdued Sandman was desperately thinking how fortunate he felt to be accompanying her for drink, albeit a work-related one.

*

"So why wouldn't you want to declare such an expensive item as stolen?" Vincent asked as he poured Fury a measure of 'Merlot Diavolo' into her marble goblet.

"Maybe it wasn't stolen, perhaps it's elsewhere in the palace?" Fury replied before taking a delicate sip from her drink. Vincent noticed that the gentle flames that constantly surrounded the impetuous Insurance lawyer momentarily faded as she gulped down her first draft of wine.

"Perhaps it's being cleaned, whatever it is?"

"No, I've checked. The main ledger is too voluminous a log to have to keep altering it every time something is sent away for cleaning. So those charged with maintaining the palace relics and whatnot keep a separate record. The Carmen Speculum was not logged in the servants' records as being cleaned," Fury asserted.

"It may be in another room?"

"No," Fury flatly stated, "Delatorian Insurance law stipulates that in any abode of more than ten rooms each room's contents must be individually disclosed – kind of like one room in a palace, in insurance terms, is comparable to a two bedroom house."

"Which would explain the location codex in the main ledger," Vincent added.

"Exactly. If one room or kitchen or vault is burgled then someone knows exactly what was in that room to begin with. Similarly it prevents anyone from claiming on an item that wasn't in the burgled room in the first place," Fury clarified as she took another sip of wine. She stretched out her arms and yawned, it was only approaching midday but it was apparent this new Insurance case was taking its toll on the Fire-Nymph.

"Welcome to my world," Vincent joked.

"How come you *do* always look so tired? We can't be working you *that* hard," Fury curiously asked.

"Bit of long story – its seasonal," Vincent replied. He found it was far easier to half explain his condition in terms of depression related states that nobody really understood than to delve into his past, where he would have to reveal that he was afflicted by something the World-Tree once considered a curse.

When their unique talent first made its appearance many Dreamrunners where accused of witch-doctory – of weaving nightmares in the weak to drive them insane. The Traums themselves, especially Vincent's father before he was dream-slayed, were often met with suspicion despite the good work that they did. In Vincent's new life as a lawyer he found it easier to keep that part of his life hidden. Everyone assumed that he was working round the clock, but never that he was an insomniac Sandman who desperately needed to top up his serotonin levels.

"So how come you ended up in Insurance?" Vincent asked, quickly changing the subject.

"Well what they say about Insurance is true, you know. It's generally an area people fall into than choose. I fell into it having rotated amongst the various other departments here. There was something," Fury continued waving a hand in the air, as if separating the good explanations from the bad, "orderly about it, elegant. Its less boisterous than Criminal, less fiddly than Research & Development… oh I don't know," she laughed, spilling a drop of Merlot down her front, which instantly evaporated on her hot chest.

"It's the money isn't it… not what we get paid," Vincent huffed, "but how much wealth is out there. It's the reason I got into Finance. There is so much amber floating around in the World-Tree and we get to decide, in our own little way, who gets a piece of it," he guessed.

Fury put down her goblet and gazed into Vincent's face. For the second time since they had started working together Fury felt a feint flutter of something pleasant… and it wasn't the wine.

"Wait a minute-turn. Surely not declaring a 250,000 amber ducat item is a good thing? From an Insurer's point of view, I mean," Vincent continued reverting back to Fury's case.

"I guess so. I mean insurance is mostly concerned with what is being claimed rather than what isn't. But in some cases it's the things that aren't being claimed that makes a Nymphet like me think twice," Fury explained.

"So what is making you think twice?"

"It goes back to my earlier question as to why someone wouldn't want to make a claim on something so expensive. Sometimes an individual's possessions can be… hmm… incongruous to the lifestyle they publicly project – it would be like a pacifist claiming his torture dungeon was robbed. That's a relatively public way of showing that you're a hypocrite," Fury replied. She had a skill for creating simple analogies when she thought her explanations might become too taxing for her audience. "So declaring The Carmen Speculum stolen and claiming on its insurance would be good if it were actually stolen, but wouldn't be good if you didn't want anyone to know it was missing."

"Like who?" Vincent probed.

"How about this – say we were married," Fury mused, much to Vincent's approval gauging the smile that quickly spread across his face, "and I owned a... oh I don't know... a crystal ball because it was given to me as a present, but I hated it because I can't stand mysticism. With me?"

"Yep," Vincent replied.

"So I lock up the crystal ball and say we shall never bring it out, ever. However you are a secret crystal-ball loving mystical freak, that absolutely has to give it a go," Fury sensed that she might be onto something and paused briefly to collect her thoughts, "so you orchestrate a robbery so that amongst other things the crystal-ball is stolen. It's not declared stolen when we both subsequently claim on our household insurance, so I'm none the wiser that it's missing. A few days later you go off to meet your hired thugs who committed the robbery, recover the ball, and stare into it to your hearts content without me knowing," Fury concluded with a deep breath.

"So what you're saying is that someone at the palace doesn't want someone else at the palace to know that this thing is missing? And why is this important in Insurance law?" Vincent posed.

"Glad you asked. The Royal Court's list of claim is valued at about 150,000 amber ducats. But if I can prove collusion then I can reject their Insurance policy altogether so they won't get a ducat."

"Because one cannot benefit from his or her own crime."

"Correct," Fury confirmed, "it would be fraud."

They both polished off their goblets of wine and looked at each other like two scheming rascals plotting something mischievous.

"So there's a conspiracy afoot in the royal palace," Vincent whispered.

"That's the hunch. It is strange that the Vigilantag Seven were released just this morning isn't it?" revealed Fury

"Released?"

"Lack of evidence apparently," Fury suspiciously stated.

"So what now?" Vincent sighed.

"Well, the original robbery needs investigating, how the Magistratum managed to recover the items, and what on earth it all has to do with The Carmen Speculum, whatever that is. That's before anyone goes about accusing the Delatorian Royals of the criminal act of fraud," Fury listed.

"Sounds like a handful, need some help?" offered Vincent eagerly.

"Absolutely," grinned the Nymphet mischievously as she ran her tongue over the top row of her teeth.

It appeared that Fury was warming up to her new assignment, and perhaps to Vincent, which made her consider their pairing up on this case that bit more alluring.

10

Fabianus spent thirty minute-turns briefing Elliot and Epona on the facts of Abigail Hood's case, which he had managed to gather from the limited documentation his preliminary case bundle contained, and during that time Elliot had managed to regain some of the composure he had lost prior to requesting the case from his uncle. Meanwhile Epona had spent the session furiously jotting down nearly every word that came from the Liberan's toothless mouth. Fabianus wasn't displeased that Elliot had poached his file, on the contrary, he left Elliot's office with a sense of relief that someone more experienced in the field had taken over the matter.

"Right, ready?" Elliot asked turning to the young Mare'ess.
"I think I've got everything down. To Delator then?" replied Epona with an air of hesitation.

"Don't worry, I remember you don't like riding things so we won't be taking the Ordo," Elliot reassured, "in fact there won't actually be any travelling at all."

The handsome attorney escorted Epona to a pentagonal room located to the middle left of the office complex. Entrance was gained from a spiral staircase that was thoughtfully and painstakingly carved from a particularly thick and twisting World-Root. Taking the steps upwards the duo emerged into the centre of the chamber through its floor – a pre-designed architectural consideration such that none of the five interior walls were breached by a doorway or passage.

"What are those?" queried the Equinmare, pointing to one of the intricate carvings that adorned each of the walls.

"This room is called a Syngraphus," Elliot replied, "this room transports us instantaneously to one of the five major capital cities of Arbor."

Epona nervously hoofed the stone floor with her right hind foot before curiously trotting up to one of the carvings. In Epona's estimation each of the walls was roughly 100 hands in height and the same again in length, so on the whole the chamber was relatively substantial in size considering how empty it was. Chiselled upon each of the walls was a great circle and in the middle of each circle a pentacle star had been delicately hewn, the double outlines of which gave the impression that the geometric pattern was formed of one continuous line that crossed from one tip to its opposite other. The star and circle mimicked a pentagram, which was not an unusual sight to Epona, given its common use in Mysticism (albeit that never before had she been surrounded by five giant ones over five times her size), but what did intrigue the young centaur was what was carved in the centre of the star-shaped patterns.

"Ah," Elliot spoke, noting the trainees curiosity, "those are sigils. There are five in this room, each unique, and each representing one of the World-Tree's major cities."

"They're beautiful," commented Epona as she ran her fingers between the smooth edges of the symbol in front of her. She suddenly realised that her eyes were closed and it was as if she could feel some primordially resonating power surging through the sigil and into her being.

"Sorry," Epona apologised with a blush as she snapped out of whatever trance had momentarily seized her.

"That's okay, hypnotic aren't they?"

"Mmm. So why are there only five?" the centaur asked taking a few steps back from the wall.

"Well most of our business is conducted in five cities: Delator, which is represented by that sigil over there," Elliot replied pointing to the wall to Epona's left, "erm, then there's Babel in Liber, the importance of which will become evident when we have occasion to visit it. Then we have Aviditas located in the archipelagos of Arabilis where many a wealthy client resides. The forth sigil is for mount Steinthor in Atlatia where the mighty Law-Bringers are stationed when they're not in circuit. And finally that one is for the Ninth Tier of Caelum." Elliot concluded.

"Why is there one for Caelum?" Epona asked stepping back next to Elliot.

"Well some of our main opposition Lawyers come from those lofty boughs of the World-Tree. Some people think of them as competent attorneys and in all honesty they can put up a good legal fight when they put their halos to it," Elliot admitted. "It's just all that forth-righteous, white cloak billowing, over-zealous drivel they undoubtedly spew that I'm not too keen on," he continued giving Epona a smile as he strolled over to the sigil of Delator. "So whenever we need a meeting with them, or they *demand* one with us," he said, not without a hint of sarcasm, "then rather than traverse the whole height of Arbor, all we have to do is step through that sigil. Easy. And it's handy to use to reach those isolated northern parts of the World-Tree, which I like doing because the Caelum Angelics hate us using their Tier as a way-station – really gets under their wings."

"Interesting. So I guess its domestic transport from any of these five locations to any other outlying region?" Epona sensibly asked.

"That's right. Now step back, this is my favourite bit," Elliot said removing a small spherical object the size of a quail egg from a pouch inside his suit jacket.

"This is a Blood-Stone," the lawyer said holding up the scarlet capsule in front of Epona.

"Blood-Stone?"

"Yep, technically it's not made of stone – that part relates to these five walls."

"And the blood part?" Epona asked wincing.

"The magic that has imbued these walls is ancient and powerful. You felt some of its residue when you touched it. In order to activate the sigils one needs to use blood," Elliot described noting that Epona looked a little perturbed. "Blood is one of the most important substances in all of Arbor. It transports everything we need to live throughout our body every minute-turn of every day. It has long been used in rituals by the Haemotites who believed that blood held the key to Plain-Shifting – to transport oneself to another location without actually crossing the real distance between them."

"But they were sadistic psychopaths who were all caught and executed," the young centaur bluntly stated.

"Their theory was correct though. Their methods, I agree, were questionable. And if you're worried about where this blood comes from, don't be. There's a bat keeper in the caverns of southern Tartarus who bleeds his bats whenever we need more Blood-Stones," Elliot reassuringly comforted the squeamish looking Equinmare.

He then gently moved Epona slightly to the left before hunching himself up into a pitching stance. He then threw the Blood-Stone as hard as he could at the sigil of Delator. Elliot quickly regained his balance and the pair of them watched as the capsule exploded in a splatter of dark crimson right in the centre of the arcane symbol.

"Bit messy isn't it?" Epona commented unimpressed.

"Just watch," Elliot replied with a knowing grin, "now what's only slightly harder than getting blood out of a stone?"

"Getting blood *into* a stone?"

"Exactly."

Quite suddenly the splash of blood looked as if it was being drawn into the recesses of the Delatorian sigil as well as the pentagram that surrounded it, like mercury to a magnet. When Elliot had witnessed this strangely macabre magic performed by his uncle for the first time, the young Criminal attorney had thought there not enough blood in the small ampoule-like Blood-Stone to fill the indentations of the immense carving. His uncle had explained that the blood was the one liquid which the porous stone of the Syngraphus was incapable of absorbing, so the thick liquid could work its way into a thin sliver through the carving without losing any of its original volume.

"That's unbelievable!" gasped Epona as the huge beige-coloured pentagramic sigil in front of her slowly turned to red.

"Keep watching," replied Elliot, thoroughly enjoying the awe the spectacle was inspiring in his tutee.

When the blood had filled the whole of the circle, the pentacle star, and the sigil of Delator, the whole outline of the pattern began to glow a shade of sunset crimson. Epona stretched a hand to the luminescent pictogram thinking how alive it now looked, only to have her arm gently retracted by Elliot who smiled and told her to wait a moment more. Then, with a sound like a tide lapping upon a shoreline, the stonework within the pattern's great circular border began to gradually dissolve away, revealing another identical looking chamber beyond.

"Shall we?" Elliot offered, waving an arm towards the new opening and the room behind it.

An apprehensive looking Epona loosened her collar and slowly wiped her perspired palms on her skirt. Then, with one foot carefully placed after the other, her four legs trotted her through the portal and into the other chamber. Elliot withheld a small giggle as he watched Epona wave her arms out in front of her like one feeling their way in pitch darkness as she stepped through the portal.

Elliot hesitated a moment before following. The realisation suddenly struck him that those next few steps would be the first in what would undoubtedly be a painful and difficult journey. How might he react to seeing Abigail after all these ring-years? Was he capable of saving her? What if she really was a murderer? All these questions flooded into Elliot's progressively weary mind.

Epona reached the other side of the wall and turned to look at her mentor. She could see the concern that had cruelly projected itself in the wrinkled brow and down cast eyes of the young attorney, who only three turns of an hour-glass ago had been full of vigour and enthusiasm.

"I'm sure she's okay, Miss Hood I mean," Epona reassuringly called through the opening.

Elliot looked up and gave the Centaur a meek half-smile, the same smile he made whenever he tried to fake a show of confidence, then took a small controlled breath and crossed the threshold into the royal city of Delator.

11

The razor sharp edge of a great iron axe glided a hair's width over Krystina Letalis' midriff as the agile female arched her back, dodging a blow intended for her head.

As her palms touched the floor she gracefully brought her legs over her body and twisted into a perfectly controlled back flip. Her movements were effortlessly executed, and as she flowed up and over and around the confused Dwarf-Giant it was like watching an Arborian Sea-Elemental toy with a tugboat.

Before the slow axe-wielder could take another swing with his savage but cumbersome weapon the pretty golden-haired Secarius delivered a swift kick to his stomach then slammed a powerful uppercut into his nose.

Shüchter's eyes welled up in agony and the Dwarf-Giant staggered backwards, dropping his axe, as he clutched at the bloody mess his opponent had made of his nose. Krystina took the opportunity to grab the disorientated brute by the belt buckle before rotating him around her. Though she was substantially lighter and smaller than her foe the assassin used Shüchter's own weight to generate enough momentum, much like a hammer thrower might a hammer, and only when his toes were carving at the ground in deep swathes did Krystina release her grip.

The helpless Dwarf-Giant was hurtled ten feet away, where his considerable bulk impacted against a broad willow splitting the tree as if it were just a twig.

As the tree folded a particularly heavy branch swung low across the Dwarf-Giant's jaw rending him unconscious. It was as if the willow took one last blow of reprisal to the creature that felled it before it would succumb to rot and decay.

"Noooo!!!" yelled Brummig as he entered the fray wielding an ivory hilted silver sword.

The female fighter looked un-moved as she turned to face the advancing figure of her new assailant. She was never a great advocator of hand-to-hand combat and her patience with the fight was swiftly wearing thin. Krystina kept her nails in immaculate condition and took some pride in displaying them in public beneath her fingerless elbow length gloves whenever she accompanied the Queen. Unfortunately, beneath her padded punch gloves, she could feel that the nail of her left index finger had broken during the last bout. She was not amused.

The assassin was surprised at how skilful Brummig handled his weapon as the second Dwarf-Giant, standing over three times Krystina's height, elegantly swept his sword to her right and then to her left.

Like someone dancing the flamenco the young woman artfully sidestepped each downward rush of the Zwerg-Riese's polished blade without so much as a flutter of her eyelids.

Krystina was an expert student of anatomy and physiology and the knowledge gained there from allowed her to predict the movements of an arm or leg by the primary flexes of their respective muscles. Her lightning reactions meant she could then judge where to place her own body when the attacker's move was subsequently carried out.

Her technique enabled her to expend as little energy as possible, and as Brummig wildly flailed his weapon in every direction – the exhaustive feeling of oxygen deprivation biting at his aching muscles – Krystina continued to dodge and duck with the same control and grace as when she had first entered the Vigilantag's hideout.

Krystina always preferred using more subtle techniques to dispose of her would-be victims. Her sister, Emilita was of a similar disposition and used an intricately carved curiae blowpipe as her weapon of choice, the darts of which were pruned from the thorns of a crimson rose bush that grew in the palace gardens – hence her alias Rose Red.

Krystina however favoured using poisons to paralyse her victims before slicing through their throats with a bleached bone-knife. Her best poison was one derived from the powdered petals of the Lilac-Rosarius, a hybrid rose bush of brilliant white. A gentle prick from the thorn of this alluring plant can induce a comatose state within three minute-turns. A concentrated dose, administered by one of Emilita's darts, could render a person immobile in a matter of seconds. Krystina always kept a snuffbox of this deadly pallid substance in her hip pouch where ever she went and as such she came to be known as Snow White.

Together the Letalis sisters secretly carried out some of the most dangerous vendettas the Delatorian royal court secretly issued. They were by far the most lethal Secarii in all of Arbor. Whenever they weren't dispatching an enemy of the Crown or accompanying the Queen as bodyguards they could be found mastering other lethal arts such as sword mastery and practising Condylus – the skill of fighting without weapons, which Krystina was at present impressively demonstrating to the increasingly dejected looking Dwarf-Giants.

As Brummig collapsed from exhaustion, without Krystina having laid even a finger upon him, the stunning Secarius wasted no time in retracting a pair of cross-handled throwing knives from her shoulder holster. With a swift flick of her wrist the weapons silently cut through the air pinning Fröhlich's hands to the tree he was camouflaged in.

The Dwarf-Giant's bow and arrow fell to the ground unused as the third Zwerg-Riese hysterically tried to free himself. In the end, for fear he might tear up his palms further, he abandoned his attempt of escape and had little option but to watch as Snow White ventured deeper into the lair beneath him.

Dok thought it quite ironic that a female who seemed more preoccupied with how her hair fell about her shoulders more than her own personal safety was playing the normally vicious members of the Vigilantag Seven for amateurs. While he had little respect for the abilities of the assassin he did however care for his own head and so the Zwerg-Riese leader, hidden amongst the forest foliage, decided to watch silently as Krystina came before Müde.

With the catlike reflexes the assassin jumped up to a low hanging branch as the bolts from the fourth Dwarf-Giant's repeating crossbow whistled beneath her.

As Müde stopped to reload his weapon Krystina swung her body round the branch like a trapeze artist before elegantly dismounting onto the shoulders of the frenzied brute. She grabbed his wrists as the thug, swerving this way and that, tried to throw her from his back.

The assassin suddenly extended her legs either side of Müde's head and wrapped them tightly round his neck. Krystina used her thighs to strangle the Dwarf-Giant with an air-constricting sleeper-hold, and in no time at all the Vigilantag's eyes rolled up and back into his skull. As Müde hit the ground with a thud he did so unconscious and snoring.

With four of the seven out of the way Krystina pressed on. The assassin finally reached the entrance to the Zwerg-Rieses' hideout only to find an ill looking Nieser standing before her swinging a huge flanged mace over his boil covered face. The sniffling giant advanced swiftly, then quite suddenly stopped. His eyelids fluttered and his nostrils began to contract and before Krystina could move into cover the Dwarf-Giant sneezed, peppering the bemused looking assassin with slimy globules of green mucus.

"Gross," Krystina winced as she looked down at what would otherwise have been a pristinely white skin-tight leather body glove.

With one broken nail and dressed in something that now resembled an Atlation's handkerchief Snow White stared into Nieser's eyes with a look of utter contempt.

The Dwarf-Giant wiped the snot from his runny nose and advanced with the same ferocity as he had previously intended. Krystina whipped a dagger from her left leather boot, ducked beneath Nieser's mace as he flung it towards her, and slotted the point of her blade into the chain link that connected the mace's great spiked ball with the massive wooden handle the giant desperately clung to.

With a sharp twist Krystina pirouetted away to the right, breaking the chain link and sending the vicious looking mace-head hurtling into the forest behind her. She continued her spin until she was behind the confused looking Dwarf-Giant and, without any remorse, swiftly delivered a sweeping kick between Nieser's legs.

"Five down, two to go," Krystina quietly whispered to herself.

She ventured into a cavern and found herself stifled by the rotting stench of dead dear carcasses around her. She raised a palm to her mouth and nose and continued forward, her left hand still clutching her dagger.

Though the light of several campfires cast flickering shadows upon the cave's damp grey walls the assassin's concentration remained unwavering, her dark brown eyes entirely focused on what was in front of her.

She followed the cave system through to a larger space where she found a sixth Dwarf-Giant sat crossed legged in the middle of the grotto.

Blöd had either not yet noticed Krystina stealthily approach him or was ignoring her advance, and his interest appeared to be directed at a shiny pebble he was rolling around in his palm. The assassin paused a few feet from the preoccupied Zwerg-Riese and began to pour some of her Lilac-Rosarius powder from her snuffbox into a blow tube.

Blöd suddenly stopped his playing and innocently looked up into the face of Snow White with a childlike grin on his face.

"Shiny," the Dwarf-Giant chuckled as he offered the pebble to Krystina.

Whilst she knew this sixth giant would put up no resistance she did realise that the most prudent way to guarantee her safety was to immobilise anyone she came across. These were twenty foot tall Zwerg-Riese after all and quite capable of crushing her head like an egg if they had half the opportunity. So without any hesitation, or feelings of guilt, Krystina took a deep breath, drew the blowpipe from behind her back, and prepared to administer a coma-inducing dose of powdered poison into the face of the unsuspecting Dwarf-Giant.

"Please, stop!" shouted Dok. "We'll deliver what the Queen requires, we just have to get it back. Please, just give us six more days."

Snow White turned to face the leader of the Vigilantag Seven.

The assassin slowly sealed both ends of her poisonous weapon and placed it into the small white pack she kept slung over her back. When her hand re-emerged from the satchel it was clutching a clouded crystal ball the size of an ox's heart. The ball began to clear and the face of the Queen of Delator melted into view.

"My son may not have six days!" boomed the Queen at the terrified looking figure of Dok. "Two days, I grant you two days to return to me what is mine."

"Very well your highness," the seventh Dwarf-Giant and leader of the Vigilantag wisely submitted.

"Two days Dok! Or Snow White will return and gut you and you band of misfit Vigilantag like fish!" screamed the Queen.

The crystal ball glazed over again and the Monarch's face, twisted with anger, slowly disappeared. Krystina replaced the mystical orb in her rucksack and made her way out of the cave and the forest and back to Delator. She paused briefly as she passed the leader of the Vigilantag, removed her glove and showed him the nail she had broken whilst roughing up his gang. She shot a stern look into Dok's face eight feet up before slowly replacing her glove and carrying on her way.

Dok breathed a heavy sigh of relief and went over to ruffle Blöd's hair safe in the knowledge that they could still use the Carmen Speculum for two more days before their lives depended on giving it back. This was more than enough time for the deviously intelligent Dwarf-Giant to come up with a plan that would give the Vigilantag Seven the upper hand when Snow White returned.

While Krystina contemptuously eyed the pathetic figures of the five foes she had defeated on her way out of Silva-Tenebrae forest, back in Delator her sister Emilita was taking considerable interest in the human lawyer and his centaur associate that had come to pay Abigail Hood a visit.

12

Elliot knew that Epona's kind words were meant to comfort him yet as he exited the Delatorian Syngraphus and stepped out onto the cobbled streets of the capital city he did so feeling drunk with despair. His very soul threatened to tear him in two. His hope felt as if it were being pulled away, drawing itself to a safer vessel, and as much as Elliot struggled to hang on to it the emotional effort in doing so was agonising. The young attorney knew, regretfully, that he had lost contact with his soul mate long ago, but now Elliot knew that to lose Abigail absolutely would be perhaps to lose his soul as well. And yet this feeling of despair was not unknown to him and, with some tragic irony, the only thing that kept him grounded was a painful moment he experienced in his youth, fourteen ring-years ago, before Abigail was sent to become a Meretrix of the royal Delatorian palace, before Elliot joined Asmodeus at Blackstone's & Associates… before Abigail was charged with murder…

*

"Son," Raphael called in a sombre tone, "something…" He wanted to continue but the Angelic's voice began to break. Elliot, who was carefully making notes from a particularly patronising text on conduct and etiquette in Arborian Law entitled 'Objectionable Objections', looked up from his pages with an air of concern about his face. Though the door to his bedroom was closed the Half-Angelic felt that his father was withholding something that was causing him a great deal of grief and pain. Elliot jumped from his bunk and ran into the hall where his father was advancing mournfully towards the young law student's bedroom.

"Father? What's wrong?"

"Elliot could you come down for a moment, there's something your mother and I need to tell you," his father quietly asked. Elliot noticed that his father's pristine white wings, the joints of which usually rose like two proud peaks above his shoulders were sunken low and the tips of his end feathers were brushing the floor. It was as if Raphael was carrying some burden he was desperate to unload.

They both walked silently down the hallway stairs and into the ground floor lounge where Elliot's mother, Sophia, was waiting. The tissue she clutched in her right hand and the raw rings around her eyes were telling signs that she had been in tears. Elliot hated her mother crying because it always made him want to cry also. It was as if the teenage boy was capable of feeling the exact same emotions as those around him, like he was some kind of conduit for sentiments and passions.

In those moments of joy, at celebrations and other happy gatherings, Elliot would almost feel overwhelmed by the power of the collective good-nature that he found himself surrounded by. This undoubtedly affected his reactions to favourable circumstances and he was often the loudest cheerer, or clapper, or whistler at any event where cheering, clapping and whistling was called for. However, in those moments of anguish and bad tidings Elliot was always the one to react the worst. So when he saw his mother there looking dejected and saddened Elliot immediately felt a lump begin to swell inside his throat.

"Mother?" Elliot whispered as he overtook his father and entered the room.

Sitting in a chair opposite Sophia was Abigail. She too was hunched forward like Elliot's mother and also showed signs that she had been weeping. Abigail's left arm was in a sling and there were a number of cuts and small bruises about her forehead.

Elliot didn't know what to feel. He had questions upon questions, the answers to which could not come fast enough for him. Abigail's parents had taken her to see her grandmother who lived in a cabin set high up in the alpine slopes south of Pannonia, and he knew that the Hoods were not due to return from their vacation for another two days.

Standing behind Abigail's chair was a tall hooded figure wrapped in a cloak of soil brown and dark shades of forest green. A bow was slung around his right shoulder and a throwing axe and quiver of arrows hung about a thick leather belt at his waist, the buckle of which displayed a scene of a similarly attired man wringing the neck of a wounded and kneeling Wolven. It was the guild crest of the Venators – a group of highly skilled huntsman who were charged with the capture and cull of the murderous Wolven clans that constantly threatened the peace and security of the World-Tree. In his left hand the hunter held a great silver-tipped spear called a Venabulum the length of which almost equalled the full height of the hunter.

"This is Venator Wilhelm Tell," Raphael told his son while placing both his hand's upon Elliot's tense shoulders. "He has some ill news."

Abigail looked up from the interlaced fingers of her hands and painfully stared into Elliot's eyes. A single tear rolled down her blushed cheeks followed by another and then another. She opened her mouth but her swollen throat prevented her from forming any words.

Elliot shrugged off his fathers hold and kneeled in front of his distressed friend. He wiped the tears from the corners of her eyes with his thumbs, but still they flowed. Abigail's body began to silently shake and fearing that she might completely lose herself at any moment she threw her healthy arm around Elliot and buried her face into his neck. As the young legal apprentice held onto Abigail as tightly as possible he could hear his mother silently sob into her tissue and his father's heavy steps as Raphael moved to comfort his wife.

"What has happened?" Elliot desperately asked looking up into the Venator's stern face. Wilhelm removed his hood and began to tell the harrowing tale of what had befallen Abigail's parents and grandmother.

"I and a party of three of my guildsmen had spent three seasons tracking a Wolven," the hunter began in a deep and sorrowful tone. "This beast had raided the outskirts of Arabilis, and was being sought on ten counts of murder and theft."

Elliot listened attentively as Abigail desperately clung to him. Her body felt weak and only the tips of her fingers showed what little strength she possessed as her nails pressed into Elliot's back. As soon as he had heard the first words leave the Venator's mouth Elliot knew that the tale would end woefully. Although he wanted to know every detail of how Abigail had come to be like this he also wanted to take the girl far away, to comfort and care for her, to wipe away her tears of grief and protect her. However hard it was for Elliot to listen to the hunter recount the episode, Elliot knew that it was harder for Abigail to hear it repeated.

"We had learnt that the beast was going to ground in Pannonia," Wilhelm continued. "Reports of his sighting were beginning to come in from the alpine woodsman who worked the forests nearby. We even found its cave where it hoped to Lunarate."

The hunter went on to describe how he left one of his kinsmen at the entrance of the cave whilst he and the remaining Venators fanned out across the alpines. They knew the Wolven would return with fresh meat and other provisions before it settled in its cave for the duration of Arbor's sixth season, within which it hoped to wait out Arbor's tri-lunarary, as such the Venators knew that if they did not find the Wolven as quickly as possible at least one life might have been lost before the day was out.

"I arrived at the Hood cabin just after Abigail had returned from picking fruit. But…" Wilhelm uttered. He looked down at the distraught young girl, then back to Elliot. The Venator had tracked and trapped and killed dozens of dangerous Wolven but he always struggled with having to deal with the desolation the beasts left in their murderous wake.

Abigail realised that the hunter had come to the worst part of the story. She pulled her head up from Elliot's shoulder and rose to her feet. Abigail searched the face of her childhood friend then she walked out of the lounge and up the stairs to the law student's bedroom. Elliot's mother tried to follow her but Raphael shook his head.

"But it was too late. The Wolven had torn her family to pieces and the girl had walked into the room just as it was collecting their..." The Venator struggled to go on. "She saw everything."

Elliot managed to drag himself off his knees and into the chair Abigail had risen from. He felt numb and his mouth was dry. He had trouble focusing his eyes on anything and everything. It was almost as if the room and all in it were in two dimensions only. All matter had lost its depth and it was as if Elliot was watching the whole sorrowing event unfold through a series of paintings in a picture book. But no tears came. In those few moments of silence Elliot wondered why he couldn't cry.

"Keep going," Elliot instructed.

"It was horrific. The girl just stood there transfixed... standing between the Wolven and me. It was then that the beast spotted me raising my spear. It lunged forwards and knocked the girl out of the way. That's why her arm... I threw myself to the floor as it bounded towards me, and as it jumped clear over me I speared his calf." The Venator had seemed to lose some of the hardiness he had been projecting when he had first entered the Blackstone's home and it was clear that the reliving of the encounter with the Wolven was beginning to take its toll on the brave hunter.

"Is it dead?" Elliot flatly asked much to his parents' surprise.

"I wounded it. Gave me time for my bow and..."

"Is it dead?" Elliot repeated cutting Wilhelm off mid sentence. The young student found that he couldn't cry because his anger wouldn't allow him too.

"I pierced its skull with an arrow as it limped away. That Wolven will never kill again."

Elliot rose to his feet with the same trance-like expressionless face Abigail had displayed a moment before. He began to walk out of the room, passed his distraught mother and worried looking father.

"There's something else," Wilhelm hesitantly continued. "She asked me to bury the remains of her family, said she couldn't leave them like that. It was the least I could do for not getting there sooner I guess. But when I had finished I found that Abigail had…"

"Had what?" Elliot's father asked.

"She had taken a knife to the dead Wolven and… She had severed its head from its body and cut out the beasts heart."

Elliot, who had stopped in his tracks to listen to the Venator conclude, continued towards his bedroom. Both his parents stared into the face of the hunter with looks of shock disbelief and horror.

As the law student took to each step of the hallway stairs it was as if his body was getting heavier. His mind clouded over. There were too many horrific details to deal with, too much anguish to overcome. For once he felt powerless. As much as he wanted to comfort Abigail and magically relieve her of her grief he found he hadn't the strength to, and as he reached his bedroom door the hopelessness of the situation came upon him in unremitting waves.

Elliot reached his bedroom door but the effort enough to open it escaped him and slowly the beleaguered student dropped to his knees and quietly began to cry.

*

Those feelings of emptiness and despair he felt as he wept on his knees to an orphaned Abigail all those ring-years ago returned to Elliot now with all the harrowing familiarity of a recurring nightmare.

Though Epona tried to engage the worried lawyer in conversation designed to distract his woeful thoughts much of the ten minute-turn walk from the Delatorian Syngraphus to the Magistratum holding cells was conducted in an ominous silence.

The young Equinmare would have been lying if she had revealed that the experience was not an uncomfortable one, and she was rapidly beginning to think that the intensity of the situation might cause her mentor to suddenly snap or bark at her at any moment. And so Epona chose to remain a half-pace behind Elliot as they ventured onwards.

"We are here to see Abigail Hood," Elliot announced clearly and authoritatively to a bored looking Magistratum officer sitting in a guard box outside the jail. "My name is…"

"Yes, yes, yes," the guard yawned as he slowly unwound a small roll of parchment upon which the daily scheduled visitations were untidily scrawled. "Ah yes…" another yawn, "it seems we see more lawyers come through here than crim…"

"I have little time for your quips or your tardiness boy! My name is Elliot Blackstone and this is Epona Brenwen. Take us to see Miss Hood at once or take us to your superior you disgrace of an officer," Elliot coolly stated taking one step closer the guard. The Magistratum looked up from his parchment and stared into the cold gaze of the impatient lawyer before him. The officer sensed that perhaps this time he had overstepped the mark and quickly fumbled for a heavy set of keys that hung from a large bronze loop about his belt.

"This way sir," the guard directed in an alert and respectful tone, much removed from his slow drawl only moments before. He unlocked the heavy wooden reinforced main door to the jailhouse and escorted the legal duo through to a hall where he then directed them to sign a logbook.

As Epona quickly placed her initials beside her colleague's on the great dusty tome, which looked like some aged book of remembrance, Elliot looked down the hall to a narrowing corridor that extend one-hundred feet to his front. Flanking each side of the passage were ten barred cells. Propped against the bars of the sixth cell on the right the lawyer's eyes met that of a female who was dressed entirely in red.

Elliot quickly rescanned the logbook he had just signed. "No other offenders," he whispered. The guard then led them on towards Abigail's cell and what felt like the longest walk of Elliot's young life. Every step that echoed from the hard stone floor was like the wails of the damned inmates of long ago, led pleading and sobbing from their cells to a lifetime behind the bars of larger penitentiaries or the shorter time under the polished edge of an executioner's sharpened axe. Still Elliot eyed the crimson clad stranger with suspicion.

The smart yet overtly ostentatious uniform the woman was wearing was in stark contrast to the dull greys and oxidised iron of the prison walls and bars. *She looks like a pirate* Epona thought to herself as her eyes fell upon Emilita Letalis. The attractive Secarius wore a red leather corset strung tight over a frilled lace shirt, the cuffs of which puffed out from her wrists like two flowery blooms. Her pantaloons flared out from under her auburn stained knee-high boots, and it was probably these last elements of the ensemble that most resembled the cutthroat villainy one might have found elsewhere in the less wholesome ports of Arbor. As Emilita shook the shoulder length curls of her brunet locks Epona spied a single red rose flower slipped behind the assassin's right ear.

As the duo advanced Rose Red turned her attention back to what looked like a tiny but intricately decorated book of hours and crossed her legs at the shin.

In the fourth cell to Elliot's left he spotted her and immediately felt as if someone had driven a stake through his heart. Abigail was curled up in the furthest corner of her cell. She had brought her knees up to her chin and was silently cradling herself.

Elliot, forgetting that cell doors were usually kept locked, pulled at the handle of Abigail's cell before turning to the guard with a look much like the one he had shot the Magistratum officer prior to entering the building.

"Sorry Sir. I'm under orders. I can't let you in."

"Thank you," whispered Epona to the officer, who nodded sombrely in response before respectfully returning to his guard box.

Abigail heard the murmurs outside her cell and slowly raised her head. It took her a moment to focus. She had still not recovered after her few hours of sleep, or from the disturbing threats the Queen of Delator had wrought upon her. *Was it Elliot*? She thought. *Was it really him*?

She brushed her dirty matt black fringe from her forehead and leaned forward onto all fours. Abigail seemed like some abandoned stray, filthy and ruffled but not without some sense of hope about her – that desperate longing to be saved, that projected self-assurance that she could be saved… that she wasn't lost. Abigail didn't cry. She simply scrambled towards Elliot who had taken a knee in front of the cell and threw her arms between the bars and round his body.

For the second time in fourteen ring-years she buried her face in his neck. It felt familiar, like an old comfort blanket. It reminded her of friendship and trust and love, but it also reminded her of that terrible day in the Blackstone's home when she witnessed Elliot receive the news of her family's murder. Little had seemed to change between that moment and this one, each forever interlocked now in some darkly twisted collage of eternal suffering and misery. But there was always hope.

"I knew you would come," she whispered into Elliot's ear. The young attorney took Abigail's cheeks in the palms of his hands and looked into her forlorn face. Soot and dirt had sullied her usually striking features and Elliot also noticed that she had dyed out the fiery red hair that had given the girl so much character and perceived energy those many ring-years before.

"Do you remember…?" Elliot worryingly queried trailing off towards the end of his sentence as he pensively gazed into

Abigail's emerald green eyes. Already his proximity to the accused was affecting his ability to adequately conduct a preliminary interview and he feared that he might fail his friend at the very first hurdle.

"It's all a blur…" she replied.

"Don't worry just take your time, do you know what has happened?"

At that moment Abigail's eyes darted up to where Rose Red was standing guard before resting back upon Elliot's. This time the lawyer noticed something different about her expression. He could *feel* it too. Elliot was fearful of opening his senses up to Abigail's emotions for he knew that the experience might be too overwhelming for him to handle. He was no good to the helpless young maiden if all he could do was cower amongst Abigail's anguish. But as Abigail's eyes searched Elliot's concerned face, with some sense of panic and urgency, the young lawyer knew that she was terrified of something other than her incarceration.

Epona had briefly noticed this too and turning towards Emilita asked, "I'm sorry this is a very difficult time, would you please give us a moment," as sincerely and as heartfelt as she could.

"I am under strict instructions not to leave her side, for her protection," Rose Red replied without looking up from her miniature textbook. "Worry not, I have taken oaths of secrecy. Whatever is said within these walls shall not be disseminated outside of them," she lied.

"It's alright Epona," waved Elliot reassuringly to the concerned looking centaur. "I fear her mind may have blocked out whatever tragedy she went through," he continued turning back to give Abigail the subtlest of winks.

As swiftly as Abigail's expression had turned to horror, Elliot's understanding of the situation turned it back to one of relative comfort and calm.

The young lawyer spent the next two hour-turns avoiding anything to do with Abigail Hood's case, and he steered the young maiden clear of any admissions and truths that would no doubt find their way back to whomever Rose Red reported to. Instead the two friends reminisced about their innocent childhood and even chuckled about the sticky situations Abigail's headstrong behaviour used to get her in at school.

Meanwhile Epona stood patiently by, advancing at one brief moment to be formally introduced before backing away again. She felt it appropriate to let the two reunited companions share this private moment together, before the investigation started, before the impersonal legal battle plans were drawn up.

"I have to go but I'll come back tomorrow, I promise," Elliot said. His heart was getting heavier as each minute-turn passed in Abigail's presence for he knew that they counted down to the point when he would inevitably have to leave her. "Is there anything you need?"

"Chocolate would be nice," she replied smiling that faked-confidence type of smile Elliot was all too familiar with. "Perhaps some clothes and some wash things?"

"Absolutely. And don't worry I'll get you out of here," Elliot said as he kissed Abigail on the cheek farewell.

The young maiden dragged herself up and nodded meekly to Elliot and then to Epona. She daren't set her eyes upon Emilita however.

With one last gentle squeeze of the prisoner's hand the young attorney turned and walked away. Epona followed briskly behind having said her small goodbyes to her first ever legal client. She felt exhilarated, sick and sorrowful all at the same time.

Elliot didn't look back. He just couldn't bring himself to do it. If he had then he would undoubtedly have given in to his desire to run back to Abigail's arms and cradle her to sleep. He found himself repeating the same two words over and over in his mind: *be strong*, *be strong*… It was meant to hold him steady, determined and prepared for the careful case preparation ahead, but he soon found himself using those same two words to will Abigail to hang on, to fight and stay alive… to hold on to hope. To trust in him like he trusted in her.

The two lawyers emerged from the prison to the blinding brightness of a Delatorian midsummer's day. Sharp rays of light stabbed at their eyes, eyes that had only just become accustomed to the grey and gloom of the Magistratum holding cell's foreboding interior.

As they exited the gated compound Elliot heard the snap of heels and as he turned he saw the previously lethargic Magistratum guard raise a rigid hand to his temple. The young attorney nodded gratefully and saluted back.

"There was something wrong wasn't there?" Epona cautiously probed. "She was frightened."

"Did you see the sash the woman was wearing around her waist?" Elliot replied.

"I saw the dodgy looking blade hanging from it."

"Quite, but the sash? Did you notice it had the Royal Delatorian crest folded within the pleats?"

"The Royal crest?"

"Abigail left to become a Meretrix shortly after her parents passed away. The disciplined life of a courtesan was what some thought best for her at the time."

"Why the tight security? Shall I find out who she is?" Epona eagerly offered.

"No need, she's known as Rose Red. Her real name is Letalis, the Secarius, Emilita Letalis," Elliot emphasised. "Only she would wear something so garish in a place like that."

"The Queen's own body guard?"

"Amongst other things, yes," the criminal lawyer replied with some apprehension. "Asmodeus was right," he pondered beneath his breath.

"About what?" Epona queried, trotting faster now as Elliot had decidedly picked up the pace.

"Oh… Uncle was right about there being more to this case," Elliot replied somewhat distracted. He was thinking hard about something, the next step perhaps, or the next destination.

"So what now?"

"Sleep," the lawyer plainly stated. "It has been a long day. Mine ran through the night on that bloody Beanstalk case. So perhaps we should call it a day."

"Get our heads cleared for tomorrow?"

"Exactly."

"And tomorrow's plan?" Epona curiously asked.

"Evidence Epona, evidence," Elliot replied turning to the centaur with a grin, "and I hope you're not squeamish."

He was beginning to get his legal head back on, having left it behind when he knelt outside Abigail's cell. Slowly but surely Elliot was formulating a plan for her defence.

Elliot had made the right choice to take a brief respite. In the time it took for the grain to fall from twenty hourglasses he had witnessed a giant crushing dead his client, had been assigned a trainee and had discovered his child-hood friend was being accused of murder, had taken on the case and had been reunited with her for the first time in fourteen ring-years. To carry on would be to risk more harm to his overloaded mind and fatigued body than good.

Epona's first day had not been uneventful either. She had almost been late for work, had been sucked into the ground like a droplet of water upon dry soil, had been caught pompously displaying her mentor's phallic headdress on her head, had met a number of animated stationary pieces, met her mentor and stepped through a Blood-Stone activated Syngraphus to assist in a proper non-hypothetical real criminal case… with a real client. All extremely far removed from the theorised tutelage of Archbold's college of Law. She was feeling equally shattered.

So as they shook hands and went on their separate ways Elliot did so thinking about a comfy bed and a good night's sleep (as well as trying not to think of Abigail being denied the same) and Epona trotted back to her recently acquired stables thinking how she might come to enjoy working alongside Elliot. *Life would never be boring* she mused, *though what did he mean by squeamish*?

13

"Sex: Male. Age: late twenties, approximately 28 Arborian ring-years at a guess, based on the subject's skeletal development."

Dr Capek leaned back from the examination table and pulled a heavy lever just to his right. At once the table's four legs retracted and the four chains that had hung loose from the ceiling to each of the table's corners were pulled taught. A gauge, also high above the doctor's head, was fixed at the apex of where the chains met and its needle now spun to life.

"Weight, hmm, remaining body mass is, 12 stone and… oh, my eyes aren't what they used to be. What do think Metri?"

"12 stone 5 and ¾ pounds to be precise Dr Capek."

"Okay that's sounds about right. Height, bearing in mind the subject's feet have been eaten away at the ankles, I should say 6 feet 4 inches had the body been intact," the doctor continued.

"6 feet 3 and – " replied his assistant.

"Yes, thank you Metri."

"Eye Colour: hard to tell given the victim's face has also been eaten away. Hair Colour: blonde but for a small amount of blood staining to the lower locks, likely the victim's own blood bearing in mind the trauma suffered to the throat region."

The pathologist quickly scanned the body again before clearing his throat and resuming the autopsy. "Finger prints: none – fingers have also been chewed away. Apparel: Wolven suit. Perhaps the deceased was into role-play, hey Aemaeth?"

"Like a playhouse actor Dr?" replied his second assistant.

"Well, but for the copious amounts of semen staining the suit I might have said yes. Something more risqué perhaps?" the pathologist mused. "Right, let's remove the costume, shall we?"

A number of efficient snips here and there and after some rolling of the corpse the Wolven suit was parted from its lifeless owner. The doctor folded this into a neat bundle and handed it to Metri who promptly spun round and placed it into a glass evidence cabinet.

"Unique features," Capek continued, "hmm, again severe head and facial traumas will make visual identification difficult. No other unique body marks. Wait what's this? Looks like scarring to the lower abdomen, likely the subject's appendix was removed at some point in his life. Now to the messy part. Pause recording Aemaeth."

Dr Capek hopped from the stool he was standing upon and scuttled over to a table laden with grim looking surgical tools, tourniquets, syringes and swabs, at the opposite end of the pathology lab. He stepped onto another stool that sat at the base of the table, quickly scanned the array of implements upon its surface before choosing a pristinely polished scalpel, a bone saw and a crescent-shaped cleaver, which had a handle at each end, which was used for cracking open breastplates.

Again he jumped down, crossed the room whilst perilously balancing the cumbersome but razor sharp tools in his arms, and stepped back up to the autopsy table.

At only three feet in height Dr Capek was not the tallest pathologist in the Magistratum, hence all the jumping up and down, scuttling around and perilous balancing. Although the desktops and the surgical assistant automata were all above his head height, the ever-cheerful doctor made do with a number of pedestals, plinths and platforms to conduct his pathology without impediment.

"Here we are Metri," he said screwing the scalpel onto one of the four of his clockwork assistant's mechanical arms, "and this one," on snapped the bone saw to Metri's lower left, "and finally… there," Capek cooed looking the automaton up and down, having fixed the breastplate cleaver to its two remaining upper arms.

"Thank you Dr," Metri stated in a voice that lacked any of the recognisable intonations and inflections of Dr Capek's human colleagues.

Metri was a copper and tin clockwork construction that, at its simplest, resembled an elaborately crafted timepiece encased in glass. The transparent surface enabled one to see right through the automaton, and Dr Capek often took pleasure in watching the cogs and pistons and pendulums turn, contract and rotate within the assistant's crystal casing. The doctor found it wondrous that the great craftsman of Horologium had fashioned such an intricate machine, so alien in appearance to any other bipedal on Arbor, whilst still maintaining the movements and behaviour and the essence of the World-Tree's sentient races. Each fluid motion of the mechanical assistant came with a satisfying hiss of compressed air, each twist of its wrists accompanied by a whir of cogs and the whiz of tightly wound copper bands.

Koestler, the only living person and founder of the clockwork city of Horologium, had crafted Metri and Aemaeth as a gift to the Delatorian Magistratum after they had rescued and returned one of his first creations that had been stolen by a travelling circus. Koestler, however, was not usually fond of human contact and having served out his three ring-year Delatorian service within the Magistratum he subsequently left the great capital city to pursue a life of solitude. He felt that his kin's propensity for violence and irrationality was something inherently illogical, an unwelcome distraction problematical to the ongoing development of intelligence. His views may have been mistaken for a Caelum Angelic had he been taller and not lacked their characteristic white-feathered wings. So when he served out his civic duties the annoyed inventor, surrounded by the barbaric brutality that threatened to impede his intellectual development, decided to move to a quiet and hitherto unclaimed part of the World-Tree known as Tempus.

No one had taken root in Tempus due to the fact that time appeared to move much faster there. People often claimed they were rushed off their feet and that day and night would come so swiftly that they didn't know whether they were coming or going. Koestler, however, knew that Tempus was located on one of Arbor's outlying branches; a great jagged mountain that rose up from the World-Tree's surface like a spike.

The particular orbit of Arbor around its sun, meant that Tempus was bathed in light for only three turns of an hourglass, after which it would be plunged into darkness for a further three, and so on and so forth.

This accelerated shift from day to night might have proved unbearable for others, but Koestler, who was familiar with working through all hour-turns of the day, whilst operating with as little sleep as possible, found the conditions quite hospitable. Besides, his speciality for timepieces meant that he could keep check with the hour in Delator, regardless of the time in Tempus insuring that his own internal body clock never got too run down. In time he renamed his new home Horologium, after the clockwork contraptions he lovingly crafted there.

While he never favoured his life as a Magistratum it was during those three ring-years of service that Koestler met Dr Mikhail Capek, a rising surgeon and skilled pathologist. The doctor taught Koestler a great deal about human anatomy, the knowledge of which the inventor used to great effect in his subsequent creations.

When Capek assisted the Magistratum in the safe return of Koestler's first creation, the clockwork architect remembered the enthusiastic forensic scientist, remembered the stimulating conversation and the refreshing feeling of being able to conduct a rational conversation with someone of his own mental ilk, and decided to send the Magistratum pathologist two assistants. Though they were meant as a personal gift he knew the Automata would prove invaluable in the enforcement of law in his home city of Delator, so he was doubly satisfied.

"Resume recording Aemaeth," Capek politely asked as he resumed the autopsy.

Whereas Metri was powered by the energy stored then released within thousands of tightly coiled self-winding copper bands, Aemaeth contained two small internal furnaces in its legs, much like a pair of boilers, and was powered by steam. Aemaeth was ever the bit as useful even if it didn't look as pleasing to the eye as its more aesthetically engineered twin.

It stood tall upon a pair of bulbous legs much like those of an antique diving suit and it had no arms. This automaton was designed to be a recorder and on the outside of the twisted bundles of Aemaeth's copper tubing, which compressed and channelled steam to various pistons and cams throughout the body, there was fixed a tin disk about the span of a soldier's buckler.

The disk had a hole in its centre through which it was threaded onto the Automaton. Three fine tubular nozzles peered out from the edges of the disk like the claw fixing of a jewel-encrusted finger ring. At the sound of Capek's command tiny bursts of flame issued from each of the nozzles as if they were miniature blowtorches, and when all three were lit the burnished disk at the centre of the robot's body began to spin.

Aemaeth was an extremely ingenious piece of engineering. Whilst the steam was used to turn the centrepiece, part of the maze like tubing within the Automaton's bottom-heavy body was also designed to channel hydrogen, which was stored in another tank fixed to Aemaeth's back, to the three burners where it was ignited by tiny pieces of self-snapping flint.

The robot was still a recorder though and therefore had to be able to adequately channel sound. In order to achieve this task a widening length of tubing coiled from the Automaton's back round its body like a Arabilisian sea snake before terminating in a great fluted head like that from some classical phonogram. Essentially Aemaeth's face was actually one giant ear.

So, with all three torches flaming, tin disk turning and great fluted ear channelling, the Automaton was ready to resume burning a fresh audio track as Dr Capek continued his autopsy.

"Internal Organs... right we'll start with the chest cavity. Metri if you could," continued the pathologist.

Aemaeth recorded the sound of cracking bone as Metri went to work on the subject's breastplate with the crescent-shaped cleaver attached to its upper arms.

"Ah excellent. Well, heart looks healthy enough, the size supports my earlier estimation as to the subject's age. Lungs look to be in good order also. Hmm, not much out of the ordinary. To the stomach contents then. Metri is now making an incision across the subjects midriff," Capek described to Aemaeth who promptly directed its fluted face towards the examination table as its three burners continued to delicately etch new channels onto its spinning disk. "And now to the stomach – "

At that moment the door to the pathology theatre creaked open and Elliot and Epona tentatively entered. Dr Capek looked up from the examination table towards the two visitors, pointed to Aemaeth before putting a finger to his lips. Elliot nodded before turning to Epona to make the same quieting gesture. Dr Capek smiled gratefully before continuing his examination.

"Yes, the stomach looks as if the subject had a hearty meal before the end. Lets take a look inside shall we Metri."

The surgeon reached inside the corpse's belly and lifted out a particularly full stomach organ together with a long length of intestinal tract. He moved to place these into a kidney dish that was placed between the corpse's legs.

"That's a…" Epona whispered to Elliot, raising a shaky finger to the faceless corpse and the bloody mass Dr Capek was hoisting out of it. "I think I'm going to…" and with that Epona quietly backed out of the room before cantering out onto the grass verge that bordered the outside of the surgery.

After she had promptly threw up the undigested breakfast she had rushed to eat two hour-turns before, dabbed at her sweaty forehead and wafted air onto her face, she re-entered the autopsy theatre smiling meekly at Elliot who asked whether she was feeling okay.

"I'm good. First time with a…" Epona replied in a manner that suggested further imminent vomiting.

"Pause recording Aemaeth," called Dr Capek.

"Wish he'd make up his mind," complained the steam-powered automaton in a feint but annoyed whisper. "I'm not made of water."

"Let's take a break shall we, Metri you can wind yourself up while I talk to our guests."

"Thank you doctor," replied the implement-burdened robot as it plodded over to its brother.

"Oohh, *thank you* doctor," Aemaeth sarcastically mimicked as Metri approached. "Just because you've got arms you think you're some big shot."

"What's got into you tanks today grumpy?" And so they continued to bicker as they did every working day when the doctor's back was turned, Metri being especially adept at winding up its brother more than itself.

Capek carefully rolled off his bloodstained surgical gloves and started to descend from his footstool.

"No need doctor we'll come over," Elliot offered stepping forward. "It's good to see you again Mikhail," greeted the young attorney with an outstretched hand.

"Good to see you too Elliot," replied Capek vigorously shaking Elliot's hand, "and how is your uncle keeping?"

"As mischievous as ever. Ah, let me introduce you. Dr Mikhail Capek this is Epona Brenwen, Blackstone & Associates' newest addition."

"Pleasure to meet you doctor," replied Epona. "Sorry about the…" she apologised gently patting her midriff.

"Not to worry my dear, and the pleasure is all mine," the doctor said sweeping up the centaur's delicate hand with his own. Dr Capek may have been 134 ring-years old but he could still play the cad if ever the opportunity arose. "Besides, I don't blame you with this one," he continued staring back down at the corpse, "even my stomach started to do the waltz when I saw…"

Epona peered round Elliot's shoulder and curiously eyed the throat that had been torn apart and the windpipe that had a bite-sized chunk missing from it, the cracked and open rib cage that looked like a Venus flytrap, and the empty stomach cavity that gave off a malodorous smell. She tried not to let her eyes wonder up to the corpse's faceless head but her curiosity got the better of her and once again she found herself trotting out of the surgery to expel what little contents there remained within her weak stomach.

"I think I'll just stay out here for a bit, if you don't mind," called the ill-sounding centaur from outside the surgery.

"No worries Epona," replied Elliot. "A bit squeamish apparently," he continued turning back to Capek.

"Like I said, this is a grim one."

"So what's the verdict doc?"

"Well I'm thinking that having his face and throat ripped out might have something to do with it," the pathologist joked.

"Very funny… were the – "

"Were the wounds inflicted by human teeth, perhaps those of the suspect the Magistratum have in custody at this moment?" Capek predicted. "Well that's the interesting thing you see. Metri could you pass me a magnification helm?"

"Erm…" replied the automaton. The doctor turned to see Metri shaking his head and holding up its four arms, each still fixed with the surgical instruments the doctor had attached earlier. Elliot thought he could hear Aemaeth let out a brief snigger.

"Don't worry I'll fetch it," offered Elliot, turning to an equipment cabinet to his left to retrieve what looked like a glass goldfish bowl the front of which appeared to be more convex than the rest, which he passed to the doctor.

"No no, you go ahead."

Elliot nodded and placed the bowl over his head until it rested on his shoulders like a helmet.

"Good?" Capek asked to which Elliot nodded in reply, "excellent, take a look at the fingers… well, what's left of the fingers. Notice the sharp scratches on the exposed bone?"

"Yep," the lawyer observed in an echoing voice, no doubt caused by the glass globe he had on his head.

"Caused by pointed teeth, perhaps a jackal, or some other feral creature."

"But not by human teeth?"

"Exactly. You can find the same markings on the bare cranium that remains… you see where the cheekbones and lower jaw should be? The same marks. And if we move down to the ankles," the doctor gestured. Elliot carefully moved down the body, still holding the magnifier in place, till he reached the area Capek had now directed his attention. "We find the same."

"But, hmm," Elliot had a thought.

"Go on, I know you're relatively intelligent, what's wrong with the picture?"

"Relatively?" Elliot grinned taking off the goldfish bowl shaped helmet and passing it back to Capek. "If I had to guess I'd say that this man was long dead before he sustained these injuries."

"…Because?" the pathologist prompted.

"Because if these wounds had been inflicted at the point of the poor fellow's death then we'd expect to see a lot more blood inside the facial cavity as well as some staining to the ends of the gnawed fingers and ankles," interrupted Epona cleverly as she re-entered the surgery.

"Quite right Miss Brenwen," Capek cooed.

"Okay?" Elliot asked turning to the trainee.

"Much better, just meat really isn't it? Anyway it's boring out there."

"Dehumanising the deceased does help overcome the squeamishness," Capek agreed.

"So that just leaves the throat area," Elliot continued.

"Exactly, this area does show more blood staining to the skin of the neck. This primary trauma point would also explain the blood patterns to the lower locks of the subjects hair."

"And this does – " Epona asked not without some concern in her voice.

"And this does match that of human jaws and teeth. Judging by the size of the piece that has been torn from the windpipe I'd say either a teenage male child or – "

"A human female," Elliot concluded.

The dejected lawyer stepped away from the corpse, Epona and Capek, and slumped himself down onto one of the doctor's stools. He put his face in his hands and let out a long sigh, as if all hope and optimism was slowly escaping him.

"She couldn't have," Elliot stated looking up at Epona's face. The Equinmare appeared concerned for her mentor yet she felt powerless to do anything.

"Anything else unusual about the corpse doctor?" Epona asked turning back to Capek.

"No, but I've yet to finish up my examination," the doctor said climbing down from his pedestal and approaching Elliot. "But if anything comes up…" he continued at eye level to the seated lawyer.

"Thanks Mikhail." With a huff and a shrug of his shoulders Elliot rose to his feet, winked at Epona reassuringly before making towards the door. Yet as he was about to exit the surgery something suddenly dawned upon him.

"What is it?" queried Epona, curiously scanning the thoughtful looking face of her colleague.

"Abigail was found with a Wolven head right? Like a Wolven mask?" asked the lawyer quickly.

"Yep, according to the witness report the Magistratum released to us, so?" replied the Mare'ess.

"Mikhail. What was this chap wearing when they found him?" asked Elliot with an increased vigour as he turned back to the Magistratum pathologist. Capek smiled up at the young attorney and dashed beneath the autopsy table to the evidence cabinet at the other side of the room. He flung open the glass doors narrowly missing his automata, which were observing the scene with increasing interest, before shooting up a small ladder and recovering the Wolven suit he had removed from the corpse. He tucked the suit under his arms, slid back down the ladder and ran under the examination table before skidding to a halt in front of Elliot, who had retaken his seat.

"This," the surgeon announced passing the garment to Elliot with both hands as if presenting the lawyer with a precious offering.

The lawyer took the costume and with a wrinkled brow looked over every inch of it while Epona and Capek watched intently. Elliot ran his fingers over the fur, turned the skin inside out, rotated it this way and that and examined the cuffs and collar. It was like watching a Seer direct physic energy through the clothing of some lost soul in order to locate them, and at one point Epona swore that Elliot had closed his eyes. The young Criminal defence attorney then stopped, thought a moment then folded the garment back up and gratefully handed it back to Capek.

"Whatever you are thinking with your relatively intelligent mind Elliot, is a full day ahead of what the prosecution has started thinking about," the doctor reassuringly stated.

"Relatively?" Elliot replied with a mischievous smile, "Thanks doc." He placed a hand on the small surgeon's shoulder, gave it a gentle squeeze and thanked him again. "Come on Epona, time we got going."

"It was a pleasure to meet you Dr Capek, despite the grimness," the centaur sincerely stated, lowering her front legs at the knees to shake the hand of the dwarfish doctor.

"Feel free to come back anytime, and you keep an eye on this one," Capek replied nodding towards Elliot, "rumour has it he's a fan of the ladies."

"Perhaps the two footed variety Dr," Epona smiled pointing to her hind legs.

As the two lawyers exited the surgery Capek looked at the Wolven suit in his hands and shook his head. Whilst he did work for the Magistratum he did have a profound respect for the human defence lawyer who took on the underdog cases and supported the no-hopers. The doctor always felt that if ever he was in trouble he could count on someone like Elliot to help him out, which is why he took a great deal of pleasure from his visits, and in reminding the lawyer of his relatively intelligent nature if ever Elliot needed reminding of the same.

Elliot appeared to be in some deep thought, as if attempting to arrange the myriad of ideas, plans and possibilities tumbling through his mind. Whenever he did this whilst walking the young attorney would invariably begin to pick up the pace, as if the physical act of a forced but disciplined march somehow ordered the chaos within his head. Again Epona found herself lagging behind her mentor, which she found quite ironic considering she had twice the number of legs as he did.

"What did he mean? He's for the prosecution isn't he? Sounds like he was helping us," Epona asked as she pulled level with her mentor.

"Erm, oh," Elliot replied, departing from whatever train of thought he had been embarking on. When the bright young attorney's mind was focused there was little that could break his concentration. Abigail used to have to throw grapes at his head to get his attention as a child, especially when Elliot was lost in some engrossing read. "Sorry, Capek was just reminding us of the head-start we had." Epona cocked her head towards Elliot with a quizzical expression on her face. "Yes, he is for the prosecution," Elliot continued, "but he's a good man… not that there are no good men in the Magistratum, just that…"

"Your rambling."

"Quite. He's reminding us that the prosecution have yet to look at the evidence… to examine the Wolven outfit… they've yet to follow that chain of enquiry."

"If Asmodeus is right and there is more to this case than meets the eye then it's bound to have something to do with Mr no-face back there," Epona stated.

"Exactly, so what do we know?" Elliot rhetorically continued. "We know that Abigail was found with a Wolven head. We also know Mr no-face was found with a Wolven body, right?"

"Yep."

"So it stands to reason that Mr anonymous was, at some point, wearing the full costume."

"Can't be that many Wolven costume makers in Delator, especially those working with the genuine article," Epona replied.

"Exactly, no poor tailor is going to have the means to acquire real Wolven pelt. So we find the tailor, we find out who the victim is."

"One step closer the truth."

“That’s the plan,” Elliot sighed. And it was a reasonable plan bearing in mind the duo had little to follow up, bearing in mind the victim had no face and that their client was under the watchful and threatening eye of a royal assassin. “So I’ll go visit some Delatorian tailors.”

“And I’ll?” Epona asked, gently scuffing a hind hoof on the cobbled street (she wanted to follow up the costume lead).

“Diminished Responsibility,” Elliot stated, which made Epona stop in her tracks. “Anything on childhood trauma induced temporary insanity case law and clauses. Babel in Liber should have it all there… a great place, all the Laws of Arbor in a huge –”

“Trauma, Babel, Diminished… I don’t understand,” the Equinmare stuttered with a bemused look on her face. Elliot stopped and turned towards the confused trainee. The rambling; he had a tendency for it when he was plotting something, and he knew that it often meant he was disregarding the capacity for others to keep up with him.

“I’m sorry… coffee?”

“What?”

“Coffee,” Elliot repeated, “you drink coffee?”

“I prefer tea… really, but…”

“Excellent, tea it is, I know this great tea house. We’ll get some food into you, given that you threw up your breakfast.”

“Hey, that was a whole lot of grimness back there,” Epona objected.

“You’re right, sorry. Tea, food and explanations, how about it?”

“You’re on,” Epona agreed.

“Excellent.”

Thus, over a cup of tea and an extremely tasty pastry at the best teahouse in Delator, Elliot, in sad reflection, revealed what happened when Abigail Hood came face to face with a Wolven fourteen ring-years ago.

“That’s unbelievable,” Epona gasped through her hands. “I’m sorry, really.”

"Thank you. So there's a chance Abigail may not have been in control of all her faculties when she was…"

"You think the Wolven costume might have been a trigger?" Epona asked.

"She was found naked but for the headpiece, that doesn't sound normal," Elliot replied.

"Neither does a thirteen year old girl cutting out the dead heart of a…" Epona suddenly stopped. She understood.

"Exactly. One traumatic event fourteen ring-years ago led to extreme behaviour. Now we're at the present and Abigail is faced with the same terrifying reality, except this time it's a man in costume which triggers the extreme throat ripping behaviour."

"Arguably," Epona reminded.

"Worth arguing," Elliot wisely replied. "So take these Blood-Stones, you'll need these to get to Babel. Don't look so worried you're going to love it. And this is the sigil for the office for when you decide to come back," he remembered removing a small quill from his jacket which he used to quickly scribble the Syngraphus symbol for Blackstone & Associates onto a spare napkin.

"And you?" Epona double-checked.

"Erm, I'll drop in on Abigail, give her some supplies and some food," Elliot dropped his gaze back to his cup of tea. Just mentioning Abigail's name made his heart heavy. "Then costume shopping," he looked up with a half-smile.

"How do you think the Magistratum is getting on putting together their case?" Epona asked.

"Hmm, faceless victim, a suspect who won't talk. It's a tough one and I'm sure their resources are focused on more clear-cut cases. Always the way, expedite the easy ones, sit on the difficult," Elliot sighed.

"So Dr Capek's right, we've got a head start."

"For now perhaps. Just for the moment."

Elliot's observation as to the Magistratum prioritising of difficult cases proved to be quite accurate as it happened. Across town the prosecution case manager on The Crown versus Abigail Hood was at that moment being quizzed by an increasingly irate Fire-Nymph about an entirely different case involving seven Dwarf-Giants and a palace vault, which meant that all thoughts of faceless victims and silent witnesses were undoubtedly pushed to the back of the overworked and underpaid civil-servant's tired mind.

14

Mirror, mirror on the wall,
Five times has it shown my fruit to fall.
Damned be my cursed womb,
From which all emerge to their sorry doom.

A quintet of gravestones it has shown me,
My first destined not to reach three.
Of the second, stillborn it was,
Her precious life a painful loss.

Yet still we strove to produce an offspring,
A son perhaps we could raise to be king.
When he came how we did rejoice,
Short-lived it was for he had no voice.
The muted cries we did not hear,
When he drowned in his second year.

As parents we outlived our children thrice,
But still a forth time we rolled the dice.
The next was born much like the second,
Threatening to take my life some later reckoned.

The fifth would be the final blow,
After many ring-years of anguish and woe.
While I bled to death she lived for a short while,
Blessing you, my love, with her first smile.
But soon her breath would start to fail her,
For this fifth soul there was no saviour.

For the Carmen Speculum I never blame you,
The gift you bought me when our love was true.
But the future it shows me I cannot bear you to suffer,
And so I leave you to take another.

I wish there was a different way,
For us to live and love and play.
Yet if I remain forever shall we be fated,
Until the moment we are separated.

My love, my life, my King,

Forgive me.

"After the King's first wife wrote that letter she poisoned herself."

"And this is the only reference to the Carmen Speculum your office possesses?" asked Fury refolding the suicide poem and handing it back to the tired looking Magistratum case officer.

"That's correct, the King ordered a formal investigation following the death. That's how we came to acquire the letter. That was thirty ring-years ago. Now I'm quite busy so if there are –"

"Just a few more questions, we'll try not to keep you," Fury lied.

Her past work to date had steered her clear of policing bodies such as the Magistratum and the majority of her cases dealt with financial institutions – great moneyed guild houses whose 'time is money' attitude undoubtedly meant that little time was wasted when it came to question and answer sessions. However, in this case, Fury was growing more and more impatient with the prosecution officer's blasé demeanour and general unwillingness to render any assistance to her enquiries. Not that the Magistratum was other wise obligated to divulge police records, on the contrary there was nothing preventing the prosecutor from placing a confidentiality status on the whole palace robbery given that it still remained open.

Whilst Fury was quite aware of this fact, it didn't stop her from increasing the temperature of the prosecutor's office by several degrees. *If you're going to make things uncomfortable for me then I'm going to make things unbearable for you*, the Fire-Nymph angrily thought to herself as the bluish hue of her flaming aura turned a subtle shade of orange. She never was one for moderation.

"The palace robbery eight days ago, how did you know the Vigilantag Seven were responsible?" Vincent interjected, instantly feeling the stifling air of the office as a result of Fury's shift in mood.

"Originally we didn't," the officer revealed, "our first visit to the vault the day after the crime yielded no material evidence of the perpetrator's identity or identities."

"But…" Fury impatiently prompted.

The Magistratum unbuttoned his collar and loosened the white frilled ruffle that he wore around his neck. "But a few days later a witness came forward, claiming that he or she had seen the dwarf-giants commit the crime. The witness also provided the location for the criminal's hideout," the prosecutor continued.

"What do you mean *he* or *she*" queried the Fire-Nymph.

"Well the witness never actually *came forward* as such, it was all written in a letter."

"May we take a look," Vincent politely requested.

"Well I guess so, just wait here please. I have to pull the file out," replied the prosecutor with a sigh as he rose from his chair. Fury noticed the man's right leg had been replaced with a wooden stump up to the knee, and as she watched him limp slowly through the open plan Prosecutions office, perhaps out of sympathy, she decided to reduce her temperature back from an intolerable heat to a comfortable warmth.

"So, bored of my company yet?" Fury asked turning back to Vincent.

"Not at all, it's interesting to see you at work," Vincent replied with smile. "I was just thinking about that poem the King's first wife wrote."

"I know, sad wasn't it?" the Insurance lawyer admitted much to Vincent's surprise. "I may be a bitch, but I'm a woman too. And there is part of me that wants to be a mother some day. I mean, imagining what that poor woman must have felt like seeing all those children, yet to be born, perish one after the other."

"I don't blame her for wanting to take her own life. It's just that… I don't know,"

"What?"

"So the Carmen Speculum was a magic mirror," Vincent continued, "perhaps it was only showing a possible future. I mean how much of life is ever certain?"

"The tone of the suicide poem suggested that she believed it to be true, which I guess is the whole point. It doesn't matter what you or I believe," Fury reflected.

"Then perhaps it was a waste of a life."

"Perhaps. People have been putting their faith in Seers and Tellers for thousands of ring-years. They believe that all of life can be foreseen because it is, in essence, already mapped out. Besides if I was going to spend 250,000 amber ducats on a magically imbued mirror, I'd want to make sure it was the genuine article."

"I wonder why the King bought it for her?" Vincent pondered.

"You know what monarchs are like, all flamboyance and no sense. He probably thought that the mirror would show him and his Queen how happy their life would be. Who knew that the future it showed the Queen was not the idyllic vision the King had intended."

"Perhaps. Then again that was thirty ring-years ago, the King has since remarried and has a son close to my own age. Why do you think he kept hold of the mirror and didn't destroy it?"

"Now that's a better question," Fury agreed, "and one we shall save when we visit the palace."

"You're not seriously going to question the King about the death of his first wife are you?" Vincent objected.

"That may not be necessary, someone else at the palace may know more about the Carmen Speculum, one of the older servants or cleaners perhaps, or maybe the accountant who keeps the royal asset ledger in order."

"And if not?"

"Then I hope you've practiced your curtsies," Fury grinned.

"Sometimes I think you enjoy your job a little too much," Vincent replied shaking his head in mock disapproval.

"Maybe a *little* too much," Fury conceded as she eyed the prosecutor with the wooden leg and a case bundle under his arm hobble back to the office.

The Magistratum prosecutor retook his seat, unwound the red ribbon that bound the case file for the Vigilantag robbery and leafed through the loose pages of parchment till he came to the witness letter.

"Here it is, relatively short considering its content," stated the prosecutor as he handed over the piece of evidence.

" 'Dear Magistratum, I know who robbed the palace vault and where they are hiding. I followed them. I shall gladly testify but my identity must remain anonymous,' " Fury read aloud. "Then it just goes on to describe the location of the Zwerg-Riese hideout."

"*Supposed* hideout," the prosecutor corrected with a grumble. "Whilst we recovered much of the palace's stolen possessions we could find nothing to link the place to the Vigilantag. It was almost as if the loot was purposefully left there for us to find. We caught the Seven on the outskirts of the city and held them on suspicion."

"Did the witness sign off the letter?" asked Vincent.

"Hansel," Fury replied, "though given the witness's request for anonymity that name is probably an alias."

"But Hansel never came forward."

"That's right, he or she… most likely a *he* given the alias, but you can never be sure, was due to identify the Dwarf-Giants yesterday morning," replied the Magistratum looking up from the case bundle to Vincent. "But as you say, the witness never came forward. Which meant – "

"That you had to release the suspects," Fury concluded.

"Unfortunately under the Incarceration Act of Arbor we can hold suspects for longer than six days only if there is substantive evidence to support their suspicion," the officer concluded.

"The lack of evidence at the vault and the hideout meant that a positive eyewitness identification and testimony was the only way to get the extension and push for a prosecution," Vincent guessed.

"Exactly," confirmed the Magistratum prosecutor. "I hate the idea of the Vigilantag running around free as much as anyone else in this office, but the Delatorian investigative and judicial processes must be followed to the letter. Otherwise what's the point in having a legal system in place?"

Apart from learning of the witness's alias there was little more that Vincent and Fury took away from their visit to the prosecutor's office. As they bid farewell to the Magistratum officer the duo began to realise how frustrating the criminal process must be for those attempting to enforce its rules and laws, especially given the Delatorian Civil laws in place designed to protect an individual's liberties. Vincent likened it to one giant game of chess and complimented Elliot on his ability to cope with it all. Fury responded by likening Criminal Law to a hand of poker… that not everyone likes to show his or her cards until absolutely necessary. She said Elliot was a bluffer, or at least that was what Vincent thought she said.

"So we know what the Carmen Speculum is and we know that there is some mysterious witness who calls himself Hansel but is apparently a bit of a coward," Vincent recapped.

"Yep, yep and yep. The palace?"

"Well you are investigating their insurance claim, so it would be within your remit to query its nature I guess," Vincent reluctantly conceded.

"It is my job," Fury stated.

"Perhaps you could try not to go all inferno in there though."

"Perhaps," Fury mischievously grinned.

Whilst Vincent was wary of the Insurance lawyer's cavalier attitude he was growing increasingly fond of her wicked streak. He found it refreshing to be in the company of someone who was comfortable taking modest risks and was strong enough to ask for what they wanted when they wanted it. Apart from Elliot, Vincent didn't know anyone else that displayed such an innately confident demeanour, except perhaps Asmodeus, but then again he was a senior partner at the firm.

The young Sandman didn't know whether Fury was fond of him however, and in some way it didn't really matter whether she was or she wasn't. Vincent always told himself that half of the attraction is in not knowing. 'It's that element of the fantastical that drives a person's dreams and desires' he would spout to Elliot whenever the Criminal attorney was being particularly lecherous. For now Vincent was quite content with being in her company and not knowing, smiling at her roguish grins and wandering what if.

The whole experience of shadowing her and offering support, granted that it had only been for a day and half thus far, was certainly more entertaining than sifting through financial statements back at his office. In a way Fury had reminded Vincent how fun the Law can be – a fact lawyers often lose sight of when their work becomes routine.

Ironically Fury's outwardly boisterousness nature and her proclivity for sharp and witty retorts sheltered a relatively lonely individual. The Fire-Nymph had questioned her brash demeanour when Vincent had walked passed her office as she was throwing ledgers about, and again when she realised that despite the Magistratum prosecutor's impatience the officer was just trying to deliver fair justice – for all she knew he was a good man and an upstanding citizen. And therein lay the problem with Fury for she never *knew*, or chose to find out for that matter. Her argumentative and combative personality traits proved to be a constant barrier in her personal relationships and even her colleagues at work knew when to give her a wide birth or even avoid her altogether.

She had originally put it down to her being a Fire-Nymph and that was just the way she was. However more and more she began to wonder whether there could be increasing room for sympathy, or at least empathy. She often mused whether the gain in social interaction as a result of being more open would outweigh any detrimental affects to her working ability, for she still considered niceness akin to weakness.

Fury was starting to realise that a change was necessary, not a drastic change but a gradual shift from aggression to compassion. Certainly spending time with Vincent helped and she used their time together as an opportunity to develop a relationship that she was admittedly keen to develop, even if she wasn't ready to admit the same to the kindly Finance lawyer.

*

"Have you seen our son today my King?"

"No. Though he did say he was going away for a few days on a hunting trip with his friends."

"Oh, are you not worried that something – "

"He is a grown man Constance, quite capable of looking after himself," the King of Delator asserted whilst scanning his daily schedule of royal engagements.

"But the proph…" the Queen hesitated.

"I am certain that this matter has been discussed."

"Do you not worry so? I love our son more than anything…"

"As do I," the King sighed. "But I refuse to believe in a lot of superstitious babble and portents nonsense."

"I do not believe that it is so my King, and for the life of our – "

"Enough!" the monarch snapped. "I have already suffered at the hands of magic and mysticism and it is not something I wish to experience again."

The royal guard accompanying the King and Queen of Delator shot sideways glances at each other yet still managed to continue their unswerving service as they escorted the Monarchs through the grand gallery to the throne room.

"Forgive me my lord. I do not mean to dredge up the past," the Queen apologised bowing her head. The King stopped and lovingly turned to his wife. The eight-strong contingent of guardsmen, four on either side of the monarchs, instantly halted with a simultaneous stamp of their right feet.

"No, I am the one who should apologise my love," the King softly said as he took the Queen's hand in his own. "I know this worries you so, but I know first hand how whole-hearted belief in a predicted future can lead to ruin. My only wish is that you can understand why I… why *we* must not unravel what is not meant to be unravelled. Now I must conduct these tiresome state affairs," he concluded kissing the Queen's cheek.

As the King continued on his way six of the guards peeled away and retook their formation, leaving two remaining guards with the Queen, which she promptly dismissed.

"Any reports from your sister?" the Queen asked Snow White, her elite bodyguard and assassin who was keeping pace two steps behind her.

"She reports that Abigail has not uttered a word your Majesty. It appears the potion may have been strong enough to cause amnesia."

"A fortunate side effect."

"Yes your highness," Krystina quietly agreed.

"And of the Vigilantag?" the Queen enquired.

"I see them again tomorrow."

"Leave no stone unturned. I shall have it."

"Yes my Queen."

Krystina realised that if the Zwerg-Riese did not deliver what they had promised then much shedding of blood and inducing of comas may result. The mission was not without its risks and for all she knew the Seven might have some surprise waiting for her. As easy as it was to disarm the Dwarf-Giants a day ago, Snow

White knew that complacency in her line of work was tantamount to tying a noose around her own neck.

"And bow," signalled the ostentatiously liveried head porter who had been escorting Vincent and Fury.

"What did he – " Vincent quietly queried, to which he received a gently elbow to the rib from Fury who was nodding towards the advancing Queen. "Ah."

Both lawyers bowed graciously as the Queen approached them. She would otherwise have kept walking given her current preoccupations but rarely did she have occasion to see a Fire-Nymph in the royal palace.

"Vincent Traum and Fury your highness, from Blackstone & Associates," spoke the porter whilst keeping his head bowed. The servants knew better than to engage eye contact with the royal family.

"Ah Blackstone's, welcome to our palace. We trust our Meretrix is in safe hands?" asked the Queen looking upon the faces of the two lawyers.

"Erm – " Vincent hesitated.

"Yes your Majesty, our greatest efforts are being employed to ensure that Abigail Hood receives the best legal care," Fury quickly responded.

"Our thanks go with you," concluded the Queen as she continued on her way.

Taking lead from their porter the duo bowed again as the Queen passed by, though as Fury lifted her head she caught the piercing gaze of Krystina Letalis staring straight at her. Others would have immediately looked away but Fury focused right back at the suspicious eyes of the royal bodyguard as she and her charge exited the grand gallery. *Now who was she*? the Fire-Nymph thought.

As the porter led the two visitors through the court Vincent could not help but feel awed by the wealth and luxuries that surrounded them. Great gilt-thread tapestries the size of barn doors, elaborately woven showing scenes of courtly life, marble statues in which so much care had been taken to represent the likeness of real life in every delicate chisel that one might be mistaken for looking upon the victims of Medusa herself. Furniture and fittings from the highest quality wood and craftsmanship. Arched glass ceilings forty feet up that allowed dazzling beams of sunlight to splash onto the polished stone floor beneath. If a royal palace is indicative of the amount of power a monarch possesses then the King of Delator was a very powerful man. Such a thought was not far from Vincent's mind as he and Fury were led to a lavish sitting room where they were told to wait for the royal accountant.

"Nice save on the Hood case," Vincent sighed as he slumped down into a deep plush armchair, which he instantly thought was the most comfortable piece of furniture his backside was ever blessed to sit upon.

"No worries, the regal rarely distinguish between individuals. As far as the Queen might be concerned we simply represent Blackstone's and whatever case the firm is currently working on," Fury replied. "Comfy?"

"Absolutely, you should try the one over there."

"I'd be afraid to burn it. Last thing we need is Asmodeus wandering why we've been invoiced for a double weave upholstered, claw footed, arch back lounge chair from the Late Romantic period."

"Good point, and good eye."

"Thanks," Fury replied as she sauntered about the room admiring the various antiquities as well as trying particularly hard not to touch the same.

It always amazed Fury how much people spent on objects which one could find an everyday affordable equivalent for. For example she noticed an extravagantly embossed solid gold candlestick holder standing on one end of the grandiose mantelpiece just in front of her. She quickly estimated the item was possibly worth a few hundred amber ducats, perhaps more.

"Now what's wrong with an every day candle holder, even a silver one would still create the same effect," Fury huffed.

"What's stoking your embers now?"

"Just think of what we're surrounded by. Now imagine if they liquidated it all into amber ducats and deposited the same into a secure depository, imagine how much the royal family would save on palace contents insurance! I bet the royal Tabularius never thought of that," Fury exclaimed.

"Actually I did," interrupted an extremely tall but thin gentleman with a long cane who slowly stalked into the room, "about 150 ring-years ago I mooted it with the then King. He didn't take to it. What was it he said? Erm, the amount of amber on paper is not what projects power but the objects one chooses to display… or something like that. So long ago."

"Forgive my crass remarks sir," Fury apologised, choosing to show some respect to the aged accountant rather that pursue the matter.

"That's quite alright my dear, I still support your view. The palace would save a great deal of amber in insurance if we sold everything. But then again you would be out of the job would you not?" queried the man with a smile. Fury really couldn't fault his logic there.

"Quite. My name is Fury and this is my associate Vincent Traum," the Fire-Nymph politely introduced.

"My name is Aerarius Artifex, and you'd like to ask me about the theft claim resulting from the robbery we had eight days ago?"

"That's correct," Fury replied. "We received the palace's insurance claim a few days ago, and I came to visit your vaults the same day."

"Oh that was you, I did wonder who had been signed off to take a peek inside," Aerarius admitted as he tapped the tip of his cane with the spindly fingers of his right hand.

"Yes, that was little old me," Fury revealed. She was starting to wonder whether there was more to the weary looking Tabularius than met the eye. Vincent also had a suspicion that the accountant was hiding something. "I take it you had a hand in completing the claim?"

"I think you'll find my signature on the claim form, and I would have checked the content of the same also. I may be old but I'm not incompetent young lady."

"I didn't mean…" Fury was trying to be civil but her naturally aggressive tendencies were also trying to break through.

"It is just that we note that you haven't made a claim for the Carmen Speculum," Vincent interrupted much to Fury's initial shock but eventual relief, it was the reason for their visit after all she later reluctantly accepted.

"And why should we have Mr Traum?"

"Well it doesn't appear to be where it is supposed to be according to your records. Prior to the robbery it was logged as being in the vault but when Fury came to visit it wasn't there. We assumed you missed it from the claim," Vincent stated in a clear and calm manner.

"Ah I see, you must have taken a duplicate of the old ledger," the accountant guessed.

"Old ledger?" Fury queried.

"Well not old, as such, just that your records may not have the current location of that particular item."

"I don't understand."

"Oh it's really quite simple my dear. Right after the robbery we decided to move some high value items out of the safe. Quite ironic when you think about it, moving things out of the most secure room in the palace because you think they'll be safer," Aerarius chuckled.

Aside from the fact that Fury was getting slightly annoyed about being referred to as 'my dear' she was not overly keen on discovering that her records might be inaccurate. She very quickly came to the conclusion that, at worst, this whole line of enquiry may actually be a total waste of time.

"So it wasn't actually stolen?" Vincent quickly asked for fear that Fury might go raging inferno on them.

"That's correct, it's actually hanging quite safely in one of the state rooms that is very rarely in use."

"Mr Artifex we are sorry to have wasted your time," Vincent apologised. Fury was more shocked now that the Tabularius had confirmed that the mirror was not actually missing which also confirmed her worst-case scenario.

"Erm, yes thank you Mr Artifex you have been very helpful," Fury reluctantly managed after some subtle signals from Vincent.

"Bit odd isn't it? Insurance lawyers being concerned with high value items that aren't claimed for. I'd have thought that you'd be happy about such an oversight," the accountant continued much to Fury's annoyance.

"Just being thorough, I'm sure you know how important it is to keep one's figures in order," Vincent replied before Fury could open her mouth.

"I certainly do young sir. Well if there's nothing else I can help you with?"

"No that's great," Vincent courteously replied as he ushered the Fire-Nymph towards the door. "Actually, I know it's going to sound silly but… oh no I couldn't't"

"Please go ahead," prompted the accountant kindly.

"Well. Would it be possible, perhaps, to take a look at the mirror? I have a love of antiquity and the imbued and my head just went in a spin when Fury here told me that she was looking into the Carmen Speculum," Vincent embellished in a particularly camp manner.

What are you up to? wondered Fury as she looked at the Finance lawyer's face.

"I guess there's no harm. It's on the way out so we pass the room anyway. I could do with a stroll as it happens," the Tabularius uttered as he rose to his feet with the help of his cane.

The spindly-limbed account led the duo back through the grand gallery and down a portrait lined corridor that peeled away to the right just prior to reaching the main entrance to the palace. This time it was Fury who was impressed by the many artistic impressions of the Delatorian royal lineage. The Insurance lawyer did enjoy a spot of oil painting, which not many, in fact nobody, knew about. She particularly enjoyed recreating sky-scapes of brilliant sunsets and serine sunrises. Perhaps it was her fondness of reds and burnt sienna and yellows and oranges; the very colours that she felt defined her personality the most. As such she did take some pleasure in casting a critical eye over the pictures of the royals in all their finery and pomp and regalia.

"Ah, here we are," Aerarius announced as he opened an intricately veneered panelled door into a relatively innocuous looking guest room.

"It's a lot smaller than I imagined," Vincent admitted as he looked at the mirror, which was comparable in size to the full length one Elliot kept in his office.

"Well not everything has to be big to be expensive. The best things – "

"Come in small packages?" Fury interrupted.

"Yes my dear," replied the accountant.

"So how is it magical?" Vincent continued as Fury scanned the room paying particular attention to the luxurious four-poster bed.

"Well watch this… one of my favourites," Aerarius said before clearing his throat. "Mirror, mirror on the wall, who is the fairest of them all."

Vincent and Fury watched intently as the mirrored surface, which had previously been reflecting the image of the bed, clouded over in a misty and eerily foggy shade of grey. From behind the dull haze a shape appeared. It looked like one figure lying on top of the other. Fury thought it was something a little ruder but restrained herself from pointing it out. After a few moments a large pair of disembodied lips pushed through the fog, blew a kiss to the onlookers and began to speak in a slightly effeminate male voice.

"The Queen is the fairest in my opinion, for never is there a more beautiful vision."

"There you are you see. Quite magical don't you think?"

"You really think the Queen is – " Fury was about to query.

"Quite magical, thank you so much for showing it to me," Vincent cooed. "Well I think we can make our own way out, just to the left isn't?"

"That's right young sir. It was a pleasure to meet you both and if there's ever anything else I can help you with just ask. Good bye," and with that the Tabularius set off down another corridor like a great stick insect.

"He was creepy," admitted Fury when the accountant was out of sight and out of earshot.

"Pssst."

"What was that?" asked the Fire-Nymph turning back to Vincent.

"Pssst," the voice repeated.

"Erm, I think it was the mirror," Vincent replied as the duo turned to look at the huge pair of lips beaming back at them.

"I correct myself… *that* is creepy," Fury said pointing a finger towards the magic mirror.

"Oh don't be like that angel," replied the floating lips, "I was just going to say that you're a lot prettier than the Queen."

"Oh, erm, thank you," Fury managed a little taken aback by the sudden compliment.

"Are you blushing, I can't tell with – Ow!" Vincent yelped as Fury lightly singed his hand.

"Don't mention it angel, I always say it's the Queen, kind of have to with all the servants about and what not, don't want to get smashed now do I. Quite vain is the Queen," the mirror whispered.

"Well I guess we had better be off," Vincent announced.

"You really think I'm prettier than the Queen?" Fury pressed smiling at the mirror.

"Come on flaming beauty let's get back to the office I think we've solved this case," Vincent joked as he tried to usher Fury out into the corridor.

"Oh just one thing," remembered Fury as she wriggled free of the Finance lawyer. "Mirror, mirror on the wall, will I ever make senior partner? Sorry it doesn't rhyme."

The mirror bit its lower lip and thought a moment, not that it was immediately apparent that the floating pair of lips was actually thinking but it took a while for an answer to come none the less.

"Sorry honey, can't help you there," the magic mirror replied.

"You mean I'm wasting my time at this bloody…" Fury ranted while stamping her feet in that stubborn sort of way she was taken to doing when particularly annoyed.

"Oh no angel, just that you're asking the wrong kind of mirror aren't you."

"Pardon me?" replied Vincent.

"Yeah, I'm a *Vanity* mirror silly heads. I do make-up and erm, hair-dos, who's the fairest (obviously), and I'm quite good with jewellery and accessories," the pouting pair of lips revealed.

"You mean you don't tell the future, like if I'm going to have kids and whether they're going to die young and stuff," Fury spurted.

"That's grim, you have issues girlfriend. No, sounds like you want Carmen, Carmen Speculum. That's the one you want, Carmen will show you all about your future and what not."

"Wait a minute-turn, you're not the Carmen Speculum?" asked Fury uncharacteristically slowly and clearly.

"*The* Carmen Speculum, well look what's climbing up in the World-Tree? No, like I said I just do pretty, or not pretty, depends who's asking really doesn't it?"

There were a few moments of silence before Vincent had to restrain Fury from storming back to the accountant's office and ripping Aerarius' limbs off 'like the horsefly he was' or something equally cutting the Fire-Nymph spluttered through gritted teeth.

"Feisty that one, pretty, but feisty," commented the mirror as the duo left the guest room. Vincent thought it best not to add anything further to the vanity mirror's comments.

15

Before Elliot left to visit Abigail back at the Magistratum holding cells Epona had managed to get the justifiably preoccupied attorney to sketch down all of the Syngraphus sigils just to make doubly sure she didn't end up somewhere a million miles away from her intended destination. It also helped her avoid stepping through the portal to Caelum, which was the last place she wanted to visit.

She cantered her way over to the Delatorian Syngraphus in relatively quick time, considering the traffic that constantly threatened to gridlock the capital, and soon found herself in the middle of five huge walls covered in pentagrams and archaic symbols.

"Okeydoke, now I just throw this little thing at the sigil and hey presto," she whispered to herself while rolling one of the Blood-Stones Elliot had given her between her thumb and forefinger. She held up the napkin upon which were scribbled the six symbols, representing her office as well as those for the five capital cities, and scanned the five walls in front of her to make a visual comparison. The wall Elliot and Epona had stepped through yesterday had the sigil for Blackstone's carved upon its surface, which made immediate sense to the Equinmare – *why have a portal to Delator when one is already in Delator*, she wisely thought to herself.

She spotted the symbol for Babel, which looked like a helix between two vertical lines, planted her hind feet firmly onto the stone floor and lifted her right front knee up into her stomach (which she did think was a little strange but she had seen Elliot do the same). Epona then spun her arm around before releasing the blood-filled capsule.

Rather unspectacularly the Blood-Stone fell short of the symbol by about a good few hands-lengths, where it burst onto the floor making a bit of a mess.

Epona embarrassingly looked over her shoulder to check that no one had witnessed her weak underarm throw, whispered something that sounded like 'bugger' before trotting over to the small pool of blood that threatened to stain the stone floor, which she rapidly mopped up with a spare tissue. Take two – this time standing much, much closer to the intended target.

The capsule exploded upon the sigil with a satisfying popping sound, and Epona watched as, for the second time in two days, the red liquid magically brought the wall to life. A moment later she took a deep breath and walked through the new opening into Liber, a region she had not visited before but one she would subsequently grow especially fond of.

*

'Seven with one blow', I wonder what that means, Elliot thought to himself as he read the shop sign hanging outside a particularly quaint thatched cottage. As he opened the front door and stepped inside a small bell tinkled overhead alerting the shop owner to the lawyer's presence.

"Good afternoon young sir," welcomed a relatively old looking tailor, Elliot reckoned to be about 80 ring-years of age, who peered up from his needle and thread through extremely thick glasses that made his eyes appear four times the size they should.

"Afternoon," Elliot replied, trying not to be too distracted by the huge pair of eyeballs that were staring straight at him. "What does your sign mean? Sounds rude."

"Someone asked me that the other day, sent him off to Madame Payne's I did. It's four doors down if you're – "

"No that's fine. The sign?" Elliot repeated curiously.

"Oh the sign. In my whipper-snapping heyday I used to be quite the hero, felled seven beasties I did, outwitted Atlations, and even served the King as his champion before scaring him off and becoming King myself. Those were the days," the old fellow chuckled to himself.

"Uh huh," Elliot replied sceptically.

"So, what can I do for you? Trousers need taking up? Cuffs need altering? Or perhaps a brand new suit sir, oh yes," the old tailor enthusiastically jabbered as he sprang to his feet and advanced towards Elliot with an uncoiled measuring tape.

"No I'm good actually. Do you have anything in Wolven?"

"Now why would you be asking me about that Mr?" the tailor asked in an extremely suspicious tone. "Everybody knows trade in genuine pelt is illegal."

"Oh, erm, is it really? Had no idea," Elliot replied with some confusion. He'd certainly not come across any fur ban legislation recently.

"Just kidding, spooked you though, didn't I?"

Completely raving mad, absolutely insane, thought the young attorney.

"Right, Wolven pelt you say? Hmm," the tailor continued as he leapt into his stock room and started throwing about boxes and clothes hangers. "I dare say they will eventually ban real fur though sir, then we'll all be buggered. People getting too sensitive about stupid fuzzy creatures… ludicrous!"

"Okay," Elliot replied, feigning interest while anxiously eyeing his pocket watch.

"I've got a lambs wool coat with a Wolven lining sir?"

"Funny, a wolf in sheep's clothing, I like it."

"Oh good, I'll put that to one side so you can try it on."

"No I meant… never mind," the lawyer sighed.

"No wine here sir just clothes," the tailor yelled from deep within the stock room.

Oh my days, I think my head is going to implode, wondered Elliot as his patience continued to wear desperately thin.

"Actually!" shouted the lawyer to which the tailor promptly poked his head back into the shop. "Sorry. Actually what I am after… oh that is a nice coat isn't?" Elliot commented, apparently distracted by the lambs-wool, Wolven lined coat the tailor had slung over his shoulder.

"Good choice sir, here let's pop it on you," the tailor offered, quickly ushering Elliot to a mirror and helping him slide each arm into the plush coat. "Oh yes, that does look good. Very dapper."

"It does actually. I think I'll take it," Elliot agreed as he posed in front of the full-length mirror, something the vain lawyer never tired of doing.

"Excellent choice sir. That will be 20 amber ducats."

"Very reasonable. Might I have a bag for it?"

"Sorry sir we don't take bags only amber."

"I meant – "

"I know, just pulling your leg sir. Of course you can have a bag."

Thus Elliot handed over two ten-amber ducat crystals and gladly received his new coat in a particularly colourful carrier bag in return.

"Many thanks, bye," said Elliot as he left the tailor's that tad bit more fashionable as when he had first entered.

Wait a minute-turn... oh he's good, Elliot contemplated shaking his head disapprovingly.

Tinkle went the front door bell and in re-entered the lawyer.

"Good afternoon sir, if you're after Madame Pay – "

"No actually…"

"I know sir, a new coat perhaps?" suggested the tailor to which Elliot stared blankly back at him. "Again just kidding, oh sir if you keep getting caught out like that your head might implode."

This is going to be a long day.

*

"Excuse me," Epona called to a passing Liberan, "can you possibly point the way to Babel please."

"It's right behind you," replied a particular obese male Biblio-Vermiculi, who made a soft squishing sound as he pulsated his way along.

"Oh, thanks," the centaur replied as the stout Liberan passed her by.

It wasn't that she found the Liberans repulsive, as many unfortunately did given that they were not the most attractive of Arbor's inhabitants to look at, it was just that she couldn't help but immediately think of caterpillars whenever she saw one of their race – specifically squashed caterpillars who were the victim of her younger cousin's regular stampeding frenzies out in the fields behind her homestead in Equinas. Now every time she saw a Biblio-Vermiculi, with their puffy babyish faces and their massive segmented bulging worm-like bodies, she couldn't help but imagine one of them squirming about in two separate halves oozing some kind of gooey puss-like matter that she imagined to be unpleasantly pungent; a grim vision but one that prevailed within her mind's eye none the less.

Turning, she suddenly realised that the Syngraphus was cast in shadow. Epona thought that perhaps the day was fading in Liber and that she best be getting on, that is until she walked around the portal building to see what was behind it.

Rising up to what must have been more than three thousand meters was simply the largest building Epona had ever laid her centaur eyes upon. She found her breath was noticeably snatched away from her as she struggled to comprehend the enormity of what presumably was the Bibliodel of Babel – a ziggurat the size of a mountain, which completely filled her field of vision.

"Bloody Caelum!" she gasped, taking a few steps back as if she feared the structure might come crashing down on her like a tidal wave.

She thought that Babel was a city with some main library within, but standing before the colossal citadel she soon realised that Babel was a library the size of a city. Epona had simply seen nothing like it in all her ring-years.

The great Arborian historian Apollodorus Dysklus, who later focused on the legalistic and founded the law firm of the same name, once wrote of Babel that it was 'like a coliseum upon a coliseum upon a coliseum forever rising from the World-Tree's surface like a great extendable telescope as if it might dare to reach, perhaps even spy, upon the celestial - if it was a natural structure one might have rightly referred to the artificial mountain as one of Arbor's more impressive branches'.

The young legal trainee tentatively trotted towards Babel's entrance where a particularly friendly Liberan librarian, who offered to give her a brief tour before showing her to the Law section, kindly greeted her.

"I can tell by your expression that you've not been here before miss."

"That's correct, it's absolutely huge. How on Arbor was it ever built? It must have taken centuries."

"Oh no miss, no-one built this structure," replied the librarian.

"So it was always here? Must have been… hmm"

The librarian paused, turned to Epona, and smiled for he guessed that the Equinmare knew absolutely nothing about Babel at all. These were the moments the librarian really enjoyed, when he could use his knowledge to enlighten and educate as well as surprise.

"Have you ever heard of the phrase 'Babel is only as big as the works that are written'?" queried the Liberan librarian.

"Actually I think I have you know, something my father told me when I was writing my Legal thesis."

"Ah yes, 'The Thorn in the Paw? – Civil Liberties in Criminal Law: A Discussion' by Epona Brenwen. I've read it. I especially enjoyed your discussion on the need for balance betw – "

"How could you have read it? I mean… well it was never released," Epona asked, absolutely astounded by her guide's revelation.

"All treatise, doctorate papers and indeed Legal thesis are submitted to Babel for registration. Every university on Arbor uses this facility to promote the works of their students, it's written into everyone's educational contract as a matter of fact."

The centaur was still reeling from the fact that someone else had read her work. Not that she was upset by the dissemination of her paper just that she would have liked to have known, however if it was a provision of her contract of education then she thought there was little point to objecting to the fact now.

"So the quote you and my dad told me must relate to some socially driven type of motivation to register and display all text – liberal acceptance of all material for the advancement of… well of pretty much everything… knowledge, understanding…" Epona mused.

"Well, yes and no. Babel does accept all complete materials on any given subject, so in essence it does promote your idea of liberal freethinking and the works that result from the same. But the thing is Babel doesn't really have a choice in the matter."

"Doesn't have a choice, I don't understand. Look at this place! I'm sure the person in charge must have some choice in the way things are run."

"Hmm, I think I'm going to have to show you something," stated the librarian as he took a swift left, detouring from his intended path.

As Epona followed her guide, still confused about a great many things, she thought that perhaps there was more to Babel than she first thought. They strolled passed small alcoves and cloisters where members from all the races of Arbor could be found scribbling away flanked by piles of research materials. The sight continued throughout the circumference of the tower where row upon row of colonnades where stacked around the perimeter, each supported by countless fluted columns with sturdy bases and

Corinthian style capitals decorated with delicate deep-set scroll and floral carve-work. Each of the pillars were the height of at least three grown men, which bemused Epona as she figured the labour involved in erecting each of the columns must have been far beyond the capabilities of the Liberans or any other Arborian race, barring the giant Atlations perhaps who could have physically performed the feat, their innate clumsiness set aside that is.

The inquisitive young centaur kept looking skyward, to a small point of light far above her that she guessed was where Babel's circular walls finally met at an apex. In fact Babel didn't have an apex or some other imagined dome enclosing the top of the structure, on the contrary the citadel just kept rising and rising for thousands of meters. The further it rose the narrower it seemed to get, it was an illusion conjured by nothing but distance and perspective, two units of measure and vantage Epona was familiar with when it came to the horizontal – staring out across the flat plains of Equinas – but never had she witnessed the optical effect in the vertical. She likened it to standing within the eye of a tornado, gazing up the funnel to the small patch of serine blue sky above, all the while surrounded by an immense power that threatened to thoroughly overwhelm her at each passing moment.

"Unbelievable, are those clouds up there?" Epona gasped with astonishment.

"That's right, Babel does stretch to dizzying heights. Worry not about the books however, the shelves are protected with magical seals that ward off damp or any other physical impacts they might otherwise suffer being housed at such altitudes."

"Amazing."

They had climbed a number of floors by way of stairways that were dotted about the colonnades at intervals of 30 to 40 metres, and at this higher level Epona took the opportunity to look out onto Babel's interior. It was akin to standing upon a hilltop to gaze upon a community.

The acres and acres of floor space contained shops, eateries and numerous stationers, which thousands of people moved busily between, quite unlike the silent and slow archetype one would usually associate with a library. What caught the centaur's attention the most however were five great towers that were set out in a cross-shaped pattern with the tallest at its centre. Each of the structures' outer walls mimicked the interior wall of Babel and Epona thought they looked much like a leaning tower tourist attraction she had seen somewhere before. Balustrade-lined walkways protruded from one of the spires every fifty floors, which served to interconnect each of the four outer towers to the central one.

"Magnificent isn't it? Remind you of anything?" asked the librarian noticing that the Equinmare had paused to take in the view. "A clue can be found in the way the walkways are staggered about the five towers."

"Its like a helix," Epona replied wide eyed, "just like the sigil for Babel at the Syngraphus," she continued clapping her hands together with some glee in correctly identifying the association.

"Very good, not many people get it. Then again many people bury their heads in books and never notice all the wonderful architectural features of this place," the librarian sighed.

"And I guess each tower houses separate sections."

"Correct again. The five major disciplines of the World-Tree: Science, Religion, Psychology, Magic and Law."

"Which one is the Law tower?"

"The middle one naturally."

"Why the middle one?" Epona queried.

"Don't you know? Being a lawyer I thought it might be the first thing they taught you," the Liberan replied with a hint of surprise. "The first ever book written was a Legal one. It was written over one-hundred thousand ring-years ago and is a loose leaf folio that lists 144,000 rules and regulations for a society that died out long before Babel was what it is now."

"That's a lot of rules."

"Strange to think that even as long ago as that, which the uninformed immediately assumes must have been a primitive age, people had a code with which to order their lives by."

Epona looked upon the central tower with a distinct feeling of pride. The conical structure looked like a giant spire that had pierced the surface from below and, like Babel, continued to rise as if to breach Caelum's dogmatic bubble. She found it quite appropriate given that as far as Blackstone & Associates was concerned they too drove to dizzying heights to protect the legal rights of Humans against undue harassment, especially if the same emanated from those celestial firebrands up in their lofty realm.

"Ah Charles, a little birdie told me you're close to finishing your book," greeted the librarian to a middle-aged gentleman who was enthusiastically scribbling away with his quill, as he and Epona entered a candle lit alcove on the tenth floor.

"It wasn't Tiresias was it? He never stops twittering that one," the writer replied with a wry smile without looking up from his page.

"Epona Brenwen I'd like you to meet Charles Perrault, one of our more famous writers in residence."

"Hello, pleased to meet you," Charles replied as he rose from his seat and shook Epona's outstretched hand. "I think he means infamous actually."

"I'm just getting the guided tour," Epona replied.

"Oh yes the old 'Babel is only as big…' business. Well you're both in luck I have just finished my new book."

"Well done Charles," congratulated the librarian.

"Thanks, what do you think?"

" 'My Life in Fairy Tales'," the librarian read. "A double meaning perhaps?"

"Exactly, it's a biography of my life writing about fairy tales in the language and style of a fairy tale," replied Charles.

"Sounds quite interesting," Epona added.

"You'll have to stay and read it if you have the time, there's another copy up – "

"Now, now Charles. You're going to spoil the surprise," the librarian objected in a tone of mock disapproval.

"What surprise?" Epona curiously asked.

"Well, for the next part of the tour we have to go all the way to the top. Hope you're not scared of heights," the librarian concluded before bidding farewell to the thoroughly satisfied looking writer and ushering an intrigued looking Epona back out towards the colonnade.

The Liberan bent his worm-like body over the balustrade that spanned the gaps between the inner wall's tall columns and peered up as if spying for something. After a few moments he let out a sigh of relief and then quite suddenly, with all ten pairs of his hands, he started clicking his fingers.

Epona looked up to where her guide was staring and saw a shadow slowly advancing to their floor from above. The young trainee squinted and began to make out what looked like a lantern being carried by some winged creature.

"Now we could take the stairs all the way to the 400th floor but I doubt my body could take it," the librarian joked as, much to Epona's astonishment, an owl the size of a house swooped down and hovered in front of them.

In its menacing looking talons the mammoth tawny owl clutched a glass box, room enough inside for at least five passengers… or at least one worried looking centaur and an enthusiastic guide who was perhaps enjoying his job a little too much.

*

The Weaving Squires... Right, don't buy anything, Elliot willed himself as he entered the second costumers on his list of retailers.

Stepping through the front door he immediately found it odd that, despite two looms being present in the middle of the spacious shop floor, he could see no clothes or scarves or hats, or even dress dummies or hangers on which to display them on. Even the looming machines lacked any spindles of thread. The Criminal attorney suddenly had that foreboding feeling he always experienced whenever he thought he might be wasting his time.

"Oh, hello," welcomed the twin owners in unison as they emerged from the back of the shop. "Not here from the court are you? Look, it isn't ready yet," they continued pointing to their material-devoid weaving devices.

Elliot stared to the empty looms, cocked a suspicious eyebrow, and turned back to the twins.

"Actually I'm not from the palace. I was recommended to come here from the owner of 'Seven in one blow'. He said you specialise in the more bespoke."

"That's right," both the tailors replied, in a synchronicity that was beginning to give Elliot the creeps. "What kind of thing were you after? Something magical perhaps?"

"I was looking for a full size Wolven costume, genuine Wolven pelt right to the headdress."

The twins looked at each other, then started rubbing their chins and making oohing sounds, and after a moment they shook their heads.

"Tricky that sir, especially a full one. Of course if you're into that sort of thing there's always Madame Payne's at the other end of the village."

"What sort of thing?"

"You know, role play sir," they replied with a wink.

"Why does everyone think I… listen can you help me or not?"

"Afraid not sir. Nope, perhaps if you were looking for something magical like we said before, but otherwise… Ah, one moment please sir," they politely stated as their attention switched to another customer who was passing through the shop door.

A gentlemen dressed in palace livery with a thick cloak draped over his left shoulder entered the room with a swagger.

Under his right arm he held a bulging velvet drawstring bag and upon his belt hung what looked like a small but full pouch of amber.

"Good afternoon sir, from the palace we presume?"

"That is correct. I have been sent to check on your progress. I have also brought further materials you have requested and your second advance payment," the royal courtier confirmed as he placed both velvet pouch and amber laden bag before the weavers.

"Oh simply excellent thread sir, yes this will compliment the garment nicely," they gasped as they drew out a length of spun gold thread, a rich material that glistened as it caught the light through the shop window. "And this should be satisfactory for now," they continued, spilling the amber ducats from the pouch across their counter.

"Excellent and may I see how you have progressed?"

"Of course sir, please come this way."

Elliot watched as the tailors lead the relatively young palace kinsmen to the empty looms. The young lawyer would otherwise have left, given that this second tailors had been another dead end, however he stayed a moment and, much to his surprise, witnessed the courtier break down and start crying.

"Oh my, it is simply the most exquisite thing I have ever laid eyes upon," blubbered the gentleman, his eyes puffy and red and his nose runny.

"Isn't it sir, just look at the delicate embroidery to the train of the cloak," the tailors pointed out.

"Magnificent work gentlemen, you are most worthy of the royal seal of approval."

"Our thanks. It is always satisfying to know that our work is appreciated," the twins sincerely replied.

Elliot squinted his eyes and looked about the shop and the looms to which the tailors were making sweeping movements with their arms, as if they were pointing out the desirable facets of some showroom centrepiece, but still he could not see the object of the nobleman's affection.

The gentleman then straightened up, brushed the tears from his face and cleared his throat.

"I shall take my leave Weaving Squires and report to the King that his garment is the most wonderful…" he stuttered again as if he was about to cry as he looked at the looms, but composed himself and confidently strolled towards the exit.

"Oh sir," the twin tailors called, "the shirt sir, you must take a look," and as they both held up what appeared to Elliot to be nothing but thin air between pinched thumb and forefinger the courtier let out a great howl as he ran from the shop in tears of happiness.

The tailors let out a sigh of satisfaction before returning to Elliot with renewed enthusiasm.

"Sorry about that sir, now what was it you were after? A magical coat perhaps?"

The young lawyer thought he best leave before he fed the weavers into their loom.

As he stepped out into the cobbled street outside he cast a reluctant glance to the slowly disappearing daylight and shook his head in disappointment. He had spent much of the afternoon rushing about from one Delatorian suburb to the other, even cutting short his visit with Abigail so that he could press on with building his legal case, however he feared that the two wasted trips to these dubious tailors was eating away at the head-start Dr Capek was so eager to encourage him of.

As a dejected Elliot was about to turn back towards Blackstone's a small child of about ten ring-years of age tugged on his sleeve.

"I think this town is going all topsy turvey," the boy dramatically announced placing his hands on his hips in that grumpy way kids are taken to doing.

"Why do you say that kid?" Elliot replied staring down at him.

"I say that because, they work night after night after night after –"

"I get the idea."

"But they never use any cloth. And people go in during the day and come back out crying like babies because it's beautiful… mental the lot of them."

"Well I think those weavers are actually more like weasels," Elliot replied as he turned to walk away.

"But you're not crying."

"Not yet anyway."

"But you saw the clothes though didn't you mister?"

"You know kid, if they're making magical clothes in there then I'm a palace jester."

"So we're not the ones going topsy-turvy then, it's everyone else?"

"Seems that way, now if I could only find a place that does Wolven costumes then maybe I'll keep from going all topsy-turvy too," sighed the lawyer.

"A Wolven costume you say sir?"

"Yep."

"I know where you can find one of those."

Elliot stopped walking and turned to the young urchin that was following him. He reached into his jacket pocket and pulled out a small amber ducat piece and showed it to the excitable boy.

"Tell you what, if you can take me to where they sell them I'll give you this piece of Amber."

"Really mister? Follow me."

*

The flying glass carriage had stopped ascending and Epona, though nervous and a little nauseous, opened her eyes and breathed a slow sigh of relief. She immediately regretted the decision.

As she peered through the transparent base of the lift her four feet were planted firmly upon she let out a small squeak of panic and desperately snatched at the handrail at her side.

As the owl made its ascent to three thousand meters her knuckles began to turn white as she desperately clung on for fear of her life. She was not the greatest fan of heights and much preferred keeping her hooves on the ground, and as the great owl-borne glass carriage continued its skyward journey she began to wonder whether taking the tour was the wisest of options.

A cloud passed by the transparent elevator as the steady but powerful beat of the Owls wings maintained the centaur and her librarian guide at their desired floor.

Gently prising the Equinmare away from the railings the Liberan slowly opened the glass door to the lift and shuffled himself onto the polished stone colonnade of the 400th floor. With much coaxing, as well as a constant reassurance from the guide that the bird above them would not suddenly fly away, Epona sheepishly followed, carefully placing one foot in front of the other whilst also repeating to herself not to, under any circumstances, look down.

She made it and immediately took to clutching the bulbous balustrades of the columned edge of the floor. Only then, with solid stone beneath her feet and with the touch of smooth strong marble under her grasping hands, did the young legal trainee look out over and across the whole spectacle that was Babel.

"Breathtaking isn't it," the Liberan whispered as, with the synchronous snap of his fingers, the huge owl swooped away, the glass box trailing behind it as it descended out of view. Epona swore blind that the bird even winked at her before it left.

"This is turning into quite an adventure," admitted Epona as she put a palm to her chest to steady her beating heart.

"Literature *is* an adventure, each turn of a page can either be a gently jaunt or a careful sidestep through lands unknown… each chapter ending an ocean port to untold possibilities," the sage-like librarian replied as he continued his tour.

As Epona followed she noticed that between every benched niche and study alcove were shelves upon shelves of books containing countless volumes of thick and slim and tall and short tomes on a myriad of subjects. As far as the Mare'ess could work out there seemed to be no order to the manner in which these texts were stacked.

"All these books are new acquisitions, yet to be sorted and individually shelved," the librarian revealed. "And here is where we reach the end."

The learned Biblio-Vermiculi, who had successfully escorted the curious young centaur to the very top of the Bibliodel, stopped and turned to a shelf to his left, which unlike any other in Babel was only half full.

"Look at the spine of the last book Miss Brenwen, notice anything familiar?"

Epona ran her gaze along the length of books, which due to their not being tightly packed were also the only ones in the great library that stood at a slant, until she came upon the last book.

" 'My Life in Fairy Tales' by Charles Perrault," she gasped, "but how on Arbor…?"

"As soon as Mr Perrault concluded his work, as soon as he knew that the work was as finished and polished and edited to his satisfaction, a duplicate of his book magically appeared on this shelf."

"I don't believ – " But before the legal trainee could finish her sentence another book, a blur at first, suddenly appeared right next to Mr Perrault's.

The whole experience; the arrival through the Syngraphus, the guided tour round the inner rim of Babel, the impromptu rise to its 400th floor and now the books that appeared from nothingness, all of the feelings from each of these elements combined to form the smallest of lumps in Epona's throat. Quite uncharacteristically the centaur found that a tear was gently running down her cheek.

"I've shed a tear or two in my time Miss," admitted the librarian as he allowed the centaur to collect her thoughts for a moment. "As long as people keep writing, Babel will keep growing."

"The great literary purge seven hundred ring-years ago, that was the reason for Babel's half-destruction wasn't it?" Epona sadly asked.

"That's right, when Caelum sought out and burned nearly one half of all the books on Arbor 150 floors of literary flare and passion and learning and knowledge disappeared in a heart beat. Even the walls supporting the shelves crumbled to dust."

Epona reached into her shirt pocket, drew out a white silk handkerchief then gently wiped the tears from her cheeks. After a few deep breaths she rejoined the Liberan.

"There are those that want to suppress the World-Tree inhabitants' creative spirit. They fear that some levels of knowledge must never be attained."

"*They* fear," Epona added nodding skywards, "that one day, perhaps even tomorrow, we'll reach the intellectual peaks that they can never comprehend. They fear their own ignorance."

"And that is why firms such as yours are so vital in protecting places such as these, in protecting the flow of creativity free from hindrance or censure. You do more good than you know. And that is why I brought you up here, to illustrate how much respect we have for people who help others who can't fight for themselves."

Whatever irrational feelings of aversion Epona had towards the appearance of Liberans prior to her visit rapidly vanished as soon as the kind librarian guide concluded his accolade.

"Right," he continued, "lets get you to the Law section shall we, I must be keeping you from your research."

"Every moment in your company has been an educational one. And for this I thank you."

As the two intellectuals strolled along a skywalk to the central spire that was dedicated to Law, Epona wondered what other marvels she had yet to witness within the circular walls of that magical place, and how soon she might have the opportunity to visit again.

*

"Come on mister we're almost there," called the young boy who had been leading Elliot to where the lawyer might find his elusive Wolven costume.

"Oh no, I've already been here," the attorney whined as he spotted the questionable shop sign for 'Seven in One Blow'.

"Not there silly, over here."

"You've got to be kidding kid."

But before Elliot could restrain the young whippersnapper the boy had quickly knocked on the great purple door in front of them.

As the sound of footsteps drew nearer to the entrance, the lawyer put his head in his hands.

"Mr Elliot Blackstone, well fancy seeing you on my doorstep."

"Hello Madam Payne," Elliot replied with a sigh.

The young boy interrupted the pair with a not so subtle cough, and as Elliot looked down the urchin held out his palm.

"Well a deal is a deal I guess," Elliot conceded placing the amber crystal in the lad's grubby paw.

"Thanks mister. Bye, bye now."

"Hey kid, say hi to your older brother for me!" called Payne as the boy contentedly took to his heels.

"*Much* older I hope?" replied Elliot disapprovingly.

"Old enough," she replied with a mischievous grin. "Now come on in, you look like you need a drink."

However much Elliot wanted to object he simply couldn't muster the energy, and with much over-emphasised dragging of feet, much to Madame Payne's amusement, the lawyer disappeared within the voluptuous vampire's satin lined boudoir, where much to his surprise and relief he found a life size Wolven-pelt costume staring up at him from the bed.

16

It was no secret that the lawyers of Blackstone's & Associates had little respect for their Caelum Angelic counterparts and Elliot especially never shied away from criticising their quality. However, even he knew that there were always exceptions: the flawless diamond in a basket of coal, a prodigal son amongst an offspring of idiots. The name of this exception was Malaphar Naberius and he had a talent and shrewdness equal only to Asmodeus Blackstone himself. He was a ferocious opponent and a forthright advocate. Every word he uttered in an open court was spoken with such passion and conviction that he had little need for bravado or spectacle. Malaphar was formidable.

"You must be distracted, you have yet to strike me. New case clouding your judgement?" queried Uriel, Malaphar's friend of eons and frequent sparring partner.

Malaphar smirked, extended his wings to full span and, with one powerful beat, thrust himself towards the sky.

"I am merely toying with you Uriel," he replied wheeling in the air as if a bird of prey caught on an up-current.

Uriel took flight and followed, clutching a metallic spear in one hand like a javelin. The blinding light of a cloudless Caelum caught the razor tip of his ferocious weapon and he flashed passed his companion like a bolt of lighting, missing the lawyer's shoulder by a thumb width.

"Well I see you have been practising your aerials dear boy," Malaphar continued to playfully mock. "I guess we all have to fly the coup at some point."

"Careful you don't get a nosebleed, this is the highest I have ever seen you," Uriel shouted back laughing. He banked to the right and lined himself towards Malaphar in preparation for another pass.

"Perhaps I have not struck you because I have yet to unsheathe this." With a widening grin Malaphar drew a double-handed broadsword from a scabbard that was strapped between the shoulder joints of his wings. "Now let us see if your skill with a weapon is as good as your skill in the sky."

The two sparring partners sped towards each other, each bearing down upon the other with all the velocity of a hawk in a killing dive. The sound of their weapons striking was like crashing thunder as blow parried blow.

"So, the case?" Uriel calmly asked as he avoided his opponent's vicious sideswipe.

"A trifle of a trial my fellow, appears the Humans are still quite cable of killing themselves without our influence," Malaphar replied in a tone of boredom.

"You are working with *Humans*? How very unbecoming of you."

"Royals Uriel, Royals… one must maintain some standards. If I am to contaminate my person with their presence, then it may as well be in the employ of those with a modicum of self respect… and power."

"Oh Malaphar, how very noble of you," Uriel sarcastically replied.

"Quite," replied the lawyer as, with a flick of his right wing he spun sharply to the left catching Uriel off-guard before shoulder barging him into a fifty-meter descent. Malaphar eyed his tumbling sparring partner and gave chase, his hands clutching his sword over his head like an executioner preparing for a final blow.

Uriel used his wings as an air break preventing him from slamming into the ground, found his feet and wheeled his spear in front of him ready to parry Malaphar's advancing blow.

With both fighters on the ground now, they circled each other waiting for that window of opportunity with which to deliver a decent strike.

Malaphar was a mountain of an Angelic. Had he not committed himself to Law then one might otherwise have found him in the front rows of some legion, putting the fear of Caelum in any that dared to stand against them. It was this commanding presence that he used to great effect in courtrooms, as well as out on the sparring fields, and many an opponent advocate was found wanting beneath the shadow of his intimidating stature.

"So who has been killed and who has done the killing?" Uriel questioned, audibly catching his breathe whilst wiping the sweat from his forehead.

"A pretty human thing by the name of Abigail Hood," Malaphar replied returning his sword to its scabbard and beckoning Uriel forward with raised fists. Uriel responded in kind by driving his spear into the ground and shrugging loose his shoulders.

"Such a shame for the pretty to perish," Uriel replied, throwing a roundhouse punch that Malaphar easily blocked.

"You misunderstand dear fellow, she is the one who has been charged with murder."

The short moment it took for Uriel to consider what the lawyer had just said was time enough for Malaphar to strike a punishing blow upon his ribs. Uriel smirked it off and threw an uppercut in response. The blow connected leaving Malaphar smarting from the impact and with bloodied lip.

"And the victim?" Uriel asked.

"Those useless Delatorian Magistratum have yet to discover that piece of information, no doubt due to the fact that the victim's face was torn from his head."

"A trial where the victim's identity is unknown," Uriel pondered. "Is it not a tad early in the proceedings to have them employ your worthy services?"

"Perhaps," Malaphar replied dodging another quick jab from his opponent, "though the Human wench seems to have retained the services of Blackstone's & Associates."

"Asmodeus?" Uriel replied with a renewed interest.

"His nephew Elliot."

"Not Raphael's son?"

"The same," Malaphar replied noticing that Uriel was eyeing the spear that stuck upright to his left. "Rumour has it that the half-breed has a certain talent for legal argument."

"How gracious of you to admit the merits of someone quite below you," Uriel replied as he shoulder rolled towards his spear.

"He is still Half-Angelic Uriel, as much as he would wish to ignore it he is still part us," Malaphar responded while reaching over his back to retrieve his sword.

"A plea bargain then?"

"Perhaps I should give Elliot the option of having his childhood sweetheart committed to some insane asylum," Malaphar grinned maliciously. "Now that would tear his little half-breed heart apart would it not?"

"Childhood sweethearts. Love is such a weakness. I shall be surprised if Elliot is composed enough to begin the trial knowing that her fate rests in his hands."

Uriel wildly kicked out towards Malaphar's midriff and as he raised up his spear horizontally to block his exposed side Malaphar brought down his sword splitting Uriel's spear in two.

"Or perhaps I should challenge Elliot to trial by combat," Malaphar laughed looking down upon his conquered opponent. "Yield."

Uriel threw both halves of his hewn weapon aside and bowed his head to concede defeat and end the bout.

"Elliot Blackstone," Malaphar spat. "I shall make him wish he never heard of the word Law."

*

"Yield."

"My sister is going to cut out your hearts," Krystina calmly stated as Fröhlich tightened a cord around her wrists and ankles.

"Yield, and you may go free to tell your Queen that there is a new arrangement," Dok repeated. "You can't win, I have foreseen everything."

"Then you do have the Carmen Speculum. If that is the case then you would have already seen my death and you wouldn't be wasting your time with your ultimatum," Krystina replied.

"Perhaps, but who said anything about killing you?"

The leader of the Vigilantag Seven reached around Krystina's waist and removed the pewter snuff box in which the assassin kept her lethal Lilac-Rosarius powder. Dok placed this to one side before searching through the Secarius' white shoulder bag for her blowpipe.

"As you well know Snow White, the powder you utilise to comatose your victims is only as potent as the measure which is delivered," Dok stated nodding to Brummig, who proceeded to tie a blindfold around Krystina's eyes. "Now I may just administer enough to put you to sleep for a day, or a month or perhaps even a ring-year… the point is you'll never know. Now imagine if you will waking up to find yourself in a wooden box. It's dark and claustrophobic –"

"Enclosed spaces do not concern me Zwerg-Riese," interrupted the assassin.

"I believe you, but being buried alive is no merry-go-round either."

Krystina faltered. She had maintained her cool head since being restrained, wisely choosing to conserve her energy than to expend it in some futile attempt at escape. The assassin had accepted her fate the minute-turn she stepped into the Vigilantag's cavernous hideout. She expected the Dwarf-Giants to mount some multi-pronged attack when she entered the mouth of the cave, but none came. Deeper she delved into the hideout but still no sign of them. Then all of a sudden they were everywhere. One had taken her sword another her bow and quiver as yet another gripped her wrists and held her aloft like a puppet. They seemed to have worked in complete synchronicity, as if they knew exactly where each had to be and when they had to be there.

It was then that Snow White realised that they had used the very item she had come to retrieve against her. The magic mirror, the prophetic Carmen Speculum, had showed the Vigilantag exactly how the fight would play out.

She had thought of the possibility of the Seven employing such a tactic but had disregarded it. Krystina had attempted to rationalise the workings of time and cause and effect and how the

Carmen Speculum fitted into each. She had thought that if the mirror only showed the absolute future and that it had showed the Zwerg-Riese being defeated then it would be foolish for them to fight. Then again she also considered whether repeated viewing of such a defeat could be used to plan a counter attack, in essence attempting to change the future. Still this did not sit well within her imaginings for she then questioned why it might have shown their defeat in the first place.

The circular argument might have caused lesser minds to suffer but Krystina Letalis was never one to panic and when she could not come to a logical conclusion, one that might have improved her odds of survival against seven fierce Dwarf-Giants for example, then she simply pushed the illogical ones aside and started a fresh chain of thought. Such a reduction to only the relevant inevitably led to her considering whether in fact the mirror had shown her own defeat at the outset.

Yet as much as she couldn't explain the arcane workings of a magically imbued mirror of divination, she also couldn't explain the profound sense of self-belief she had in her own abilities. Defeat was a worst-case scenario she simply never entertained.

"Do you really think the Queen will entertain anything you have to offer? You have stolen from her. She will send the entire Delatorian army after you. They will hunt you down," Krystina asserted as best she could, trying to buy more time for herself. If perhaps she could twist her wrists free or…

Suddenly she realised her window of opportunity. She heard Müde and Shüchter rummaging through her shoulder pack while Fröhlich and Nieser were bickering over her ornate jewel encrusted weaponry. Brummig was still behind her tightening the blindfold and she guessed that only Dok was looking at her now. Blöd, the seventh and the largest, though least threatening Krystina remembered, was in the corner of the cavern sat cross-legged whilst rocking back and forth, the sight of which she recalled being quite disturbing.

Taking on two Dwarf-Giants was certainly more favourable than seven, and as she felt Brummig's touch leave her head and as she heard Dok opening her snuffbox of Lilac-Rosarius powder she took in a deep breath and made her move.

In a flash she slammed into Brummig's nose with the back of her head, immediately feeling the spray of his warm blood upon her neckline. The momentum had rocked her onto her back and estimating where Dok's face might be she kicked out with her bound feet catching the leader square between the eyes.

Panic reigned and shouts and grunts and curses were bellowed. In those split seconds of commotion she had looped her wrists under her feet, brought her knees up to her chin and fed the rest of the lower half of her body through the oval gap between her restrained arms.

She was on her feet. The mental map of the cavern still fresh in her mind, committed to memory before she was deprived of her sight, she elegantly back flipped again then again stopping inches short of a weapon rack she had previously noticed in the far corner of the grotto. Hurried footfalls came towards her and more deafening roars of anger. She sliced the binds from her wrists upon the blade of a vicious looking scythe to her right. Her hands were free, little did it matter that her feet were still bound, but at least she could now wield something. As she reached up to her blind fold she thought of how wrong the mirror must have been, how foolish it was for the Zwerg-Riese to trust in such –

Then silence. Numbness strangely came over her and she suddenly felt her knees buckle. Her head felt light. She reached for the blindfold again.

It was just in time to see a maniacal looking Fröhlich deliver his second blow to her jaw.

The assassin's eyes rolled into the back of her head and like a withering flower she collapsed into a twisted heap.

"How predictable," Dok sighed. He leant towards Krystina's bloodied face and blew a fine mist of the assassin's own drug over her nose and mouth. "Let the Queen send her armies," he continued, "let them come to their deaths."

Blöd, who had witnessed the brief spate of disorder, shot a downcast look to the hessian covered Carmen Speculum, which was propped behind the racks of fearsome weaponry, slowly rose to his feet and solemnly left the cavern. Had his six fellow Vigilantag seen him depart, they would have glimpsed a tear of sadness gently trickle down his face.

17

From a dream of books and words, towering libraries with the knowledge of ages and labyrinthine complexes of endless shelves stacked tall with dusty tomes, Epona awoke refreshed, invigorated and eager to start her third day in work.

The previous day's journey into the awe and spectacle that was Babel had left her with a renewed appreciation for her chosen profession – such was it known to wane amongst many a student lawyer after four or maybe five long ring-years of learning.

The excursion to Liber had not only been eye opening but it had also been a productive research trip, and as she left her rented stable in Delator she did so carrying three dense and tightly bound scrolls tucked under her arm, as well as carrying a wide smile upon her face.

Elliot, on the other hand, had not returned to his own house following the wild goose-chase that was yesterday's costume tracking extravaganza, which had concluded upon the doorstep of the vampire seductress Madame Payne.

As the dishevelled attorney dragged his feet back to the office he did so dressed in the same clothes as the previous day, with skewed bed-hair, and with what looked like rouge lipstick on his collar, beneath which he swore he felt the delicate wound of a fresh love-bite.

His 'research' and impromptu tour round Delator's mix of morally questionable and arguably insane tailors and dress merchants had not been in vane however, and as he made his weary way to work he did so carrying a new coat inside a particularly attractive designer carrier bag as well as the identity and location of a, possibly *the*, Wolven costume vendor that had supplied Abigail's victim inside his head.

The Criminal attorney reached the office thirty-minute-turns before Epona, enough time to fix his hair in his full-length mirror, throw himself into his comfortable office recliner and jot down the address of the costume merchant before it disappeared from his busy mind. His Valkerie quill-holder was especially keen to help in the latter task, handing Elliot his crow-feathered quill whilst beaming with enthusiasm. Then, quite suddenly a Hermes messenger swooped into the office and hovered in front of Elliot's desk before fluttering a message to the lawyer with her long blonde lashes.

"Ah thank you, could you have it pushed over behind that desk over there, please," thanked Elliot, pointing to Epona's new non-coffin shaped desk – he felt the young Equinmare might perhaps have preferred something more traditional to write upon.

A few moments after the Hermes exited the office a particularly large Mongolian Deathworm, from office supplies, nuzzled a tightly bound bale of hay to where Elliot had directed.

"Perfect," Elliot announced quite contentedly, "just in time."

Epona promptly arrived five minute-turns later, stopped briefly to admire her new desk, neatly placed her reference scrolls on its surface before turning to Elliot with her hands on her hips in mock disapproval.

"You know I do actually eat *normal* food," she said eyeing Elliot, who had his feet up on the desk and was playing noughts and crosses with his quill-bearer.

"Oh the hay… I thought you might like something comfy to sit on," Elliot replied with a smile.

"I know… just kidding, it's perfect, thank you," replied Epona pulling apart the brown packing rope and teasing out the straw into a full and level pad. She set herself behind her desk with a grateful sigh and looked up at Elliot, positively bursting to tell him of yesterday's adventure.

"Come on then," Elliot acknowledged, "how was your first trip to Babel?"

"Unbelievable…" and so Epona continued for a good half-an-hourglass describing the great library with the magically appearing books, the five towering spires rising like great stalagmites and her helpful, respectful, and enthusiastic guide, employing every complimentary adjective she could conjure to pay proper lip service to her overwhelming experience.

"I must admit it is one of my favourite places in all of Arbor," Elliot admitted.

"It looks so imposing from the outside and then…"

"And then once you enter it's really magnificent… classical, almost mythically beautiful."

"Exactly," Epona grinned, "and how was your shopping trip?"

"I have doubts as to the sanity of Delator's dress-making community I'll tell you. Complete fruit-loops the lot of them, anyway I got the information we needed, and a new coat as it happens," he replied pointing to the designer carrier bag propped against his mirror.

"Good for you. I found a number of cases on diminished responsibility and insanity clauses, not directly relevant but all quite interesting as a pointer to how one might employ such a defence."

Elliot strolled over to Epona's desk and unfurled one of the silk-tied scrolls the centaur had brought from Babel.

"The Wood Dove case," Elliot read aloud, "sounds familiar."

A small town called Dvořák, 15 miles southwest of Delator, was the setting for the particularly interesting case of 'The Wood Dove'.

150 ring-years ago a cold-hearted woman poisoned her husband because he refused to give her a divorce.

Covering up the murder, the duplicitous widow, in fake mourning for her recently deceased husband, subsequently met a handsome gentleman who was quick to comfort her and quicker still to ask her to marry him.

A clause in the deceased's Will was that he be buried within the grounds of his estate, the same estate that passed without challenge into the hands of the murderous widow. She continued to live in the palatial abode and luxurious grounds of her ex-husband's estate with her new lover, though their romance was to be short lived.

An oak sapling took root on the deceased's grave, which grew strong and thick and fast as the days went by. Before the grounds persons realised there was a large tree, seemingly ages old, atop the murdered husband's grave, the shadow of which cast an ominous shroud over the main residence, blotting out the sun and preventing daylight from spilling into the woman's main bedroom. It was if the blood of the dead man had accelerated the growth of the towering and imposing oak, as if his hand had extended beyond the grave to condemn his killer to a life of eternal darkness.

Lost in a lustful bliss the woman and her new husband disregarded the old oak and, eager to awake to the bright rays of morning, they merely moved to one of the residence's other spacious sun-facing bedrooms. The woman had considered cutting down the tree, but knowledge had spread as to its unearthly rate of growth and many a lumberjack refused to split the trunk for fear that it was cursed.

One cold morning the woman awoke to the coos of a Wood Dove, a solemn but melodious warble that brought her great unease and unrest. The woman convinced her new husband to snare the Dove and quell its racket, which he succeeded in doing with much efficiency. The next morning, however, the woman rose to the eerie calls of another Wood Dove. This bird, which appeared to look identical to the one before it was also swiftly disposed of… only for another to take its place the following dawn.

This cycle continued, the stress of which slowly pecked away at the woman's sanity until she whole heartedly declared that the Doves were actually speaking to her, mocking her with demands and insults, not unlike those her ex-husband previously burdened her with. The new husband, unable to cope with her insane ranting and raving, had little choice but to abandon her. After three long ring-years the woman committed suicide by hanging herself from the oak tree above her deceased husband's grave.

"How did this matter ever see the inside of a courtroom?" Elliot queried, half-testing Epona's ability to extract and recall the cogent facts from the lengthy law report.

"Following the suicide," Epona began, "the woman's new husband… the one that abandoned her, staked claim to his wife's estate. However the executors of the woman's estate found a journal amongst her possessions. The journal was full of disturbing scrawls and inane babble… but between the tome's pages was also written a confession. In the height of the woman's guilt induced madness, the woman revealed how she thought the Wood Doves were sent by her dead husband to torment her for bringing about his un-natural death. The murdered ex-husband's family used this confession as a basis of a counterclaim to the new husband's stake in the estate. They maintained that because the woman had originally killed her first husband, this voided her original claim to the estate. Nullifying her original claim would then prevent the new husband from, in essence, staking a claim to an estate that was never one that the woman was entitled to pass on in the first place."

"Because it would have been against the deceased's husband's wishes to enforce a Will that would benefit his killer," Elliot concluded.

"Exactly, a view that the Delatorian Forum Domus unanimously agreed upon."

"Very good. What parallels can you draw from the case of 'The Wood Dove' and Abigail's?"

"Whilst the order of events differ, the murder, the insantity then the subsequent suicide in the case of The Wood Dove, as opposed to the arguable insanity Abigail experienced, then the murder then what looks to have been attempted suicide, what was interesting about the former case is that the Delatorian Judge dealt briefly with what might have been the case if the deceased husband had maltreated the woman enough to bring about her total loss of control at the point she killed him. This hypothetical order of events does partly mirror Abigail's circumstances, albeit that Abigail experienced her mental breakdown 14 ring-years after the trauma she suffered when her parents were killed, which resulted in the desecration of that Wolven's corpse. The proximity of the trigger is the key to whether such a defence might be accepted."

"What did the Judge have to say?" asked Elliot.

"The Judge said that could it be proved that the Wood Doves or abuse or… well let's just say a trigger, may have caused the woman's insanity prior to her killing her first husband then, as that would arguably be a defence to a charge of murder, then his Will, and her subsequent Will, may be held valid," Epona summed up while running her fingers through her hair, "but note the use of the words 'may', 'could' and 'arguably'."

"Ambiguity, a valuable skill to know, especially during negotiations… never show you're hand until the game is over."

"You do like your gambling aphorisms don't you?"

"The Law can be a game," Elliot replied, "one that is inherently difficult to play if you don't know the rules, and not the Legal text book rules either, but something more."

"The grey areas?"

"The moment a Lawyer starts seeing everything in black and white, right or wrong…"

"Then he or she closes their mind off to those areas which can't be defined, which have more scope for interpretation. You're saying that the moment you deal in absolutes is the moment you forfeit your right to… barter, *perhaps*?"

"In a manner of speaking," Elliot replied with a smile, noting Epona's use of an ambiguous term at the end of her sentence. Eliot's favourite term was 'arguably'.

"Then can I tell you an *absolute* viewpoint, which has been troubling me?"

"Of course you can Epona."

"I don't believe Abigail is crazy, I don't believe you think so either. And I still think we *are* missing something… so…"

"So why did I seem so preoccupied with insanity cases?"

"Well, yes. Aren't you worried we're wasting our time?"

"Ironically your research trip may actually buy us more time than we might seem to waste. I don't wholeheartedly believe Abigail is crazy, and I'm not just saying that because I know her… or *knew* her. There is something more that we're missing but the sooner we rush to court without a stalwart defence… without knowing all we need to know, then…" Elliot didn't conclude. He and Epona both knew the repercussions of failing in their task. "*Perhaps*, the insanity argument will prove fruitless. But it will *definitely* buy us a week or more."

"Because the prosecution will have to assign a psychologist to examine her, maybe repeatedly, to validate our claim," Epona guessed.

"Exactly. Time enough for us to get to the bottom of this whole thing, hopefully."

Elliot rolled up the scroll of 'The Wood Dove' case and placed it beside the other cases and legislative text on Epona's table.

"How is she?" Epona tentatively asked.

"All the better now she knows she has friends with her. Thanks for asking. But I still can't risk conducting an open interview in earshot of that flamenco costumed assassin."

"Emilita Letalis?"

"Rose Red… if ever there was a more inappropriate alias…"

"There must be a way," Epona whispered to herself.

"Huh?"

"There must be a way of finding out what she knows without alerting Emilita to the fact. What we need is a Dreamrunner."

"If only I had one of those in my list of contacts," Elliot sighed.

At that moment Fury stomped by Elliot and Epona's office huffing and puffing and shouting something that didn't sound particularly appropriate. A moment later followed Vincent who was shaking his head, in grief or irritation or perhaps in defeat, but evidently not attempting to quell Fury's temper. Vincent strolled past Elliot's office before back tracking to the doorway and popping his head round the doorframe to enquire as to whether Elliot and Epona were having any more luck with their case than he and Fury was having with their own.

"Fury's case not going well?" Elliot queried with his right eyebrow raised mischievously.

"Don't even start," sighed Vincent turning to Elliot. "You look cosy Epona, settled in okay?"

"Absolutely, I went to Babel yesterday and it was…" then she paused and realised she was acting like a giddy schoolgirl.

"It is great isn't it," Vincent replied.

"Wait a minute-turn, there's something different about you," Elliot teased, "you look… well, *normal*. Not tired… awake etc. Been getting a good nights sleep have we?" He said with an enormous grin while nodding his head in the direction Fury had stormed off in.

"As a matter of fact I am *sleeping* better, thanks for asking… anyway come on, Fury's gone to Brimstone's to put out those flames of hers."

"Wait you have changed, you're asking *me* to the bar?" Elliot replied with puzzlement.

"And Epona, come on you two… problems shared…"

"Over an alcoholic beverage are problems soon alleviated?" Epona guessed.

"I'm impressed," commented Vincent, "third day here and you've turned her into an alcoholic Elliot, well done," he continued mockingly.

Epona smiled, rose from her straw seat, gently brushed the loose strands of hay from her skirt and trotted towards the door.

"Who said he *turned* me into anything?" she grinned as she passed through the doorway, which triggered the same reflexive smile from Elliot and Vincent also.

"Lipstick on your collar Elliot? Apparently *you* haven't changed at all," Vincent concluded, following his colleagues to

Brimstone Bar as Elliot tried not to turn and look at Epona, who was giving him a curious gaze, as she craned her neck to see if it was true.

*

"I don't believe that old codger lied to us," Fury protested, referring to the Royal accountant Aerarius Artifex. "So bloody unassuming my arse," she continued, unceremoniously gulping down a half-goblet of blood-red wine, a droplet of which slipped from the edge of her glass and onto the side of Fury's chin evaporating into a fine mist of heady aroma.

As well as studying people's faces Elliot also enjoyed watching people lose themselves in their own excesses. Living to excess was something he did quite spectacularly, taking a measure of sadistic satisfaction in recalling a previous night's revelry to a normally bemused looking Vincent the following morning. As Elliot watched Fury in full non-blazing but unrestrained glory he momentarily thought back to why he had originally found the Fire-Nymph especially alluring.

"The accountant could be mistaken you know? He was quite… well, old," Vincent added as the four lawyers sat at their usual recessed booth at Brimstone's.

Vincent rarely chose to let go, and Elliot had soon realised that his colleague's sleeping disorder – which had seemingly disappeared of recent – might have been the reason why Vincent wasn't the party animal he was.

"I heard Aerarius was getting on to over 200 ring-years," Epona pro-offered, while sipping her sweet-water and bourbon mix on the rocks.

She couldn't slide into the booth, but Brimstone's barkeep had already thought of that and had produced an upholstered pad that looked like an antiquarian chaise longue. As Epona sat there with her front right leg and both hind legs tucked beneath her equine body, Elliot thought the Mare'ess had promise and was looking forward to unwinding with her in a non-sexual-harassment-resulting kind of a way. Not that the alternative hadn't crossed his mind either, especially now, as he watched Epona gently sway her free leg in a languid sort of fashion. Half-Angelic and Equinmare – he couldn't quite make it work in his head, though even he would admit that with Abigail behind bars physical relationships were the last thing on his mind. This was partially why he didn't feel the need to tell his colleagues that he hadn't actually slept with Madame Payne last night, for it just didn't matter.

"So apart from the Vigilantag Seven on the loose, a missing mirror and an arguably voidable insurance policy, my friend being charged with murder watched over by a deadly royal assassin and a faceless corpse of unknown identity… how is everybody… generally?" Elliot asked deadpanly.

Silence.

"Well I am sleeping better," admitted Vincent.

"As it appears you are Elliot," Fury slyly whispered as her eyes fell upon the curious red stain that was sullying Elliot's otherwise brilliantly white, though slightly ruffled, cotton shirt.

"So everybody's good then," Epona summed up with a sardonic sigh. "What now?"

"We've got to check out the lead on the costume merchant," Elliot clarified turning to the centaur, "and I guess you two – "

"What?" Fury asked. "Break the accountant's limbs?"

"Bit harsh… a re-interview perhaps? What do you think Elliot? Or would that put the palace on the defensive?" Vincent asked.

No reply.

"Elliot?" Vincent repeated.

Still no reply.

The Criminal lawyer's attention was apparently elsewhere. That sudden realisation that someone has said your name across a crowded and noisy room, when all else is filtered out as your ears search for the source of who said it – something similar had momentarily seized Elliot's senses. It wasn't noise though, nothing spoken. More like something *felt*, as if some external force was gravitating Elliot towards it.

"Elliot?" Epona softly said, gently brushing her mentor's shoulder with her glass-free hand.

It was enough to shake the lawyer free from whatever had come over him.

Elliot pulled his eyebrows into a stern but focused expression, like he was trying to analyse what had just happened, and in a manner not far removed from the ghostly moans of a theatrical séance host Elliot turned to his three colleagues and announced, "someone's here."

Half a minute-turn later the same Hermes that had previously conveyed her hay delivery message to Elliot floated into Brimstone Bar. Hovering on the spot she gently wheeled to the left then to the right as if looking for someone. She soon picked out Elliot and, with two silent beats of her huge butterfly wings, pushed herself towards him.

Weaving in and out through Brimstone's stalag-tables she came to a graceful halt in front of the three lawyers and the trainee, turned slightly to face Elliot and nodded.

"Twice in one day Eve, people are going to start talking," Elliot grinned.

The Hermes rolled her eyes upwards and shook her head. A brief eyelash-fluttering moment later and she was gone again, leaving Elliot with the same expression he had moodily projected to his colleagues before the messenger's sudden arrival.

Elliot looked down into his goblet of 'Merlot Diavolo', swirled the last of its contents then slowly sipped it down. He then rose to his feet, threw on his suit jacket, fixed his tie and turned to Epona.

"Asmodeus wants to see us in his office."

"Anything serious?" Epona replied.

"It appears we have a visitor."

"Elliot would you stop with all the tension building… who's here?" Fury half-slurred.

"Naberius, Malaphar Naberius," Elliot soberly replied.

*

Elliot had never met Malaphar, and the young Criminal attorney only knew him by reputation. In a tragically ironic sort of a way the Caelum Angelic was the very reason Elliot had a post to fill when Asmodeus took him into the firm.

The Arborian Law Reports state, in perhaps too graphic a detail, how Michael Quartz, Elliot's predecessor as well as one of the originally banished Caelum Angelica, once agreed to try a case based on the still barbaric legal ritual of Trial by Combat.

His opponent was Malaphar Naberius, at the time a contemptuous young Caelum barrister who still relished destroying all those who stood to defend Human causes.

By the end of that trial and after near twenty hour-glass-turns fighting – each blow a legal-argument victory, each wound a defeat, Michael threw down his fiery sword and conceded the case.

The gesture was not enough for Malaphar, and he stood over the back of his opponent and ripped the wings from his Caelum Angelic cousin. Michael would never fly again.

It wasn't enough to kill Michael, no. Malaphar wanted to take away from his opponent all that had been divinely granted. In Malaphar's opinion bi-pedal born wings was the province of those in Caelum. All those banished to Tartarus, like Asmodeus and Raphael Blackstone and William Dante, were deemed unworthy to return to those elevated realms. Malaphar lived to ensure no 'traitor' ever set foot upon his celestial bough-land.

Under his sword, his brute force and legalistic fanaticism, three Blackstone's & Associate's Tartarus-Angelic lawyers would soon regret ever meeting Malaphar at trial.

With wings torn from his body, and though he would never admit it during his last ring-years of service, Michael retired, his pride mortally wounded – and not because Malaphar had taken his identity, his wings, but because Malaphar had taken away the Criminal lawyer's want to fight in a courtroom thereafter. Malaphar had broken him, had left him the wingless Caelum outcast whose only consolation was to otherwise soar and tear through the air like all the Angelic, Caelum or Tartarus, were born to do. Malaphar had taken Michael's spirit. Break a hawk's wings and it soon loses its veracity – this is what Malaphar hoped to do to all of Caelum's traitorous, and this is what he longed to do to Raphael Blackstone's firstborn son.

Elliot had hated the idea of being appointed to replace Michael, hated that Malaphar had broken one of his own kind and created such an opening. There was no justice in that, no legal principle that rationally differentiated right from wrong. It was simply a powerful Caelum Lawyer who was fighting his own private battle centuries after the civil war of that celestial realm had ended.

Elliot often thought that the only reason Malaphar became a lawyer was in direct response to Asmodeus establishing Blackstone's & Associates – as if it were a ready source of argumentative, hopefully violent, encounters, which the World-Tree's inhabitants had for ring-years successfully stifled. Malaphar, in those jurisdictions which recognised Trial by Combat, such as Delator, could now throw down the gauntlet, and in so doing exercise his client's legalistically protected right to the same – to trials that were nothing more than gladiatorial arenas where sharpness of tongue was rendered useless to a blade's sharpened edge.

Delator still administered the ancient right of trial by this brutal form, but not in four hundred ring-years had it been called upon. Never could one, after the torture inflicted upon Michael, thereafter bring him or herself to agree to the archaic ritual. And so Malaphar's reputation lived on, unchallenged. It was doubly unfortunate in Blackstone & Associates case as Asmodeus had considerable trouble finding anybody to fill the post left empty by Michael's departure. Though Asmodeus personally handled a number of Criminal Defence case, it wasn't until Elliot arrived 393 ring-years later that Blackstone's criminal department could fully resume its business.

When Elliot discovered that Malaphar may indeed be prosecuting the case of Abigail Hood, it wasn't the fear of losing his case in an open court that scared him, and his legal reputation was precious little compared to the repercussions Abigail might face if he lost. Rather it was the momentary realisation that he might perhaps lose his own head in the process. A headless lawyer was no use to Abigail. A single-minded Caelum fanatic was a Defence attorney's worst nightmare.

Elliot knew that someone had raised the stakes. He knew that perhaps on this occasion even his talented ability for addressing an audience might fall by the wayside. That for all his Half-Angelic strength, for all his want to overcome, all this, was nothing compared to the physical strength of Malaphar Naberius, to that Angelic's want to wreak havoc upon all those that would seek to protect Humans.

For once, during the brief but full three days of optimistic pre-trial preparation Elliot feared that the case might have been doomed from the very outset.

*

Epona trotted quietly behind Elliot from Brimstone Bar to Asmodeus' office. Like her mentor, Epona had only seen Malaphar's name in print and had never met the attorney in person. A thick tome on Arborian legal Institutions and Methodology, a requisite module in any World-Tree Law course, contained a brief chapter on Trial by Combat in which the Angelic's name was mentioned twice. Judging from her colleagues' reactions at the bar however, Epona guessed that there was more to Malaphar than just three pages in a legal textbook.

Elliot momentarily paused paces from his uncle's office and turned to face a worried looking Epona.

"Malaphar is not a nice person. He is also not one to be trifled with either. For all his outward charm and eloquence he is no more than a cold-hearted bastard and everything he says is tainted with vindictiveness. You are better than he, if I hadn't known you before this week I'd still know that your appointment to this firm was enough to better the likes of that ruthless Angelic."

"Thank you," Epona blushed. It surprised her that for all Elliot's apparent womanising and drinking, there was a controlled and inherently good person within. His kind words, spoken in a reassuring tone, lit a fire in her belly that burned away the butterfly nerves within. If ever she had the reason for knocking at the gates of Caelum she knew that with Elliot by her side she could summon the courage to do it.

Before Elliot pushed open the door Epona gently hoofed at the floor and looked up into the Criminal lawyer's face.

"There is more to the Law than brute force," Epona whispered.

"Absolutely. That's why I'm not kicking down this door and fronting that ignorant bastard right this moment."

"And because it's your boss' door and that wouldn't go down so well," Epona smiled.

"There is that," Elliot grinned, and with those few tension breaking exchanges he reached for the ornate brass handle and gently pushed the door open.

Asmodeus and Malaphar were standing by a polished basalt fireplace behind Asmodeus' desk. Each had a quarter glass of what smelled like almond liquor, and had Elliot not been privy to Malaphar's chequered history he may have otherwise mistaken his uncle and the Caelum Angelic for friends. It was all outward appearances however and Elliot sensed that Asmodeus wanted Malaphar out of Tartarus as much as he did.

"Ah Elliot," Asmodeus greeted, "this is Malaphar Naberius from Caelum."

Elliot took three confident paces forwards and offered an outstretched hand. "Your reputation precedes you Mr Naberius."

"As does yours," Malaphar replied with a firm handshake, "and please, call me Malaphar."

"And this is Epona Brenwen, new to the firm," Asmodeus introduced.

"Charmed," replied Malaphar gently taking Epona's hand as one might a delicate flower.

For a moment Epona was transfixed with how handsome the Angelic was. But it was just for a moment. Even the fullest fruit can have a rotten centre she thought to herself. She politely retracted her hand and made a, albeit faked, respectful nod in reply.

"And how is your father Elliot? Well, I hope," Malaphar continued turning to the young attorney.

"Very well, I had no idea you two were acquainted," Elliot replied, fighting back a burning desire to tell the Angelic to mind his own business.

"A long time ago, was it not Asmodeus?"

Asmodeus answered Malaphar's assertion with a gentle nod. The Angelic was referring to when all of Caelum knew each other, before the war destroyed such bonds... before Malaphar sided against Elliot's father and uncle.

"And what do we owe this visit Malaphar?" Epona ventured.

"How I wish it were under more joyous circumstances that I come upon your firm Miss Brenwen," Malaphar lied. "But then again these Legal nuisances do always get in the way of a good drink, wouldn't you say Elliot."

That legal nuisance is a good friend of mine Malaphar, I'll warn you to watch your tongue in future – was what Elliot wanted to say but instead he ground his jaw and half-smiled in response.

"Then I take it you shall be representing the prosecution in the case of Abigail Hood?" Elliot asked.

"And how tragic a case it appears to be," Malaphar replied looking into his glass of liquor.

"Then you are perhaps here to see if we'll plea bargain?" Elliot continued, trying not to lose patience with the Caelum lawyer's theatrics.

Malaphar placed a hand on Elliot's shoulder. "I fear Master Blackstone that there may be no room for such manoeuvring," he replied with hint of the patronising.

Elliot felt his shoulder tense and in his minds eye he imagined his fists clenching. He moved to Epona's right hand side and away from the Angelic's condescending touch.

"Just as well, for it may have been a wasted journey. It is likely that we shall defend the case. Miss Hood *is* innocent," Elliot confidently declared.

"No trip is ever wasted," Malaphar replied, passing Elliot a silk-tied folio that was undoubtedly a copy of the Prosecution's pre-trial bundle, "and as for Miss Hood's innocence. Well, I guess that will be for a swor… I mean, a *court* to decide." The slip of the tongue was purposeful and Malaphar relished Elliot's reaction. *Sword dear boy, sword – I shall have your head by the time this trial has reached its end* were the thoughts that went through the cunning Caelum lawyer's mind.

Malaphar downed the last of his drink and gestured to Asmodeus that he was ready to leave. As Elliot's uncle walked Malaphar to the door and the Syngraphus thereafter, the Caelum Angelic turned and bid farewell to his opponent. "I shall see you in court Master Blackstone, Miss Brenwen," and with a wry smile he left.

Elliot shook his head and stepped out into the corridor.

"Malaphar," he called out to the departing Angelic, "the Magistratum must be worried if they are wasting your precious time and skill with this… what was it… *nuisance*. I shall read your court documents with interest."

"Well Elliot, the Delatorian Palace can be demanding," Malaphar replied before he turned once more to leave, a smug grin painted unsubtly across his chiselled visage.

Elliot stood there a moment watching his opponent leave, and the thought of running a blade down the Angelic's spine admittedly flashed through his mind. He made the same stern expression as he had made back at the bar and re-entered his uncle's office, where Epona had sat her equine body beside Asmodeus' desk waiting patiently.

Elliot gently placed a chair so that it faced his tutee, slumped into its welcoming arms and padded cushion, rested his elbows upon his knees and his chin in his palms, and sighed.

"Well that was… civil," Epona smiled. "You know I once knew a guy that frowned like you but more often. One day the wind changed and he ended up a mono-brow."

Epona was right of course, no use worrying about the inevitable.

"What a dick!" Elliot spluttered with a chuckle. "I thoroughly dislike that man."

"He's a slime bag. Unfortunately there are still many of his sickly kind to be found sullying our noble profession," Epona added.

"So what do you think the purpose of his visit was?" Elliot queried.

"Well, it certainly wasn't to make friends. Intimidation; to show us how brave and powerful he is," Epona continued in mock machismo, "by strolling into the lair of the enemy."

"Yep, quite transparent really isn't he?" Elliot replied untying the Prosecution's court bundle Malaphar had left them. He quickly flicked through the loose-leaf folio before passing the pages to Epona.

"Ridiculous, we already have all this information," Epona objected.

"I know. He's not even provided a list of witnesses."

"Trial by Combat," Epona gasped looking up into the curiously unperturbed face of Elliot.

"Exactly, no need for witnesses or exhibits or cross-examinations – "

"But the Magistratum would never allow it, not even the High Court of Compenso would entertain such a farce."

"It's out of the hands of Compenso or the Magistratum," Elliot guessed. "Malaphar said his appointment was at the demand of the Delatorian Palace."

Epona sat there jaw agape.

"Unbelievable isn't it? The prosecution in the matter of the royal Meretrix Abigail Hood has been chosen by the Royals," Elliot continued, rising to his feet to make his way to his uncle's decanter of Almond liquor and two fresh glasses.

"But Abigail is a royal servant, more than that, she's a Meretrix, one of the Queen's ladies-in-waiting, why would they allow – "

"Well the few pieces we have seem to fit don't they, there is a royal assassin watching over Abigail at this moment, and I'm damn sure it's not for her protection," Elliot replied returning with two glasses of sweet smelling alcohol, one of which he offered to Epona, who surprisingly swallowed the lot in one swift gulp.

"So…" Epona was about to recap, "wait a minute-turn, why don't you look more worried?"

"Because I have you on my side Epona," Elliot grinned, "and because section 47 of the Delatorian Judicial Process Act was amended 150 ring-years ago."

"I don't – "

"It's a surprise, a surprise you are going to deliver when the time is right, until then Malaphar's motion for Trial by Combat will go unchallenged."

Epona, though a little confused, accepted that her mentor had more legal knowledge than she did, rose to her feet to kick away the pins and needles in her hind legs then trotted slowly to the fireplace.

"So we concentrate on finding the rest of the pieces of the puzzle rather than worry about me having a soon to be headless tutor."

"Thanks for the vote of confidence," Elliot laughed, "and *yes*, we refocus on the case. And in that respect we return to your earlier flash of brilliance."

"A flash of brilliance? So early in her training, that is encouraging," Asmodeus jovially added as he re-entered his office.

"Ah uncle just the man," Elliot replied turning in his seat, "you wouldn't know any Dreamrunners would you?"

"Why?" Asmodeus replied intrigued.

"Abigail is currently under the watchful, and no doubt, threatening eye of Emilita Letalis," Epona explained.

"And you fear Miss Hood would be unwilling to agree to an open interview in the Secarius' presence?"

"We fear uncle that what little Abigail might know may condemn her even before the matter sees the inside of a courtroom."

"Then perhaps you need to re-acquaint yourself with Vincent."

"Vince knows a Sandman?" Elliot replied with surprise.

"Not exactly Elliot, Vincent *is* a Sandman, third generation, and a very capable Dreamrunner," Asmodeus revealed. "But whether – "

Before Asmodeus could finish his sentence Elliot had downed the last of his glass of liquor and was already out the door and on his way to Vincent's office. Epona made a nervous kind of half curtsy to the firm's Senior Partner and then followed Elliot, collecting the Prosecution papers as she left.

"Miss Brenwen," Asmodeus called, "Elliot can get excitable, but he's a fine lawyer… a risk-taker, but of noble heart."

"In the short time I have known Elliot I would have to agree. But, if I may ask, why are you telling me this?"

"Because this case may call for more risk-taking than usual, and if at any point you feel you can't continue with the matter, for which I shall not look upon such a choice unfavourably, I want you to know that Elliot will also understand."

Epona reflected upon those words for a moment, about how the case was unfolding into something previously unforeseen, about the risks Elliot, and she, may have to take. Then she remembered the words Elliot had spoken to her before they met Malaphar. *Perhaps it's not brute force or intelligence that wins a fight, perhaps its courage*, she mused, and with that thought she thanked Asmodeus and galloped after Elliot, confident that she had the abilities to face whatever this case and those thereafter would throw at her.

18

"I'm not sure this is the best way Elliot."

"Listen Vince, the only way we can get you close enough to Abigail to do… whatever it is you do, is *this*," Elliot replied waving an out-swept hand to the bustling party that was going on around them.

"I can't get arrested."

"Yes you can. Focus. Just do what I do."

"Get wasted and end up sleeping under some jetty somewhere?" Vincent mocked.

"Yes."

"You know they'll disbar me?"

"For having a good time? Don't be ridiculous. Bloody Caelum, if I thought *that* was ever a possibility do you think I'd carry on the way that I do?" Elliot reasoned.

"Perhaps, but then a again you do have a reckless sort of a disposition." Vincent shook his head despairingly, made a slow sigh, then whipped two glasses of 'Merum-Nitidus' from the tray of a passing waiter and gulped them down in four extremely animated and overdramatic swallows.

"That's the spirit," Elliot grinned approvingly before giving his companion a vigorous slap on the back.

"So what happens when I get absolutely obliterated on this *stuff*?" asked Vincent holding up his two empty glass flutes.

"I don't understand."

"I'm not going to be any good to Abigail if I'm blind drunk," Vincent sounded the last two words very slowly and precisely so that there could be no misunderstanding.

"Worry not my sad little friend. I have this."

Elliot reached into the inside pocket of his tuxedo and retrieved a delicately blown glass vial that was full of some greenish glowing liquid with a consistency much like treacle.

"What is *that*?"

"This Vince is the sober-up-erer of all sober-up-erers."

"What's in it?"

"I have no idea, I had an apothecary mix it up before we left."

"It looks wrong," Vincent winced.

"And it tastes wrong, believe me. But, somehow, by consuming this liquid all the alcoholic nastiness in your system is immediately…" explained Elliot flexing his hands in front of Vincent like a magician casting a spell.

"Immediately what?"

"Look, I don't know. But it works, get this down your throat before the Magistratum cart you off and you'll have a clear head for the rest of the mission."

Vincent blew out his cheeks in a moment of hesitation, then took the potion from Elliot and tucked it inside his waistcoat.

"So whose party is this for anyway?"

"Erm. It's… no idea."

"So how did we get on the guest list?"

"What's with all the questions? Just drink and be merry. Ooh look at those two over there… this must be the annual Delatorian pre-fashion-show launch party," Elliot laughed clapping his hands together like a delighted schoolboy.

"They are quite pretty actually, apart from the stick."

"That's a bit harsh… oh no, your right she's a Wood-Nymph."

"Very willowy," Vincent chuckled while retrieving two more glasses of fizzy wine, one of which he handed to Elliot.

"How in the World-Tree do you manage to get invited to this type of shindig?" the Dreamrunner huffed with a hint of jealousy in his voice.

"Networking my dear boy, networking," Elliot replied smugly. "Do you see that woman over there?" he continued pointing to a tall, slim, stunningly attractive girl sporting an obsidian-black cocktail dress, the hem of which clung tightly to her upper thighs.

"Why am I not surprised?" Vincent rhetorically replied. "Yes I see her."

"Excellent. Now she has a twin sister, who should be… erm, ah yes… there she is just over by the buffet table."

Elliot pointed out another tall, slim, stunningly attractive woman who was also wearing a high cut, low bust line, slip of a dress, only this one was ruby red.

"Ok, I see her too."

"Excellent. Now we had a… relationship."

"Relationship?"

"Of a sort. Anyway she has a friend… where is he… he never misses a thing like this… ah there he is," Elliot pointed out, directing Vincent's attention to a haughty looking fellow who was wearing a kaki safari outfit, tanned leather riding boots and hat that had a line of what looked like gator teeth sewn into the peak.

"Who in bloody Caelum is that?"

"That is Lucian Archbold the… erm, fifth or six… can't remember. His great, great so on and so forth, father established Archbold's school of Law, the one Epona graduated from."

"He doesn't look Lawerish," Vincent added.

"Well, that's because he's not," Elliot replied gulping down some more wine. "As you can see he is more predisposed to hunting things."

"Really," Vincent sarcastically interjected. "I never would have guessed."

"No really, that fellow, who admittedly everyone thinks is a bit of a ponce, actually did a few ring-years hunting Wolven with the guild-house of the Venators."

"Pull the other one," Vincent replied in disbelief.

"No really his name is still attributed to the greatest number of kills in a single tri-lunar cycle."

"Okay, that's quite impressive."

"Exactly. Anyway, he once got into a spot of trouble."

"Spot of trouble?"

"Exactly," Elliot replied in a fashion slightly attributable to the mildly drunk variety.

"What was the trouble?" Vincent queried equally inebriated.

"The trouble involved the illegal importation of certain... furs."

"Furs?"

"Yes furs."

"Bit boring isn't it."

"Not really."

"Please elucidate," beckoned Vincent who was tactfully intercepting another drink-laden waiter.

"Well. It would break my client's confidence... wait a minute-turn, do you want to know how I got invited to this party or the minor infringements of Mr Safari?"

"Interesting choice... well, as there is undoubly a rational explanation boring-type assertion as to the manner of your invite, then I'd rather know the dirt on Mr I've-Got-Teeth-In-My-Hat Wolven-Killer."

"Undoubtedly," Elliot corrected.

"Yes it is."

"Exactly... erm... as I was saying... certain furs, Wolven being not yet one of them, are illegal to... procure."

"Procurance, yes," Vincent replied slurring.

"Exactly. Mr Thingybob was caught... I don't know if I should tell you," Elliot teased.

"Tell me."

"Sure?"

"Erm... yes," Vincent confirmed, pausing a moment for fear he might vomit.

"Mr What's-his-face-the-sixth-whatever was caught wearing," Elliot continued tapping his nose in a secretive sort of a fashion, "Hermes-wing underpants."

Vincent turned to his colleague with vigorous shaking of the head in objection.

"Yes he was," Elliot confirmed with a slight uncontrollable sway to the right.

"You my debauched friend are pulling my – "

"Leg? Todger? Moppy-type hair?" Elliot mockingly guessed.

"All of the above. I don't believe you."

"Fine."

"What do you mean fine? Prove it."

"Ok I will. But," Elliot retorted raising a finger, "if I am right, then…"

"Then what?"

"Then erm… you have to spank the bottom of the female of my choosing."

Vincent thought good and hard, weighed the pros and the cons, of which there appeared to be more cons, then turned to Elliot and drunkenly proclaimed, "You're on."

"Excellent, come with me. And stop dribbling."

*

Having spent much of the day attending their own affairs, Epona especially enjoying putting her new desk in order whilst Fury avidly scribbled down all that had been found out about her insurance case, the two talented lawyers met and decided to while away the remains of the day following up Elliot's lead on the Wolven costume vendor before trading hours closed.

"So, how are you finding things at our merry little firm?" Fury asked as they strolled along a particular fashionable promenade in the southwest of the Delator.

"It's really great and everyone is so friendly and helpful, and yesterday I went to Babel for the – "

"Yeah, whatever. Ooh look at those shoes," the Fire-Nymph interrupted.

She peeled away from Epona's side and drew herself temptingly towards the window display of one of Delator's more bespoke, and expensive, designer cobblers.

"Clogs? Really not my thing I'm afraid," Epona admitted.

"No, not the clogs you moron, those."

Fury wasn't purposefully being rude, it was just that she kept little company with females and, though she would never admit it openly, she always felt awkward around them, as if she were being scrutinised or criticised or one of the other competitive-type observations females are predisposed to making when surrounded by their own.

Fury pointed to a pair of fine glass slippers. The light fittings within the shop made them sparkle like polished diamond.

"Now those are nice. Don't think I could afford two pairs though," Epona giggled clopping her four feet on the cobbled walkway. Whilst the centaur couldn't wear high heels, owing to the fact that the weight of her equine body would invariably break them, she much preferred wearing flat shoes to horseshoes.

"They are a bit pricey," Fury agreed wincing at the extortionate price tag.

They took one last longing look at the slippers then continued on their way.

"Sorry, you were talking about Babel."

"Oh, well I guess it's probably old news to you, the last thing you need is some naïve trainee harping on about dusty books and mouldy tomes."

"I remember my first trip to Babel," Fury recollected. "Asmodeus sent me there on a research trip to look up something or other about Insurance Law… what was it… never mind it's gone. Anyway, do you know they wouldn't let me?"

"Why ever not?" Epona replied taken aback by the idea that such a place of learning would turn anyone from its gargantuan doors.

"Well, they feared I would ignite the precious volumes within," Fury grinned.

"Never. Why would they say that?"

"Well as accepting as Babel appears to be, the Librarians still revere books above all, certainly above the rights of a researcher if they deemed her a threat."

Fury suddenly stopped at an artist's shop where she scanned a selection of oil paints and a particular attractive brush set. She shook her head and continued then stopped again and this time perused the canvases, before shaking her head once more and walking off.

"Art can be an expensive hobby," she sighed to Epona.

"I can imagine. So did they let you into Babel in the end?"

"Yep. I assured them I was a lawyer from Blackstone's and that the protection of literature… blah, blah, blah, anyway as soon as they heard the firm's name they were as nice as pie."

"I had similar praising when I went. They are fond of lawyers," Epona smiled. "So come on, did you end up burning anything?"

"Well I did manage to track down my legal thesis… and singe my name from its cover. As if I want anyone attributing that pretentious piece of work to me," Fury mischievously giggled.

They continued strolling and chatting and finding out more about each other for longer than they thought, and only when Epona reminded Fury that there was a risk their lead might be shutting up shop for the day did they rush themselves over to its address.

Fury had warmed to the new trainee. Epona reminded her of what it was like to be starting out as a Lawyer, full of eagerness and enthusiasm and that delusional sense of moral superiority. The Fire-Nymph told Epona of her first few days at the firm, about the constant fire evacuations Blackstone's had to endure whenever the hot headed lawyer combusted a case file or set fire to a facsimile, especially taking pleasure in her fond memory of coming into her office one morning to find everything conveniently replaced with flame retardant equivalents and non-flammable furniture.

Epona enjoyed the story of Fury's less than perfect introduction to the firm, and immediately felt more comfortable sharing her own trepidations about being the first four-legged lawyer in the office. She was even bold enough to admit to Fury that she found the Fire-Nymph a little intimidating during her interview, to which Fury confided that she often put on a harsh front in order to rappel those she didn't take fancy to, after which she admitted that her first impressions of Epona was that she was some stuck-up snooty horsy-set type; all pomp and polo. So with the air cleared, and a new friendship forged the better for it, Epona and Fury set off on their way to a quaint tailor's called Tres-Porcus.

"Is this the place?" Epona asked looking up towards a shop sign that was displaying what appeared to be three pig's trotters pressing down upon the peddle of a spinning wheel.

Fury glanced through the window, her eyes falling on a particularly eye catching display involving a female shop dummy dressed in a red hooded cape flanked by what looked like embalmed Wolven.

"Certainly looks suspect. Shall we?" Fury replied pushing open the front door.

The interior of the shop resembled more a hunter's store than a tailor's. Each of the walls was draped in a myriad of furs and the stuffed heads of numerous feral animals, and Epona turned to Fury with a look of concern.

"Looks like a taxidermist's. Are you sure this the place?"

"That's what Elliot said," replied Fury.

At that moment a young gentlemen appeared from behind the shop counter. Though he was draped in the unique style of a Venator, his boyish good looks and un-masculine frame betrayed the stocky features that were possessed by that noble guild.

"I'm afraid we are shutting up shop ma'ams," the boy politely spoke, "unless you have come to collect an order?"

Fury looked round to Epona who instinctively gave a quick nod.

"Yes, I'm here to collect a Wolven costume, and I cannot spare another moment."

"I'm afraid miss that I have no orders pending for that particular design," the vendor courteously replied to Fury, "maybe if I took your name?"

"Maybe if we spoke to your manager sir," Epona confidently replied, "this is an important order, one I hope your good establishment has not overlooked."

"One we certainly would not have miss, but I fear the owners of this store have departed for the day, for the hour is late."

"And where might we find them?" Epona inquired.

The young merchant studied the Fire-Nymph and Centaur with interest for this was the first time he had ever spoken to either of their species.

"Let's see. One has gone to market, the other town and… erm… the other has gone all the way home."

Epona seductively trotted toward the shop counter and gazed up into the young man's eyes.

"Such a bother good sir. We were assured your fine establishment would have been able to service our *needs*."

"Oh yes," Fury followed up, "the royal palace shall be disappointed."

"Oh… erm… the Palace of course… I shall have to check our ledger," the shop assistant nervously stuttered, before retiring to a back room.

Epona shot Fury a sideways glance. "What are you talking about?" the Centaur quietly rasped.

"Shut it and act demure," Fury replied. "What's he to know the difference."

The shop assistant returned a few moments later with a thick order book, which he thumped down upon the shop counter. He quickly thumbed through the heavy tome while looking up now and again to check whether his efforts were still being scrutinised by his two female customers.

"And when might you have placed your order?" the shop attendant asked.

"Seven days ago," Epona quickly replied, having swiftly added up the number of days of Abigail's incarceration then added a few more for good measure.

"And you said it was a Wolven costume?"

"That's correct," Fury confirmed.

The shop assistant shook his head and worriedly scratched at his temple.

"It appears that the most recent order we have for that particular outfit was actually placed two weeks ago, and erm… it has since been collected."

Fury stamped her feet on the floor in annoyance sending small embers spraying from her toes.

"This is highly irregular, perhaps there has been a mix-up?" Epona complained.

"We pride ourselves on delivering a high quality service, we do not make mix-ups miss."

"Well it appears that on this occasion your services are found wanting. Now give us the name of the person who ordered the last Wolven costume then perhaps we can get this thing sorted out," demanded Fury.

"Erm I'm afraid we can't – "

"Do not be ridiculous young man, it is quite clear there has been some mistake on your part and orders have been wrongly taken. Now I must insist on the name. It would be a terrible bother if we had to call in the Delatorian Palace Guard to sort out this minor mishap," Epona sighed.

The shop assistant looked at Fury who confirmed what her colleague had said by a slow nod of the head.

"It *would* be a terrible bother to involve the…" the young man nervously agreed. "Anyway, yes, the name of the customer was…"

His index finger traced down a column of delicately quilled entries.

"Ah here we are, his name was Hansel."

Fury froze as if rooted to the spot. She must have misheard she thought.

"I'm sorry could you repeat that."

"His name was Hansel, no surname, just Hansel."

Fury looked blankly at the shop assistant. She wanted to tell him that it couldn't be, wanted to tell him that Hansel was a witness in *her* legal case… that he couldn't possibly be linked to Elliot's, *could he*?

Epona, noting that the Fire-Nymph's aura had markedly shifted, turned to Fury and gave her a slight kick to the shin.

"Hansel… oh yes, Hansel. Our mistake my good man, it was actually he that we were inquiring for… yes… we must have got our dates mixed up. I'm sure he probably came to collect – " Fury murmured as she back stepped to the front door.

"Yes our mistake, apparently. Please forgive us for wasting your valuable time," Epona apologised, following her colleague towards the exit.

"Not at all good women, a misunderstanding I'm sure. By the way miss," the assistant called to Fury, who was momentarily shaken from the countless questions and answers and associations that were crowding her mind. "I know it is probably something I *should* know, considering the occupation I have chosen to… erm… but I was wondering how is it your clothes do not catch on fire miss."

Epona curiously turned to Fury for she had wondered how her colleague's clothes didn't burn away also, but was too polite to ask.

"Oh, it's a thermal insulated ceramic weave apparently," Fury blushed. "Keeps my body temperature constant and retains heat. And its also flame retardant which makes it especially handy… otherwise I'd just walk around naked I guess."

There was a brief silence during which time the three of them contemplated the last part of Fury's statement.

"Well, may I be so bold as to say that it does you justice miss. And you also miss," the young man added turning to Epona, "your livery is expertly tailored."

The two women thanked the polite assistant, apologised again for wasting his time, then left, stopping a moment outside to check their reflections in the shop window.

"Charming young man," Epona stated brushing down the sleeves of her expertly tailored herringbone patterned jacket.

"Very charming man, I almost feel guilty for chastising him about the Wolven costume thing," Fury admitted.

"Speaking of which, who in all of Arbor is Hansel?" Epona asked.

*

Without the benefit of a magical, green, treacle-like hangover cure Elliot awoke to a gentle wrapping at his front door with a head that felt as if someone had cleaved it open with a two-handed axe.

He cast a bleary-eyed look at his bedside timepiece and disappointingly discovered that it was only three hour-turns since he had left the fashion party. His disappointment was only momentary however, as to his pleasant surprise, he found that he was lying sandwiched between the two stunningly attractive twins he had previously pointed out to Vincent before the both of them had got horrendously drunk.

As for Vincent, Elliot vaguely remembered that the Sandman went to spank the bottom of Lady Alicia Arrogans, a relatively pretty socialite of little cultural worth, missed, and actually spanked the bottom of an Ecquart Silverback, a haughty noble Equinpare from Equinas, whose instinctive response was to plant a particularly fashionable silver-shod hoof in the centre of Vincent's chest. The Centaur's mule kick sent the Sandman hurtling backwards though the air. Unluckily for Vincent an intricate drinks display consisting of a merlot fountain, punch bowl and a wine glass pyramid less than cushioned his ungraceful landing.

The last thing Elliot saw was a five-strong Magistratum Peace Team carrying Vincent away and into the back of a waiting wagon cage. The plan had been executed without a hitch, relatively speaking, and all Elliot worried about was whether his colleague had remembered to drink the contents of the small glass vial he had handed Vincent at the beginning of the night. Quite how he ended up between the twins was still a mystery however.

There was a heavier knock at the door, which caused the twin on Elliot's right to stir slightly. The lawyer painfully drew himself out of bed, wrapped a towel around his waist and made his way towards the front door.

Elliot swore he was still drunk when he reached for the door handle. But what subsequently met his eyes would prove more sobering than any alchemical concoction.

"Hang on, I'm coming," Elliot yawned. His eyes strained against the harsh light of a street fire-lamp overhead, and only when Elliot's visitor moved to blot out the piercing rays did his identity become startlingly apparent.

Standing before the Lawyer was a twenty-foot tall male Dwarf-Giant. Under one arm he cradled an unconscious, possibly dead, body of a young maiden dressed in a white leather body-glove and upon his back was strapped what looked like a barn door.

Elliot was under no illusion that the scene was less than suspect, and correctly guessing that his visitor was in fact one of the notorious Vigilantag he instinctively reached for a polished sabre that was conveniently kept by the door amongst an array of rain shields and walking canes.

Blöd, however, was quicker than his bulky stature projected, and left with little choice the Zwerg-Riese raised a clenched fist and struck Elliot clean across the jaw.

Apparently Elliot's evening was far from over.

19

Vincent tore through the forest with all the – *wait*, he thought, *why am I running*.

There was always a period of disorientation when waking into a dream, and it was not much different to rousing from a dream-state as far as Vincent was concerned; those first feelings of reality flushing out the subconscious, the feeling of strained eyes blinking into the light-emitting world of the waking.

He slowed to a steady pace then stopped. He turned round and peered into the dense foliage he had just ran from but he could see nothing chasing him. As far as he could deduce he wasn't running away from anything.

Vincent looked to his left and then to his right. Nothing but thick dark forest vegetation filled his field of vision. It *was* night however, that much was clear, and not because he was in a dreamscape and all dreams were traditionally conjured at night. In his time, before joining Blackstone's & Associates, the Dreamrunner had experienced dreams of burnished skies strewn with piercing crimson sunlight. He had been bathed in such golden hues that everything seemed bioluminescent. However, this experience, this dreamscape, was the first he had woken into that was black and grey and, but for the tall trees and shrubs around him, deadened… ominously so.

He tipped his head skywards. No stars, no lunar bodies, no clouds, just blackness. It felt unsettling, like looking up into the dark clouds of a pre-storm that blotted out the sky above. It was as if someone had thrown an impenetrable cloth covering over the entire realm, as if someone had placed a death-shroud upon the dreamscape.

Vincent hated this. He hated the unfamiliarity of someone's subconscious. However beautiful or in this case ugly a Scape was, under the surface, they were nothing more than the uncontrolled forms of a mind let loose. The dream is a playground where the mind unwinds. If it is a mind that is predisposed to destroying galaxies to unwind, then it didn't matter that the conjured constellations of swirling nebula were perhaps beyond description. To a Dreamrunner it only mattered that at any point during such a dream the whole Scape could be torn or crumpled or consumed without so much as a flicker from the dreamer's rapid eye movement.

This is why Vincent chose a Lawyer's life over that of a Sandman like his father and his father before him. Until someone came along and proved that the World-Tree and everything in it was the subconscious creation of some deity or being or even the imaginings of a small child, Vincent was safe in the knowledge that everything in the real world was tangible and measurable and to all intense and purposes predictable.

Such luxuries as gravity or solidity, feeling, smell or even sight, even life itself, were never ones afforded a dreamer in dreaming. They were certainly not absolute senses a Dreamrunner could depend on within someone else's subconscious.

There was a sound within the undergrowth beyond, a faint rustling, like a feral creature scratching at the forest floor. Vincent pressed ahead and thought that *he* might have been chasing something or someone did cross his mind.

A chill wind blew through the air and Vincent pulled his suit tight around his body, until he realised that it was a dreamscape at which point he formed a thick coat to wrap itself around him. That was until he realised that sensory information was false in this realm at which point he told himself that the cold was nothing more than a subconscious illusion created by a sleeping mind. So as Vincent ventured into the forest he did so without the feeling of a chill wind biting uncomfortably at his skin.

It troubled him that he had easily forgotten the ability a Sandman has to separate himself from the dreamscape around him. Only that way could a Dreamrunner help a dreamer defeat a nightmare. Only in the most inhospitable of marescapes could a Sandman become attached to the illusions within. This was how

Vincent's father died, and it was the one thing Vincent promised himself he would never forget.

'Never underestimate a dream,' his father once told him 'for it can turn on you in a heartbeat.'

Vincent came to within a few paces where the scratching sound was emanating from when it suddenly stopped.

Then a figure rose up and flashed passed him in a blur of naked flesh. It was Abigail, or at least Vincent guessed that it was Abigail from Elliot's brief description.

The Dreamrunner shouted out for her to stop but still she ran. Vincent looked down to where Abigail had been pawing at the ground and found a tattered nightdress and a torn red hooded cloak. There were palm prints of blood on the otherwise white undergarments and Vincent immediately feared that Abigail was in some way injured.

He looked up in the direction of where Abigail had run to and gave chase.

A few minute-turns later Vincent burst through the forests exterior wall and found himself on the outskirts of a vast orchard, where row upon row of apple trees heavy with fruit extended into the horizon.

Ten rows ahead he could see Abigail standing upon a stool picking apples that she placed neatly into a willow-woven basket she had hanging from her free arm.

She was not naked this time, she was wearing cleaner, fresher versions of the clothes Vincent had seen discarded moments earlier. She looked happy and was humming a tune Vincent couldn't make out.

Vincent took a few more steps towards her pausing only briefly to pick an apple of his own. It was perfect, a full shade of healthy green, large and plump and unblemished. The Dreamrunner was tempted to take a bite, but soon shook the impulse off. The quickest way to merge with a dreamscape, to allow it to attach to oneself, is to believe in it wholeheartedly. To bite from something as tempting as a succulent food substance is to consume the Scape and in so doing allow the Scape to consume oneself.

Vincent let the fruit drop from his hand and continued towards Abigail.

She sensed she was not alone and the humming stopped. Abigail turned with a look of utter terror and let out a piercing scream that sent sound waves blustering passed her unknown visitor like a gale force wind.

Vincent tried to calm her by approaching more cautiously, and he would have verbally introduced himself but for the deafening shrieks she strenuously produced. Abigail then stumbled from her stool and fell to the ground scattering her apples over the lush green orchard floor.

The Dreamrunner looked round but saw nothing that could elicit such a reaction from Abigail. Then he looked down at himself and instantly realised that he was the cause of the maiden's distress.

He had turned into a Wolven, or at least that was now the image he was projecting. Even a simple touch of the Scape's fruit had been enough to allow him to be incorporated into Abigail's dream structure.

Vincent shrugged off his own stupidity and spoke a few chosen words of Sandman incantation, which with a Wolven's jaw came out in nothing but grunts and barks. But the intent was there, and by the time he had concluded the chant the Wolven projection had dissolved away completely.

He saw Abigail continue running and once again gave chase.

Vincent noticed that each row of apple trees Abigail ran passed seemed to hyper-age and wither, the fruits borne on their branches turning mouldy and diseased.

"I've been sent by Elliot, Abigail, Elliot Blackstone!" Vincent called out, hoping that Abigail was still within earshot. "Please, I'm here to help."

The Dreamrunner watched as Abigail stopped suddenly and tentatively turned to face him. The decaying had also ceased when the maiden halted, and turning his head momentarily Vincent noticed that the dead trees of rotten fruit he had ran passed were now healthy and blossoming. Elliot appeared to be Abigail's calming influence, which Vincent had hoped for upon first entering the dreamscape.

"Elliot?" Abigail called out with a smile. "Is he coming to see me today?"

She skipped to where Vincent was standing, but as she drew nearer she appeared to grow shorter. Vincent blinked, thinking that the horizon line was playing tricks with him, but when Abigail came before him, she had changed into a younger version of herself, seven, perhaps eight ring-years in age.

"Abigail?"

"Is he coming, is he? You know sometimes he's a big meenie-head. But I don't think he's that bad really," the young Abigail cooed.

Vincent took a knee, so that he was at eye level with the girl, and smiled a big reassuringly kind smile. With a snap of his fingers he produced a butterfly net from behind his back and offered to it the now excited and fear-free Abigail.

"A present from Elliot. He said he's very sorry but he can't come today. He's very busy. But he's thinking of you. He said for me to look after you till he can come."

"Are you one of Elliot's friends?"

The question had not been one Vincent had had previous occasion to consider. He guessed that between all the banter and playful mocking that perhaps Elliot did consider him a friend.

"Yes I am," Vincent confidently stated. "You know he's worried about you?"

"Elliot's worried about me?" Abigail replied blushing while swaying from left to right.

"He said that you might be afraid of something, something you can't tell anybody about. Is that true?"

"Not reeaaally. We have this scary teacher, who I don't like very much. Elliot thinks she's a witch with a broom and a cat and a cauldron and everything."

In some Criminal cases Elliot had partaken in there was a need for the deposing and questioning and cross-examining of child witnesses. After each of these cases Vincent remembered Elliot returning to the office mentally drained and exhausted and in desperate need of alcoholic refreshment, such was the effort expended in trying to extract a precise piece of information from children whose minds would wonder and trail off in any other direction but the one a lawyer had set them upon.

As Vincent knelt in front of the young Abigail he realised how hard it must be, how eternally patient one has to be, to coax something from such a young distractible mind.

"I remember having scary teachers myself. And do you know what I learnt?"

"Nope."

"I learnt that sometimes they're not scary at all," Vincent replied. "Shall we go catch some butterflies with your new net?"

"Ermmm, nahhh. Ooh do you want to see something really gross?" Abigail asked pulling an ugly face.

"Is it really gross?"

"Yep!"

"Go on then, but you have to stay close by me so I don't get lost okay?"

"Okay, it's just over there by the water," Abigail pointed.

Vincent looked up and noticed that the previously endless rows of apple trees to the horizon had now vanished and were replaced by a thick sculpted hedgerow that marked the boundary of the orchard. Ominously the hedges were sheared to resemble the heads of Wolven. More worrying was that this didn't seem to have any adverse effect on young Abigail's excitable disposition.

Beyond the hedge line Vincent could hear what sounded like the sea, the hypnotic sound of an immense body of water washing upon a shoreline.

Vincent rose to his feet and took Abigail by the hand. She skipped him through the leafy Wolven heads while lala'ing the same tune she had previously been humming as an adult when she was picking apples.

As they left the apple grove Vincent looked up and noticed that the solid, bodiless black sky suddenly terminated and from then on continued in all its recognisable star and full-moon filled celestial glory. The Dreamrunner thought that Abigail's subconscious must have been trying to lift the shroud from her dreamscape.

Abigail and Vincent finally came upon a shoreline, the sand of which reflected an iridescent glow from the moonlight, as if the sand were a multitude of fine precious stones.

Then Vincent's expression changed to one of horror as he now looked upon what Abigail had taken him to see.

Lying lifeless at the water's edge was a dead body.

The young Abigail released her grip from Vincent's hand and skipped over to the corpse. She then slumped herself down and started stroking the dead man's hair.

Vincent slowly approached the body. It was dressed in what looked like a Wolven suit that was covered in patches of blood. His neck had been violently torn asunder and what was left of his windpipe was splayed open.

"Abigail come away… its…"

As he looked towards Abigail he found that she had changed back into her adult self. She was crying and instead of stroking the dead man's hair Abigail was now cradling his head in her lap.

A small trickle of blood was falling from the edge of her lips.

"Abigail who is this? Please, Elliot needs to know so he can help you."

"He always liked it when I called him Hansel," she managed as she tried to fight back the tears that began to flow from her bloodshot eyes.

Vincent recognised the name immediately and he was taken aback, almost enough to have pulled him out of the dreamscape altogether. He looked back to the face of the corpse. There was something else, something familiar but… Tried as Vincent might he couldn't remember where he had seen the face before.

"This man's name is Hansel? Are you sure Abigail?" There was an air of urgency now in Vincent's voice. He was close to the truth and he sensed also that he might be close to some danger – that point in the dreamscape that can turn at any moment.

"Please tell Elliot I'm sorry, please tell him I…" then Abigail's voice trailed away and her attention shifted to the moon overhead.

"No Abigail stay with me, please, stay with me," Vincent pleaded.

It was no use. Abigail had succumbed to whatever had taken over her ten days ago on the banks of Restless River. Her eyes glazed over and she was gone.

Vincent rose to his feet and tried to pull Abigail away but she remained steadfast and rigid. Then a rustle came from the hedgerow behind him. Slowly the sculpted shrubbery was coming to life. The Wolven heads turned from foliage green to matted greys, before they rose from the ground with a savage writhing and twisting, as if the earth beneath was giving birth to them, their bodies materialising from the undergrowth into the unmistakably full forms of a terrifying clan of vicious Wolven.

They turned to face Vincent and slowly stalked to where he had fallen backwards. He turned to face Abigail but she had disappeared, so too had the corpse.

He had just enough time to utter one last incantation before the Wolven fell upon him.

He opened his eyes. Grey shapes came into view and he feared that he had not been quick enough to escape the dreamscape.

To Vincent's relief the shapes became walls, then a ceiling, and then bars on a high set window opening.

He awoke in the holding cells of the Magistratum two cells opposite from where Abigail was sleeping. She was muttering indecipherable words and she was turning in her sleep. It was apparent that the fears in her subconscious had caught up with her. Vincent knew of the nightmares she was having and he hoped and prayed that she would wake soon and leave them behind.

To Vincent's surprise Fury was waiting at the doors of his cell.

"Come on you drunkard, I'm here to bail you out," she complained in earshot of Emilita Letalis who was still watching over Abigail's cell. Fury then threw Vincent a subtle wink to let him know everything was taken care of.

A Magistratum guard unlocked the cell and helped Fury to heave Vincent out. The Dreamrunner was covered in sweat and appeared to be physically exhausted.

"How many times have I told you?" Fury continued to complain. "You can't go competing with those drunkards you call friends." Of course she was talking about Elliot. "It's a good job you can't read my mind because…"

Vincent took the hint and mustered enough energy to momentarily dip into Fury's mind.

Remember don't say anything till we're outside and bloody Caelum do you smell, Fury thought much to Vincent's amusement. Then he remembered the instructions from Elliot not to look over to Abigail, not to attract any attention, to just act like a hung-over drunken bum till he was outside.

Fresh air hit Vincent in the face like a rigorous slap, which Fury had considered doing to make the whole affair look more realistic but reluctantly decided against it.

"I do smell," Vincent said with surprise as Fury linked his arm through hers.

"You're telling me," Fury joked. "So, find out much?"

"You are not going to believe it."

"Try me."

"Abigail said the victim's name was…"

"Hansel by any chance?"

Vincent stopped in his tracks. "How do you know that?"

"Aha, while you and Elliot were getting yourselves drunk and spanking bottoms… I mean *really*, such a *subtly* executed plan, my… anyway, Epona and I followed up Elliot's costume lead."

Vincent remained silent. Whereas Fury had spent the night with the knowledge that her case and Elliot's were associated, and having had a good nights sleep to clear her head, Vincent on the other hand was still reeling from the revelation and was still trying to order the jumbled thoughts that were stacking up in his mind. He was also trying to retrieve the image of the man's face, that recognisable visage he had sworn he had seen somewhere before.

"So the same person Abigail is charged with murdering is the same person who saw the Zwerg-Riese commit the Palace robbery," Fury recapped, allowing a moment for the association to sink into Vincent's thoughts.

"Unbelievable isn't it?"

"In the wrongest kind of way. So, did you get a face?" Fury pressed.

"You know questions and bright light and empty stomach, don't really go well together in the morning-type hours," Vincent moaned.

"Oh, you're such a wimp. Come-on, while it's fresh in your memory… what does he look like?"

"Erm, he was, oh I don't know."

"Concentrate, do you want a quill and ink, maybe if you drew his – "

Vincent suddenly stopped in his tracks.

"What did you say?" Vincent asked with a stern expression.

"I was saying, Mr Moody, that perhaps if you made a picture of his face it might help you remember the details."

"You're a genius," and with that Vincent planted a kiss on Fury's cheek, which turned a redder hue of crimson as if the Fire-Nymph was blushing. Then Vincent took her hand and started running.

"Oi, where are we going?"

"To the Royal Palace," Vincent announced.

"You can't possibly be serious."

"Why not."

"Because you smell. And you look like a bum," Fury joked. "Come on, you can come back to mine and wash up."

"You sure?" Vincent queried. He had never been to Fury's place before.

"Yes I'm sure, as long as you don't sneak any more kisses, you cheeky bugger," Fury grinned.

As much as Vincent wanted to have his suspicions as to Hansel's identity confirmed he did realise that sweaty, smelly, shoddy-looking individuals were not readily admitted to the Delatorian Royal Palace. So without much resistance at all Vincent followed Fury back to her house for a clean up, a strong coffee and a full breakfast, though perhaps not a cheeky kiss.

20

Elliot Blackstone had been drunk many times before and had suffered many a painful hangover as a result. The dehydration, the lethargy, the general slowness in response time, all of these debilitating effects the lawyer had grown to find familiar. Others of the depressingly pessimistic disposition may have claimed that a hangover was the fitting punishment for a night of debauched excess. Elliot however always considered himself optimist. Those first few steps back into the realm of the conscious always gave Elliot a feeling of liberation, as if he were being reborn. He wasn't devoutly religious, but if pressed to draw a spiritual comparison he might have claimed the experience was something akin to leaving a confessional booth with the satisfaction of attaining a morally clean slate.

Elliot Blackstone had been punched across the face considerably less times than he had been drunk, and as aggressive as he tended to get when inebriated he made it a rule not to get into situations were being punched across the face might be a likely outcome. He felt there was nothing soul cleansing about receiving a beating.

He didn't fear getting into a fight should the need arise however; it was just that he realised that he wasn't built to brawl. Elliot's Half-Angelic strength may have compensated for his lack of height and build, but it didn't detract from the point that there were still individuals out in the World-Tree more predisposed to fighting and more favourably designed to carry out the same. The pugilists of Pannonia for instance, when not hewing the forests of that mountainous region, could be found cage fighting for prize purses. Their arms were like pile drivers, their chests like barrels, their shoulders like those of a horned bull and their fists like mallet heads. They were built to fight. Elliot was not. So when Elliot awoke the second time that evening, his hangover having been replaced with that jaw-achingly strained-neck feeling of being knocked out, he immediately thought of the defeated opponents of the Pannonian pugilists, and whether they ever grew used to feeling the same pain that he was experiencing at that particular moment.

"My sincere apologies for rendering you unconscious Mr Blackstone," spoke a voice of deep baritone from somewhere behind Elliot's head.

The lawyer opened his eyes and found that he was lying on his couch in his front room. Curled in the recliner opposite was the maiden he had seen upon opening his front door. Elliot immediately recognised her as Krystina Letalis, the Secarius and sister of Emilita Letalis. He raised himself into a seated position and put a hand to his jaw to assure himself it was still attached to the rest of his head. Elliot then twisted slightly and looked around to see where the voice was coming from.

"I did have little choice in the matter, for I feared you may have run me through given the opportunity," Blöd called out from Elliot's kitchen. The Dwarf-Giant then returned to the front room, crouching as he passed through the kitchen doorway, and handed the drowsy and disorientated lawyer a cup of something hot and herb smelling before slumping down upon Elliot's Arabilisian rug. "That should help with your head," the Zwerg-Riese added.

Elliot was speechless. He was trying to deduce how on Arbor a member of the Vigilantag Seven was sitting crossed-legged in his lounge.

"Why have you come here?" Elliot finally managed.

"I have come bearing gifts," Blöd half-smiled pointing to the comatose figure of Snow White.

"I'm sure there's a saying about being wary of bandit murderers bearing gifts," the attorney mordantly replied, "or is it 'never accept gifts from strangers?' That sounds about right."

"If you do not wish to talk rationally then I shall leave and find someone who does… someone else who *is* interested to know about the mirror and the Meretrix."

"The Meretrix?" Elliot replied rising from his seat. "Abigail? Abigail Hood?" There was panic in his voice now, and concern, and he had an overwhelming urge to unfurl his wings and beat an explanation from the intruder who had come uninvited into his home to turn all reason on its head.

"Abigail," Blöd solemnly replied looking into nothingness, "I did not now her name, only that she was a Meretrix."

"Who are you? Which one? Dok? Brummig? Answer me."

"Blöd, just Blöd."

"You can't be. Reports have it that Blöd is – "

"Mentally deficient? A simpleton? A dumb ogre?"

"Yes," Elliot quietly replied dropping his gaze to his cup of herbal mixture, which was somehow dissolving the pain from his jaw, neck and shoulders.

"Ironic is it not? That the one person who delivers you answers is the last person you might think could ever –"

"Enough! To be completely honest I care little whether reports of your demeanour or intelligence or… everything, are accurately documented. All I know is that your merry band of men have been killing and pillaging and…" Elliot paused, his voice had become raised and his temper was flaring. It wasn't getting him anywhere. "All I care about…" he continued in a dejected tone, "…is Abigail."

"Then I shall start from the beginning."

"You have my undivided attention."

"No judgments?" Blöd asked.

"That depends on how your story ends."

"So be it."

*

Fury's house was not as Vincent had imagined it. He had thought the Fire-Nymph's dwelling might be something akin to the lava pool below Brimstone Bar, all carbon briquette, ashen stained walls and superheated bubbles of glazed rock and sand, cooled over time to produce eerily organic-looking stone formations; a subterranean environment of harsh temperatures and a steady iridescent glow much like Fury's constantly flickering aura. In actual fact the Nymphet's home was nothing of the sort. It was, well… homely.

Fury lived in a small cottage on the outskirts of Delator surrounded by a rich scenic countryside and acres of sky. It was far removed from the bustle of the capital city and Vincent found it quite out of character for someone who always seemed so busy and bothered.

The house was built out of irregular blocks of stone bound together with mortar and from the outside it looked almost patchwork, like a tessellated mosaic. Vincent found the sight oddly appealing and likened it to the aged stone walls, now crumbling and in disrepair, that used to enclose the whole of Delator in ring-years less safe than those at present. It looked as if the cottage had stood there resolutely for eons, unwavering and admirably arrogant to the bitterness of the Delatorian winters or its scorching summers.

The roof was of polished slate and when the daylight rays shone upon its surface it seemed as if the pyramidal structure was on fire. Vincent thought that perhaps a traditional thatched roof might have given the cottage more character, but studying the charcoal blacks of the slates merging into the myriad shades of grey of the outer walls he found them aesthetically correct in an intensely mysterious sort of way. Fury told him the house looked at its best when framed beneath grey storm clouds or surrounded by winter's snow.

The interior of Fury's dwelling was much like the outside, moody greys and solid blacks. A buffed basalt table weighing several tonnes was the centrepiece of Fury's dining room and was flanked by six intricately carved but sturdy high back chairs of burnished fireproofed oak. The Fire-Nymph had original wanted matching dining furniture but subsequently thought against the idea when she realised that her guests might suffer somewhat from pulling stone block seats from under the table every time they sat. Not that Fury ever entertained many guests for dinner.

The front room had a sofa fashioned from the same fine ceramic weave as Fury's clothes, which meant that she could forego the fire protection in favour of comfort when it came to the Eiderdown cushion stuffing. A similar approach had been taken in her bedroom, though Vincent dared not request a tour of that particular part of the house, at least not on his first visit.

A traditional log burning fire was set in the west wall of the front room which provided heat during the colder days, as well as considerately bathing each of Fury's hung oil paintings in a wash of oranges and reds.

"Oil paintings by firelight," Fury mused, "the glow really brings out the pigment."

"As if the paintings are alive," Vincent added.

"I like to think so. Right sweat bag, in the shower you go. There's a fresh towel – "

"Towels?" Vincent queried. "You take showers? But doesn't that?"

"Extinguish me?"

"Well, yes."

"Yeah it does… sort of, any kind of intense application of water can cause my skin to crack."

"Then how *do* you drink? Wouldn't you just crack from the inside?"

"Do you want to talk about Fire-Nymph biology or would you rather just take a shower."

"Erm," Vincent hesitated. He wanted to know all there was to know about Fury but also realised that there was a pressing legal case to be fathomed that demanded their utmost attention.

"Go on, off with you," Fury sighed ushering off the Sandman much like a mother might a reluctant child on bath day. "They'll be fresh clothes hanging up for you in the spare bedroom."

"Men's clothes? Why do you – "

"Go!" Fury commanded, to which Vincent skulked away, all the more intrigued but none the wiser.

Half an hour-turn later and Vincent was bathed and refreshed and wearing a freshly pressed pin-strip suit with matching waistcoat.

"Very suave, looks like something Elliot would wear," he joked as he stared at his reflection in the spare bedroom's full-length mirror.

Fury didn't reply. She could hear him clearly enough, she just chose not to tell Vincent about her past relationship with Elliot. Not yet.

"That's a bit more like it," said Fury, popping her head round through the bedroom door, with a nod of approval, "just fits you."

"So, the palace?"

"Breakfast first. You sure are eager. Do you remember yet?"

"No," Vincent replied gazing out of the bedroom window to the rolling hills beyond. "Well, I… it just doesn't make sense."

"The idea of Abigail killing our robbery witness?"

"Sounds insane when you say it like that," Vincent sighed.

"Perhaps it is, perhaps she was… perhaps everything's gone topsy-turvy," Fury replied with a reassuring smile. There was one thing she did know that wasn't topsy-turvy, and it warmed her heart to think it. If only Vincent knew what that was, then perhaps it would have warmed his heart also.

"Perhaps," Vincent replied, "we should have breakfast. Don't want my stomach rumbling when we interrogate the Queen."

Fury stood there jaw agape.

"Just kidding, I'm sure Elliot will want to do that."

"You're withholding something Mr!" Fury said skipping to the kitchen. "Let's see if a full fry-up will make you give it up."

"I'd give up a lot more for a lot less," Vincent quietly reflected. "For you I'd –"

"What was that?" Fury called from the kitchen.

“Nothing,” Vincent sighed.

*

My nightmares are getting worse, Abigail thought to herself as she opened her eyes and stared up at the now too familiar sight of her prison’s concrete ceiling. She felt clammy and exhausted and she had that dull feeling about her head, like when one sleeps for longer than one should.

She got up from her bed, which was considerably more comfortable since Elliot had brought her a sleeping bag and cushion, and stretched her arms above her. Abigail heard her bones creak and felt her muscles pull taught. How she longed to be outside, running through Brewer’s field like back when she was a child, when she was innocent and carefree… and free. Then suddenly she hung her body loose and tried to recall the dream she had awoken from. *Something about fields… no, an apple grove… and something else, someone else.*

She raised her head and looked through the bars of her cell. Emilita was still there, still there reading, propped up against the bars of the cell opposite looking nonchalant. Abigail wanted to throw something at her, wanted scream at her, to get the assassin to react… to interact with her. It was the forth day that the Meretrix had been imprisoned and she had heard nothing from Emilita but the terrifying threat she had overheard those few mornings before. But Abigail fought the urge to talk to her. The Secarius had betrayed her.

In better days, before her incarceration, Abigail had seen Emilita around the Delatorian Palace. The assassin always followed the Queen wherever the Queen chose to go. Abigail imagined that if the Monarch decided to rattle the gates of Caelum Emilita would have been right behind, ready to protect, ready to die. The Meretrix grew to admire the assassin, as well as her sister Krystina, for how strong and confident she always looked. But those memories meant nothing now. Abigail was experiencing first hand how ruthless the sisters could be. Admiration had originally turned to fear that first day behind bars, but now the fear was turning to anger.

Elliot had promised to save her and for that Abigail knew it might take all the lawyer's courage and strength. Now it was time for her to show those same traits too.

Abigail may have yelled at the assassin right there and then had it not been for the faint clop of hooves on stone that came drifting down the corridor towards her cell.

"Epona," Abigail greeted with a smile, "I'm grateful you've come."

"Well Elliot thought you might like some… well some friendly company," the centaur whispered cocking her head over to the direction of Emilita. "And I would have come even if he hadn't have asked me."

"Thank you," Abigail replied sincerely.

"How are you holding up?" Epona asked slowly lowering her equine body to sit opposite the Meretrix.

"I just wish they'd let me out once and a while, to stretch my legs… to look up at the sky."

"They should be," Epona replied with a frown. "I'll speak to the Magistratum."

"How's the case going?"

"We're all working very hard, Elliot especially."

"He's a good man, cheeky as a boy but I guess people change."

"Oh, he's still cheeky I think. He cares about you a lot," Epona reassuringly replied.

"He always was a soppy one too," Abigail chuckled.

"Really? Everyone says he's a womanising alcoholic."

"I can believe that, but I'm sure that's a front."

Abigail paused a moment as another fond memory of her and Elliot came to her thoughts.

"I've been told I'll be in court in two days. Will you be there?"

"Who told you that?" Epona replied with a look of confusion. Blackstone's had yet to inform the Meretrix of the impending proceedings. In fact Epona was there to talk it all through with her this morning.

"I think he was from Caelum, tall guy… cocky. I really didn't like him."

"Malaphar, that bastard!" Epona sputtered. "He knows better than to… what else did he say?"

"Started asking me some questions about why I'm here."

"What did you say?"

"Nothing about all this," Abigail replied with a wry smile. "I told him I wanted my lawyer present."

"I bet he didn't like that. Serves him right."

"He said he was looking forward to seeing Elliot in court, then he left."

Epona dropped her gaze to the floor. She knew exactly why Malaphar was eager to see Elliot in court.

"I brought some things for you, some food," Epona continued changing the subject.

"That's very kind. The food here is not quite to palace standards."

The centaur began unpacking a number of items from her saddlebag, a small face towel, some bread and cheese and hams, grapes, which Abigail was extremely grateful for, and some fresh green apples.

"So what Malaphar told you was true, you will be court in two days. But," Epona hesitated, "the format for the proceedings is going to be… well, not what you expect."

"Will I be called as a witness? I've already told the Magistratum that first morning that I don't remember anything," Abigail replied picking at the grapes and consuming them with a satisfied sigh.

"There'll be no witnesses, as such."

"I don't understand, what's wrong?"

"Malaphar has pushed for Trial by Combat, it's an archaic practice but one which has yet to be repealed, somehow he – "

"But Elliot!" Abigail interrupted, "He can't… what if something happens… I don't understand, what about legal argument, what about the Law?"

"It *is* the Law Abigail, aged as it is and infrequently exercised."

"Elliot will fight Malaphar?"

"Yes he will," Epona lied. As the centaur's eyes darted to Emilita she could see the tiniest of grins curl upon the assassin's narrow lips. The lie had reached its intended recipient. "But you don't need to worry, he's tougher than he looks."

Abigail put aside her grapes and picked up one of the apples Epona had given her.

"It may be overwhelming Abigail, there hasn't been a trial by means of combat in sometime, and news is sure to spread quickly. There may be many people watching but we'll be there and a judge will oversee the proceedings as is usual. Elliot has his own theories as to why the prosecution might have pushed for this type of trial," Epona continued sifting through her bag for any other items for Abigail she may have overlooked. "It may be that the prosecution's material case against you is weak, and that Malaphar wishes to end it using brute force rather than brains. Then again Malaphar has been known to – "

Epona looked up and caught Abigail staring intensely at the apple she had just bitten into.

"Abigail?"

There was no reply. A single tear rolled down the Meretrix's cheek.

"Abigail, what's wrong?"

"Something… I don't know, something familiar, sad almost."

Emilita's trained peripheral vision had closely watched Epona and Abigail's movements during the course of the session. Each of the items passed from one to the other had been automatically committed to memory and she could even recall the tiny initials sewn into the face towel, a small detail that may have been lost on the less attentive.

The assassin knew that all items would have previously been scrutinised over by the guard at the front of the cells prior to Epona entering the compound. This was standard practice to ensure nothing of harm or, worse still, nothing that might help a prisoner escape was passed over by any visitors. Still Emilita watched. If a scroll had been given to Abigail or a written message passed back to Epona then the Secarius would have known about it, would have known to report the same to her Queen… and to Malaphar. Whether this reporting betrayed the sanctity of Epona and Abigail's attorney-client privilege mattered little.

The laws of Arbor meant little to the assassin's guild. They abided by their own laws, passed down from master to apprentice, their own modus operandi that was accepted by their subsequent clients as beyond reproach. In the relatively law abiding World-Tree of Arbor the Secarii was a law upon itself, dedicated entirely to the service of those that retained them, by whatever means necessary.

Emilita had one eye staring intensely at the apple Abigail was holding. *That's right Abigail*, the assassin thought, *you shall remember soon enough… then you'll wish you were dead.*

21

"Now are you going to tell me what we're doing back here?" Fury queried as she and Vincent approached the palace gates.

"It came to me, well nearly came to me, when you mentioned giving me a quill and ink to see if I could draw the person I'd seen in Abigail's dream as opposed to trying to force it from my memory."

"Well I am a genius," Fury grinned.

"Absolutely… anyway, then it *did* come to me… where I'd seen his face before."

"So?"

"I think you'll find it more of an impact when you see for yourself, just a few more moments," Vincent replied.

"You're teasing me aren't you?"

"Maybe just a little bit."

The two lawyers reached the main guard box beside the palace gates and duly announced their arrival to a senior guard standing sentry.

"Sir, Madam, I regret that the palace will be receiving no guests without prior appointment today," the guard greeted in a regimental and forceful tone.

Vincent curiously glanced through the gates. He saw other guards rushing here and there and several servants milling about in groups in the courtyard. There were looks of concern on all the faces he saw.

"An emergency?" Vincent replied.

"I'm not a liberty to say sir, none-the-less as I have said the palace is – "

"We are here to see Aerarius Artifex," Fury interrupted stepping forward, to which the guard's natural reaction was to reach for the hilt of his sabre.

"That's correct, tell him Blackstone & Associates are here about the Carmen Speculum," Vincent added.

"The Carmen Spec – " the guard stuttered.

"The Carmen Speculum," Fury clearly enunciated.

"Tell him we regretfully inform him that the palace's recent insurance claim is likely to be rejected, and we are here to discuss the situation. This is no trifle of a matter and he shall be very disappointed if we are turned away."

The guard stared at Vincent a moment. He knew that it was easy enough to send the lawyers away, but then he didn't know when they might be granted entrance again thereafter. The guard realised the matter was of some urgency however and resolved himself to at the very least send a message to the royal accountant before taking any further action.

"I shall have to see if Mr Artifex is available to see you sir," the guard replied as he beckoned over one of the two royal message runners that always stood ready on the other side of the gate. "Who shall I say is requesting his presence sir?"

"Vincent Traum and Fury. He knows who we are," Vincent confidently replied.

The guard poked his head inside the guard box, nodded and then marched over to the approaching messenger. Another guard emerged from the sentry box and immediately replaced him. This one looked surlier than the first, of broader shoulder and possessing an expression on his face that suggested he was not overly amused with the Lawyers' impromptu visit. Looking upon him made Vincent thankful that he and Fury had come across the other guard first.

"A few moments sir, miss, your arrival is being announced to Mr Artifex," the first guard reported as he retook his sentry post. The other guard huffed and then disappeared back inside the guard box. "Of course if Mr Artifex is unable to see you – "

"We understand," Fury replied as she eyed the message runner sprinting through the courtyard, weaving in and out of the groups of servants before, almost, colliding with a royal guard who was also conducting himself in a similarly hasty manner.

Fury didn't feel too comfortable waiting in front of the guard box and turned to Vincent to politely request a word in private. The two lawyers crossed to the other side of the cobbled street that ran parallel to the palace main gate and out of earshot of the guards.

"What do you mean we're thinking of voiding their insurance claim?" Fury frantically queried, her back turned to the palace so as to not advertise her alarm to anyone who might be watching them.

"Well, it is looking more and more likely isn't it?"

"Well, perhaps, but – "

"And it did seem like the only way we were going to get inside today."

"Agreed, but – "

"But?"

"Oh bugger it!" Fury conceded in a dismissive tone. "I don't know… you put on – "

The Fire-Nymph was about to say that Vincent putting on Elliot's suit had made him just as cheeky as Elliot.

"What?"

"You put on *a* suit and suddenly you become just as cheeky as Elliot," Fury replied as she playfully poked Vincent in the ribs. "I thought suits stand for serious?" she added rhetorically.

The two of them stood there a moment observing the peaceful goings on outside the palace. It was in stark contrast to the commotion behind the palace gates. More groups of servants, chambermaids, porters and kitchen staff had come out onto the courtyard and were gossiping in groups of between three and ten. It would have looked like a garden party but for the servants' uniforms and the odd guard running purposefully between the groups.

"I wonder what's going on?" Fury queried.

"Maybe some kind of fire evacuation drill."

"I'll give them something to bloody evacuate about if they don't let us in… the suspense about the victim's identity is killing me."

"The main reason I haven't told you yet is because I need it confirmed, I'm going to look a bit stupid if I'm wrong and I've gotten your hopes up."

"Vince, like I care about how stupid you look… wait that didn't come out right."

"Stupid *if* I'm wrong, *if*. You're saying I look stupid?"

"All I'm saying is that you've done so much already to advance both mine and Elliot's cases and well if you get something wrong… even something as important as this."

"That's reassuring, thanks."

"Let me finish," Fury gently whispered looking up into Vincent's eyes, "even if it is wrong, I'll always think agreeing for you to help me was the right thing."

"That means a lot," Vincent replied staring back into Fury's wide eyes.

"So who do you think it is?" Fury whispered stepping closer to Vincent.

"You really want to know?"

"I'll think no less of you if you are wrong."

"Ready?"

"Always," Fury replied straightening Vincent's tie.

"Ok it's…"

"It's?"

"Oh, wait up we're being called over, I hope it's good news," Vincent grinned as he sidestepped an annoyed looking Fury before dashing across the street to the guard box.

"You sod!" Fury quietly cursed.

Five minute-turns later a boy servant of about eleven ring-years of age, whose frilly pages uniform made him look like a girl, was leading the two lawyers to Artifex's office.

The commotion outside the royal palace was mirrored by the fuss that was going on within. It appeared that most of the servant's were being rounded up and ushered outside and more guards were running between the innumerable palace rooms and corridors as if securing each area. On a number of occasions Fury and Vincent were stopped and questioned to which their pageboy eloquently informed the guards that the duo had been granted an audience with the royal account. The guards muttered something about things being highly irregular until the boy chastised them, the sight of which entertained Fury greatly.

For the second time in as many days the two lawyers were shown to another lavish stateroom where they were told the Tabularius would be with them shortly.

"You know Aerarius isn't going to be too pleased with your threat Vince."

"If I'm right then the insurance claim is going to be the least of his worries."

"So what's our justification for rejecting the claim, he's sure to ask you know."

"I don't know, this is *your* area of expertise," replied Vincent. "What do we know? We know the mirror isn't the one which Artifex showed us, so?"

"So he's either lying or he's a little confused."

"Which one would you gamble your cottage on?"

"I wouldn't," replied Fury, "but if I was to gamble your home, then I'd go with the former. There's no way a Royal Accountant misses something that expensive, they're trained not to."

"So?"

"So if he's lying then that suggests that the mirror may actually have been stolen, in which case it goes back to our suspicions that the original vault robbery may have been an inside job, which has subsequently been reinforced by the fact that a palace Meretrix has arguably obstructed justice and killed the witness."

"Ergo…"

"Fraud, just as we discussed on day one," concluded Fury.

"So we pre-warn the accountant of our intention to void the policy and pass our suspicions of the fraud to the Magistratum," Vincent summed up.

"Purposes being?" Fury tested.

"Well with the impending trial of Abigail the Magistratum will have their hands full, I mean you saw how preoccupied they looked when we went to see them… so even if we're wrong then we may still have time to backtrack before we have to give up all this new evidence for scrutiny."

"And the Tabularius?" Fury queried.

"It may be likely that Artifex will be called as a witness by Elliot, especially once he learns that his case has something to do with a palace robbery and a magic mirror. Hopefully the aged Artifex will be so confuddled with the whole thing that he'll subsequently come across all confused when Elliot questions him about the fake mirror he showed us."

"Does that really help things though, proving that the accountant is inept?" Fury wondered.

"In a way it does, I guess that Malaphar may actually want to call Aerarius first to testify – "

"I get it… Malaphar will make him out to be a stellar witness beyond reproach, only for Elliot to tear him to pieces under cross-examination. I like it. You thought about all this outside?"

"Not all of it, some of it I just remembered from discussing the finer complexities of Insurance law with you a few days ago."

"Remember anything else?" Fury pressed, "say the name of the victim maybe?"

"You're terrible," Vincent chuckled.

"And you're a spoil sport," Fury said sulking.

At that moment the heavy handle of the stateroom door turned and in stalked the tall, thin, slow moving figure of Aerarius Artifex, displaying a look of displeasure on his face.

"So what is all this I hear about the rejection of our claim? I must say it is extremely displeasing to say the least, I trust you have a full report with appropriate reasons?"

The accountant chose to remain standing this time and his imposing height detracted enough from his frailty to project a much more foreboding impression than Fury and Vincent had experienced on their previous visit. It was clear the Tabularius wanted the meeting short.

“We are in the process of finalising our report sir,” Vincent replied.

“But we thought it best to come visit you in person, out of respect, rather than have you receive an impersonal memo or rejection letter from your insurers,” Fury eloquently added.

“And your gesture is very much appreciated my dear,” replied Aerarius, “Blackstone & Associates has always done us the greatest of services.”

“And your insurers has always valued your custom, which is why we decided to keep you as informed as possible,” Vincent replied.

“So what can I do to alter your views on the claim? Something about The Carmen Speculum I was told?”

“That’s correct,” Fury confirmed, withholding the urge to chastise the accountant for previously lying to her and Vincent about the mirror in the first place.

“I was under the impression that had been covered?”

“The anomaly in our records, which you pointed out, is something your insurer’s wish us to, well… double check,” Vincent replied.

“It’s a disclosure issue that touches upon the Palace’s policy of insurance as a whole sir,” Fury added.

“And you wish to satisfy yourselves again before producing your formal report?” Aerarius queried.

“Exactly,” Fury replied.

“If we may examine the mirror again sir, then I’m sure we may be able to appease your insurer’s as to the innocence of the non-disclosure.”

“And this is all you request?” the accountant probingly asked Vincent, whilst eyeing the Sandman suspiciously.

“It is sir,” Vincent confidently replied, “and our apologies if this small request has taken you away from more pressing business.”

"Not at all Mr Traum, Miss Fury, whatever I can do to be fully compliant," Aerarius smiled with a reassuring nod.

"We are grateful," Fury thanked.

"But as you guessed my time is limited, so I shall leave you in the capable hands of Tom to escort you to the east wing and the mirror," and with that the accountant slowly turned to leave.

"By the way sir, may we ask as to the reasons for the commotion?" Vincent called.

The Tabularius seemed to ignore the query completely and continued through the door of the stateroom after which he disappeared round the corner. It appeared that, however civil a manner the brief meeting had been conducted in, the accountant's displeasure remained uncomforted by the lawyers' fair assurances.

"Do you think he bought it?" Fury whispered.

"Well we sounded genuine enough," Vincent replied, "and I think our friendly tone helped."

"I still don't trust him."

"Don't worry he'll get his day in court, I'm sure of it."

The two lawyers exited the room and found Tom, the girly-looking pageboy, waiting quite patiently on the other side of the door. He jumped up from his chair, from which he had been swinging his dangling legs a few inches from the floor, straightened his ruffle and proceeded towards the grand gallery, stopping to turn his head after a few steps to ensure the lawyers were following.

Though the palace hustle and bustle continued around them, this time Fury and Vincent's walk to the guestroom located in the eastern wing was unimpeded. Each time a guard looked to approach them Tom would only have to turn his head and frown to send them back to whatever duties they were busying themselves with. Fury had thought to ask the boy what all the fuss about the court was but her thoughts had been given over to what Vincent might reveal to her at the end of their journey.

After fifteen minute-turns and much for the benefit of their young escort, whom they guessed Aerarius would later question, the lawyers finished measuring up the Vanity mirror that was the false Carmen Speculum, as well as making fake notations in an official looking ledger, and exited the guestroom trying best to project an air of satisfaction, though Fury was tempted to ask the Vanity mirror whether it still thought she was fairer than the Queen.

However, instead of walking back through the portrait lined corridor on their way back to the grand gallery and the main palace entrance, Vincent paused a moment and politely asked Tom if he and Fury might take a brief moment to admire the paintings. The pageboy cocked his head to the right and shrugged his shoulders, before installing himself in the nearest chair in sight where he took to swinging his dangling legs and twiddling his thumbs.

"You know I much prefer your paintings," Vincent complimented Fury, examining each of the royal portraits in turn.

"What are you doing?" the Fire-Nymph whispered as she slowly followed Vincent down the length of the corridor.

"They always look so serious in these paintings… royals I mean. Never smiling, I mean you'd think with all their pomp and power they'd be quite happy."

"Vincent?"

"Maybe they're taught to look smug at a young age."

"What are you babbling on about?"

"I mean if I were *this* guy for instance…" Vincent stopped, pointing out a particularly large canvass upon which was painted a handsome young man, "… dressed in such finery and jewels, then I'd be very pleased, positively beaming in fact. The rest of my rich life to look forward to… I might think I'd never *die*."

Vincent turned to look at Fury and with the subtlest of eyebrow raises he gently nodded his head.

Fury felt her jaw drop. *It can't be*, she thought, *Vincent's mistaken*. She broke eye contact with the Sandman and gazed up at the painting. It was of a young noble with a square jaw, kind eyes and shoulder length blonde hair that was brushed behind his ears. His age was comparable to perhaps Vincent's though the confident manner in which the man was posed seemed to project wisdom beyond his ring-years. He was dressed in a military uniform with starched black lapels pressed flat against his neck, and a polished silver breastplate upon which was engraved two horned stags rearing up at each other. The man's trousers, replete with red piping running up the sides, were flared in the militaristic style and protruded at the knee from a pair of black leather riding boots. Draped across his shoulders was a scarlet robe that fell to his ankles. Fury looked back to his face. *It can't be.*

"Oh yes, if I were he…" Vincent continued oblivious to the growing panic that was building up inside Fury, "Tom! Come over here."

The pageboy looked up, sighed a bored sigh, and slowly marched himself next to Vincent.

"Tom, can you tell me who this fine looking fellow is?"

The boy lazily looked up to the high vaulted ceiling and to the gardens on the other side of the corridor's glazed wall, which ran parallel to the paintings, and one might have thought he was ignoring Vincent but for his outstretched hand turned palm up. The Sandman obliged and placed a shard of amber in Tom's hand. But before the boy could open his mouth Fury spoke…

"Its Prince Phelan," she gasped, "the only son to the King and Queen, heir to the throne of Delator."

Vincent turned to look back at the painting then to Fury, who looked as if she had seen a ghost, and then to Tom, who snatched his amber clutching hand behind his back for fear the Sandman might take the precious crystal back.

"Don't worry you can keep the amber. Is she correct?"

"Of course she is mister," replied Tom, "everyone in Delator knows who he is."

"As so they should," Vincent tentatively replied, his voice trailing off towards the end of his sentence as he turned back to face Fury.

He could see fear in the Fire-Nymph's eyes.

"Funny you should point him out sir," interrupted Tom.

"What… sorry, erm… why is it funny?" Vincent enquired.

"Well, all the too'ing and fro'ing about the palace sir," the pageboy whispered, "he's gone missing… they can't find him."

"Erm, oh… that's," Fury began, shaking herself from the shock that had taken over her, "… that's a shame Tom, but… I'm sure he'll turn up. By the way, how long has he been missing?"

"Erm, must be five… maybe six days."

The two lawyers looked at each other but none could conjure the words required to suitably communicate what they were thinking. For the first time in their short relationship the pair were left utterly speechless.

"Doesn't surprise me though," Tom started up again, strolling off down the corridor towards the palace entrance.

"What do you mean?" called Vincent, whilst dragging Fury away from the painting.

"Well sir, he's always sneaking off that one. Has a fondness for the Meretrixes he does."

Fury and Vincent couldn't believe what they were hearing. The Fire-Nymph felt her temperature rise and had an overwhelming urge to grab the pageboy by the collar and shake all the information he had out of him. Vincent's shock was momentary, and with his yearning for evidence slowly dissipating he now seemed more subdued, deep in thought and quiet. The Sandman appeared more preoccupied with thinking about how he was going to tell Elliot that his childhood sweetheart Abigail Hood had, in the absence of an alibi, murdered Prince Phelan… the next in line to the thrown of Delator.

22

Elliot arrived at his office three hour-turns before a scheduled meeting with Epona, Vincent and Fury, and he was fatigued and confused and lost.

He had spent the morning in the company of a member of the Vigilantag Seven and a comatose Snow White, and slumping down into his office chair he found that his nerves were shattered. The Half-Angelic couldn't concentrate on anything, on the paperwork on his desk, on the grains of sand spilling through his hourglass, even on the magic mirror he had recently installed in Blackstone's main boardroom… but more worryingly, he found that he couldn't focus on the case.

The morning's encounter and the information gleaned from the same had been too much for the young attorney to handle. Elliot thought that a visit to Brimstone's might put him right, but he couldn't even muster the motivation to drag himself to his feet, and besides seeking solace in alcohol would have been tantamount to running away from his worries, not rectifying them. He stared into nothing, silent, brooding almost, and anyone observing may have thought that the lawyer was stooped deep in legal contemplations. But he wasn't. In truth he was trying to silence the thoughts in his mind, to find a moment's clarity in a haze of confusion, to stop thinking before his brain imploded.

He put his face in his hands and took three deep breaths. Elliot then straightened up, took a loose piece of parchment from his desk draw, gently took his quill from his concerned looking bronze Valkerie, and began to write.

Anything you don't do you can't do, anything you do do you were always supposed to.

At his most anxious Elliot often wrote little messages to himself like the one above. Sometimes they were titbits from his stream of consciousness: clever conjunctions or amusing anecdotes. Sometimes he didn't know what his messages meant as he wrote them, he just knew that getting them down on parchment was preferable to them perhaps being lost in the back of his mind. But as he wrote those words Elliot knew exactly what he was trying to convey. He was describing his resolve, his ability, and his strength to overcome. The lawyer hated being told he couldn't do something, so to prove otherwise he would do those things… to demonstrate that he could… that there was nothing he wasn't capable of doing.

Before those three deep breaths he imagined his peers telling him Abigail Hood's case was a lost cause, he visualised Asmodeus advising him to step away from the matter, he even saw Malaphar laughing at him. Had he remained in those thoughts he may have heard them say that he couldn't defend Abigail… that it was beyond his capabilities. But that was the last thing Elliot was willing to accept. So with three hour-turns to go till his debrief with his colleagues he rose from his seat, folded up the little piece of paper, tucked it in his waistcoat pocket, and made his way to the Syngraphus and to the land of the Law Bringers thereafter.

*

The Giant population of the World-Tree, of which many still lived in Atlatia, numbered only ten thousand. Life in that mountainous region was slow, ironically mimicking the manner in which its inhabitants aged. The reason why their numbers were so low was perhaps the realisation that raising a family was a facet of life that needn't be rushed, especially considering Atlations lived to at least 400 ring-years.

When the great Law Bringers of Atlatia were not meting out justice upon the realms of Arbor, one can find them residing upon Mount Steinthor, a region Elliot had never before visited. He had once heard Fabianus eloquently describe its gargantuan buildings and roadways, ten times the width of any in Delator, upon which plodded the heavy-footed populace. Other paths ran alongside the main roads and were devoted to those non-indigenous species of Atlatia such as Humans and Nymphs and Centaurs. These distinctly narrower pathways were clearly separated by thick double yellow lines and all Giants knew that to overstep such a boundary mark would be risking a particular gruesome end upon any who would unluckily find themselves under the wagon sized foot of a clumsy Atlation. For such reasons drunkenness in public was made illegal many ring-years before.

Whilst most Giants regarded those non-Giants as something akin to a minor nuisance, such does the big often regard the small in Arbor, there were those Atlations that had forged trade agreements and business dealings with those not of their kind. For instance some Giants in the mountain-breaking business benefited greatly from the engineering prowess of those Humans entrepreneurial enough to enter into advisory contracts with them. Though it might look an oddly union, the relationship suited both parties quite satisfactorily, and when one mountain had to be hewn to make way for another throughway there was sure to be a human or other non-Atlation engineer lending their expertise to the endeavour, as well as subsequently benefiting from some of the precious ore which might be collected as a result.

Strolling the human-sized paths high up in Mount Steinthor, Giant legs walking what might have appeared to be perilously close to him, Elliot was unusually un-phased by the shear scale of his surroundings. Perhaps it was because he had only recently concluded a case not more than seven days before in front of a judge, jury and public gallery, made up entirely of Atlations.

Occasionally the lawyer found himself craning his neck to peer up at the vast dwellings. Had he still been of the worried disposition, as he had been upon entering his office back at Blackstone's a while before, he may have imagined his present position as reflective of the current situation of his legal case: that his small and outwardly insignificant presence in the vast and overwhelming realm of Atlatia was akin to his handling a case that seemed so far above him and which odds of winning seemed so stacked against.

Since learning of the truth from Blöd he might have thought that his subsequently making an impact on the case, rising up against the Queen of Delator for instance, would be like trying to arm-wrestle an Atlation. But his thoughts were elsewhere. Elliot knew the desperation of the situation and the futility of doing nothing but dwelling on the same. Instead he thought back to the first case he ever tried and what he learnt from it…

Six ring-years ago in the rich princedom of Arabilis a young Human orphan boy, who had been sold into servitude, was accused of stealing a magic lamp from one of the archipelago's many underground sacred treasure tombs. Any act of thievery in this realm was dealt with severely and the punishment for the boys crime was the cutting off of his left hand, such was it believed that all sin emanated from that appendage.

The boy maintained that he had been duped into taking the lamp by a nefarious figure by the name of Ahban Nazzeer, a morally devoid and unprincipled horse trader whom had long swindled the island occupants of Arabilis out of their hard earned amber.

The young boy's master believed him, and in an effort to clear the dishonour that the boy's charge had brought upon his estate, and perhaps in realising that a one-handed servant was substantially less efficient than a two-handed one, he requested the services of Blackstone & Associates in defending the boy's case in court.

Elliot was only a quarter ring-year at the firm when the scroll of appointment landed on his desk and he was impetuous and arrogant and eager to make his mark on the Arborian legal landscape.

But for all of the Half-Angelic's fiery bravado he could only manage to convince the Prince of Arabilis to reduce the charge against the boy to one of petty thievery, the punishment of which was the cutting off of the boys left little finger – such was it believed that all minor sins projected from this minor digit.

It pained Elliot greatly to see the young boy led crying to the swordsman's stump, and he began to doubt whether he had done all that he could have done for the boy's defence. He even began to wonder whether his overzealous assertions, used to almost theatrical proportions whilst making his case, had detracted from the essence of his legal argument.

After the sword had come down and the boy's wound had been seared and sealed, and when all tears shed by the boy had dried up, he approached Elliot, looked up into his face, and smiled.

'I like to think I serve my master well sir, which is why I think he has blessed me by hiring you. For this I shall be eternally grateful. You may think that you could have done better but I know that you have served your master, the Law, well also and in so doing, whilst you may have cost me a finger, you have saved me a hand. Even if losing a finger were all you could have offered me, I would have welcomed it gladly compared to the other. So I want you to remember whenever you're sad about a case and how it turned out… to think about when you saved a boy's hand, and how that made the boy feel.'

The boy's words humbled Elliot greatly and they stayed with the lawyer to this day. As the ring-years passed the Half-Angelic attorney remembered those words of comfort from the boy whenever a case turned sour. Gradually Elliot's demeanour altered considerably and arrogance gave way to compassion, and, though he still conducted himself in court with a certain amount of flair, he always remembered that without a solid legal basis and learned reasoning to his submissions he wasn't serving his master, the Law, as best he could.

As Elliot approached the residence of the retired Judge Hallbjorn he didn't think of what he might subsequently request from the aging Atlation, how it might put him at odds with the Royal Delatorian family and what he might lose as a result. All he thought about was how he saved that boy's hand, and how if

Abigail was still imprisoned rather than executed at the end of this case then at least he would have saved her life.

*

"He's late," Fury sighed, looking at the candle-clock in her office.

"No wonder really," Vincent joked. "He's probably shacked up with those twins from the party."

"I'm sure he's trying to figure out what to do about tomorrow," Epona added with a frown, and with the tiniest hint of jealousy in her voice.

"What's tomorrow?" Vincent asked

"He meets Malaphar for Trial by Combat."

"You're kidding… he didn't mention anything about – "

"He probably didn't want you to worry about it… anyway I think he has a plan," replied the centaur turning to Fury.

"That sounds like Elliot… always something up his sleeves," Fury added with a grin.

"I hope so," Elliot interrupted entering Fury's office with a determined step and a thoughtful expression on his face.

He gave a nod and a smile to Epona, who returned the gesture, before strolling over to Fury's desk where he perched himself on its corner.

"So what have we got?"

"Well Elliot, I'm glad to report that your plan to get me drunk and arrested worked," Vincent huffed shaking his head disapprovingly.

"Did you remember to take the potion?" Elliot asked.

"That I did. Abigail's dream was weird to say the least. First she was running naked from something. Then... well, then she was in an orchard picking apples, I turned into a Wolven when I touched one… which freaked her out a bit until I turned back and told her that you'd sent me and I was there to help."

"You turned into a Wolven?" Epona queried in a tone of disbelief.

"I know, it was a stupid mistake on my part. I let the dream realm affect me… in essence I bought into its fake reality and even for a moment that can lead to dire consequences. You become part of the dream."

"What did she say? Abigail… when she realised you was a friend?" Elliot pressed.

"Now this was quite odd. She turned into a child version of herself, and what was it… oh yes, she said that some time's you're a big 'meenie-head.'"

Elliot smiled and shook his head. He'd forgot how the young Abigail had been so cute in her observations of him all those ring-years ago.

"Then…" Vincent hesitated.

"Go on," Epona urged on, thoroughly engrossed in the Sandman's story.

"Then she showed me a corpse of a man. His throat was ripped out… and well, he was wearing a Wolven costume. She said his name was Hansel."

"Magistratum records have it that Hansel was witness to the palace robbery Vincent and I have been investigating the insurance claim for," Fury added.

"Okay keep going," Elliot sighed.

"What do you mean keep going," gasped Fury, "this links both our cases!"

"I know."

"What do you mean you know Elliot?"

"Fury, we'll get to that, just tell me the rest… what did you and Epona turn up at the costume place?"

"Well," Epona began, "we found out that a Wolven costume order was placed something like a week before Abigail was formally arrested."

"Placed by someone calling himself Hansel," Fury concluded.

"Did you manage to find out who Hansel is?"

"No *we* didn't Elliot," Fury replied looking down at her feet, "but Vincent did."

Elliot looked over to Vincent. The Sandman got up from his chair and paced about the room. He had been trying to adequately word his next revelation to Elliot in such a way as to not alarm the Criminal defence lawyer but he found that he couldn't.

"It's Prince Phelan."

Fury couldn't remember a quieter period in the presence of her colleagues. Even alone in her office the Fire-Nymph was known to rant and rave and spurt general obscenities at troublesome files. Had she not been with Vincent at the time he had pointed out the painting of the Prince, she may have started ranting and raving and spurting general obscenities at that very moment. Epona, who had learned of the harrowing news from an overly eager Fury as soon as the centaur arrived at the office, watched her mentor intently. The Mare'ess' own reaction had been one of horror, then one of nausea, then one of galloping to the bathroom to throw up. She was under no elusion how serious the situation had become with the mention of that royal name.

Vincent, Fury and Epona, each having reacted in their own way to the victim's identity, now watched Elliot with marked concern. What was the Half-Angelic going to do? Would he dramatically fall to his knees, throw his hands in the air and yell 'why'? Perhaps he might unfurl his wings in anger and try to break Abigail out of prison. Or perhaps he would just sit there, perched on Fury's table with a blank expression on his face.

"I think you've broken him," Fury whispered to Vincent after a few more minute-turns of unbearable silence.

"Just give him a moment, let him process..." Vincent replied.

"Elliot?" Epona called out placing a hand on the attorney's knee.

It was the second time Epona and seen her mentor phase out completely and she liked it no better than when she witnessed it the first time, when Elliot received word that Malaphar had come to visit him.

Suddenly Elliot blinked, looked down at Epona's hand and gently placed his own on top of it, then he kindly looked into the centaur's eyes. Though he would never openly admit it, the attorney found something soothing about the Mare'ess face, even in those moments when she looked her most concerned.

"Well I guess we all knew it had to be someone's son," Elliot simply stated.

"Someone's son, yes… but not the bloody Royal heir Elliot!" Fury objected, trying best to keep her voice down.

"Does it make any difference? A man is still dead," Elliot replied, "this much we've known from the beginning."

"Delator will bring down all its power on us when they find out," Vincent reflected to himself.

"Then they don't find out… not yet."

"That's with-holding evidence Elliot?" Fury criticised.

"And no one tells Abigail either," Elliot continued ignoring the Fire-Nymph. "By the way how is she Epona?"

"Erm, she's good… she seems well enough. She turned a bit strange when I gave her some apples."

"Apples!" Vincent interrupted. "Just like in the dream, I saw hundreds of apple trees decay and die."

"And she told me Malaphar had come to see her," Epona added.

"Bloody Caelum Elliot!" shouted Fury, "you're not listening, the palace is already looking for the Prince… they'll find out soon enough, then they'll come down on you for obstructing justice."

Elliot walked over to Fury and placed his hand on her shoulder and looked deep into her eyes. He saw the same fear in her eyes that Vincent had seen back at the palace.

"I'm afraid too Fury, I may seem a little detached but inside I'm… I'm terrified. And Fury's right, the identity of the victim does raise the stakes," he continued to Vincent and Epona, "but I must ask you all to wait a moment more before we tell the whole of Delator that their Prince is dead."

"And what do we do in the meantime?" Vincent asked.

"Well, now it's my turn to tell you what I've learnt, and Fury?"

The Fire-Nymph gazed up into Elliot's face. She looked tired and weary, and the gravity of the situation seemed to weigh heaviest on her shoulders.

"Yes," she exhaustively sighed.

"I have something to show you," Elliot revealed, "something that might just rekindle your fire."

*

"Where in all of Arbor did you get that?" Fury gasped as Elliot dramatically pulled the cloth covering from the Carmen Speculum.

"Is that really the Carmen Speculum?" Vincent asked as he ran his hand up one side of the mirror's intricately carved frame.

Epona was just speechless.

"I'm led to believe so," Elliot replied.

"Why is it boarded up?"

"Well Epona, Blöd told me – "

"Blöd, of the Vigilantag Seven, Blöd?" Fury interrupted.

"I think you'd best start at the beginning Elliot," Vincent added, "because something tells me that your night wasn't just spent with those twins."

"Well not all of it," Elliot grinned. And so he began to recount how a twenty-foot tall Zwerg-Riese knocked on his door in the early hour-turns of the morning with an unconscious assassin tucked under one arm and a magic mirror strapped to his back. Elliot further revealed how, upon waking from being knocked out (to which Epona's reaction to this news was to put her hand to her mouth in shock), the Dwarf-Giant proceeded to tell him that the palace robbery was in fact orchestrated by the Queen of Delator, and how Snow White had acted as a go-between for the Vigilantag Seven and the Monarch during the whole insidious affair. Elliot went on to describe that when the Magistratum later caught the Dwarf-Giants, the Queen for fear that the gang would implicate her in the robbery, organised for the only witness to the crime to be killed.

"As we thought," Fury interrupted turning to Vincent, "without the eyewitness testimony from Hansel... I mean the Prince, the Magistratum had no choice but to release them."

"Exactly," Elliot confirmed.

"So the Queen had her own son killed for fear of going to jail?" Epona queried in disbelief.

"That's the thing, I don't think she knows who she ordered killed… and the mutilation of the corpse, whilst ironically covering up the identity of the witness, something I'm sure the Queen welcomed, meant that no-one was to know the victim was in fact, as you have discovered, Prince Phelan."

"Hence the reason the royal guard is turning over the palace to find him," Vincent agreed looking up at Elliot from his boardroom chair.

"Exactly."

There was a pause whilst everybody considered what had been just been said. Now that the whole plot was out in the open, and open for discussion, Elliot's heart felt a little lighter and any doubt he had prior to the meeting was slowly, though not completely, ebbing away.

"So how does Abigail fit into all this?" Epona finally asked breaking the silence.

"I'm not too sure on that one," Elliot replied.

"Well a pageboy at the palace told us the Prince was fond of Meretrixes," Fury added.

"Still doesn't explain one: how or why the Queen chose Abigail to kill Hansel, and two: how Abigail knew Hansel was the Prince… or simply, how she knew who to kill," Vincent pointed out.

"Two things that we need if we're going to have any chance of convincing a jury that the robbery and the murder were connected," Elliot sighed.

"So how do we get those facts?" Epona asked.

"I'm still working on it."

"You know Elliot there's a chance that even if we discover the missing links, that… well, that Abigail may still have accepted to have done this thing for the Queen – "

"Of her own free will Fury?"

The Fire-Nymph nodded mournfully.

"That's something I've thought about… at length, but I'm just not ready to accept that. The Abigail I knew could never –"

"I believe you Elliot. I know I haven't known her for very long at all but she seems like a good woman," Epona offered comfortingly.

"Ditto," Vincent agreed, "there's something else we're missing. There's got to be."

Elliot turned to his colleagues and nodded thankfully. He would have told them there and then that he would always be in their debt for the effort they were putting in, but there was still much to do, and as Vincent had pointed out there were still a number of questions that needed answering.

"Well I guess the majority rules," Fury summed up with a smile, "so she's innocent. Now what do we do to *prove* it?"

"Okay. Epona, tomorrow I meet Malaphar – "

"But why don't we just petition – "

"The fact is the Angelic has made an oversight, and I want him to suffer for it… The palace pushed for Malaphar's appointment and sanctioned his request for trial by combat – they're trying to sweep the whole thing under the carpet before this goes to court. And it will go to court… and before the trial proper begins I want that arrogant bastard on the back foot," Elliot resolutely stated.

"So you still need me to fish for that 'section 47' thing?"

"As amended," Elliot clarified to Epona, "find that and I keep my head, literally."

"And such a pretty head too," Fury replied with a grin, "and what about us two?" she asked gently nudging Vincent in the ribs.

"I think the mirror still has a part to play, so Vincent I need you to take its dimensions and find me a glazier and a mage."

"And a mage?" Vincent queried.

"Trust me, I know what I'm doing… I think I know what I'm doing."

"And me?" asked Fury.

"Well Blöd is still keeping low at my place. He's agreed to testify so we need a formal witness statement. Don't worry, I've told him your coming," Elliot added noting Fury's reluctant look on her face.

"Worry! Why should I worry? He's only a dangerous killer Dwarf-Giant wanted across the whole of the World-Tree," the Fire-Nymph sarcastically replied. "And what do we do about his other Arborian warrants of arrest while we're at it? We are technically harbouring a fugitive Elliot."

"Well there's no outstanding warrant for him in Delator, so in the meantime he falls outside of the this jurisdiction. This much I have had clarified."

"From who?" Vincent asked.

"You guys do ask a lot of questions," Elliot grinned.

"Fine, what ever you say, you're lead Counsel anyway," Fury conceded.

"Yes oh great leader, we trust your judgement," Vincent also conceded but much more light heartedly, before bowing and leaving the boardroom with Epona.

"Listen Elliot, I'm sorry about earlier. I don't mean to lose my temper, it's just sometimes…" Fury whispered when she and Elliot were alone.

"No Fury, I'm sorry. I shouldn't expect everyone to just follow me blindly on this one. I need someone like you to point out when I've crossed the line."

“Well you can count on me to slap your wrists when you’re naughty,” Fury giggled. “You really believe she’s innocent?” she continued in a more sombre tone.

“With all my heart.”

“There is one way to find out how this whole thing is going to turn out you know?” the Fire-Nymph suggested looking up at the Carmen Speculum.

“There’s a reason I had it boarded up Fury, I forgot to say. There’s just something wrong about it, everyone who has used it has somehow suffered some great tragedy. I can’t use it to compound the desperate position Abigail is already in,” Elliot sincerely replied.

He had previously considered using the mirror’s powers of divination since it had come into his possession, but the more Blöd told him about the whole affair, how the Vigilantag used it to capture Snow White for instance, the more Elliot decided against it. Part of him felt that the future was still in his hands, and now his teams’ too, and relying on such an artefact, in essence to cheat, was something that Elliot considered a subversion of everything he believed sacred about the Law. As he told his colleagues, he would use the mirror but not for the purpose for which it was somehow imbued.

“Fair enough Elliot, I trust you,” Fury admitted giving the attorney a kiss on the cheek. “Erm, oh another thing. Vincent was quite worried about breaking the news of the victim’s identity to you, I don’t know if you noticed.”

“Yeah I did, he’s a good man.”

“That he is. Just that… have you thought about how you might break the news of the Prince’s death to the King and Queen?”

“Yeah, they do have a right to know… I’m working on that one too.”

“Elliot Blackstone against the World-Tree, I don’t know which one I feel more sorry for,” the Fire-Nymph joked.

“Well with friends like you, I’d feel more sorry for the World-Tree.”

"There is that. Well I best be getting to my chores, I've a Dwarf-Giant to interview," Fury concluded edging towards the door. "What about you?"

"I'm in court tomorrow… I've got to see a man about a sword."

23

Before today, the largest ever attended trial in Arborian Legal record occurred in a backwater town called Dearing, a quarter-trunk away from Delator, 207 ring-years ago…

Having been hard at work all morning picking apples a young boy decided to take a nap upon a hilltop before returning to town. The hill had a tall oak in its centre, the thick branches of which provided welcome shade to anyone who chose to rest beneath the tree's leafy bough.

The boy took off his cloak and wrapped it into a bundle so that he might lay his head upon it. However, before he shut his eyes to sleep he took the amber shards he had earned that morning and hid them in a deep hollow at the base of the tree and covered the hollow with a hefty rock. This didn't look too out of place as the hill was not the lush green kind, as can be found in Pannonia, and there were already a number of loose rocks and large stones sprinkled about its surface.

The boy yawned a big tired yawn, closed his drooping eyes and fell asleep, safe in the knowledge that anyone who tried to rob him whilst he was asleep would find nothing of value upon his person.

A few hour-turns later the boy awoke refreshed. Before making his way back into town he took up his cloak and unbundled it, before shaking it out and throwing it over his shoulders. He then slowly rolled away the rock that was covering the oak's hollow and reached inside to retrieve his shards of amber.

To his great distress the boy found that his hard-earned amber was nowhere to be found. He looked around the hilltop to no avail, and thought back to before he slept and whether he remembered anybody walking by that might have seen him hide his precious crystals. He couldn't.

Panicked, the young boy ran into town and declared, quite animatedly, to the guard standing sentry at the gates that he had been robbed. The guard, ever patient, listened to the boy's story before suggesting that he see the mayor at his office at the other side of the town. Still distressed, the boy made his way to the mayor's office shouting that he had been robbed to whomever he passed, which was a great many people. The townsfolk kindly enough to listen told him to calm down and see the mayor.

The boy reached the mayor's office, eventually, and threw open its doors. He stomped up to the mayor of the town, placed his hands on his hips and declared that he had been robbed. He asked the mayor what he would do about it to which the mayor asked him whether he knew who had taken his belongings. The boy said that he was asleep and that he neither saw nor heard anyone approach him. The boy, who had calmed a little, also said that he hid his amber well and that someone very sneaky must have taken it.

With very little evidence to go on the mayor asked the boy to take him to the hilltop and to the tree beneath which the boy had slept.

After a slow walk, during which time the mayor learned a great deal about the boy, they eventually reached the hilltop. The mayor did his best to investigate the site himself, but he could not come up with any explanations for the robbery. Slowly the boy began to cry because he knew that the much-needed amber to help his family was lost forever. The mayor also felt sorrowful at the sight of the boy's tears.

After a few moments of thought, the mayor strode up to the tree and stated in his most authoritative voice: "Old oak, old oak. I hereby place you under arrest for the theft of this poor boy's possessions." The boy wiped the tears from his eyes and looked at the mayor curiously. The mayor then took a knee and to the hefty stone, which the boy had used to cover the tree's hollow, and stated equally authoritatively: "Hefty stone, hefty stone. I hereby charge you as an accessory to the theft of this boy's possessions." Again the boy, who had now stopped crying, titled his head and wondered how the tree and stone might have committed such a crime.

"Old oak and hefty stone. You are hereby summoned to the town square at noon tomorrow where you shall be tried for the crimes for which you have been accused," the mayor concluded, before escorting the bemused looking boy back to town.

As the rest of the day went by word soon spread that the mayor had arrested and was intending to put on trial an old oak tree and an ordinary looking, though hefty, stone. The townsfolk gossiped through the day about how this might be done, though none questioned the mayor's wisdom, which had served them well for many ring-years.

The next morning the mayor entrusted some of his best foresters to carefully uproot the tree and replant it in the town square. He also entrusted an officer of the peace to bring the stone from the hilltop to the town.

When noon was approaching the whole town, which numbered 2437, spilled out into the town square where they found the old oak, and the hefty stone beside it, waiting for their trial to begin. When the townsfolk saw the mayor slowly approach the square from his office they began to whisper amongst themselves. 'What would happen?' they asked. 'How will the mayor put this tree and stone to trial?' they wondered.

Beside the mayor walked the boy, who looked quite afraid seeing the whole of the town's population come out to witness the proceedings.

"Old oak. Hefty stone. You have been charged with the theft of three shards of this boy's hard earned amber. How do you plead?" the mayor asked. The crowd hushed and waited for a reply.

The tree and stone were silent.

"Court recorder, will you enter into the record that old oak and hefty stone have chosen not to enter a plea," the mayor directed, to which a nervous looking court clerk hesitantly obeyed.

"Very well oak, stone. A plea of *not guilty* has been entered on your behalf," continued the mayor. In the back of the crowd of onlookers a young girl suppressed the tiniest of giggles for she found the whole affair extremely amusing.

With great bravado the mayor began to question the tree and the stone in turn: "Where were you both when the crime took place?" to which the there was no reply. "I put it to you that you were both at the scene of the crime aha! Deny it if you will." Still there was silence.

A middle-aged man who had been standing next to the giggling girl in the back of the crowd felt his shoulders begin to shudder, and for fear that he would burst out laughing at any moment he clamped his hands over his mouth, to which his neighbour also did the same in response for the hilarity of the event was proving infectious.

Still the mayor pressed on with his questions: "So you both choose to remain silent. That is of course your right. But it only compounds your guilt!" A soft breeze blew through the square which made some of the tree's branches gently sway, but still the old oak remained silent. The rock remained still, and was equally silent.

The town butcher who had been watching the trial caught sight of the giggling girl, and the man standing beside her, and his neighbour trying to withhold their laughter, and quickly found that he had the sudden urge to laugh also. Though he pressed his lips tightly together he could think of nothing but how funny the trial was, and with no other choice left he put his knuckles in his mouth and bit down hard. A small teeter escaped however and an old woman standing next to him was the first to hear it. She slowly chuckled to herself also, though it came out in low whoops and wheezes.

The mayor began circling the tree and stone and declaring how stealing was wrong and if they had done it or if they had not done it, to speak up. Still there was nothing but silence from the tree and stone. The butcher who had bitten down upon his knuckles felt his face turn red and his stomach tighten. He bent double and pressed his palms to his knees and began breathing very slowly and carefully, such do people do when they choose to fight against the uncontrollable fit of laughter soon to erupt within them.

Then it happened.

Halfway through the mayor's next question, as to which one of the tree and stone planned the robbery, the butcher burst out laughing in a great booming chortle. With tears of joy streaming from his eyes the middle-aged man who had been standing next to the giggling girl, joined the butcher and started laughing also. The giggling girl who felt as if knots had taken her stomach started rolling around on the floor of the square in fits of uncontrollable giggles. The laughter and chortles and giggles and guffaws rippled through the townsfolk until all; young, old, woman, man, bright, not so bright, were slapping each other on their backs and laughing so hard that it made them cry. When they found it hurt to laugh and they felt they could laugh no longer, they would burst out laughing some more.

The young boy looked around and felt a smile appear on his face. He stood next to the mayor however who was looking extremely stern indeed, which made the young boy keep from joining in the hilarity.

"Order!" boomed the mayor. Still the laughing continued. "Order!" he repeated in a louder more commanding tone. Slowly the townsfolk, seeing the look of anger upon the mayor's face, began to take control of their selves and the laughter gradually died away completely.

"You should be ashamed!" stated the mayor disappointingly, "this boy has come out to see justice be done and you have all turned this trial into a mockery. I find you all in contempt of this court!"

There was a murmur amongst the crowd, and each bowed their heads in shame.

"Yet I have no wish to imprison all of you this day so this will be your punishment. Do you all see this boys little finger nail?" the mayor asked holding up the boys hand up high so that the boy was almost on his tip toes. "Each one of you shall bring me a shard of amber equal to the size of this boys little finger nail, so it might teach you that the Law is no laughing matter."

The mayor then adjourned the proceedings and dismissed the court. The next day each of the townspeople visited the mayor's office and deposited their small shards of amber. When the day was through and normality had returned to the town the mayor turned to the young boy and said: "please accept these amber shards in reparation of this court being unable to deliver you appropriate justice." The boy, who was overjoyed, collected the amber into a small pouch and found that it weighed nearly the same as what was stolen from him.

"But what about the tree and stone?" the boy asked.

"Well," replied the mayor, "I think they have had a good talking to and I doubt they shall do it again. I'm minded to set them free and return them to their hill, what do you think?" The boy thought hard and eventually agreed, for deep down he didn't want to see the old oak and hefty stone punished any further.

And so the oak was replanted upon the hilltop and the stone placed next to it, the boy recompensed and the mayor happy that he had delivered some form of justice.

Used as a case law example on the perils of being in contempt of court, Elliot regarded the case with great fondness during his days at law school. To this day the young attorney never made any attempt to decipher the motives of the mayor or the legality of the trial itself. It became his favourite case because the copious amounts of reported joviality reminded him of his own immaturity. The case also had a happy ending, which Elliot considered had some intrinsic moral quality about it.

He occasionally thought back to the case of the tree and the stone whenever he felt down about something. And as he laced up his white padded sparring tunic he ran through the case in his mind. The last thing he wanted Malaphar to see upon exiting his tent was that he was afraid. So taking his mind elsewhere he chuckled along with the rest of the giggling townsfolk of Dearing and reminisced about how it made him feel the first time he heard it.

The hour was soon approaching and the sun was high in the sky, an the assembled masses, significantly outnumbering those that gathered for the trial of the tree and the stone, basked in the glorious sunshine waiting for Abigail Hood's Trial by Combat to begin.

The whole of Delator must have turned out for the spectacle for not a patch of grass could be seen between the sprawling populace, save a cordoned path that ran from the entrance to Fulmen field to the square of grass in its centre upon which Malaphar Naberius and Elliot Blackstone would soon draw swords.

Pegged at opposite ends of the fighting ground were set two tents within which the attorneys were each making their pre-trial preparations. Installed at the third edge of the square between the two tents stood a dock where a nervous looking Abigail Hood sat waiting, and beside her was a great judge's bench where a relatively young Delatorian judge, not much older than Asmodeus Blackstone, sat perched on a high chair ten feet from ground level. This aerial view afforded him a suitable vantage from where he might adequately conduct the proceedings, as well as halt them should there be any breach of conduct from either of the lawyers.

Abigail looked as if she might throw up at any moment. Having been a Meretrix of the Royal palace she was not unfamiliar with mass gatherings of people, who turned out to see the King and Queen and the Prince, but this was considerably different. She felt each of the tens of thousands of eyes from the spectators glaring at her accusingly, and she desperately tried to avoid making eye contact with any one of them for fear that her heart might give out as a result.

The noise was deafening. Groups of watchers chattered amongst themselves at a volume enough to compete with the next group of chatterers who were conducting their conversations that bit louder… and so on and so forth until there were those sitting next to each other who almost had to shout to make themselves heard to their neighbour.

Some people had turned out with picnic baskets and parasols, apparently intent on making a pleasant afternoon of the whole violent affair. Others had brought instruments and games and the whole sight may have been mistaken for a festival of music to those not privy to the impending proceedings. Those intent on bringing refreshments of the alcoholic variety were soon deprived of their much-loved liquor by a Magistratum force that must have numbered over a thousand. The officers formed a perimeter around the field and carefully watched over the crowd to ensure that no two spectators watching would mimic the bout that would subsequently occur between Abigail Hood's Half-Angelic defence lawyer and the Caelum attorney sent to prosecute.

An official headcount conducted by five court clerks recorded those in attendance: watching, guarding, judging and participating, as numbering 32,459. The trial of Abigail Hood would thereafter be known as the biggest attended trial ever to have occurred upon the World-Tree's surface.

Vincent, who had been keeping Elliot company as well as lending a certain amount of moral support to his friend and colleague, stepped out of the defence tent and was immediately awestruck by the shear number of people who had turned out to watch the trial. The amount of spectators had considerably increased whilst the Dreamrunner had been within the tent and part of him was not prepared for the sight of the sprawling masses.

Though nervous that he was now being scrutinised by those that had seen him leave the tent he managed to make his way over to where Abigail was sitting. Much to Vincent's relief the Secarius, Emilita Letalis, was nowhere to be seen. He thought that perhaps now it didn't matter to the Queen whether the Meretrix said anything or remembered anything, for if Malaphar proved victorious in his bout with Elliot, which looked the likely outcome, then Abigail would subsequently find herself convicted of outlawry and would also perish beneath the blade of a sword. *Where is the justice in this?* Vincent disapprovingly wondered.

"How are you holding up?"

Abigail, who had been staring at her lap, her head bowed as if ashamed, looked up and gave a meek smile to the approaching Sandman.

"It's you," Abigail sighed in relief, "from my dream."

"I'm sorry I had to do that but Elliot needed to know what you were afraid of. And I'm sorry if I scared you by turning into a… you know."

"I've had worse dreams of late."

"Elliot's still inside preparing," Vincent advised, deciding to change the subject, "but he wanted me to tell you not to worry… that everything's going to be okay."

"Ever the optimist, eh?"

"He is that."

A hush suddenly fell over the crowd and Abigail and Vincent looked up to see what was going on.

Confidently striding up the cordoned path towards them was Fury, who was seemingly enjoying the reaction she was getting from the crowd. Most people in Delator, having been content in living out their whole lives within the boundaries of their great capital city, had never seen a Fire-Nymph before. Some watched with her with awe, some little children cowered beneath their mother's shawls fearing that the woman was some evil daemon, and others – woman of the jealous disposition – regarded the attractive stranger with indifference, especially when one or two wolf-whistles, which were directed at Fury, broke the silence. Fury loved every minute-turn of it.

She reached the edge of the square fighting ground and beckoned Vincent over with a nod.

"That's Fury," Vincent explained to Abigail, "she works at Blackstone's as well… bit off a show off but she's damn good."

"Your firm sure is varied," the Meretrix replied.

"That's how Elliot's uncle likes I think. I'll be back soon."

Taking his leave of the accused, Vincent walked over to Fury to fill her in on the format of the proceedings.

“It’s more like a bloody festival of music than a court of law. It’s a farce,” Fury stated shaking her head.

“I agree. These people don’t care about the law, or justice, to them it’s no different from a Pannonian prize-fight.”

“How’s Elliot doing?”

“Surprisingly calm actually, considering,” Vincent replied.

“He’s probably got something dramatic planned. Speaking of which, where’s Epona?”

*

Epona was dressed in her best suit and was confidently cantering her way to the field where she would subsequently deliver a crushing blow to Malaphar’s plan.

Tucked in her saddlebag were two copies of section 47 of the Delatorian Judicial Process Act (as amended), which Elliot had instructed her to procure. Having read the same she immediately understood why Elliot originally chose not to challenge Malaphar’s motion for trial by combat. The Half-Angelic wanted to publicly humiliate Malaphar. It may have been a petty way of getting back at the Caelum prosecution lawyer for his ruthless involvement in the case, but Elliot knew all too well how important it was to strike the first blow. Forcing Malaphar to alter his plans would mean that the defence would start the trial proper at a considerable advantage. In other words Elliot would be prepared for the examination and cross-examination and serving of exhibits and Malaphar wouldn’t be. Or at least Elliot hoped he wouldn’t be.

The centaur felt quite good about herself. Five days at the firm and she was already being relied upon to assist Blackstone’s premiere criminal lawyer in chastising an equally famous Caelum Angelic attorney. The responsibility made Epona feel as if she were really contributing to the firm and to Elliot’s case for that matter. Having heard horror stories from other legal trainees at other firms, of the endless copying and proofreading and anything else that wasn't quality legal work, Epona had always feared whether Blackstone's would subject her to those same mundane tasks. It was a fear quickly allayed however and as she made her way to Fulmen field she did so with her head held up in pride and with a very smug grin on her face.

That is until she found herself approaching a field that considerably lacked the thousands of spectators and lawyer's tents and judge's bench and the dock of the accused, which she had expected to find after her relatively problem free trot from Delator.

The only person she did come across was a human female of about fourteen ring-years of age who was dressed in a white frock, tied at the waist with a pink cotton belt, and a large white bonnet which was fastened under her chin. In the girl's right hand was clutched a shepherds staff, which was the same height as the girl and curled into a spiral at the skyward end.

"Excuse me?" Epona called out. "Where is everybody?"

"You're a centaur," the girl replied with surprise. "I've never seen a centaur before."

Epona smiled and moved forward a little closer.

"Hello, my name's Epona. I was wondering if you could help me?"

The girl curiously cocked her head to her shoulder before walking round the Equinmare to get a proper look at all of Epona's four legs.

"Can I ride you?" the girl innocently asked.

"Hmm, us centaurs don't really do that… unless it's an emergency of course," Epona replied with a smile. "As I was saying… where is everybody?"

"Well the shepherds have moved the flock on to where there's greener pastures, but we lost one… that's why I'm still here. Will you help me find him?"

"Flock? This *is* Fulmen Field isn't it?"

"No miss, this is Fulmin Field, Ful*min*. Fulmen field is three hills away over in that direction," the girl replied pointing towards the east.

"Oh dear," Epona nervously whispered to herself. "This is not good."

*

Judge Coerceo removed a pocket sundial from his judge's robes and checked the time. He then nodded to one of his court ushers who promptly sounded a large horn to signal the beginning of the trial.

The crowds silenced and with restrained excitement they watched as both Elliot Blackstone and Malaphar Naberius exited their tents.

Elliot looked calm and collected and the gravity of the situation appeared lost on him. Even his heightened senses, which would have picked up and amplified within himself the tide of emotions that was rippling through the spectators, seemed uncharacteristically unresponsive.

This was in fact a show of fake confidence to the greatest degree and Elliot actually felt fearful and nervous, and his heart was pounding beneath his sparring tunic... more so when he realised that Epona was no where to be seen. Adopting the best poker face he could he eyed Malaphar who was advancing towards him.

"Nice day for it, wouldn't you say?" whispered Malaphar when he was shoulder to shoulder with Elliot facing the judge.

He was dressed in the same padded fighting jacket that he had been wearing a few days before, when sparring with his friend in Caelum, only this time he wore a cuirass of polished steel over it, upon which was etched the symbol of his celestial realm – a pair of angelic wings folded around a fiery sword.

"I don't know Malaphar. Always room for improvement," Elliot calmly replied.

Both attorneys had chosen to wear plated bracers to protect their forearms and wrists as well as thick leather shin guards to protect their lower legs. They had the choice of wearing full armour, albeit with knees and elbows left bare (in accordance with the rules set down for such proceedings), but each realised that such weighty protection meant sacrificing speed and agility, two qualities which one needed in spades if one was to rapidly deliver a blow or swiftly sidestep the same.

"This court is now in session," Judge Coerceo began. "Miss Abigail Hood you stand convicted of murder. How do you plead?"

Abigail just kept looking at Elliot and she found that she couldn't take her gaze away from him. The next two words could condemn his life and perhaps save her own, or save his life and condemn her own. Never would she have wished this choice on anyone. She would rather give up her own life than see Elliot suffer under Malaphar's sword. How had it come to this?

Elliot, noting the delay in response, turned slightly to face Abigail. He could only guess what she was thinking but he knew, in every facet of his soul, what his friend was feeling. He looked upon the face of the Meretrix, smiled a small but reassuring smile, and gently nodded his head.

"Not… not guilty," Abigail forcibly replied through the lump in her throat. Then, as a tear rolled down her cheek, she nodded her head back at Elliot. It broke his heart in two, seeing her like that, vulnerable, forced to make decisions she wasn't accustomed to making.

"Let a plea of not guilty be entered into the records," the Judge continued. "Abigail Hood, by petition of your defence, your proxy has been nominated as Elliot Blackstone. Do you have any objections?"

Again more questions. *Please let it be over*, she exhaustively thought to herself. She raised her head to the judge and nodded her head.

"For the record miss Hood," the Judge gently directed acknowledging the grief he could see in the young woman's eyes.

"I… have no objections," she replied, her voice breaking towards the end. She slowly put her face in her hands and quietly sobbed. *I'm sorry Elliot, I'm so sorry.*

"So be it. Mr Naberius, Mr Blackstone if you will now recite the oath."

And together Elliot and Malaphar spoke the following words:

"Hear this, ye justices, that I have this day neither eat, drank, nor have upon me, neither bone, stone, ne grass; nor any enchantment, sorcery, or witchcraft, whereby the law of Deus may be abased, or the law of the Serpine exalted. So help me Deus and his saints."

The declaration varied from jurisdiction to jurisdiction. For instance in Atlatia Deus was replaced with Thor and Serpine with Nidhogg, but the meaning remained the same. Each combatant was swearing that he had utilised no evil lore or magic, which in Delator was associated with Serpine – a vile serpent that religion would have those believe was the cause of all evil in the World-Tree – to give himself an un-natural advantage. On the battle field the supreme victor was always the one who Deus or Thor, or Enlil in Arabilis, granted their divine favour upon. In essence the victor always had the strength of the deity in his arm, the strength of Justice. This was how the Law had rationalised such a barbaric form of trial. It was a rationalisation that had its many critics, Elliot and Vincent being two of them.

Elliot and Malaphar turned to face each other, bowed, and then retired to the weapon racks beside their respective tents. But before they did so, Malaphar stepped up to Elliot.

"You do remember the call of submission don't you Elliot? I'd hate to do any more damage than necessary," the Caelum attorney taunted.

"The only one calling 'craven' will be you Malaphar," Elliot calmly replied, to which Malaphar strolled to his weapon rack smirking.

Please be late Epona, just a few minute-turns, Elliot thought, *just give me enough time to slice that smile from his face*.

*

"Bloody Caelum I'm going to be late," Epona gasped as she eyed the angle of the sun in the sky. "Sorry Mere, Pere, Blackstone's had to let me go because I let one of their lawyers die because I'm a dufus."

She galloped as fast as her legs would carry her. She eventually reached the crest of the first of three hills, which the shepherd girl had pointed out, and paused briefly to get her bearings, then she bolted towards the next hill in sight.

"Fulmen, Fulmin… fair mistake really Elliot," she muttered to herself, "oh that's right you can't hear me because your head's been severed from your body, silly me."

She shook off her self-chastisement till less pressing times, gritted her teeth and pushed onwards.

When in the right mood she was one of the fastest runners in Equinas. What she had told Asmodeus and Fury at her interview had been true and she loved nothing more than galloping the shoreline of her home realm whenever she found herself back there. The pastime had strengthened the muscles in her hind legs, which when factoring in her low body weight meant that she could compete at speed with any male centaur. Epona would have otherwise taken up professional racing had the unfortunate incarceration of her father not steered her towards a career in Law.

From the crest of the second hill the Equinmare suddenly heard a faint cheer emanate a short distance to the east, which she reckoned was about three-minute turns away.

"Oh no, it's started."

*

Malaphar had used his trademark shoulder-rush to knock Elliot onto his back, and the young Half-Angelic had to perform a quick backwards roll to evade the Caelum's swiftly descending blade.

Elliot pushed himself back onto his feet and gripped the hilt of his sword as tightly as he could, having almost lost it in the roll. It was his father's sword, the same one Raphael had refused to turn upon his brother Asmodeus during the civil war in Caelum, and Elliot had collected it the previous day from a reliable weapon smith who had polished and sharpened the blade and rebound the hilt. The irony was not lost on Elliot, how a weapon unsheathed in the Caelum civil war a thousand ring-years ago was now being employed to parry the blows from one of that realm's most notorious advocates.

The crowd had gone ballistic, and with each metallic crash of sword on sword their cheers became louder. Some were on their feet now to get a better look at the bout, each encouraging the fighter of their choice with words not meant for younger ears.

Elliot spun his sword in his right hand and viciously swiped it at Malaphar's head. With lightening reflexes the Caelum Angelic parried the blow and turning Elliot's sword away from him Malaphar countered with a powerful downward stroke, which scraped the steel of Elliot's breastplate.

Visibly shaken Elliot sidestepped another attack before deflecting Malaphar's sword high enough to manage a smarting hit to the side of the Angelic's ribs. Malaphar noticeably reeled backward, pained and un-amused by the Half-Angelic's blow. In a rage he brought his sword down upon Elliot's five times in quick succession, the vibrations of each blocked blow progressively weakening Elliot's arm. Malaphar's final strike swatted Elliot's weapon away and sent it hurtling thirty feet to the Half-Angelic's rear, where it slid into the ground in front of a particularly nervous looking spectator.

Having disarmed his opponent Malaphar saw his window of opportunity and lunged at Elliot's stomach. Elliot had no choice. From the slits in the back of his tunic he rapidly unfurled his wings and with a powerful reverse beat he propelled himself backwards.

Malaphar had overextended his last strike and had fallen upon one knee. The Angelic looked up just in time to see Elliot dive towards him shoulder first. Elliot, moving at a considerable midair pace, managed to knock Malaphar onto his back, but as the Angelic un-gracefully fell he managed to reach up with his free hand and grab Elliot's ankle. Malaphar gritted his teeth and slung Elliot skyward.

Elliot tumbled through the air for a brief moment before he finally managed to use his wings as an air break. The brave defence lawyer's aerial advantage soon dissipated however as, with a great roar from the crowd, Malaphar extended his own wings, which were considerably larger than Elliot's. Not only was the defence lawyer lacking his weapon but he was also lacking the strength enough to compete with Malaphar off the ground. The Half-Angelic was still the more agile however and as he saw Malaphar quickly fly towards him he bravely decided to meet the Angelic head on.

"Elliot, don't!" Abigail cried out as she desperately tried to leave the dock. Vincent quickly ran to her side and gently restrained her back as two Magistratum officers of the court, who had spotted Abigail's erratic movements, advanced towards them.

"It's ok, she's going to stay here, she is," Vincent reassured the guards, "won't you Abigail, for Elliot."

The Meretrix gave up her struggle and buried her face in the Sandman's neck. She couldn't bear to watch anymore.

Only a few swords lengths separated the lawyers as they rapidly accelerated towards each other. Then at the last possible moment Elliot dipped and dived beneath Malaphar. Frustrated, the Caelum Angelic snarled as he wheeled back round to face Elliot. But Elliot's gambit had paid off and as Malaphar's eyes fell upon the small figure of the Half-Angelic it was to the sight of Elliot retrieving his sword from the ground in which it had been stuck. The crowd was quick to show its support to the previously weaponless defence lawyer who had outwitted a considerably more powerful opponent, which appeared to incense Malaphar even more than Elliot's tightly executed manoeuvre.

*

"Out of my way!"

"I'm sorry miss, but no one is allowed to enter the arena when the trial has begun," replied a particularly heavyset Magistratum officer guarding the cordoned entrance to Fulmen Field.

"I don't have time for this. My name is Epona Brenwen and I'm with Blackstone & Associates. If you do not let me pass then you will be allowing a gross injustice to occur. Do you understand me?"

Epona had trotted right up to the guard and shoved a bound scroll under his nose.

The guard hesitated and looked around his shoulder to his fellow guardsman. Everybody was still engrossed in the bout at the centre of the field that little attention was being paid to the perimeter.

"Erm. I'm going to have to check with my superior miss," the guard replied as he continued to look around his shoulder. "Now where is he?" he mumbled to himself.

"This is ridiculous," and with that Epona reared up on to her hind legs and jumped clean over the cordon and the guard, who had stumbled onto his backside in panicked response.

"Wait miss! Stop there!" yelled the officer as he took to his heels in pursuit.

A number of other Magistratum officers had seen the Mare'ess' minor infraction and were already moving to assist their confused comrade. Some spectators had even allowed their attention to be torn away from watching the combat to see what was going on.

Epona could see Elliot pulling his sword from the ground up ahead, as well as Malaphar slowly descending from the sky back to his feet.

"Your honour!" Epona shouted out. It was no good for the cheering crowd, still appreciative of Elliot's dive, was drowning out the Equinmare's plea.

*

"Come on you Caelum bastard," Elliot cursed under his breath as he eyed Malaphar stride towards him.

"Bravo Elliot," Malaphar greeted as he stood two sword lengths away from the brave defence lawyer. "How unlike your father you really are."

"You don't know anything about me Malaphar," Elliot spat.

"I know that you would fight when he would not. It would appear cowardice does not run in your blood after all. Then again I suppose it is tainted by Human."

"You son of a…"

To call his father a coward and his mother's blood a taint was about as much as Elliot was going to take. He raised his sword high above his shoulder and swung with all his might.

Malaphar, taking pleasure from eliciting such a reaction from Elliot, grinned and arced his weapon just in time to parry the Half-Angelic's blow.

Suddenly a great cheer came from the crowd, which seemed relatively far away and unconnected with the duel. Elliot briefly glanced to his right to see what the disturbance was. It was a costly mistake.

Malaphar stepped inside of Elliot's range preventing the young attorney from making good any subsequent attack. The powerful prosecutor then grabbed Elliot by the throat and hoisted him a foot from the ground.

"I believe the word you are looking for is 'craven'," Malaphar whispered into Elliot's ear.

Elliot was being choked to death and as much as he wanted to tell the Caelum Angelic where to go, he found that all that came out of his mouth was a splutter.

"What was that Elliot? Do speak up won't you, the noise from the crowd is quite overpowering… no? Well have it your way."

Malaphar locked the guard of his sword under Elliot's and with a sharp flick of his wrist he managed to dislodge the hilt from the young attorney's grip. It was the second time Elliot had lost his weapon and left with little other choice he kicked his boot into Malaphar's groin.

The Angelic released his throat hold over Elliot and stumbled backwards. Though his hand was still clutching his sword Malaphar was now bent double with his free hand cupping his groin.

"Sorry Malaphar didn't quite catch that," Elliot called out as he got to his feet, "wasn't 'craven' was it?"

"You little - "

"Oops too late," Elliot grinned.

As Malaphar was slowly straightening up from the particularly un-sportsman-like kick from his opponent, Elliot gleefully watched as Epona, who he had seen come charging towards them when Malaphar was choking him, stopped short enough to spin the back of her Equine body full at the recovering Angelic.

Malaphar was thrown ten feet to the left where he landed with an unpleasant bump. Elliot had never been happier to see Epona's hind.

"Order!" shouted Judge Coerceo. "I will have order in my court!"

The crowd had gone wild. There was whooping and cheering and clapping and nothing could be done to quell it.

"Order! Or I shall hold each and everyone of you in contempt!"

The cheering and whooping and clapping abruptly stopped from the spectators, bar one who only ceased when his neighbour elbowed him in the ribs. Elliot thought back to the trial of the Old Oak and the Hefty Stone and smiled.

"Arrggghhh!"

Malaphar had retaken to his feet and was wildly rushing towards Elliot with his sword held high above his head.

"I said order Mr Naberius," the judge repeated. "You will stay your hand sir or find yourself in contempt," the judge warned.

The Caelum Angelic came to a stop only two feet away from Elliot and it took him a further moment for the judge's words to register in his angry mind. Slowly, and not without some reluctance, Malaphar lowered his weapon. Elliot could see from the corner of his eye that the Angelic's chest was heaving and his usually pallid face was flushed. Malaphar was furious and Elliot loved every minute-turn of it.

"Mr Blackstone," Judge Coerceo continued, "this is highly irregular. I trust there is an adequate explanation for this intrusion?"

Elliot took a deep breath and glanced over at Abigail, who had pulled herself away from Vincent and was watching the change of proceedings with a look of trepidation, before turning to face Epona, who was still clutching a bound scroll in her hand whilst visibly catching her breath.

"Your honour," Epona interjected, "I must apologise for this untimely intrusion, but it has recently come to our attention that this trial is illegal."

There was a gasp from the spectators and even Malaphar raised a disconcerted eyebrow.

"Illegal you say? And I trust you have appropriate precedent to back your assertion, miss?"

"Miss Epona Brenwen," Elliot replied on his trainee's behalf. "Junior counsel for the defence."

"Miss Brenwen," the judge acknowledged, "I am sure the scroll you clutch in your hand is not for dramatic purposes. Please state your case."

Epona looked about her and immediately felt the weight of several tens of thousands of eyes bearing down upon her. To say she felt a little pressurised would have been an understatement, and she was certainly aware that her intrusion into the proceedings was not receiving the warmest of welcomes from those that had turned out to see a good brawl.

The centaur turned to Abigail who was still installed in the dock of the accused and gave her the same reassuring smile that Elliot had given the Centaur on numerous occasions during the first week of Epona's employment.

"Your honour, I hold in my hand section 47 of the Delatorian Judicial Process Act," Epona began conscious that she was now the centre of attention. "This section, which was amended 150 ring-years ago, stipulates that all petitions for trial by combat in criminal cases must be brought on behalf of a named wronged."

Judge Coerceo looked at Epona with interest. Unlike his fellow Delatorians he had seen Centaurs before and in fact one of his close friends was the same individual who had instinctively hoof kicked Vincent across a busy fashion party two days ago. He beckoned Epona forward with a slight wave of the hand, to which the Mare'ess turned to Elliot for approval to approach the judge's high bench. Elliot smiled and nodded, inwardly impressed with how his tutee was coping with the pressure of her surroundings and the situation as a whole.

Epona slowly trotted to the Judge and stretched her arm upwards to pass her scroll into Coerceo's patient hands.

"It appears, Mr Naberius, that section 47 indeed renders this trial illegal. Do you have any submissions in response?"

Malaphar ground his teeth but was quick to temper the fury that was welling up inside him. He soon realised that the trial had taken an unforeseen turn and was also quick to realise that any falter here on his part may be seen as a weakness in a matter that may subsequently go to a proper trial.

"I must say your honour," Malaphar began with all the self control he could muster, "the objection to these proceedings appears a little late in the day. I respectfully submit to my learned colleague that any objections to the petition for Trial by Combat should have been lodged soon after the same was being petitioned."

It was a relatively calm assertion given Malaphar's current state and Elliot feared that his plan might fail.

"Your honour –" Elliot replied clearing his throat.

"Your honour," Epona quickly interrupted, "I believe the fault for the delay in the serving of this new counter-motion may lie upon my shoulders. It has been a considerable task to track down a servable copy of the said section and I am relatively new to this vocation."

"Mr Naberius?" asked the judge, checking to see if the Angelic had any further objections.

"The fault of a trainee is hardly a call for a trial such as this to be delayed. I respectfully suggest, your honour, that my learned colleague returns to law school where she might learn of due process and etiquette," Malaphar replied with a hint of malice.

Elliot was about to come to Epona's defence but the judge was quick to reply.

"Yet it seems that this trainee has identified a gross illegality in your original petition Mr Naberius," the judge pointed out. "It is quite clearly stated here that in charges of a criminal nature made against an accused, where a petition for Trial by Combat is made, that said petition must be brought by a close relative or trustee of the victim's estate. This insures that only private actions might be settled in this manner, and that prosecutions brought by the crown are not expedited by this form of trial. I am sure you realise that the crown, the royal house of Delator, does not challenge to combat those beneath it merely to see swift justice done, for the strength of Deus always rests in the arm of the Monarchy and all those who act as its champion. Such are Kings divinely ordained is it not?"

Malaphar quickly collected his thoughts and confidently strode towards the judges bench.

"Your honour, it is the case in this trial that the victim's identity is presently unknown – "

"Ah yes Mr Naberius, extremely unfortunate," the judge interrupted, "yet perhaps if the prosecution's case had been finalised… perhaps if your petition was legally lodged following the Magistratum's full investigation into the identity of the victim Abigail Hood is accused of murdering, then perhaps section 47 would have been subsequently followed to the letter, yes?"

Malaphar didn't reply.

"Do you have anything to add Miss Brenwen?" the Judge continued.

"Your honour, only that if this illegal trial continues, then the subsequent verdict of the same will be built on unsafe ground and possibly open to appeal and possible overturning," the centaur confidently replied.

Elliot immediately felt a distinct sense of pride for Blackstone's newest addition. Not only had the Mare'ess correctly asserted that the illegality of the proceedings would lead to a question over the validity of its outcome, but Elliot was also quick to appreciate how Epona had placed emphasis on how Judge Coerceo's judgement on the same may also be open to an overruling by a judge far above him. Elliot new that the only thing Judges hated more than a prejudiced trial was in having their subsequent judgements being overturned. Epona had not only put pressure on Malaphar's petition, but she had also put pressure on the judge's original decision to grant it.

"Malaphar?" asked the Judge.

The Caelum Angelic, whose ruffled-browed expression had been intensely directed at Epona, turned again to the Judge and conceded the point by bowing.

Judge Coerceo gestured to his court usher herald who, though a little vexed by the turn of events, promptly sounded his horn. The gathered crowds, who had been whispering amongst itself since the impromptu arrival of the four-legged female legal trainee, hushed and turned their attention to the judge.

"I hereby declare that this trial is held to be null and void and is to formally cease upon this hour-turn. I further declare that this trial shall resume at Compenso two days from now. Court dismissed," Coerceo concluded with a heavy sigh.

Malaphar, ignoring Elliot and Epona completely, threw his sword to one side and advanced towards the Magistratum officer who had administered the case before the Angelic was instructed to prosecute. The Caelum Angelic shot the civil servant a penetrating glare that chilled the officer to the centre of his soul.

Whilst Malaphar was not totally blameless (in not checking section 47 of the aforementioned act) he knew that if the Magistratum had done their job properly and identified Abigail's victim, then sought permission from the victim's relatives, then he might have concluded the trial there and then with a quick snap of Elliot's neck. The prospect of taking the matter to Compenso, and a proper trial, was something the Angelic was little prepared for, and he was quick to put the nervous looking Magistratum officer on notice of the same.

"Malaphar!" Elliot called out, unable to abate the temptation to have the last word. "Well fought! Now let's see if your bark is as good as your bite."

With the judge having retired from the arena Elliot could chastise his opponent without the risk of being criticised for bad etiquette.

Malaphar fought off his compulsion to finish the job he was so successfully doing during the bout and merely continued to his tent.

Elliot breathed a heavy sigh of relief. Although he had wished that his trainee arrived late so he could have a good go at Malaphar, the young defence attorney knew that perhaps on this occasion his wish might have cost him his life. Whilst he had fought with bravery and skill, he knew that only one winged combatant would have subsequently left the field victorious, and that was Malaphar. Elliot turned to Epona, who was looking noticeably shell shocked from not only addressing a judge but also declaring the biggest ever attended trial in all of Arborian Legal history illegal, and smiled in gratitude.

Epona shook the tension from her shoulders and advanced towards her mentor, but before she could reach him Abigail vaulted over the edge of her box, wriggling free of Vincent and several Magistratum guards, and threw herself at the tired looking attorney.

"You bloody… you could have got yourself killed," Abigail sobbed pounding her fists upon Elliot's chest, "you fool, you bloody heroic clever fool!"

"Well fool and heroic perhaps," Elliot replied cupping Abigail's face in his hands, "but I'm not sure about clever."

The Meretrix looked into her childhood friend's kind eyes and couldn't help but smile through her tears.

"Two out of three is not bad I guess," she replied hugging Elliot as tight as she could.

The guards who had been watching over the accused turned to each other and shrugged. They decided to let Abigail have this one moment with her heroic defence lawyer.

Suddenly the silence that had previously descended over the thousands of spectators was broken by the feint sound of clapping, which emanated from a young girl who had taken to her feet. The girl was showing her appreciation for the courage that the young Half-Angelic had shown in protecting Abigail. The sound was joined by another and then another, and before long the whole gathering was cheering and clapping and congratulating Elliot on a fight well fought.

Over the shoulder of Abigail, Elliot looked at Epona and again nodded gratefully. The centaur curtsied in response, before she turned to Vincent and Fury who were giving her the thumbs up from the edge of the arena.

Better late than never, Epona contentedly thought, *better late than never*.

24

The Letalis sisters were not always assassins, and both had previously shared a loving, nurtured childhood much like any other pair of sisters might, not withstanding that they were orphans who never knew their parents. Their transition from lovable twins to deadly Secarii was not one for which their orphanage was to blame for theirs was a place of great joy and merriment and endless pyjama parties and picnics. A single death marked their change from Emilita and Krystina Letalis to Rose Red and Snow White, and it was the death of a dwarf named Méreg…

Méreg was a rude, bad-tempered, impatient dwarf who lived in a dank cave in the small realm of Bodmin, which was southwest of Equinas. When he wasn't partaking in thievery, for which he was extremely skilled, he was practicing alchemy, of which he also had some talent, and although he had yet to turn glass to amber he did have knowledge enough to turn one living thing into another.

During the twenty six days of Delatorian high summer, when the heat becomes unbearable so as to make even the most medial task Herculean, the royal family retreat to Bodmin where the weather is cooler and the air less stifling. So it was in one particular ring-year, when Prince Phelan was but ten ring-years old as were the Letalis sisters, that the Queen found herself in the troublesome position of having been transformed into a bear cub.

The Queen had interrupted a particularly daring heist in which Méreg hoped to acquire the Carmen Speculum. Following the suicide of his first wife fifteen ring-years before, the King, disgusted at the sight of the mirror, relocated it to a secure vault in the royal family's summer residence. Only a few of the palace staff knew of its location and when they drunkenly and audibly discussed the item over three pitchers of ale one midsummer's evening the dwarf was by chance at the same watering hole to overhear them.

Méreg conceived of a plot whereby he would enter into the service of the summer retreat, under the guise of an able cook, and steal the keys to the vault – a task not difficult for one as skilled at pick pocketing as he was. The second stage of the plan involved temporarily turning the mirror, which was substantially larger than himself into a something considerably smaller. And the plan would have worked, Méreg having been accepted as assistant chef to the head cook of the palace, but for the Queen walking into the vault at the exact time as the dwarf was preparing the next stage of his heist. With little time to subdue the Queen, change the mirror, and escape, for the Monarch had pulled on an alarm bell beside the vault's entrance and the guards would have soon been upon the dwarf, Méreg threw his potion at the Queen instead and ran.

Instead of changing into a hand mirror, the transformation intended for the Carmen Speculum, the Queen turned into a young bear. Convinced that the guards would entrap her in this state and without the regal voice to tell them what had happened, the Queen bounded out of the vault and her summer residence and followed the dwarf into the forests that flanked the palace grounds.

The bear-queen soon became lost in the forest and had lost the tracks of the dwarf several miles before. It was then that Emilita and Krystina came upon her. The children were afraid at first, but when they saw the cub roll upon the ground and whimper they approached and began stroking the bear's fur. The bear-queen did not growl or claw at the children, and allowed them to take liberties no non-regal had ever taken with her for she knew that the children could lead her out of the forest and perhaps to some food and water. This the children did and as the bear-queen was looked after by the twins in an outhouse beside their orphanage the King sent men far and wide to try to find her.

Each day the Letalis sisters came to play with the bear and each day the bear led them back into the forest, where she hoped to find the dwarf's lair.

One afternoon in a clearing, while the bear-queen was bathing in a nearby stream, the twins came upon the dwarf. He was angry for his long beard was stuck in a log he was splitting.

Tugged as he might he couldn't free himself and all manner of profanities issued from his mouth, more so when he saw that the twins were having a good giggle at his expense. They were still kindly children however, and as much as the dwarf cursed them so, they still picked up his axe and sliced his beard so as to free him.

The ungrateful dwarf berated the children for cutting his precious beard and he had little thanks to give them. He snatched back his axe and turned to leave, grumbling to himself and cursing the children. He was evil enough to have perhaps taken their heads clean off there and then but for his attention being suddenly directed to a small bear cub that was appearing at the clearing's edge.

Méreg recognized the bear as the Queen immediately, as did the Queen recognize him, and he swept up his axe and charged at the cub.

The twins, fearing that their bear friend would come to harm, gave chase and managed to trip the dwarf up. Over and over the dwarf went and when he got to his feet he found that the sisters were upon him beating him with their fists. He struggled them both off and gave Emilita a swift backhand that smarted the poor girl almost to the point of tears. Krystina rejoined the fray as did the bear cub each swiping at the Dwarf, who was no taller than they, with all their combined might. Their efforts were little compared to the strength of the sturdy and stalwart dwarf and he soon threw Krystina aside and kicked the bear cub in the stomach.

The dwarf then made for his axe but it was nowhere to be found. As Méreg clenched his fists and advanced towards the cub once more Emilita who had been waiting behind the log, from which only moments ago she and her sister had freed the dwarf, pounced on the dwarf and imbedded his own axe into his back. Méreg gave out a great howling cry and fell to his knees.

It was then that the Queen began to change back to her former human self. But the retransformation was not complete and in place of feet and hands still she had paws. She saw that the dwarf was not completely dead and because of this his magical power, with which he had imbued all his alchemical concoctions, still held sway over the Queen. The Queen could not pick up the dwarf's axe and finish him off however, owing to her paws not being able to handle such a tool, and so she asked the twins to cut off Méreg's head.

The twins were awestruck at the transformation of the bear into a fully-grown human woman however, and Emilita especially was still in shock from plunging an axe into the dwarf's spine. It wasn't until the woman told the twins that she was the Queen of Delator that Krystina took up the axe and decapitated the evil dwarf. Thus the Queen returned to her former glory.

She took the twins back to the orphanage and made them promise that if they kept the whole affair secret she would return with gifts the following day. The twins believed the Queen and fell asleep together in their bed, but their innocence was lost at the murder of the dwarf and nightmares descended upon them.

When the Queen returned the next day the Letalis sisters threw them selves at her and sobbed uncontrollably. When the Queen had comforted them enough to stop the flow of their tears she explained to the twins that she was to act thereafter as their guardian and move them into the royal palace.

Though the twins had a wholesome and full life at the palace in the ring-years that followed, still they were plagued with the occasional bout of melancholy and sleepless night owing to what they had done. It was then that the Queen decided to tell them of other warrior woman from Delatorian and Arborian mythology that had bravely fought against insurmountable odds to prove victorious or that died honorable and noble deaths. The twins were so enthralled by these stories that when they were came of age they requested to join the palace guard. The Queen refused their request and instead sent them to her Secarius mentor, a Pannonian elder by the name of Jacqueline Mortel, for before the Queen married the King of Delator she was a guild member of that secretive assassin's society – it was actually the Queen's skill with a blade, wielded during a warrior tournament in Delator, that first attracted the King towards her.

So the Letalis sisters learned the deadly art and when their training was complete they returned to the palace and, after a demonstration of their skill against the Queen herself in a private training quarter, the Queen agreed that they become her personal bodyguard. The twin's loyalty would subsequently prove unwavering and each act of vendetta was carried out in such a cold and calculatingly morally devoid fashion, for when they killed they killed in the Queen's name and at her command, just as it had been when they were children. The only thing that changed was that now, after each kill, they could sleep peaceably thereafter.

*

Krystina never knew whether those subjected with a comatosing dose of Lilac Rosarius ever dreamt whilst in their state of unconscious. Now she did.

As her eyes opened to the view of the interior of Elliot's home she remembered her dreaming, the myriad of images from her childhood, her training, and her first kill.

Not all of her body had regained its strength and she found that she was still unable to move. There was a dullness to her senses too, and only after a few more moments did she realise that the whistling sound ringing in her ears was that from a boiling kettle. She tried to think back to how she could be in such a position. She recalled receiving more than one blow to her jaw, and as the feeling slowly came back to her face she felt the soreness of a wound that had yet to heal. Her body had fallen into a state of hibernation, her heart just slowed enough to allow the faintest trickle of blood to pump through her body, and as such her system had little energy enough to repair the wounds she had received from her last encounter with the Vigilantag Seven.

She had been outwitted, and outmanned, and she had been defeated. For long she and her sister had mused that their new lives were deity ordained, like the warrior women of myth. They imagined that they were immortal, exhibiting capabilities far beyond that of any other Arborian race. They even believed they might fair well in a wrestle with a Wolven if it ever came to it. However as she lay there, temporarily paralysed, she began to accept that she had weaknesses just like any other person. Had she awoken in a coffin deep within the World-Tree's surface, just as Dok had threatened, then she may even have shed a tear or two. But she was still a Secarius and as soon as Krystina began to recover enough to wiggle her fingers her mind began to work out a plan of escape.

While the assassin was gradually rousing from her slumber Blöd was busying himself in Elliot's kitchen. It was far removed from the inhospitable caverns he and his fellow Vigilantag had long endured, and the Dwarf-Giant found great satisfaction in handling the clean and shiny implements that were dotted about the kitchen.

He was working on a herbal remedy, that he might give to Krystina should ever she awake, as well as preparing a fine dinner that he and Elliot might sit and eat when the attorney came back from his bout with Malaphar. He was having difficulty however and though Elliot's ceiling was still in the classically tall design Blöd still had to conduct most of his culinary efforts sat cross-legged in the middle of the kitchen. As he lifted himself up slightly to stretch for a knife that was just out of reach his head brushed an overhead pan rack causing the pans hanging from it to clang together. It was then that Krystina realised that she was not alone in the house.

Having regained most of the feeling in her upper body now, she managed to strain her neck to survey the immediate area and search for where the noise had come from. At that moment Krystina watched as a thick long arm crossed the width of the kitchen entrance before pulling back again, the hand of which now clutched a large polished carving knife. The assassin immediately thought the worst and imagined her captor readying himself to slice through her neck or wrists. She looked around what she now realised was a sitting room for something she could use as a weapon. Her eyes fell upon Elliot's sabre, slotted in amongst a number of rain shields, and she resolutely decided to retrieve it when the feeling returned to her legs.

It took another hour-turn before Krystina felt mobile and confident enough in the re-found use of her limbs to make her move. During this time she lay there wondering why and how a Vigilantag had chosen to bring her into such an abode. She was unbound and bathed and she began to think whether in fact she was in any kind of mortal danger at all. These thoughts soon dissipated however as she remembered the manner in which she had been captured. Perhaps this was another ploy to disorientate her. Perhaps the Vigilantag Seven were merely toying with her.

There was a shuffling sound now as Blöd carefully edged his huge bulk through the kitchen door and into Elliot's front room. Krystina immediately screwed her eyes tight and lay still giving the impression that she was still in a comatose condition. Beneath the shawl that covered her, however, her right hand slowly tightened around the handle of Elliot's sabre.

The Dwarf-Giant moved beside the couch Krystina was peacefully resting in and gently brushed her hair from her forehead. In saving the assassin from the clutches of his gang Blöd had made a decision to which going back was not an option. In a way he felt relieved to be leaving behind that bloody part of his life. For long he had convinced himself that his criminal past had been a necessity, the need to survive in the wilderness. But now, looking upon the face of the fair maiden before him, Blöd began to think that his life could now change for the better. He leaned in closer as if to take in each delicate detail of Krystina's face, as if looking upon something of beauty could make clean his soul. How different life could have been had he stayed in his home realm.

Suddenly the assassin's eyes flashed open. Blöd reeled back surprised and almost knocked the couch onto its side. Krystina's gaze darted to the Zwerg-Riese's knife. The Dwarf-

Giant raised his hands as if to calm the maiden who grew more distressed as each short moment passed. It was too late however and upon seeing Blöd's weapon, the assassin instinctively threw off her covers and brought up Elliot's sword.

The Dwarf-Giant suddenly felt cold. The expression on his face turned to one of confusion and his brow wrinkled as he tried to fathom this strange new sensation. Krystina was sat up now, close to him, and she looked deep into the Dwarf-Giant's eyes. In the blink of an eye she had pushed the sabre deep into Blöd's heart right up to the hilt. Another quick flick of the wrist and she knew her assailant would be gone.

Blöd looked down and the realisation of what had happened suddenly dawned on him. The hand which clutched the carving knife slowly opened and the implement fell to the floor with a soft thud. He looked to the coffee table to the side of him, turned the assassin's attention to the plated meal set upon it as if to offer some explanation.

"I only wanted to help," Blöd slowly whispered, the life ebbing away from his body. He felt his eyelids droop but fought hard to keep them open. He felt so tired.

Krystina's grip on the sword loosened and she looked down to see what she had done, to understand what she had done. It was then that she knew, as she began to look wildly about the place as if searching for some aid… knew that she had taken the life of an innocent. This wasn't a Vigilantag hideout, this was a home, not Blöd's but a home none the less… a safe haven.

A tide of emotions came over her… guilt, confusion, helplessness, even sadness. They were the same feelings she had experienced long ago, before her assassin's life, as she tried to sleep next to her sister the night she took Méreg's head from his body, the night everything changed.

She saw the Dwarf-Giant's head droop back and fearing the he might fall backward and dislodge the sword, and to prevent of torrent of blood which might issue forth if it was disturbed, she gently cupped Blöd's face in her hands and drew him towards her chest. She could feel the pulse in his neck slow and knew that soon he would be gone.

Krystina had killed on command for the better part of her adult life, always with reason, always for the good of something else, for the protection of someone else. Now she was at a loss to explain her actions. All of her twisted assassin rationale, which had long dictated her life's choices, gradually began to unravel. Yes, Blöd was part of a dangerous mob, which killed indiscriminately, but was that all the Dwarf-Giant was. She had seen his figure on the first occasion she had visited the gang's hideout to retrieve the magic mirror and thought then that the docile looking Dwarf-Giant was not a threat. But she had been mistaken. It wasn't docility that she had witnessed; it was gentleness… the same sight that was before her eyes now.

She rested her head on his shoulder and as she saw the tip of the sabre protrude from Blöd's back she imagined the pain he must be going through. Someone of lesser bulk would have perished long before.

Krystina began to weep gently now, as the flood of all those long-restrained emotions returned to her. As she wept she felt as if she was that little girl again, all those ring-years ago, crying herself to sleep at the horror of what she done.

Blöd had energy enough to lift his head and he noticed that the maiden was crying, though he couldn't feel her tears on his shoulder. He raised a hand to brush away her tears, to run his fingers through her hair, but failed. He felt so numb, so tired and cold. Life enough for one more thing he thought easing back from the maiden's body. He forced his eyelids open and whispered.

"Remember your laws… in saving you your life passed to me, now that I am perished your life shall pass to Elliot. It need not go on like this."

Blöd's chin fell gently onto his still, barrel-like chest, and then he was gone.

25

" 'Dear Diary, once upon a time a poor orphan girl met a dashing young prince and they lived happily ever after. I fear such a simple story of love will never come true. I fear that somehow I may be destined to a life of sorrow and despair. Perhaps I am cursed. Hansel grows more… distant by the day. I think he fears falling in love. Perhaps one can never have the things in life one truly wants, because of fear… our own fears and those of others. Perhaps only by being fearless can we live happily ever after. I fear he shall lose his love for me… I fear it may be the last thing I shall be able to bear. And so because of this I do not fear death…' "

Malaphar closed the small journal from which he had been reading and looked solemnly upon the faces of the thirteen jurors before him.

"Abigail Hood wrote this entry two days before killing her lover… two days before she almost killed herself," the Caelum Angelic continued. "There is one undeniable fact that screams out from the last entry in her diary, one frightening realisation that cries out from these anguished words of reflection and it is this: if I cannot have the one I love then no-one else will."

When Elliot was a trainee his uncle once taught him that making an opening speech is much like planting a seed. During the course of a trial that seed grows. Each new piece of supporting evidence is like fresh water upon its roots whilst the evidence against is akin to a harsh drought. Each witness called to build up an argument is like the rays of sunlight that fall upon the plant's leaves whilst each witness called to tear an argument down is like the dark of an eclipse. If one has successfully nurtured their case then, come the conclusion of a trial, all will be able to see one's argument in all its healthy, flowering, fully grown splendour. If one is not successful then one will see the argument whither and die and one shall lose.

It was perhaps an overly simple analogy and Elliot admittedly felt a little patronised upon first hearing it, but as the prosecution in the case of the Crown versus Abigail Hood concluded its opening statement, the young attorney thought back to his uncle's words. Elliot realised that Malaphar did not know what he did, that the Caelum Angelic knew nothing of royal conspiracies and magic mirrors, and because of this Elliot had wondered what motive Malaphar might argue as the reason for the Meretrix committing the crimes for which she had been charged. Jealousy, love and obsession… a few of the oldest motives in the book. Malaphar may have planted a bad seed in the minds of the jurors, one that had no basis for rational assertion, but Elliot knew that it was composed of the base elements of human weakness, which were elements that could easily be watered.

In any other circumstance Elliot would simply have introduced some aggressive weed right next to such a seed, something designed to directly attack the root of Malaphar's argument before it began to sprout and flower. But instead of arguing Abigail's virtues, instead of being pulled into a character debate, Elliot would choose a completely different tactic, and a far riskier one.

As Malaphar retook his seat Judge Coerceo, who had been listening intently to the prosecution's opening speech while scribbling notes as an aid-memoir, looked up from his quill and turned to Elliot.

"Mr Blackstone, the Defence may proceed with its opening statement," the Judge directed.

"Thank you, your honour," Elliot replied, clearing his throat and taking to his feet.

The High Court of Compenso takes its name from the Delatorian term for weighing one thing against another.

From the outside the court building looked relatively unassuming and only a weathercock shaped in the image of a set of scales differentiated the building from others such as the

Magistratum Headquarters or the Delatorian Municipal offices. The purpose of the uniformity in build style of all of these centres of administration was one of balance and equality. Each centre of Delatorian governance could not therefore outwardly claim to be as grandiose or as important than any other. Only the Palace could make such claims.

The inside of Compenso was anything but unassuming however, and stepping through the court's entrance could be likened to walking into a great marbled mezzanine amphitheatre of polished alabaster.

The main idea surrounding jurisprudence in Delator is that the accused, or the aggrieved in civil matters, stands in the centre of the court. Thus the individual is positioned in the middle of the perceived Scales of Justice where, all things being equal, the scales would be balanced. Yet given that one is in court in the first place more often than not means that those scales are imbalanced. It is then the job of the attorney in criminal cases to tip the scales, to demonstrate that the client is actually wrongly accused and thus show that he or she actually is 'balanced' – the Delatorian Legal term for the law abiding citizen. Given the weight of the evidence against Abigail Hood, Elliot was under no illusion that he would have a great deal of tipping of scales to do.

"Once upon a time," Elliot solemnly began, "there was someone who wanted something she knew she could never have… something of great power. Over time the denial of this thing drove the woman to despair for so great was her want for it that she could think of nothing but it being in her possession. This madness turned to desperation and the woman employed means unlawful to acquire what had long eluded her."

The young attorney paused and looked upon the faces of the jury members, searching for those signs that might show what he was saying was being suitably absorbed.

"This tale is not something found in Abigail's diary," Elliot continued. "It is not written from some heartfelt plea for love and happiness, for the woman I speak of is not the woman who stands accused before you this day. This tale is one based in fact and from actual corroborated events. Some of you shall not enjoy what I shall present to you during the course of this trial for at its centre is the story of a girl… a girl who was used and taken advantage of and broken. This is the truth of Abigail's portion of the story and when I come to its conclusion you shall know that Abigail Hood is innocent."

Elliot took one last look at the jurors before turning his gaze to Abigail who was sitting in the dock of the accused in the centre of the court thirty feet below him.

Another facet of Delatorian jurisprudence is the idea that all judgement is delivered from above. This belief attempts to bridge the relationship between law and religion and is used to reinforce the idea that every being residing in the capital, though equal to each other, live in the light emitted from Deus' grace high above, magnified on Arbor's surface by the rule of the deity ordained Delatorian Royals.

This hierarchy was achieved architecturally in Compenso by the introduction of several tiers into its interior. As aforementioned the accused stands in the centre of the court and at ground level, ready to receive his or her judgement from above. Behind the accused and set into the circular interior wall above the main entrance are two staggered rows from which the jurors observe the proceedings. These stalls were approximately ten feet above the courtroom floor, such is the height of the entrance way and such was the intention for jurors to deliver their collective judgement to the accused below them.

Standing directly opposite the entrance and the juror's stalls, propped against the rear wall were the Colossi of Compenso, two sculptures of staggering proportions each fifty feet in height and twenty feet in width. Rumoured to have been sculpted from one block of stone, each was carved in the effigies of Iustitia and Justitia, two forms of the same goddess that symbolised Justice in Delatorian mythology.

Iustitia stood facing the right side of the accused and was dressed in a knee length robe tied at the waist with a belt of simple chord. Her face was fair and her long hair spilled over her shoulders and down her back in intricately carved locks, which Elliot fancied must have been worked with utmost devotion. In Iustitia's left hand was gripped a shield which she held guarding her front, upon the face of which was inscribed a passage from the Lexus Codifium that described the goddess's mythic birth origins, her battle with injustice and her selfless death. Her right arm was stretched across her breast and the side of her upturned palm brushed the topmost part of the shield. This was where Elliot Blackstone conducted the Defence's case and from Abigail's viewpoint it looked as if the great statue was literally offering her a defence in the form of the brave young attorney.

Elliot's palm shaped platform, accessible from a doorway in the shield behind it and reached by climbing a twisting staircase inside Iustitia's hallowed yet hollow body, was approximately thirty feet from the ground. Thus continued the hierarchy where the place of the attorney was above that of the juror for an attorney's words act to sway those opinions of the latter. And so it was that Malaphar also stood upon the palm of Iustitia's celestial alter ego Justitia.

This effigy of the goddess of Justice, though similarly robed, looked far more foreboding and vengeful than her World-Tree incarnation, and in her right arm was held aloft a great bolt of lightning, which looked as if it threatened to smite all those found ultimately guilty. Her face was carved with a grim expression of clenched teeth and fury and Abigail found that she could not hold her gaze upon this statue's stern visage for long without feeling a great deal of discomfort. Covering the front of Justitia's robe was carved a breast-plate upon which was engraved the myth surrounding how, upon death, Iustitia was granted a place beside Deus from where she could deliver just punishment to those evils that had not only brought about her end but which also continued to plague the Arborian landscape. In so doing she became Justitia.

As Elliot looked upon the proud figure of Malaphar stood beneath the jagged stone lightning bolt of his fearsome statue, the young attorney wondered whether the arrogant Caelum Angelic realised the irony of his position, that he was being held aloft by a goddess who above all fought against the illegal incursions of Malaphar's own kind, for there were no greater and more ruthless crimes than those historically committed by the winged inhabitants of Caelum upon the lives of Humans. Elliot imagined Justitia, sat at Deus' right hand side, grinding her teeth in response to such a travesty.

"Mr Naberius you may call your first witness," called Coerceo from the judge's bench – an elevated pulpit that protruded from the rear wall of the court between the heads of the Colossi.

The judge's bench was a semicircular platform carved in the relief of a tree and more than fifty thousand delicately chiselled leaves decorated its frontage. The leaves fanned out onto the court's domed ceiling and it was as if the tree's solid canopy was offering protection to all the individuals present within Compenso. The sculpture continued towards the ground in a thick trunk that bowed inwards at its middle, before continuing down where it widened into a number of roots that intertwined amongst the feet of the two Justice statuettes standing either side of it. This great monument was an artistic representation of the World-Tree that was Arbor and below the bough, 75 feet from the floor of Compenso, was where Judge Coerceo conducted the trial, perched above all bar Deus himself.

"Your honour if it pleases the court the Crown calls Paul Bonjean," Malaphar clearly stated.

A doorway opened to the left of the courtroom floor and from it a nervous looking clerk tentatively emerged. Behind him followed a heavy-set human man who stood near seven feet tall. The clerk ushered the man to the prosecution witness box, which was located beside the statue of Justitia, before bowing low and taking his leave.

"Please state your name for the record," Malaphar directed.

The man didn't reply immediately and he seemed to be more concerned with the three hundred sets of eyes scrutinising him from the gallery, which ran the circumference of the court above the jury stalls and terminated either side of the statues of Justice, than with the piercing gaze of the Caelum Angelic who had called him.

"Sir!" Malaphar barked, "Your name for the record."

"Bonjean, Paul Bonjean sir… pronounced Bonyenne sir, if you don't mind sir," the witness apprehensively corrected, much to Elliot's personal amusement.

"And your occupation?"

"Lumberjack sir."

"And you conduct your work where Mr Bonjean?"

"Where ever there's trees need hewing sir," Paul innocently replied to which a brief snigger emanated from the gallery in response.

Malaphar who seemed relatively calm, considering his first witness appeared not as stalwart as perhaps first witnesses should, smiled and continued in a more patronising tone, half in the hope that if he spoke more slowly the seemingly slow witted witness might understand him better.

"Where were you on the 43rd day of this month Mr Bonjean?"

"Silva-Tenebrae Forest sir, good trees there."

"I am sure there are. And what set that day apart from any other?"

"Sir?"

"What did you find Mr Bonjean?" Malaphar rephrased.

"Her," Paul replied pointing a finger towards Abigail.

Abigail considered the lumberjack a moment and she tried to remember whether she had seen the man before and, more importantly how he might have known her.

"Let it be known for the record that Mr Bonjean is pointing at the accused," Judge Coerceo ordered.

"Please would you describe how you came across Miss Hood sir," Malaphar asked.

"Well. I had just been at a tough oak for… well, must have been two hour-turns… when I thought this bloody thing… oh pardon the language sir," the witness apologised looking up to the judge's bench.

"Please continue," Coerceo replied with an understanding grin.

"Erm, right. Well I thought this is going to take another two or three hour-turns to fell… massive great trunk it had… almost as wide as your sculpted tree there your honour – "

"And?" Malaphar interrupted, quickly losing patience with his witness.

"And I went to get myself a drink from the river because I was a bit thirsty."

"And did you notice anything odd?"

"Restless River was still sir. Usually its – "

"Anything else?" Malaphar pressed.

"Oh. I saw, erm, Miss Hood is it? Well I saw the young maiden on the banks of the river sir."

"And how did Miss Hood seem?"

"Well, she seemed… well," Paul paused, "she was naked sir and… well she seemed very fine indeed," he continued blushing, "not that I was staring or anything."

Even Abigail, who was at first nervous at the sight of the man who had found her, allowed herself a tiny grin in response to the lumberjack's bashfulness.

"I am sure you were not," Malaphar replied. "Was the accused totally without dress?"

"No sir, she had a mask on her head."

"A mask you say?"

"Yes sir."

"And what manner of mask was the accused wearing?"

"It looked like a Wolven mask sir," Paul replied.

"A Wolven mask," Malaphar dramatically repeated, much for the benefit of the jury. "My you must have thought that a little odd?"

"Objection your Honour. Leading the witness," Elliot interrupted. Admittedly it was a small point to take but Elliot took the opportunity to break his opponents flow. He knew Malaphar would have done the same.

"Sustained," replied the judge.

"What did you feel when you found her there all naked but for this Wolven mask?" Malaphar rephrased, shooting the slightest of grins across to the Defence's platform where Elliot cocked his head mischievously in response.

"I felt quite… I don't know… afraid I guess. Not by the mask because, well, I've seen masks before… I was afraid that she might have been dead," the lumberjack solemnly admitted.

"Was the accused conscious when you found her?"

"No sir, she looked like she was sleeping."

"And how might you have known that if she was wearing a mask Mr Bonjean?"

"Oh, I took it off to see if she was breathing sir, and she was. I wrapped her up too sir… to protect her modesty."

Abigail was grateful that a kind soul had come across her unconscious body, and she looked up and nodded kindly to the lumberjack. Paul appeared to be too embarrassed to return the gesture.

"What did you do next Mr Bonjean?"

"Well sir, I scooped her up and took her to a healing house I know on the outskirts of the city. I would have taken her to the main one in Delator but it's a little further and I didn't want to waste any time."

"And did you reach this healing house?" Malaphar continued.

"No sir, an officer of the Magistratum came upon us just as I was leaving the forest. Quite lucky it was. He managed to get a proper nursing wagon to take her into the city."

"One more question Mr Bonjean."

"Yes sir?"

"Did you notice any blood on the accused when you removed her mask?"

Elliot, unsurprised from the relatively mundane questioning Malaphar was conducting thus far, subtly raised his head and carefully studied the reactions of the jurors to the last question. He found that some were staring intently at the witness while others had allowed themselves a curious glance over in the direction of Abigail. All the faces looked as if their owners were deep in thought.

"Erm. A little sir."

"Where?"

"Her mouth sir… and her teeth," Paul added hesitantly.

There was a murmur amongst the gallery members, which Judge Coerceo quickly suppressed with the knock of his gavel.

"No further questions your honour," Malaphar concluded with a thorough look of satisfaction on his face. The witness may not have been a stellar one but he had elicited a response from the court. For all intents and purposes the lumberjack had done exactly what Malaphar had intended him to do.

"Mr Blackstone, do you have any questions for this witness?" Coerceo asked.

"Just a few your honour," Elliot replied rising to his feet. "Mr Bonjean, your accent is Pannonian?"

"That's right sir."

"I thought I recognised your face," Elliot smiled, "you're also a prize fighter. I saw your last bout. Quite a fight."

"Thank you sir. The purses sure do beat chopping down trees."

"I'm sure the bruises are worth it."

"That they are sir," Paul replied glad to be quizzed on anything other than unconscious blood stained maidens.

"You mentioned that when you found Abigail Restless River was… well, not as it should be."

"Yes sir, I've been working Silva-Tenebrae for a while now, pays better than the woodland in Pannonia you see, and I've noticed the river is always moving… quite a torrent it is."

"But not this time?"

"No sir, it was still."

"Have you ever seen such a change as that before?" Elliot probed.

"Erm… yes sir I have now you mention it," the lumberjack reflected, "back in my home town."

"What happened?"

"There used to be a river that ran through it and in all my ring-years I never saw it still. The elders used to say that it was the pulse of the town… always flowing."

"But not forever?"

"One day it suddenly stopped. I was told only great magic could have stopped it flowing so."

"Did you believe that?"

"I did sir."

"Do you believe that is what happened to Restless River? That some magic… some unknown force quelled its torrent?"

"I do sir."

"Mr Bonjean, going back to the time you found Abigail. Did you notice any marks on her body? Any wounds?" Elliot asked.

"A few sir. A deep cut on her back… I noticed it when I carried her off. Looked like a thorn had caught her skin. I've been cut by a lot of thorny vines in my time and that's what it looked like."

"Any other marks?"

The witness looked down again bashfully. "There was a claw mark on her breast sir. It wasn't deep but it was a mark none the less."

"Thank you Mr Bonjean. No further questions your honour."

"Mr Bonjean you may step down," Judge Coerceo directed.

The lumberjack rose slowly and was escorted back through the doorway at the side of the court. Before he left he turned and gave Abigail a nod and a smile, relieved as he was that she was safe though sad at the same time that the maiden was in the position she now found herself in. The Meretrix nodded gratefully and mouthed the words 'thank you'.

"The prosecution calls Priam Alcedo of the Magistratum," Malaphar stated to the court, to which a man, not much older than Elliot took the prosecution witness box. "Please state your name and rank for the record," the Caelum Angelic asked when the officer had made himself comfortable. Unlike the lumberjack before him, the officer looked un-phased by the grandiosity of his surroundings.

"Priam Alcedo, Magistratum Sergeant second rank," the officer proudly replied.

"Mr Alcedo, after you arranged for a healing wagon to take the accused back to Delator what did you do then?" Malaphar began.

"I left the lumberjack who found her with a colleague of mine who took his statement. Then I made a preliminary search of the immediate area."

"And what did you find?"

"I found the Wolven mask that the lumberjack had stated the woman was wearing."

"Is this the mask of which you speak?" Malaphar asked, as a younger Caelum Angelic with short silver hair, whom Elliot guessed was his junior counsel, stood abruptly from the prosecution bench beside Malaphar's platform and held up the Wolven head mask for all the court to see.

"Yes it is," Priam confirmed.

Both the co-counsel for the defence and for the prosecution were located to the side of their lead counsel's elevated platforms, separated from the gallery by a shoulder high brass rail that ran the perimeter of each box. Opposite Malaphar's junior counsel, at the defence's half of the court and paying close attention to the proceedings sat Fury. She was dressed in a black full-length body glove with fitted fire-retardant gown. Sat behind the Fire-Nymph in the gallery were Vincent and Epona, who were both taking notes of anything of interest and relevancy.

Abigail looked up at the Wolven mask and immediately felt a chill run down the back of her spine. She had no recollection of wearing it and it unnerved her to think that she had donned a likeness of that which had butchered her family all those ring-years ago.

"If it pleases the court your Honour the prosecution enters in to the records exhibit alpha," Malaphar requested.

"Very well," the Judge replied.

"So after you found the mask what did you do then Mr Alcedo?" Malaphar asked.

"Following protocol I logged the position of the mask and the rough position of where Miss Hood had been lying. An impression left in the grass provided that information. Then I went on to scout the surrounding area."

"And what did you find?"

"I was about to give up the search, but after ten minute-turns of walking up the riverbank I found a body."

"Hansel's body?"

"At that point in time I did not have that information. Visual identification was not possible and only recently have we learned the identity of the body."

"You say visual identification was not possible, how was this so?" Malaphar asked.

"The body was without a face."

"You mean he was wearing a mask also?"

"No. I mean his face had been eaten away."

"No eyes, no mouth, no – " Malaphar mused.

"Objection your honour, I think the officer's words are fully understood by the court," Elliot interrupted, in response to the growing whisperings and gasps from the gallery members, as well as the squeamish reactions of a particularly perturbed looking female juror in the front row of the stalls.

"I have just never known a face to be eaten away your honour… a corpse to be disfigured so," Malaphar countered in a tone of mock innocence.

"Neither have I," replied the judge with a brief frown, "objection overruled."

Elliot would have otherwise pressed the matter, that Malaphar's attempts to shock those present in court with graphic and gory detail was a mere theatrical device, however the Half-Angelic knew Dr Capek would soon take the stand and that the pathologist's evidence may be far more disturbing than that of officer Alcedo's.

"As I was saying officer, the victim had no…?"

"No facial features of any kind, as my report states the whole face had been literally eaten away."

There was something authoritative about how this witness conducted himself; a kind of youthful arrogance yet clear and concise and much a measure of the quality of officer the Magistratum prided itself on producing. There was no hesitation in his testimony even at its most bloodiest parts.

"Was there any other wounds apparent on the victim's corpse?" Malaphar continued.

"His throat was ripped open."

"And?"

"The body's fingers and feet had also been gnawed," Priam replied.

"Officer Alcedo is there any reason why someone might want to disfigure a corpse so?"

"The most obvious motive would be if someone wanted to hide the identity of the deceased."

"And that someone would be?"

"The individual responsible for committing his death presumably."

"And a very thorough job she did too would you not say officer?" Malaphar summed up turning to the jury.

"Very thorough," Priam confidently confirmed.

"No further questions your honour," Malaphar concluded, to which Elliot slowly rose to his feet to begin his cross-examination.

"Officer Alcedo, let me run through a scenario with you and tell me whether it *may* have possibly occurred," Elliot began. "Imagine that perhaps Abigail and Hansel had been sharing a special moment as young couples in love are want to do, and that afterwards they fell asleep." The officer listened carefully to each word nodding at those points were Elliot paused for breath. "Imagine then that Abigail awakes in the night with a thirst for water and as such makes her way quietly to the river's edge so not to wake her lover. With me?"

"Yes sir."

"When her thirst is quenched she returns to where her lover is sleeping in time to witness some feral beast fix its jaws around Hansel's throat. She panics, she's afraid and vulnerable. She picks up the Wolven Mask and attempts to fight off the beast with it. As a last resort she dons the mask herself and attempts to make herself as big as possible, to frighten off such a beast – "

"Okay."

"But she is overcome by the strength of the animal that has just killed her lover and she falls into Restless River where she is dragged away by the river's torrent. As her body is washed downstream the beast returns to the corpse of Hansel to take its fill of the poor man's flesh. Officer Alcedo is it possible that this scenario could have occurred?"

"Its possible," the officer honestly replied.

"In your professional opinion… as an astute officer of the Magistratum," Elliot flatteringly continued, "do the wounds on Hansel's body suggest that perhaps he was the victim of an animal attack, and not an assault committed by Abigail?"

"The wounds are suggestive of that, yes."

"And the claw wound on Abigail's body, could that have been inflicted by such a frenzied animal attack?"

"I guess it could have," Priam admitted with a shrug of his shoulders.

"No further questions your honour," Elliot announced.

The cross examination had gone better than Elliot had expected and, whilst the officer's testimony for the Prosecution was a credible one, the Half-Angelic had been successful in planting his own seeds of doubt in the minds of the thirteen jurors.

Elliot's hypothetical scenario had been totally plausible and was as likely to have occurred then any scenario Malaphar might subsequently devise.

It was fortunate for Elliot, and Abigail Hood for that matter, that the jurors were learned and astute enough not to take everything at face value. They were made up of the Councilarius of the thirteen districts of Delator – wise individuals who ran each area, with autonomous powers granted to them by the Palace, in the best interests of the whole Capital city. It was the Monarchy's way of delegating the everyday running of Delator so that the King, Queen and the Prince could partake in more stately engagements. In major trials where the charge called for a high court hearing the thirteen councillors sat in proxy for the King. As such their subsequent collective judgement had an equal rigidity as if it had come from the King's own lips.

They were of a varied age, each a leader in their own vocational fields prior to taking up their council posts, and they had enquiring minds. Elliot knew that if he could introduce doubts in the prosecution case then the Jurors' reasoning minds would seize upon the same and use them to pick apart Malaphar's argument. If the young attorney did his job right then the real breaking down of the case would take place not in the great courtroom floor of Compenso, but in some back area reserved for the jury's deliberations.

Next to appear as witness for the prosecution was the palace physician, who was summoned to examine Abigail upon the Meretrix's admittance to the Royal infirmary.

Dr Asklepia was a human woman of average height, willowy in frame and defined in facial features. Her sharp cheekbones protruded from her face such that she projected an air of refined beauty laced with a certain astuteness. Propped upon her thin small nose was a pair of rimless spectacles from behind which two wide eyes of brilliant blue surveyed the court in front of her. As with the Magistratum officer who appeared before her,

Asklepia looked unconcerned with the proceedings almost to the point of looking bored.

Her responses to Malaphar were short and succinct, answering questions directed to her much like a doctor might read from a medical examination chart. She revealed how Abigail was unconscious when first admitted into her care and how only briefly did the Meretrix stir from her sleep to utter a number of undistinguishable words. Asklepia then described what her preliminary examination revealed – staining to Abigail's teeth and gums and beneath her finger nails with blood which was not her own.

In the whole the doctor's testimony was unspectacular and merely confirmed the statement previously given by the lumberjack. That is until Elliot stepped up to begin his cross-examination.

"Doctor, shortly after your examination of Abigail she was released into the custody of the Magistratum."

"That is correct."

"So she was given a clean bill of health then?" Elliot asked.

"Miss Hood left my care in the same condition as when she came into it, unconscious but healthy," Asklepia replied.

"Is it the practice of physicians to release patients in such a state?"

"In the whole we prefer to keep such a patient until consciousness has been regained, at which point we might better understand whether the patient has suffered any mental damage which a preliminary physical examination might not at first reveal."

"But on this occasion, such a protocol was not followed."

"No."

"Dr Asklepia, why was such a protocol not followed?"

"As I have said," the doctor began, "the practice is more preferential than protocol based. Many patients, those suffering from excessive liquor intake for example, may be admitted to a surgery in a state of unconsciousness however when satisfied that the patient is in no immediate danger we may decide to release them to sleep off such a self induced stupor in their own beds. This allows valuable ward space to be freed up for patients suffering more severe injuries."

"And on this occasion, was it your preference to release Abigail to the custody of the Magistratum and a cold, dank holding cell thereafter, because you were satisfied that the patient was healthy enough to be in no immediate danger?" Elliot questioned in a more direct tone than previously adopted.

"It was not my concern what the Magistratum wanted with her and I have little knowledge of the inside of their cells. However I can assure you that I considered that Miss Hood was stable enough to be released," Asklepia replied impatiently, not used to her learned opinions being called into question.

"So Abigail's state may have been akin to a self induced drunken stupor then?"

"Her state yes, but there was now outward signs of such an intake of alcohol."

"Did you attempt to rouse her from her state of unconsciousness?" Elliot pressed.

"All attempts to bring her round proved unsuccessful."

"Dr Asklepia, could it be perhaps that Abigail had been drugged?"

The doctor's quick replies were slow to come on this occasion, and it was the first sign that the royal physician was perhaps not as forthcoming with the truths of her decision to release Abigail than she had at first made out.

"Dr?"

"Yes, Miss Hood could have been under the influence of some drug."

"And yet you chose to release her?" Elliot asked.

Again there was a pause in reply, a hesitation.

"Dr Asklepia, did you actually approve the release of Abigail that morning?"

"No."

"Did you sign the patient's release form?" Elliot continued to press more forcefully.

"No," Asklepia replied, her voice having lost some of its earlier authority.

A murmur went through the courtroom as Elliot, much to Malaphar's displeasure, took apart the doctor's testimony.

"Order," directed Judge Coerceo with two light knocks of his judge's hammer.

"Dr Asklepia," Elliot began, "who did sign Abigail's patient release form?"

"Emilita Letalis."

"And in what capacity does Miss Letalis work at the royal infirmary?"

"She does not."

"She doesn't?" Elliot repeated, "and in what capacity do you know Miss Letalis to act doctor?"

"She is one of the Queen's own bodyguard."

"And does one of the Queen's own bodyguard have the necessary authority to have granted the release of Abigail, over that of perhaps your authority to have granted the opposite."

"Under the Delatorian royal seal, yes she did," Asklepia replied, almost to the point of dejection now.

"Just one more question doctor. Do you know of any other name which Miss Letalis goes by?"

"Yes I do… Rose Red."

"The same Rose Red who is a member of the Secarius? The assassin's guild?"

"I believe so."

As the thirteen jury members shot each other curious glances, looks within which were imbedded yet more queries, Elliot confirmed that there were no further questions and retook his seat, satisfied that he had suitably seized the attention of those that would decide the case. As was the case in the court of the giant Atlations not more than seven days ago, all Elliot had to do now was hold himself together enough to slowly reveal the bigger picture, the grand conspiracy.

Asklepia left the witness box under the frowning gaze of Abigail, who had regarded the doctor's testimony with increased anxiety. The doctor knew, as did Abigail, that her professional pre-concerns with the protection of health and life had been found wanting. As the doctor left she did so with her head bowed in shame.

Elliot half expected his Caelum opponent to be left reeling from that last cross-examination but to his surprise Malaphar was a vision of utmost calm. Elliot knew that an attorney's show of outward frustration can often be as telling as the testimony of a credible witness upon the impressions of a jury, and he realised that Malaphar was perhaps with-holding his rage for this very reason. There was something more though, almost sinister, and as Malaphar shot Elliot the slyest of grins, Elliot felt that the Angelic was perhaps taking some sadistic enjoyment out of the whole affair. Enjoyment of the challenge, to stand against a worthy opponent, may have been a plausible reason, but the truth of the matter was that Malaphar was enjoying watching Humans suffer – the increased woe of Abigail as each new piece of evidence was produced, even the discomfort of his own witnesses under Elliot's cross examination. The reason Malaphar did not look as rattled as Elliot had hoped was because he simply didn't care about anybody's wellbeing in that courtroom bar his own.

As a recess was called, signalling the end of the morning session and a welcome break for lunch for the court members, Elliot kept thinking of what else Malaphar had to produce, for his witnesses thus far had not been particularly supportive of the prosecution's case. The Caelum prosecution lawyer had two more witnesses to call – Magistratum pathologist Dr Capek, and the Meretrix Nemain Morrigan, close friend and confident of Abigail Hood. *What are you up to Malaphar*, Elliot suspiciously thought to himself.

26

"He's gone."

It was a relatively short statement and the one least expected of all to have issued forth from Elliot's mouth, so it was of little surprise then to find Fury, Vincent and Epona sitting jaw agape in response.

"What do you mean he's gone?" Fury queried, eager to break the ominous silence that had descended upon the small Compenso conference room.

"When I came back from Trial by Combat with Malaphar, Blöd was nowhere to be found," Elliot replied.

"And Krystina?" Vincent asked.

"Also gone."

"Elliot, what the bloody Caelum are we going to do?" Fury asked desperately.

Elliot didn't reply. He seemed to be deep in thought, his gaze focused on the grains of sand spilling through the hourglass that was in the far corner of the room.

"Elliot?" Fury snapped.

The Half-Angelic attorney slowly turned his head and looked at his colleague. His demeanour was less than confidence inspiring and he could feel the tension slowly building in the room.

"We progress as planned. Fury I want you to cross examine the Meretrix Morrigan, I trust you have read her statement?"

This time it was Fury who sat silently, slowly shaking her head in disapproval.

"Fury," Elliot gently repeated, "remember what I said to you last week."

"You should have told us Elliot," Fury sighed. "We are here to help and still you think you can take this all on by yourself."

"It's not that, really. Our prime witness is gone, yes. But this is not the end. We pick ourselves up and we go on. I had to be focused for the morning session and to have your worries weighing on my mind, had I told you, would have kept me from performing to the best of my abilities," Elliot solemnly replied.

Fury looked up to Vincent and then to Epona who both shrugged their shoulders as if to offer nothing further.

They had all come this far trusting Elliot's judgement and all knew that there was perhaps more to the matter than he was willing to divulge. Epona thought that perhaps Elliot's elusiveness with certain facets of the case was through a want to keep his colleagues free from harm, for in essence they were taking on the throne of Delator – a task not without its perils considering the involvement of the deadly Secarius sisters who might stop at nothing to prevent them, one of which was now seemingly unaccounted for. And yet Epona also felt saddened that her mentor was taking this burden solely upon his own shoulders, as it was so great a burden. However, no sooner had she wished how she wanted to do more to help when Elliot slowly approached her. He took a wax-sealed envelope from his inner suit pocket and passed it the doting Mare'ess.

"Very well, I shall tell you all what I have planned," Elliot conceded.

*

"You say that the primary cause of death had been the injury sustained to the victim's throat?" Malaphar asked, ten minute-turns into the afternoon session.

"That is correct," replied Dr Capek, sat perched on a stool to the side of the witness box. Malaphar would have otherwise had the small doctor inside the witness box but for the fact that he would have been totally invisible to the rest of the court.

"And this injury, how was it inflicted?"

"A single bite to the throat."

"And not that from an animal either doctor."

"No," Capek replied.

"Dr Capek," Malaphar confidently continued, "in your medical opinion what could have caused such a wound?"

"The wound was made by the jaw of a human."

"A human female perhaps?"

"Yes."

"Abigail Hood's jaw perhaps."

"The size of the wound is comparable to the dimensions of Miss Hood's jaw, yes."

"You are saying, then, that the sizeable and violent wound inflicted upon Hansel was caused by the accused having torn the flesh from his throat with her own teeth?" Malaphar sought to clarify, in a reserved tone so that each of the jurors would adequately register every word of his question.

"It does appear to be the likely cause of death – "

"Yes or no," Malaphar forcibly interrupted.

"Yes," Dr Capek slowly sighed.

"Thank you doctor. No further questions your honour."

The doctor sat with his head held low. As much as he loathed assisting the Caelum Angelic attorney in pointing an accusatory finger at Abigail, he could not escape the facts gleaned from his thorough autopsy.

"Dr Capek," Elliot greeted taking once more to his feet.

"Ah Elliot, good to see you. I wish it could be under other circumstances," the doctor replied looking up at the young attorney.

"As do I," Elliot smiled. "Doctor is there anywhere in nature that this method of kill is repeated?"

"Oh yes, it is quite common. Many predators take their prey by the throat… the method constricts the airway and may indeed sever the jugular causing massive blood loss. Some predators use the hold as a pivot point, perhaps thrashing the prey's body about in order to break its neck."

"I'd imagine it would be quite an effort to successful carry out such a kill, what with a prey that may be larger trying desperately to escape."

"Yes, such predators have adapted over time… they have developed into more efficient killers," Dr Capek replied.

"Doctor, how big was Hansel, roughly."

"Average build… just shy of 13 stone had all his organs and head and limbs been intact."

"And how much does Abigail Hood weigh?"

"Unfortunately I have not had an opportunity to examine Miss Hood."

"Roughly?"

Dr Capek turned atop his stool and scrutinised the Meretrix.

"I do hope I don't overstate your weight miss, that would be awfully embarrassing for me," the doctor cooed, causing a momentary chuckle to escape from the jury stalls. "I would say 8 stone," Capek guessed turning back to Elliot."

"You have already established that the neck wound was the primary cause of death, so doctor, what amount of effort would a 8 stone human female of slight frame have to exert to inflict such a wound upon a 13 stone medium built human male?"

"I would say a considerable amount."

"Because nature necessarily hasn't evolved Miss Hood to the point of being a natural born killer, such as the World-Tree predators you have recently described?"

"That's correct."

"Because Miss Hood is but a dainty Delatorian Meretrix perhaps?"

"She certainly looks so. No offence Miss," the doctor added turning to Abigail, to which the Meretrix looked up and smiled forgivingly in response.

"And I imagine that Hansel would have had little difficulty shaking Abigail off had she indeed been in the process of ripping out his throat," Elliot pro-offered, his head shaking in mock disbelief with his last four words.

"Considering Hansel's bulk… considering that the killer would have had to have bitten through several layers of subcutaneous fat, let alone the windpipe which is relatively tough… then yes, I would think that Hansel would have had ample opportunity to perhaps subdue his attacker before any fatal injury was sustained."

"Was Hansel drugged in anyway, to perhaps dull his ability to fight off such an attack?"

"Tests carried out on his blood did not reveal the same," Capek replied.

"Doctor, what do you know about the Wolven?"

"They are a race of mutated feral killing beasts, who possess an uncontrollable urge to satisfy their blood lust."

"And those bitten by the Wolven, what happens to them?" Elliot probed.

"Depending upon the amount of the Wolven virus introduced by the bite, the recipient of the same will experience a violent change in their biology."

"So those bitten by the Wolven become Wolven?"

"Yes, if indeed the Wolven responsible does not kill its prey."

"Doctor," Elliot began slowly now, for the benefit of the jury, "is it known for those to have suffered from the Wolven virus to *not* undergo the change into a fully formed Wolven?"

"Yes."

"In what circumstances might this occur?"

"If the Wolven virus was not directly injected… if it was perhaps introduced into the recipient's blood stream gradually," Capek replied.

"And whilst they might not change into a fully formed feral beast, they would nevertheless possess other Wolven characteristics?"

"Yes."

"Such as?"

"Increased strength is a certainty, heightened senses… increased stamina," the doctor listed.

"And a capacity for moral detachment?" Elliot added.

"The want for blood would still be apparent, so yes, I would have to agree."

"Doctor Capek, would it be beyond the realms of possibility that Miss Hood has been infected with the Wolven virus."

"Hmm, I guess it would not be, no. It would certainly explain how one so dainty could overwhelm one so much larger."

"Thank you doctor. No further questions your honour," Elliot concluded.

The Half-Angelic had come to accept that Abigail did perhaps commit the bloody crime she had been accused of, however the obvious question arose as to how she might have been capable of conducting the same. He still, however, believed that Abigail was not of sound mind at the time she conducted the crime and Elliot had pondered several possibilities as to what might cause the temporary breakdown of her mental state and the actual physical increases in strength needed to carry out the act itself. Had she temporarily regressed back to that point in her youth, when she mutilated the Wolven that had murdered of her parents? This was certainly something which the young attorney had originally thought and was the reason he had sent Epona to research insanity clauses and case-law at Babel, but it was the manner in which the kill was executed that failed to sit well within Elliot's mind. Of sound mind or not, Abigail could just have easily have cracked Hansel's skull open with a rock or perhaps have sliced his throat open with a fruit knife. Both of these methods could have been carried out while Hansel was asleep. But to use one's teeth… to consume… to cannibalise almost, was much more personal, much more primitive… more unhinged.

Elliot had only recently touched upon the theory that Abigail had perhaps been tainted with the Wolven virus. Vincent's dream-running of the Meretrix at the Magistratum holding cells had revealed something eluding to the possibility these vicious beasts were somehow involved. The fact that Hansel was dressed in a Wolven outfit, and Abigail's history with the Wolven, simple produced too many coincidences to merely ignore. Then there was the involvement of the Queen and the Vigilantag Seven and the Carmen Speculum. Perhaps the Queen of Delator knew of

Abigail's tortured past, and if she did then the Monarch could easily have used this information to groom her Meretrix into a killer, especially given the Queen's previous life as a Secarii. Had Elliot known that the Queen had approved the training of Emilita and Krystina Letalis in their youth, then this would have compounded his theories.

Elliot was determined to discover the truth of the matter within the next 36 hour-turns, after which time he would come face to face with the Queen, and although he now lacked the valuable testimony of Blöd he did at least know where to find others which might corroborate what that Zwerg-Riese had earlier revealed to the young attorney.

"I think that shall be all for today," Judge Coerceo called. "Court dismissed."

As the court members slowly dispersed, Elliot gently unfurled his wings and glided down from his elevated podium to the dock of the accused to check how his client was fairing.

"Everything is going to be okay Abigail, I want you to know that whatever happens over the next day and a half I will get you out of this."

Abigail looked up and smiled meekly. Delatorian justice worked fast in the capital city and the first day had taken its toll on the Meretrix. She extended her hand to her defence attorney and childhood friend, which Elliot cupped with both of his own.

"Just be careful Elliot. I know you… you'll risk more than others are prepared to suffer. Please just be careful, there are those here that would see you sooner suffer than me."

She paused and looked up to Malaphar who was engaging his junior counsel in brief conversation. The Caelum Angelic attorney then stopped, realising that he was being watched, and returned Abigail's gaze in a manner that chilled her soul to the core. Elliot looked over his shoulder and cocked his head up to his opponent. Malaphar would have taken his life just the other day had Epona not intervened, and in a way the greater peril had passed. There were however a few more challenges that Elliot would have to endure before the trial was over.

Elliot waited till Abigail had been escorted away before joining his colleagues outside of the court.

"You're sure you don't want me to come with you?"

"I'll be okay Vince, I'd like you to keep Abigail company tonight. I can't stand her being alone, especially since she's learned so much about the case today," Elliot replied.

"Don't worry, I'll head over to the holding cells when I've taken care of the mirrors."

"How are they coming along?" Elliot asked.

"They'll be ready for tomorrow's afternoon session. Will you be?"

"I hope so Vince. Fury, ready for Morrigan's cross-examination?"

"Her testimony's a lie, I just know it… I'll get the truth out of her."

"And don't let Malaphar bully you," Elliot advised. "I take it you'll be at home this evening… I'll send you further instructions regarding our other witnesses by candle light, but here's a letter of authority from Hallbjorn should Malaphar challenge the introduction of them, as well as a list of questions you may want to use for your examination."

"You really have thought of everything haven't you? Well good luck Elliot and be careful," Fury stated with more conviction now than concern.

Elliot's short conference and the plan revealed there from had enthused the Fire-Nymph with a certain amount of determination, and she was eager to return home and scrutinise the Meretrix Morrigan's witness statement prior to taking her testimony to pieces tomorrow morning. She gave the young criminal defence attorney a gently stroke on his arm and departed with Vincent in tow. Elliot then turned to Epona, who was looking down at the sealed envelope her mentor had entrusted to her during the lunchtime recess. The Centaur's brows were frowning and she looked more than a little perturbed.

"Are you sure you're okay with this?"

"You know, just after your uncle told us that Vincent was a Sandman, he took me to one side and told me that you would understand if ever I was hesitant about taking instructions from you."

"That sound's like Asmodeus, he knows I can be a bit impulsive."

"*A bit?*" Epona grinned.

"Okay, maybe a little more than a bit. But he is right you know, if ever you feel you can't do what I ask of you then I shall not berate you for telling me so," Elliot reassured his young trainee.

"I've never met a Monarch before," Epona reflected with a sigh.

"I can still ask Vincent to do it if you don't want to."

"I'll do it."

Elliot felt a distinct sense of pride for Epona at that particularly moment. What he was asking from her was no mere trifle and any lesser individual may have turned down the task. In one week, Epona was proving herself to be resourceful and courageous and loyal, three virtues that Elliot felt would bode well for the Mare'ess in cases to come.

"Remember, the message you are about to deliver will not be easy to accept, I can think of no harder news to hear actually, but you must leave the Palace with the counterpart to the letter signed. Wait there for as long as it takes. Afterwards give the letter to Fury, she'll know when to use it," Elliot carefully instructed.

"Guess I'd best be getting along then." Epona began trotting towards the direction of the palace when she paused momentarily and turned back to her mentor. "By the way, take care of yourself Elliot, I don't think even my hooves are quick enough to rush to your aid this time."

As Elliot watched his defence team members depart he began to think of how valuable they were, not only as colleagues but as friends also. He then shrugged his shoulders and shook his head at the thought of what he was asking them all to do, and what he was about to do himself. *Not bad leadership skills for a womanising drunkard,* Elliot mused self-mockingly. He then turned away from the high court of Compenso and made his way to Silva-Tenebrae forest.

27

As Epona stood before the throne room's amber studded, red-leather padded double doors, that were three times her height, she felt a nervousness that she had never felt in all her ring-years. The canter over to the palace from the court of Compenso had been a relatively serine one and the throughways and cobble paths had been unusually devoid of the bustling rush of traffic she had come to expect of the capital at that hour. It had been time enough to mull over what she might say at the palace gates, how she might introduce herself… how she might tell the King his son is dead. The letter she had received from Elliot had been wax-sealed and she had only been told the crux of its contents from her mentor. Nothing had been mentioned of the letter's tone, and therefore she could not know how its royal recipient might take it in. *I wonder if they are in the habit of shooting messengers in Delator*, she had thought to herself, trying above all to adopt Elliot's light-hearted approach to dealing with moments that were less than light-hearted… attempting to quell the pounding heart that beat within her chest as she stood flanked by two heavy-set, polearm-wielding Delatorian guardsmen, waiting for a sign that her admittance before the Monarch had been granted.

'Make sure you get the King to sign the letter', Epona had remembered foremost of Elliot's instructions. Yet what if the King broke down in tears, an emotional wreck of a man, at the news of the death of his first-born? What if he turned to rage and had her ejected from the palace in a blaze of untamed passion? All of these possible reactions to the harshness of the message she was about to deliver had gone through the Mare'ess' worried mind, and tried as she might to compose herself, to keep her course steady and her thoughts focused, it was little compared to the weight on her shoulders of what that small enveloped tucked away in her saddlebag represented. But above all of these woes was the fear that the Queen might be sitting in session beside the King, for the message was intended for the King alone and no doubt implicated the Queen within its revelatory pages.

Could she have said 'no' to Elliot… heeded Asmodeus' words of comfort and declined the task guilt-free? As much as she wanted to do the very best in her new job, especially within the first week, she had thought more than once that this first assignment, this first case, was all so far above her own untrained abilities that she risked doing no more than falling ungracefully at the first fence. Her mistake with the name of the field, upon which Elliot met Malaphar for combat, almost cost her mentor's head and whilst in the end it did not, and that Elliot actually relished taking his Caelum opponent on hand-to-hand, it did not detract from the fact that it could so easily have gone the other way. Elliot might not have been a believer in worst case scenarios but Epona certainly was and each worst case imagined, and the myriad of mistakes she might make that preceded the same, reminded her that out in the real World-Tree a wrong decision, a misread situation… a misjudged opponent, all had consequences of the direst kind. It was so far removed from the hypothetical studies of the law school lecture halls, and on some level Epona doubted her mentor's faith in her… she doubted whether in fact she was ready to become a lawyer at all. And as she waited there at the palace for what seemed like eons she began to doubt whether she truly had the conviction to follow through with Elliot's plan.

*

"All of your horses and all of your men are currently predisposed with locating the Prince your Highness, unfortunately none are currently spare to attend the repairs."

"Very well, I trust the rest of our defences will not start to fall from our ramparts unexpectedly Captain," the King replied.

"The rest of the guns have been secured by my own retinue your Majesty."

"And the search for my son, how do your efforts fair?"

"Your Highness, I fear that so far they prove unfruitful, yet the men continue to search from dusk till dawn. Enquiries are also being made of other cities, in case the Prince has perhaps made himself known at those locations."

"Your efforts are much appreciated Captain. Are there any other matters that require my attention?"

"Erm, actually there is someone here to see you your Majesty… by the name of Miss Epona Brenwen from Blackstone and Associates," the Captain tentatively reported.

"Has she reserved an audience?" the King asked turning to one his courtiers, who promptly unfurled a large scroll and began thumbing down the entries.

"No your Majesty," the courtier replied after a brief moment of silence.

"Then send her away Captain, the throne is far too busy to grant audience to those who simply turn up at our gates."

The Captain of the royal guard took his right earlobe between thumb and forefinger and wiggled it gently. The King beckoned him forward and stooped slightly so as to receive what information the Captain wanted to impart only to him.

"Yes your Majesty, of course, but she maintains that she has pressing news regarding the trial of Abigail Hood, news she insists can only be shared with your Highness," the Captain whispered.

It was an intriguing request to say the least, and the King weighed it up against the more mundane appointments scheduled for his attention. He had been showing a keen interest in the proceedings against the Meretrix and hoped that Blackstone & Associates' efforts would prove successful and that she would soon be released to return to the palace. There were a number of Meretrixes at the royal palace and he was particularly fond of Abigail, of her roguish demeanour and brazen manner born from a past life less comfortable than her present one. The King found her presence refreshing and a welcome break from the mindless servitude that unquestioningly attended his every need.

"Send her in… and clear the throne room."

"Yes your Majesty," replied the Captain. With a loud snap of his fingers the Captain sent the King's courtesans shuffling to the throne room's side exits, and a few nods to the King's own bodyguards dismissed the retinue to stand sentry at the other side of the closed doors. When the room had been cleared and the King's safety insured, the Captain marched to the grand entrance way and struck the heavy doors with three firm raps.

Epona's heart leaped into her throat at the sound of those few dull thuds. She tentatively took a hoof-step backwards as the guards either side of her took hold of the two great brass handles and with an ominous silence, free of the creak and stress of entrances equally as aged, they slowly pulled the doors open.

The Captain stepped forward and scrutinised the Centaur with a curious gaze.

"Has Miss Brenwen been…?" he asked turning to one of the guardsman that had opened the door, whilst eyeing Epona's saddlebag.

"Yes Captain."

"Very well Miss Brenwen," the Captain continued turning now to Epona, "the King may see you, and if you might keep it brief for there are other engagements which demands his Highness' attention this evening."

Epona nodded respectfully and made to move past the Captain but stopped short.

"Is the Queen sitting in session sir?" she asked, unable to see past the Captain's wide shoulders to the thrones beyond.

"No, just the King. Does this matter require the presence of her Majesty also?"

Epona thought a moment about that question. Essentially the Queen had every right to know about the fate of her son as well as the King. Yet she knew that to have her present would be to risk Elliot's preparations… would be to jeopardise the course of the Defence's case. Could this be ethical she suddenly found herself thinking, legal even? Is this the only way of absolving

Abigail? – By asking a husband to refrain from reprimanding his wife, to request a King show restraint at the death of his blood heir and only child? Of course she knew that the answer was yes, but that answer was one that came from somewhere other than her legalistically predisposed mind, even somewhere other than that part of her moral centre that dictated what she knew to be right and wrong.

"No," Epona finally replied after a brief pause. The Captain then stepped aside allowing the Mare'ess to enter.

*

"What in all the World-Tree are you doing here," Elliot sighed to himself as he carefully picked his way through the twisted and thorny undergrowth of Silva-Tenebrae forest.

The attorney had reached the woodland as the sun was descending and the day's heat had yet to dissipate and succumb to the chill of the Delatorian night, and Elliot could feel the clammy residue of sweat that had uncomfortably laced his chest and back. There was humidity in the air too, which was not so stifling as to make one turn back to cooler retreats, but made venturing into that foreboding forest more strenuous than the long trek might otherwise have made it.

"Come on, where are you?" he whispered into the thick vegetation, his eyes scanning from left to right mimicking the sway of his outstretched lantern as if he were some pioneer or raider of tombs searching eagle-eyed for hidden treasure.

A twig snapped in the distance somewhere behind him, and he turned sharply and came to a halt, an unnatural stillness as if he feared the ground would fall away beneath him if he made the slightest movement. Quelling the jangle of his nightlight so as to return his immediate locality to quiet, he peered down the broken path of loose stone and weed and decaying leaves that he had come from, searching now more with his ears than his eyes for further sounds of disturbed foliage or the faint rustlings caused not from the forest's wildlife.

The light of the day had all but faded now and the sky above took on a pastel-shaded look of deep blues and dark purples, as if the sun was being slowly suffocated beneath the horizon, refusing to give up its last desperate rays to the night. The first of Arbor's moons had subtly wheeled into view and the fierce luminosity of the same was already cutting sharp highlights into the jagged vegetation surrounding Elliot. The lawyer chose to extinguish his lantern at that point and took a moment to survey the sky without the diffusion his lamp was causing. Elliot was always taken aback at how swiftly day turned to night when one's attention was fixed elsewhere. On some level he felt it quite arrogant of people to ignore this daily cycle, to show the night a lesser respect as one showed the day upon waking. There was a time in his youth when he liked nothing better than to lie on his back on a cool night and watch the stars above arc overhead, imagining other World-Tree's far away and other Elliot's looking right back at him.

The sound of stalking footfalls emanating from deep behind the forest's edge brought Elliot swiftly back to reality and he instinctively reached for his sword that hung loose at his side, the same sabre that had been used to fatal effect by Snow White in the dispatching of Blöd the previous day.

He closed his eyes and tried to focus his Half-Angelic abilities. Had he been entirely Angelic his senses may have honed in on the six Dwarf-Giant hearts that were racing with anticipation thirty feet away, or perhaps the smell of the beads of sweat that were collecting in the small of Dok's back… but he couldn't. What he could sense were six distinct feelings of fear and passion and anger, ambition, vengefulness and hysteria, which were all far removed from his own calm and defiant demeanour.

Elliot slowly opened his eyes and found himself surrounded by the six remaining members of the Vigilantag Seven, their swords drawn, bolts loaded, and maces swinging. He had found his witnesses… or perhaps, one might say, he allowed them to find him.

*

Your Royal Highness,

It is with the deepest regret that I find myself writing this letter to you, but as the trial of your Majesty's Meretrix, Abigail Hood, progresses I find that I am left with little choice. I sincerely apologise for not being before you in person but if all has gone to plan, or rather if all has gone beyond hope, then I am currently risking life and limb to secure those individuals who would be able to corroborate the tragic series of events I am about to describe to you.

Less than two weeks ago your Highness' palace was broken into and its safe plundered. The individuals responsible were those vicious and deadly members of a band known as the Vigilantag Seven, I trust your Majesty has heard of this devious group before and I shall not here recall their criminal exploits upon Arbor's realms.

The band was caught by the Magistratum following their raid on your palace and was held pending identification by the one and only individual who had witnessed the crime. The individual in question went by the name of Hansel. By now your Majesty may have learnt through the course of Abigail Hood's trial that the victim of her alleged crime was also called Hansel. It is with sorrow that I report that these two incidents are indeed connected. I have received testimony that Hansel was killed so that the Vigilantag Seven would escape being formally identified, and it is causation and not coincidence that they were released the same morning as Abigail Hood was taken into custody for the crime she now stands accused.

Amongst the possessions stolen from your Majesty's palace, items that are still unaccounted for, was the Carmen Speculum. I know it must pain your Highness' heart to hear of this item once more, given what I have learnt of its history from the Magistratum, but it has been revealed to me that the basis for the robbery, the sole reason for the planning and subsequent execution of the Vigilantag's heist was for the purposes of obtaining this unique magic mirror.

Whilst the reasons for committing such a crime may appear to be obvious, given the value in amber the item is worth, as well as the powers of divination it possesses, the Vigilantag did not steal this item for themselves. It has come to my attention that the intended recipient of the mirror, the individual who had hired the Vigilantag to commit the robbery, was her Majesty the Queen of Delator.

I realise that this accusation may be taken as treasonous and I fully accept the consequences of making the same. If I am wrong then be my head parted from my body in recompense to both your royal graces. Yet what I fear more than being wrong is being right, for if it goes that her Highness the Queen employed the services of the Vigilantag to steal the Carmen Speculum then it also goes that she arranged for the disposal of the witness to their crime, Hansel, in order to have the band subsequently released from Magistratum custody.

This may sound like the ravings of a man desperate to save his client, Abigail Hood, but alas the events I have so far told you are true.

And it is because they are true that I find myself compelled, nay, obligated, to report this to you at this point in time. And yet I fear this act alone may not be enough to save Abigail Hood's life, whom I whole heartedly believe has become embroiled in this whole affair, whom has been used as the instrument to end poor Hansel's life, against her wishes and against her own will. It is such that I humbly request your Majesty's royal seal of approval to question the Queen before the court of Compenso, for I fear this may be the only way to get to the truth of the matter. Your royal seal is required to authorise the manner by which the Queen's testimony might be acquired (the details of which are found attached to this letter), and it is with all hope that I trust your Majesty will see fit to agree to my proposal.

I know it must seem unreasonable of me to request that your Highness does not put your Queen on notice of the above, for that is your right as King and as husband, yet I fear that if the Queen learns of the above then the truth may find itself buried under more bodies than just Hansel's.

I humbly ask this not for myself but for the life of a faithful Delatorian Meretrix who at this moment lies vulnerable in a dark cell afraid and alone and whose fate may yet rest beneath the blade of an executioner's sword.

I trust your Majesty will see fit to do the right thing.

Your ever-faithful servant,

Elliot Blackstone

The King looked up from the pages of Elliot's letter to the Equinmare standing patiently before him. Epona had noted that the monarch's face had taken on a sterner expression than the one he been displaying when she had first entered the throne room. Yet she also noted the absence of grief, the absence of some inner pain that would have indicated a heart torn asunder by the loss of a child.

"This is true?" the King finally asked, his voice broken yet still authoritatively regal.

"I have not read the contents of the letter your Majesty, but if what is written within those pages is what I believe it to be then yes, it is all true," Epona replied, her head bowed low in respect.

The King rose from his throne and paced about the room in deep contemplation. He paused in front of a portrait of the royal family and he perused the face of his Queen and wife with marked concern. The Monarch knew that she had wanted the mirror for some time now, and that her want of it had turned to obsession on those occasions when he had denied her request, yet the King did not expect the Queen to have gone to such desperate measures. A part of him longed to dismiss the contents of Elliot's letter but deep within his heart he knew that the facts the young attorney from Blackstone's had revealed were engrained with a certain truth. He was not angry, as Epona might have expected him to be, but was more disappointed. That his Queen might go to such lengths for the purpose she had set herself, to secure the life of their son, was born of passion and love and caring, yet the lengths she did go to also showed disobedience, of the King, his rule and of the Delatorian laws he had written.

He looked down from the painting to the letter in his hands and weighed the options in his mind. The King could disregard Elliot's heart-felt plea and chastise the Queen in the privacy of the palace walls, which would prevent the populace from learning of her insidious plotting and save the Royals the inevitable backlash, or he could grant the lawyer's request and have the Queen cross-examined in front of all the public to see. Yet it was not the fate of Abigail Hood, which also concerned him greatly, that assisted him in coming to a decision, rather it was his belief in the Law: that all should be held accountable before it, regal and non-regal alike, and that it should be public and free from censure. These were the foundations of his rule in Delator and these were the reasons he chose when he approached a bureau behind the royal thrones, and to the red sealing candle that stood upon it, with the intention of granting Elliot his request.

He pressed the royal signet ring into the soft wax he had dripped onto the authorisation form attached to Elliot's letter before sombrely marching back to where Epona had been waiting.

"Very well, Miss Brenwen, do what you must."

The Equinmare graciously took the signed and sealed form and letter from the King and bowed low. Still with her head tilted she took four slow steps backwards before turning to depart the way she had come, all the while thinking that something about the whole situation was definitely amiss.

*

"Elliot Blackstone, I presume," Dok asked, his mouth twisted into a sadistic grin.

"And you must be Dok, the leader of this desperate band," Elliot coolly replied, his eyes slowly moving round the group. "Here to surrender?"

"Not really. Where's our mirror?" the Vigilantag leader snapped.

"Your mirror? That's not quite correct is it? I understand the Carmen Speculum belongs to the Delatorian Royal family."

"Enough Dok, let me make him tell us. By the time I've carved away the soles of his feet he'll be begging to give it back," Brummig threatened stepping forward, brandishing his Zwerg-Riesen butcher's cleaver menacingly.

"I wouldn't come any closer if I were you," Elliot warned.

"Veil threats human," Müde yawned, raising his cross bow so that it was aimed at the attorney's head.

Dok nodded to Shüchter, Fröhlich and Nieser, who were stood at Elliot's flank, and with a blood curdling roar the six Dwarf-Giants rushed the Half-Angelic all at once.

"Suit yourselves," Elliot sighed as the wings upon his back sprung from beneath his coat. The young lawyer propelled himself into the air as the half-dozen Vigilantag were almost upon him. Those caught off-guard clumsily ran into their opposite number in the circle and were left sprawling on the forest floor.

Müde looked up and released a salvo of steel bolts from his crossbow at the attorney who was hovering near the forest's thick canopy. His shooting was erratic and each of the missiles flew wide of their intended target.

Dok grabbed hold of those on the ground and forced them up to their feet, but before he could rally his band a sudden darkness came upon them all. Dok checked himself before quelling the shouts of the rest of the group. It had turned pitch black all of a sudden and the leader of the Vigilantag was momentarily disorientated, bumping into his band as the rest trod upon each other's toes in some vain attempt to escape their darkened prison.

"Silence! Hold fast!" Dok ordered. "Fröhlich, a light."

A torch was lit, immediately illuminating the group in a flickering blaze of light. Dok snatched the torch up and proceeded to stalk to the edges of what seemed to be some kind of solid cell, much like those the Venators used to temporally imprison their captured Wolven, albeit this one was substantially larger. He struck the wall in front of him with his fist, which caused a dull metallic clang to echo off the prison's four thick walls and ceiling. The other gang members followed Dok's lead and began swinging their sturdy weapons at the interior walls in a furious attempt to break free.

The whole noisy affair was futile as the prison was wrought from unbreakable Dwarven steel, and as the last of the dull thuds from within the trap rang out Elliot slowly descended from the forest canopy to land gracefully and unharmed upon the top of the metal box.

"Finished?" Elliot asked, tapping the roof with the tip of his sword, to which further beating of weapons from within sounded in reply.

"We can do this all night, the air within this cage permitting," the attorney continued.

The clanging ceased and the forest clearing was returned to quiet.

"Good. Are you listening Dok?"

There was a low disgruntled snort in response, which Elliot reckoned was sign enough that he had the Vigilantag leader's attention.

"Under the joint laws of Arbor," Elliot began, "and by authorisation of the Law-Bringers of Atlatia, I hereby place the six of you under arrest."

No reply came from within the steel box.

"I am to take you to Steinthor where the Zwerg-Riese have requested the Atlations pass sentence over you. I myself am privy to the particulars of the sentence, would you like me tell you?" Elliot taunted.

Silence.

"Well I'll tell you anyway. I hear that you are all to be executed?"

A number of panicked whispers came from within the prison, followed by a sshhing sound that came from Dok, who was still listening intently to the attorney's sombre words.

"I know… and without a trial at that. It appears that such is the demand for your demise from all the races of the World-Tree that on this occasion the Law-Bringers are prepared to forego what would undoubtedly be a pointless show trial. Of course I questioned the justice of the same," Elliot lied, "but would they listen? Nope."

"Then why waste your breath here?" Dok replied, his voice turning to one of dejection at the realisation that for now he was as good as caught.

"Just making chit chat," Elliot yawned in mock boredom. "Did you know I've even been granted authority to kill you all right this very moment should you put up any resistance? With the snap of my fingers Halvard here can press this prison into the ground till you are all as flat as pancakes." Elliot looked up to the giant, who less than two weeks ago had squashed his client Jack, and smiled.

Halvard, who had been put under Elliot's charge by the retired Judge Hallbjorn, rubbed his huge hands together in joyful anticipation. It was he who had slammed the great prison down upon the six Zwerg-Riese as soon as Elliot had flown clear of the group, and he was eager still to pop each one of their heads as if they were grapes.

"What do you want?" Dok asked.

"Blöd has told me everything. *Everything*," Elliot slowly and clearly repeated. "What I want is for you testify the same in court. If you do this then I shall appeal to the Law-Bringers to spare your lives."

There was a brief pause as Dok considered the attorney's deal. Although he was ruthless and brilliant and cunning, he certainly wasn't compassionate or self-sacrificing. If saving his own head meant revealing the Queen's plot concerning the Carmen Speculum, the involvement of the Vigilantag Seven, as well as what he knew about the disposal of the witness Hansel, then his instinct for self-preservation would have made him start talking there and then if it could have saved his head that bit faster. Honour among thieves was not something Dok held in any kind of regard, and as such he had little qualms with testifying against the Queen or any other in that respect, even his own gang.

"Why not ask Blöd? It would appear he's been more than co-operative thus far," Dok asked.

"It is my belief that he is dead. Now tell me how many more must die before this comes to an end?"

If Dok had his way it would be just one more, and that would be Elliot. Yet it wasn't going his way, and if he refused to comply with the attorney's wishes then the next victims of the whole Royal conspiracy would be himself and his five companions. This was not an eventuality the leader of the Vigilantag was about to let happen, certainly not so the Queen of Delator could then wash her hands of the affair publicly guiltless.

"I shall do it," Dok conceded.

Elliot stood up and glided back down to the forest floor. He breathed in a great sigh of relief for the first part of his plan had worked.

"Halvard I want you to stay here tonight with the prisoners. I'll send someone to escort you into Delator tomorrow morning."

"Why not now?"

"If an Atlation shows up with a box full of Vigilantag then the whole of Delator will be desperate to know what's going on. No, you stay here and wait for your escort."

"And if they try to escape?" Halvard asked tapping the side of the prison with his foot.

"Kill them," Elliot replied. "Did you here that Dok, don't try anything rash for it *will* be the last thing you do. You appear in court midday tomorrow."

There was no reply and Elliot guessed that the gang was more than likely sulking. The young lawyer expanded his wings once more, cleared Silva-Tenebrae's leafy canopy and flew back to his home and to a soft comfortable bed.

It had been a long day of Defence cross-examination and daring Vigilantag capturing and he was in need of a much-earned rest. There was however one thing left to do before retiring for the evening, and when Elliot reached his house thirty minute-turns after leaving the forest he made his way straight to his study, where he promptly lit a scarlet candle and focused his mind on the image of Fury.

"Ah Fury, you're still up, excellent."

The candle's flame flickered in response. "Yes I got them… no I'm not hurt. Because I had a little help, well a big help really. Did you study the questions?"

The flame danced about the candle's wick.

"Good, good," Elliot continued. "If all has gone well with Epona at the palace then she'll deliver to you what is required for my part of the Defence to be valid… yes I think she'll get it… anyway, after she's seen you send her over to the northwest clearing of Silva-Tenebrae forest to meet Halvard. She'll have to escort him into Delator."

A puff of fine smoke came from the flame as a piece of candlewick was consumed.

"Well I would have sent Vincent, but he's working on the mirrors and then he's going to see Abigail… Epona will be fine.

No I don't fancy her," Elliot sighed, responding to each of Fury's candlelight queries with rapidly diminishing strength.

"If all goes well, I'll see you when this whole thing is over. Take care," Elliot concluded.

He blew out the candle, stretched his arms into the air and pulled the stress knots from his back, before wearily making his way to bed, where he peacefully drifted off to sleep as soon as his head hit his pillow.

28

"What do you mean he didn't tell them?" Fury barked, snatching up Elliot's letter to the King from Epona's outstretched hand.

The Mare'ess had contemplated not telling Fury the small fact that Elliot's letter had omitted to reveal that Hansel was actually the Royal Prince, and she had spent all of last evening re-reading the letter and fathoming what motives her mentor might have for not disclosing the same. None-the-less when she saw Fury and had handed her the counterpart to the letter signed by the Monarch the information just slipped, uncontrollably, from her lips. She immediately regretted it.

"You know, I'm sure he has his reasons," Epona replied. The Fire-Nymph was too busy scanning Elliot's letter and didn't reply straight away.

"Well, I guess there's nothing can be done now," Fury conceded with a sigh, much to Epona's surprise, as the Fire-Nymph finished reading the handwritten manuscript. She then looked up from the pages and locked her colleague with an expression of concern more than anger. She hated the idea that they were taking more risks than necessary during the course of the trial and above all wanted a few truths revealed in order to alleviate the burdens that had been heaped upon them. The fact that they were in essence with-holding the true identity of Abigail's victim was not something which she had any qualms about from a legal perspective, although that too might have had worrying professional repercussions. It was more the fact that there were parents out there who didn't know their son was dead. It felt wrong on some moral level and it was Fury, the most unlikely of the Defence team to have such problems with this given her sly and unwieldy disposition, who was having trouble getting to grips with it the most.

Epona, on the other hand, still had the utmost faith in her mentor and believed beyond doubt that Elliot had his reasons for the omission. This feeling didn't come from some sense of duty or loyalty, although she considered each of these traits in high regard, yet more the realisation that Elliot however rash or risky his actions absolutely knew what he was doing. In her opinion Elliot only made calculated risks, educated guesses and gambles so well conceived that they appeared not to be gambles at all.

She often thought what course of action she might have taken had her childhood friend or family members had found themselves in Abigail Hood's position. One conclusion rang true each time – that she would stop at nothing to help them. This was a realisation born from witnessing her father imprisoned in her youth, and it was the one moment she always thought back to when she imagined that the subsequent act of rendering assistance might outweigh the demands on her morality or pose any threat to her personal safety.

"It's easier to take risks when a loved one's life is at stake," Epona whispered.

Fury passed back Elliot's letter to Epona and nodded her head slowly in agreement.

A knock broke the melancholic silence then and Vincent popped his head round the conference room doorframe.

"Court is about to begin session, we best be getting back in there."

"Thanks Vince," Fury replied before turning to Epona, "Elliot told me that there's an Atlation awaiting escort from Silva-Tenebrae's central clearing. The giant has six Vigilantag to bring to town."

"You're kidding… Elliot caught them?" Vincent asked with a gasp of disbelief.

"Yep. He wants Epona to bring them into Delator," Fury continued.

"Fun never ends," Epona replied with a meek smile.

"Beats proof-reading I'm sure," Fury added.

"That it does… and when Delator's alarm bells begin to ring at the approach of an Atlation?"

"Asmodeus has alerted the Magistratum to the impending visit so your journey should go unhindered, they'll know what to do with the Vigilantag when you arrive, apparently," Fury replied.

"Unbelievable," Vincent sighed. "I don't know about proof-reading but this sure beats Finance Law."

"How are the mirrors Vince?"

"All done Fury, Elliot took possession of the Carmen Speculum some time this morning."

"Right… lets help Elliot end this, I guess I can always chastise the cheeky bastard tomorrow," Fury grinned.

*

The Meretrix Elspeth Morrigan had been a Royal Delatorian Courtesan for two ring-years longer than Abigail and had been responsible for chaperoning the young Miss Hood and in teaching her the ways of the court. She was strikingly attractive, possessing a classical beauty that mimicked the alabaster statues surrounding the Goddess temple of Mira in Arabilis. Her cheekbones were high and well defined and when she smiled her whole face lit up. A petite nose and two eyes of piercing purple completed a face of such beauty that it made men stop in their tracks and blink their eyes as if standing before a mirage. Elspeth was tall and slender with a small waist and was the envy of every maid in the palace as well as the fantasy of every butler. But to Abigail she was a friend and companion and because she was it made her appearing for the prosecution that bit more difficult for Abigail to accept or to understand.

The work of a Meretrix was not a sordid one, which the less knowledgeable city folk of Delator might have one believe, on the contrary it was a role which demanded much eloquence and elegance. Essentially the Royal Meretrixes were hostesses. They were charming and beautiful woman who would keep those unaccompanied guests to the palace company, dancing with them at grand masqueraded balls or sitting beside them at formal dinner tables, or perhaps even just walking them around the sculptured grounds of the palace gardens on a pleasant afternoon. On the whole these guests were often visiting nobles from the other Arborian realms, wealthy Princes on 'seasonal rotation' (Elliot's term for their finding a wife), or Amber laden landed gentry who had risen to lofty peeks enough to rub shoulders with royalty.

They were mostly male, though not all Human, and always without exception enjoyed the company of attractive women. Each of these guests knew that the Delatorian Meretrixes were the most beautiful in all the World-Tree. But there were rules. Even the cad Liberan Viceroy Tibuleus' wandering ten pairs of hands never strayed too far from his flamboyantly embroidered twenty-pocket waistcoat when under the roof of the palace, for whilst a guest of the Royals one was not to make any improper advances or lewd propositions towards the Meretrixes as to do so would be to show disrespect to one's hosts and risk being ejected from the court altogether. Not that impropriety or lewdness did not take place behind closed doors, for it did, yet only at the instigation and wish of the Meretrix.

Elspeth taught Abigail everything from the new waltzes to come out of Pannonia to the current states and affairs of Arborian nobility (enough to conduct oneself knowledgeably if engaged in light conversation) to the often yawn inducing fancies of high society, not to mention the rules of etiquette and formality. Abigail relished every moment of her new palace life and took great pleasure from learning the ways of courtly life from her friendly fellow Meretrix, albeit Abigail still had a wild predisposition to gallivanting around forests naked on her time away from the palace. In time Elspeth became a close confidant of Abigail and together they shared their dreams and aspirations and stories of loves, past, present, and hopefully future.

"Miss Morrigan, how long have you been in the employ of the Royal Palace?" Malaphar asked. Considering the first day of the Prosecution's case had not been as watertight as the Caelum

Attorney had intended he looked decidedly smug. Elliot was away from court, preparing his defence for the afternoon session, and Malaphar had already taken advantage of the Half-Angelic's absence to shoot more than one patronising glance towards Elliot's co-counsel Fury. Delatorian Law reporters would later describe what a sight it was to behold. Only human attorneys had graced the elevated platforms of Compenso prior to Abigail Hood's trial and the spectacle of an aura flickering Fire-Nymph, which up-lit the face of the Goddess statue Iustitia with a golden hue, standing off against a comparative giant in the form of Malaphar, whose intimidating bulk was amplified by the manner in which, on this occasion, he had unfurled his wings at forty-five degrees to his back as if he might swoop forward upon his opponent at any moment, left a great deal of the court members taken aback.

"Fourteen ring-years," Elspeth replied. She was dressed in formal courtly attire comprising a bodice of delicately woven silk a subtle shade of off-white dotted with polished amber droplets, over which she wore a three-quarter length Arabilisian fur-lined satin coat which appeared to hang effortlessly from her graceful shoulders. An ankle-length pleated skirt split to the thigh, to offer some mobility whilst maintaining the wearers alluring air, completed the ensemble. A number of male jurors had already locked eyes with the Meretrix and had given her approving nods. Had they seen her glass slippers hidden beneath the witness box and the perfectly formed feet upon which the shoes were slipped, they may have lost themselves in their fantasies altogether.

"For all these ring-years you have been a Meretrix?"

"That is correct." Even her voice possessed all the harmony of a caressed harp.

"And for how long have you known the accused?"

"For twelve ring-years."

"Since her uncle installed her in the court?" Malaphar asked, taking a brief moment to look over at Abigail.

"That is correct."

"Because her parent's were killed and she was left orphaned?"

"Objection your honour," Fury interrupted, "and the relevance to such a question being?"

"Merely to ascertain whether Miss Morrigan was aware of how the accused came to join the palace your honour," Malaphar replied simply, as if aloof to the effect his last question was having on Abigail's already faltering demeanour.

"Over-ruled Miss Fury, please continue Mr Naberius," the Judge directed.

"Miss Morrigan, how would you describe your relationship with the accused?" the Caelum attorney asked.

"We are Meretrixes sir, relationships are forbidden."

"Your friendship then?" Malaphar rephrased.

"The best of friends, she was new to the court and I took her under my wing, proverbially speaking," Elspeth added as her gaze wandered over Malaphar's wings.

"And you taught her everything she needed to know to conduct herself about the palace?"

"That is correct. A charge I enjoyed as much as Abigail enjoyed learning from me I think."

"But that has all changed?"

"Yes," Elspeth sighed, dropping her gaze to lap.

"How so Miss Morrigan?"

"Over the past few ring-years Abigail has become increasingly… detached."

"How so?"

"I'll notice her absence from her quarters, and sometimes she'll be gone for days. Then she'd return and always with some bruising or cuts to her face or arms. It concerned me greatly," Elspeth added turning to look at Abigail for the first time since taking the witness stand. "A Meretrix is meant to be… well perfect." This last comment caused Fury, who thought the witness very modest, to roll her eyes skywards as if in desperation.

"You thought the accused might be harming herself? Because she perhaps was not perfect?"

"No. Well, yes… I thought that she might be harming herself, yes… but not because she wasn't perfect, for she was. I thought that perhaps she was unhappy with some other part of her life, so much so that she was taking other risks to her personal safety and wellbeing."

"Other risks?" Malaphar pressed.

"I knew she enjoyed the woods and was aware that she went to visit them on a number of occasions when we were permitted time away from our duties."

"Did you ever follow her out on these excursions?"

"No. But there were rumours."

"Go on."

"Rumours that she… danced naked in the forests, conversed with the flora and the fauna." Elspeth had believed the rumours at first, then, wanting to protect Abigail's palace reputation, she dispelled them, asserting that no Meretrix would behave as such. But now, as she spoke, she found herself believing again, realising that there was a part of her friend that she might never know about or understand.

Abigail wanted to object so much yet she remained silent. She wanted to tell everyone why this was, why this fascination with Nature, and that it was innocent. Fury could see it in her eyes as they glistened with tears the Meretrix hoped to hold back.

"And you believe this is where she got her injuries?"

"Sometimes, but there were occasions where the palace guards would report she had not left the grounds and yet still she was absent and yet she would still return to her room in such a state. As I was trying to say, I was concerned because I knew that if she marred herself any further… if any of her injuries ever became permanent, then her life as a Meretrix might be over."

"For you are supposed to be perfect?"

"Yes."

"Did she ever explain her injuries?" Malaphar continued.

"No. I tried to ask her when she returned but she was always in such a daze, always so weary, so I would just help her into bed. Then in the morning she would claim not to remember or tell me not to worry."

"Very odd behaviour for a Meretrix," Malaphar asserted turning briefly to the jury. "Now, Miss Morrigan, you have maintained that relationships are forbidden."

"Yes."

"But the accused, she talked of one did she not?"

"Hansel."

"And did she tell you of this relationship?"

"Only of how she felt about him. How she loved him," Elspeth replied.

"A forbidden love."

"I tried to warn her, I tried to tell her that it couldn't last."

"But she felt otherwise?"

Elspeth nodded gently. She began to feel weary of the questions. Weary of the betrayal of the trust Abigail had placed in her as confident. "She loved him. Abigail used to say some loves last… last through everything."

"And then?"

"Things changed. She told me Hansel was having second thoughts, that there was no way they could continue because of who she was, because of who he was."

"And who was he?"

"She never said."

"What else did she tell you?"

"That she could not live without him, that she could not bear for his love to be elsewhere other than with her… she said she would rather die."

"And?"

"And that she would…" Elspeth faltered.

"She would what?" Malaphar pressed.

"That if this was a betrayal, that if Hansel in fact loved another… then…"

"Then what Miss Morrigan?"

"Then… she would kill him."

As those last words of prosecution testimony left Elspeth's mouth Abigail put her face in her hands and quietly cried to herself.

*

The view from Halvard's shoulder was astounding and Epona could see the whole of Silva Tenebrae's forest canopy laid out before her like a patchwork quilt. She had allayed her own objections to riding things on this occasion for fear that if she were galloping far below the Giant on the forest floor, out of Halvard's sight, then she might have risked being trampled under his huge boots.

She had arrived at the forest clearing to find Halvard wide-awake and slightly irritable, having not had the benefit of the soft lullabies of his golden harp to coax him gently to sleep the previous night, or for several nights since it escaped at Hillock Court for that manner. Epona soon found him willing enough, however, when she asked him to give the Vigilantag's steel prison a shake to rouse them from their own slumber. Halvard then threatened to eat them one by one if they did not give up all their weapons through the small hatch at the top of the cage, a consideration Elliot had mistakenly overlooked. Epona considered that her mentor's thoughts must have been elsewhere. So with the six Zwerg-Riese disarmed, as much as they claimed to be anyway, Epona leaped upon Halvard's palm and was duly lifted to his shoulder.

"You do realise that if you are all lying to me then there will be a contingent of Magistratum officers at Delator who will not hesitate in shooting you all?" Epona calmly called down to the steel cage that the Atlation was effortlessly swinging beside his right leg as he slowly trudged through the forest. Two daggers, a sling and shot, as well as some brutal looking knuckle-dusters were suddenly thrown out of the hatch, much to Epona's approval and amusement.

Halvard was not the greatest of conversationalists and after Epona had learned of his current charge at the request of the great retired Law-Bringer Hallbjorn she contented herself with sitting as comfortably as she could and watching the World-Tree trees go by. Every now and again the ground shaking vibrations of the Atlation's footfalls would send the feathered population of another oak scattering to the wind like the seeds of a blown dandelion. The scenery was so much different from her home realm of Equinas, which on the whole was much more sparse and lacked the dense mass of forest that could be found in Delator and Pannonia. The first few days of her new job had been so hectic that Epona had little time to contemplate how much she missed home and how much she missed galloping the shoreline of Equinas at sunrise.

"Miss Brenwen," Halvard softly spoke, for he did not wish the power of his booming voice to carry the Equinmare clean off his shoulder. "I don't think there's room enough in the streets of Delator for my big boots. I think I'll have to wait outside the city limits."

"That's correct Halvard," Epona replied reassuringly, "my boss has already spoken to the Magistratum about it, and with luck there'll be a great number of them waiting at the city perimeter when we get there."

"I do hope they won't be running under me feet, I wouldn't want to squish anymore of Mr Blackstone's friends."

"Don't worry Halvard, I'm sure they'll keep well clear." Epona patted his shoulder, though afterwards doubted whether the Giant could have felt it through his thick coat.

*

"Miss Morrigan it can't be easy for you, testifying against your friend like this?" Fury began.

"No."

"Especially considering the trust and confidence she placed in you."

"Like I said it's not easy, but some things need to be known."

"The *truth*," Fury replied suspiciously. "So you were offered nothing to appear in court today?"

"I don't understand?"

"Hmm, well we shall get back to that one," Fury smirked. "Abigail wasn't the only one who indulged in personal relationships was she Miss Morrigan?"

"We are Meretrix, we offer companionship to – "

"That's not what I mean," Fury interrupted. "You were, or should I say *are*, having a relationship of your own are you not?"

"Objection your honour, I'm sure Miss Fury is eager to know the sordid details of every affair that goes on within the Palace walls but I'm at a loss to understand the relevancy of this line of questioning," Malaphar asserted rather snidely.

"It goes to the credibility of the witness your honour. Evidence suggests Miss Morrigan is in fact not the perfect Meretrix which Mr Naberius has led us to believe."

"If my learned colleague has such evidence then, albeit for me to tell Miss Fury how to do her job, I suggest she produces it," Malaphar replied.

"There is a Palace employee your honour," Fury replied turning to the Judge, "who has agreed to appear as a rebuttal witness for the Defence should Miss Morrigan prove to be economical with the truth. I just thought it only just to give Miss Morrigan an opportunity to tell us her story first." Secretly Fury hoped she would not have to call Tom the Royal pageboy, for child witnesses, Elliot once explained to her, can prove none too reliable under the pressure of a court environment.

"Very well Miss Fury, you may continue. Objection overruled," Judge Coerceo stated.

"Miss Morrigan, are you currently conducting a relationship outside the confines of your duties as Meretrix?"

"Yes," Elspeth replied after a moment of contemplation.

"Apparently you are both to be wed."

"You've spoken to him?" Elspeth looked up suddenly into Fury's eyes.

"I am sure he is very happy. Strange though that the Palace should release someone such as you… to free you from your duties forever, to be married to someone so… common."

The Meretrix remained silent.

"I ask you again, were you offered any incentive to appear in court today."

"No… I – "

"Perhaps I should call your husband-to-be as a witness, yes I think that is for the best."

"Wait," Elspeth gasped, "just wait. It's not what you think."

"Then please explain Miss Morrigan, for the benefit of all us… for the benefit of Compenso," Fury pressed, sweeping her arm dramatically over the court.

A hint of the old Elliot extravaganza, Vincent thought to himself as he watched the Fire-Nymph. The Sandman had taken co-counsel's seat at the bench beside the platform Fury was making her cross-examination from, and was growing increasingly impressed with the manner in which Fury, whose first legal discipline was not Criminal Law, was conducting herself. Vincent recognised the Fire-Nymph's fervour, that methodical way she followed through an argument and the fierceness of her delivery. She was doing Elliot a great justice in agreeing to take up the Defence in his absence.

"Yes they said they would let me go – "

"*Who* said?" Fury pressed.

"The Queen. Her Majesty said that I would be free to marry whomever I chose if I appeared today."

A stunned silence had descended upon the court. Malaphar would have objected at this juncture yet realised that it might show weakness and may only compound the Defence's arguments.

"So she knew that you were seeing someone?"

"Yes Her Majesty knows everything that happens with the Meretrixes."

A thought dawned upon Fury at that moment and she paused.

"But everything I have said is true," Elspeth called out, frantically attempting to rally herself for fear that the Queen might be none too satisfied with her performance. "Abigail did say she would kill him."

"Whatever you say Miss Morrigan," Fury replied derisively. "Just one final question. Did the Queen know that Abigail was conducting a personal relationship?"

"Yes, I told Her Majesty that Abigail was seeing someone… I told her about Hansel."

Bingo, Fury thought to her self, *that's the missing piece.* "No further questions your honour," she concluded, and turning to Malaphar she showed the Angelic a triumphant grin.

29

Six large horse-drawn cages, each normally reserved for the capture of Wolven and on loan from the guild house of the Venators, were waiting for Epona, Halvard and the remaining Vigilantag at Delator's boundary. Accompanying each cage were five heavily armed Magistratum officers as well as two armoured reserves from the city's standing army. Asmodeus' instructions were being followed to the letter. This time the Zwerg-Riese would not be treated so easily as the last time they were in Magistratum custody.

Halvard lowered the prison box he was carrying to the ground making sure to drop it the remaining five feet to ensure the prisoners inside got an uncomfortable jolt at their journey's end. Then, as if presenting the officers with a freshly prepared banqueting platter, the Atlation unclasped the top of the prison and pulled it away. Standing wearily on the Dwarven-steel floor of the prison, eyes straining against the harsh light of the day, were six particularly dishevelled and dejected looking Dwarf-Giants. At the snap of the Magistratum Captain's fingers, thirty crossbows were raised and pointed at each of the gang members.

"I wouldn't try anything if I were you," Epona playfully called out to the Vigilantag leader as Halvard gently lowered her from his shoulder to the ground.

Dok turned his head to the side and shot the Equinmare a threatening gaze. Although she had put on a courageous front, an almost mockingly brave one, when Epona was sat atop Halvard's shoulder on their way through Silva-Tenebrae, now that the cage top had been lifted and she could see Dok and the five other Vigilantag in all their twenty-foot tall menace she felt less than safe, even if surrounded by near forty armed officers.

"Not so brave now are we Mare'ess?" Dok smirked.

"Silence!" the Captain of the guard barked.

"Cuff them, and I suggest you take them to the city oubliette until such time as their fate has been decided," Epona said to the Captain, a distinct authority and urgency intonating her words.

"But the holding cells should be adeq – "

"They'll bend the bars of your prison cells as if they where circus props," Epona interrupted, "put them underground."

"Very well miss," the Captain conceded. "And that one?" he continued pointing at Dok.

"He's coming with me to Compenso," the Mare'ess replied. "Halvard! If the Vigilantag resist the Magistratum's efforts to shackle them then you may crush them."

Epona then slowly trotted up to Dok, causing the officers surrounding the gang to perspire a little more and tighten their grips on their trained crossbows.

"Do not toy with me," Epona warned looking up into stern eyes of Blackstone's & Associates newest Defence witness.

*

"That's how the Queen knew how to get to the eye-witness… unbelievable," Fury chuckled as she paced about the Defence's conference room at Compenso. A short recess had been called following the appearance of the Prosecution's final witness; time enough for Fury to make last minute-turn preparations before she called the first witness for the defence.

"What are you talking about?" Vincent queried, preoccupied with sifting through the statement for the palace accountant Aerarius Artifex.

"That was one of the missing pieces! Whether we could prove the Queen actually manipulated Abigail Hood to murder Hansel was always one problem, but a greater one was proving how the Queen knew Abigail knew Hansel."

"That's a good point actually," Vincent replied looking up from his pages with a look that projected some surprise in not having posed that question much earlier in the preparation of the case.

"I wonder why the Queen did use Abigail though… I mean she had her Royal assassins."

"I guess that's for Elliot to find out Fury."

There was a knock at the door, then came the voice of an usher who notified the pair that court would begin session in three minute-turns.

"The accountant?" Vincent asked, collecting up his papers and rising to his feet.

"Absolutely," Fury replied.

*

"Are you sure about this Fabes?" Elliot worriedly called from the other side of their transport.

"I've been steering these things for ring-years Elliot, stop worrying… did you know that in Liber we actually race them, oh yes, the first took place – "

"Not a good time Fabes," Elliot replied as he struggled to strap down the huge frame and mirror of the Carmen Speculum to the shifting carapace of their wagon-sized Woodlice. "Why couldn't we just get a regular type wagon thing… with wheels… and horses?"

"Have you seen these through-ways?" Fabianus remarked, waving four pairs of hands at the cobbled streets outside the Delatorian Syngraphus. "Wooden wheels on stone would shake your precious mirror to shattering point. Oh no, this is by far the smoothest form of transport for something this large… actually did you know that the legs of a Woodlice can take the load…"

Elliot would otherwise have been listening to his colleague's encyclopaedic knowledge of Woodlice weight distribution and traction over rocky terrain, but he was more concerned with how he was going to conduct his questioning of the

Queen of Delator. Nobody had ever deposed a monarch in this realm before and Elliot was not ignorant of the extremely delicate nature of the task ahead of him. Subjects had been beheaded for taking lesser liberties, and the Half-Angelic knew that he risked being charged with treason if all did not go to plan.

"…Yes truly exceptional creatures, Elliot. Elliot?"

"Quite fascinating," Elliot lied. He then took the pocket sundial from his jacket pocket and studied the time. "We best get going Fabes. We've still to get this through the Palace gates remember."

Fabianus made one final rope adjustment to his side of the transport then pulsated his way up to the driver station at the front of the Woodlice; a raised platform anchored onto the creatures strongest carapace plates, room enough for a driver and a passenger. Elliot then climbed up to join him. The Half-Angelic looked over his shoulder and cast a concerned eye over the not-too-secure looking manner in which they had tied down the mirror.

"Trust me," Fabianus reassuringly stated, taking up two extremely long Griffin feathers from the compartment underneath the driver's seat. With three sets of hands on each feather, the enthusiastic looking Liberan began to tickle the feelers that protruded from the head of the Woodlice up over the front-most lip of its carapace. Slowly and, much to Elliot's surprise, smoothly the creature began to make its way through Delator's bustling streets.

"Unbelievable, I can hardly feel a thing."

"Told you Elliot, the smoothest way to travel. Stimulate the right feeler and the creature goes right, do the same to the left and it goes left. Tickle them both for forward"

"What about backwards?"

"They don't do reverse, that's why they curl up into balls when they hit things. I guess that might shatter your mirror," Fabianus reflected. "Fancy a go?"

"No thanks, just keeping going. And try not to hit anything."

Elliot needed for himself and the Carmen Speculum to be in place at the palace for the beginning of Compenso's afternoon session, any later than this would risk delay to the proceedings, something Judges greatly disliked.

By the Half-Angelic's reckoning Malaphar should by now have concluded the case for the Prosecution. Two witnesses to be called by Fury for the Defence and then the cross examination of the same and then a long recess for a late lunch would in turn lead to Elliot's part of the defence; the riskiest part of the proceedings yet, even more so than going sword to sword with a Caelum Angelic.

*

"The Defence calls Aerarius Artifex," Fury clearly stated.

Appearing as a witness for the Defence was not something the Royal accountant agreed to lightly, or without some objection, and in the end Elliot had to issue a formal summons in order to guarantee the presence of the aged Tabularius at Compenso. Fury was looking forward to this, to leaning on a witness who had so blatantly lied to them regarding the state of the Carmen Speculum.

A side door opened in the court, but the thin frail cane-wielding accountant did not emerge. Instead a perturbed looking court clerk tentatively stepped through the opening, nodded graciously yet nervously to the Judge before quick stepping to the rear of the statue of Iustitia. A moment later and the breathless court clerk, who had climbed the spiral staircase within the hollow Goddess stature, emerged onto Fury's platform and leant forward to whisper his message into the Fire-Nymph's impatiently waiting ear.

"What do you mean he's not here?" rasped Fury underneath her breath. Her temperature rose a degree or two and the court clerk backed away for fear his head might catch fire.

"Nowhere to be found Miss, we have looked everywhere."

"You didn't think to perhaps tell me this sooner?"

"You said you were not to be disturbed Miss, as you were in conference during recess."

Fury narrowed her gaze and if she could have channelled her heat through her eyes she may just have set the poor clerk's head ablaze.

"Leave, now," Fury spat.

"A problem Miss Fury?" called the Judge from his elevated bench. Fury took a deep breath, cracked her knuckles and slowly turned to face the Judge.

"An unforeseen circumstance has arisen your honour," she replied through a fake smile, "might I graciously request a moment to confer with my colleague?"

"You may."

"My thanks your honour." 'Always preserve the niceties, etiquette is everything,' Fury remembered of her limited advocacy training.

She walked to the edge of her platform and took a knee in front of Vincent who had moved to the corner of co-council's box.

"Where the bloody Caelum is he Vince?" Fury whispered with a hint of panic.

"The old bugger probably knew he was going to get caught out, he's probably left the city."

"When I find that bastard I'll…" Fury turned to look around the courtroom. Those Delatorians who had been patiently waiting in the gallery for Fury to begin Abigail Hood's Defence were already shifting about in their seats, and those in the Jury rows were beginning to guess that something was not quite right. It was not the best start to Abigail Hood's defence, and Malaphar was positively relishing every moment of the unfortunate mishap.

What nobody knew was that Aerarius Artifex had in fact not left the city. He was actually buried four feet beneath a freshly planted bush of Lilac Rosarius outside Emilita Letalis' palace quarters, his throat slashed from ear to ear. His body would never be found.

Upon hearing news of the accountant's summons the Queen deduced that it must be in connection with the Carmen Speculum; that Abigail Hood's meddlesome Defence team had finally discovered the association between the Meretrix's incarceration and the theft of the magic mirror. The Monarch promptly ordered the accountant's swift dispatch. With Snow White otherwise engaged at the time, lying comatose in Elliot's front room, Rose Red had obliged with ruthless efficiency.

"Where's Brenwen? Where's anybody?" Fury whispered in annoyance.

At that moment the entrance to the public gallery slowly creaked open and Epona, noticing that all was uncharacteristically silent, slowly trotted through like a teenager tiptoeing to her bedroom long beyond her curfew. She raised her head and saw that every member of the courtroom had turned to face her. With a face flushed with embarrassment she looked up to Judge Coerceo and nodded, then curtsied (not a courtroom requirement), then stuck both her thumbs up at Fury and Vincent and smiled.

"She looks pleased with herself," Vincent whispered to Fury.

"Her last-minute, save-the-day type timing's unbelievable," Fury replied. "Your Honour," she continued turning back to the Judge, "our sincere apologies, the Defence in fact calls Dok, leader of the Vigilantag Seven."

A gentle murmur of whispers and gasps rippled through the courtroom. The Jury members turned to each other baffled, shrugging their shoulders and shaking their heads. Unsurprisingly Malaphar promptly rose from his seat.

"Objection your honour," the Caelum Angelic responded. "I am not sure where my learned colleague actually studied legal method, but it is common place to produce a list of witnesses prior to the beginning of the trial, so as to give the other side adequate notice of the same. I am sure my learned colleague understands that in Delator attorneys are not in the habit of calling witness as their fancy takes them."

Arrogant bastard, Fury maliciously thought. "Your Honour the Vigilantag have recently been re-apprehended having made an attempt on the life of Miss Hood's lead counsel Mr Elliot Blackstone. We believe that this witness possesses information that goes to the very crux of this trial, the truth of the matter. I have a signed diktat from Steinthor your honour that authorises their presence here above all those other realms of Arbor where this group is wanted. Perhaps the graciousness of your court, your Honour, might allow this witness the opportunity to reveal what he knows before he and his band face their fate elsewhere?"

"Very well, I shall allow the witness… on this occasion only," Judge Coerceo agreed.

Malaphar clenched his fists behind his back. The Fire-Nymph was proving to be an annoyingly resourceful opponent, whose seemingly spontaneous witness selections, as if some magician pulling bunnies from bonnets in a travelling sideshow, as well as her mode of cross-examination was already waylaying the Angelic's methodical and carefully prepared prosecution. He also felt some dislike for the Judge, and not because he was Human and the attorney was not of the Human-liking disposition but, because the Judge appeared willing enough to entertain such unprofessional behaviour. Yet the attorney was beginning to realise that perhaps there was more to this trial than he was led to believe, and part of his reasons for not continuing his objection was his want to know what the Defence had up their sleeve.

The only time the accused gives up the centre of the courtroom floor is when the calling of a certain witness might threaten the safety of the court. Such witnesses are not brought in through the side entrance of the court and are not lead out by some disgruntled looking court clerk. These witnesses are in fact held beneath Compenso, in holding cells, or the cages they were transported in, and individually guarded. When the time comes for them to be called to testify their cage or cell is repositioned below the centre of the court, ready to be drawn up into the interior as the floor slowly retracts above the witness's head.

So, to the wide-eyed horror of those Delatorians that only knew the Zwerg-Riese as Ogres, Dok emerged from below the court like a caged pit-fighter. Though he was not of the physical stature of those remaining members of his gang, Dok still stood sixteen feet tall and was as imposing to fearful eyes as perhaps a fully-grown Atlation may have been. To Humans Giant or Dwarf-Giant makes little difference… both are still menacingly larger.

"Please state your name for the record," Fury asked in a broken voice, also taken aback by the sight of the witness.

Dok smirked. It had been a long time since anyone had said 'please' to him. "Dok," he replied simply.

"Dok…?"

"Son of Astaroth." This was not spoken with a smile but with a look of almost sad reflection. It briefly reminded him of Stolz, the home he had abandoned in his youth.

Malaphar raised an eyebrow in recognition, for the name Astaroth was not unknown to him – an Angelic who was as ruthless as Malaphar in his lifetime, who had died long ago but not before spawning Dok's paternal line.

"And your current occupation?"

This question did elicit a sly grin from the Dwarf-Giant. "Mercenary for hire, Miss."

"And your last client?"

"I'm afraid I'd be breaking client privileges if I were to tell you Miss," Dok replied. Ever defiant in the face of authority, Dok found he was enjoying the attention of a full court, having previously only had the company of his six-gang members to while away his time in hiding, and was not willing to comply without some mischief. Both he and Fury knew it wouldn't last however, not if he wanted to save his neck from the noose of Steinthor's Law-Bringers.

"The Royal Queen of Delator," Dok continued slowly and with emphasis. Those words elicited such a reaction from the court that Judge Coerceo spent the next few minute-turns knocking his gavel in an attempt to bring about some degree of order.

"What was the job for which you were hired?"

"The retrieval of the Carmen Speculum."

"Do you not mean theft?" Fury asked flatly.

"Well, as I understand it the item did belong to the Royal family and the Queen is a part of that royal family… can one steal from him or herself I wonder?"

"So the Queen, or someone in her charge, welcomed you through the door, opened the palace vault and handed the mirror to you?"

"No."

"The King then perhaps?"

"No."

"Then pray tell what was you mode of entry?"

"A stealth entry," Dok replied proudly, "through the Palace kitchens and then through the – "

"A break in?"

"We tried not to break anything, stealthy remember."

"A robbery then."

"If you like."

"Did you *steal* any other items when you were in the palace vault?"

"We took a few items."

"And did the Queen ask you to 'retrieve' those items?" Fury pressed.

"Not all of them."

"But you said the main reason for your being hired was the Carmen Speculum, so why the other items? What were the Queen's instructions?"

Dok smiled. If he was going to play along with the terms of his incarceration then he was going to ensure that those charged with his treatment had to work hard for their rewards. Finally the Fire-Nymph had asked something for which there could be no ambiguity.

"She said she wanted it to look like the vault had been plundered. Her primary item was the mirror though, as long as we got out of the palace with that then – "

"Then your mission would be accomplished."

"Yes."

"Your Honour," Malaphar interrupted with a look of bemusement that was not totally disingenuous. "I am wondering what any of this has to do with the murder Miss Hood has committed." It was not so much a question as a statement of fact.

"It concerns the individual Abigail is accused of murdering. If the Defence could be allowed a little latitude your Honour?" Fury quickly stated.

"I am sure you are as eager as I to know this *truth* the Defence claim to be able to produce Mr Naberius?" the Judge asked.

"I am positively on tenterhooks your Honour," Malaphar replied with some element of sarcasm, before shaking his head at the jury and animatedly rolling his eyes in mock despair. The display was lost on the jury members who were still dealing with the knowledge that their Queen had been party to a crime.

"But you were caught?" Fury continued.

"Eventually," Dok replied.

"Do you know how?"

"A witness."

"That's correct. Hansel," Fury stated to the rest of the court. "You considered threatening the Queen did you not?"

"When one's back is to the wall, one considers all means of possible escape."

"Did anyone visit you while your were in the custody of the Magistratum? The Queen perhaps?" Fury asked.

"One of her servants. A Secarius who goes by the name of Snow White."

"What did she say?"

"Nothing, until I told her that only our release would guarantee our silence."

"And then the next thing you know you are released and the eyewitness Hansel is dead. Many might not see this as mere coincidence."

"Objection," Malaphar called in a disinterested tone.

"Dok, do you believe that the Queen ordered that Hansel be killed before he identified you so that you and your gang could be released… to 'guarantee your silence' as you put it," Fury re-phrased.

The court had silenced and the various whisperings that had been conducted throughout the examination of the Dwarf-Giant had been quelled by a number of raised forefingers to the lips by those desperate to know more.

"Yes."

"Thank you. No further questions your Honour," Fury concluded, receiving a nod of approval from Vincent as she retook her seat.

"Did this Snow White individual tell you that the Queen was having Hansel killed?" Malaphar asked sharply.

"No," Dok replied.

"Did she say she was going to kill Hansel herself?"

"No."

"Did she say Hansel would in fact be killed at all?"

"No."

"Did she even mention anybody called Hansel?"

"No."

"And yet you believe that your original release was owed to this Hansel being killed."

"Yes. I'm sure you're familiar with Delatorian jurisprudence enough to know that in the absence of any material evidence an accused may only be held in custody for a limited period of time. Hansel would have provided that material evidence would he have not?" Dok didn't particularly like being barked at by anybody, especially some seemingly arrogant self-aggrandising Angelic who had no part in his deal with Elliot.

"Dok," Malaphar began patronisingly, "is it not arguable that the charges against you were dropped by the Queen? After all it was *her* vault as you state."

"It's arguable."

"Then it would be equally arguable that Miss Hood's murder of Hansel had nothing to do with you or the Queen or some magic mirror?"

"Awfully coincidental though isn't it?" Dok replied, mimicking Malaphar's highbrow accent.

"Is it arguable? Just as likely as any other ridiculous conspiracy the Defence are hoping for us to believe?"

"It's arguable."

"No further questions your Honour." Malaphar retook his seat but not before giving the Dwarf-Giant a disapproving shake of the head. Whilst the Vigilantag had bartered a deal to avoid execution they still had to answer to the crimes they had committed all over Arbor, and Malaphar hoped that he would be retained to prosecute Dok and his band of criminals in the trials to come. The Angelic promised to himself that he would deliver something more scathing than a number of direct questions should next they meet.

"Your Honour, the Defence respectfully requests a conference in chambers so that the complexities of the next witness may be discussed. The manner of its presentation may be... unorthodox," Fury stated.

"Now that is a surprise," Malaphar criticised under his breath, just audible enough for the Judge and Fury to have heard him.

"Of course Mr Naberius may also be party to the discussion, if he so wishes," Fury added in response.

"And how long do you think these discussions might take," asked the Judge."

"Thirty minute-turns perhaps, your Honour. It would really depend upon Mr Naberius' input and of course your own, your Honour."

"Very well Miss Fury," Judge Coerceo acceded. "Court adjourned. We shall reconvene for the afternoon session, after lunch, little point stopping and starting."

"Quite, your Honour," Fury smiled.

Fury had made the request for closed conference for two reasons. The first reason was to buy Elliot enough time to make it to the Palace and be prepared for his portion of the Defence. The schedule had been pushed up due to the Royal accountant being unaccounted for, and Fury guessed, quite correctly, that Eliot was not ready. By asking for a conference session the Fire-Nymph hoped to sway the Judge to reconvene after the mid-day break for lunch, as there would be little point in continuing after the conference only for the afternoon ring-hour recess to be called soon after. Given that two witnesses had already been heard today the disruption to the proceedings would only be minor. It was to Fury's relief then when the Judge agreed to her request.

The second reason was that Fury felt it prudent to seek the Judge's opinion on the complexities of the next part of the Defence's case. Their first witness had bent absent, and the second had been riskily introduced, albeit a signed edict from Steinthor had been obtained, as such Fury did not want to risk Malaphar openly objecting in court to the next. She couldn't risk the Judge subsequently denying the Defence the opportunity to present evidence pivotal to the case if such an objection was sustained. Elliot's presence at the Palace would be useless if nobody could bear witness to the same. Fury felt confident enough that the evidence would be allowed if she could convince the Judge that it was valid and, more importantly, legal.

Thus, while the court members dispersed for a lengthy recess and a long luncheon, Fury collected her thoughts and her papers and made her way to the Judges chambers, having paused briefly to explain her motives to Vincent and Epona (who both approved), where she would reveal to Judge Coerceo why exactly the Defence's next witness (more in the form of an exhibit) was actually a magically imbued mirror. Fury was ready for a great deal of criticism from Malaphar.

30

Elliot and Fabianus pulled up outside the Royal Palace to find the gates wide open and a number of uniformed stable hands ready to slowly usher the lawyers' Woodlice into the courtyard. Several more servants promptly assisted in the unbinding of the Carmen Speculum, after a few words of warning as to the delicate nature of the item from Elliot, and proceeded to carry it off towards the main Palace building.

"Surprisingly helpful aren't they… considering," Fabianus commented. Elliot nodded in agreement.

Must be the King's wanting, the young attorney thought to himself.

The lawyers flanked the ten-man strong procession, such was the number of bodies it took to shift the mirror, all the way to the throne room, and received more than a few curious looks from the palace staff as they went. The captain of the Delatorian Royal guard then ordered the mirror placed in the corner of the room with the reflective face towards the centre of the room… much to Elliot's relief.

"Wait here, the Queen shall be with you shortly. And don't look so concerned, I hear that she is quite pleased with your recovery of an item her Highness believed quite lost," the Captain re-assured the nervous looking lawyers, before clearing the room of staff and proceeding towards the throne room's grandiose double-doors.

"Thank you Fabes," Elliot said turning to his colleague and giving him a pat on the shoulder. "Perhaps it's best if you were not here when… you know."

"Good luck Elliot," the Liberan replied before departing the room solemnly.

"Thanks."

The great doors to the throne room slowly closed behind the Liberan and Elliot found himself alone. He looked towards an intricately crafted clockwork timepiece the size of a chest of drawers positioned to the rear of the room, which he recognised as having been produced by the great craftsman Koestler of Horologium, and sighed a deep sigh. He then turned to face the mirror, cast an eye over his reflection, to his surprise finding that he did not look as weary and exhausted as he felt, then nodded before oddly giving himself the thumbs up.

Three heavy knocks upon the throne room's side entrance brought the lawyer's attention back towards the centre of the room, and he watched with a quickening pulse as the Queen of Delator gracefully entered.

*

The closed conference at Compenso concluded, much to Fury's surprise, after only fourteen minute-turns. Of course Malaphar had objected profusely following Fury's presentation to the Judge, argued the legitimacy of the evidence, how the prosecution had no right of reply to the witness, even how the whole affair was tantamount to entrapment. Judge Coerceo was not ignorant to the Angelic's objections yet gave Fury ample opportunity to answer each of the prosecution attorney's concerns in turn uninterrupted. The Fire-Nymph conducted herself admirably and resisted the temptation to flare up in response to her opponent's criticisms. It was not until Fury produced the signed counterpart to Elliot's letter to the King that the Judge agreed to allow the Defence's new evidence. Judge Coerceo was not about to ignore the written authority of the Monarch, yet before dismissing the lawyers he did point out that the subsequent evidence had just an equal chance of failure as it did success.

Whilst Vincent made preparations for Blackstone's magically imbued mirror to be moved to the courtroom, Fury shared a long lunch with Epona in the substandard eatery that was Compenso's canteen; it often being the case that courthouse restaurants are not the greatest of Arbor's culinary establishments.

Both had little to say to each other about the case, and Fury still seemed preoccupied with the Judge's closing words. Epona picked at her unappetising omelette and reflected upon the case thus far.

"Is it always like this at Blackstone's?" Epona finally uttered.

"Sometimes its normal. Elliot does enjoy mixing it up," Fury nodded.

"That's good… at least I won't get bored," replied the Mare'ess with a meek smile.

The court clerk, whom Fury had criticised for failing to find Aerarius Artifex, entered the canteen and informed Fury that court would reconvene in ten minute-turns.

"Here we go," Fury sighed turning to her worried looking colleague. "Don't look so distraught, if Elliot fails and they kill him, at least you'll have a shot at promotion," Fury added with her own meek smile.

Epona promptly galloped to the nearest female restroom and emptied her nerve-wracked stomach of her undigested omelette.

A slightly off-colour Mare'ess re-entered the courtroom to find everyone staring intently into its centre as if under some strange spell. Abigail's stall remained retracted to the edge of the floor and Dok's cage had been lowered back down into Compenso's underground complex during the recess and the floor had closed back up above it. Another object now held centre stage; a great pyramid, the apex of which stood near twenty feet above ground. It was draped with a potato sack weave of heavy brown cloth. Vincent was stood at one of the corners of the pyramid, his head hidden under its covering.

Epona looked up to Fury, who had already re-established herself upon her statue's platform, and gave her a curious glance. Fury quietly beckoned her over to co-counsel's row with a subtle nod of the head.

Then suddenly Vincent reappeared, breathed a slow heavy sigh, and pulled away the cloth covering to reveal what truly stood beneath.

A simultaneous gasp sounded across the whole of the court from those present as if all had just witnessed some sideshow conjurer produce a pink mammoth from where before there was nothing.

Three triangular faces of polished mirror pane protruded from the courtroom floor like a crystal stalagmite, each side viewable from the dock and jury box, the attorney's platforms and the gallery, and the Judge's bench respectively.

Yet the mirrored surfaces did not reflect those open-mouthed, wide-eyed faces of those in the gallery, or Malaphar's curious gaze complete with cocked eyebrow, or Fury's somewhat surprised expression, or even Abigail's look of panic from the dock of the accused. Instead each surface showed Elliot Blackstone kneeling quite peacefully open one knee, head bowed in respect, before the great gilded thrones of the Delatorian Royal Palace.

Everyone could hear footsteps now, growing louder, and those of the worrisome disposition turned around in their seats or craned their necks to fathom where the sound was coming from. Those more spatially aware knew exactly from where the footfalls were emanating. Not only could the population of Compenso see into the Delatorian throne room, the great glass pyramid also allowed them to hear all that was going on within.

*

Two sets of feet? Elliot thought, *no three... two wearing boots the other soft soles... that means...*

"You may rise Mr Blackstone," the Queen graciously commanded.

The young attorney did so and immediately his heart began to sink. The Queen was already seated upon her throne, wrapped in a figure hugging dress of icy blue and a shawl of pale Wolven pelt, the toothless head of which covered her left shoulder like a piece of tribal armour. Upon her head was a ringlet crown of translucent amber, a rare shade of ivory, which caught the light like a halo. Standing to her left behind her throne stood Rose Red, Emilita Letalis, dressed in an armoured body suit an uncharacteristically sombre shade of dark ochre. A brace of daggers hung loose about her small waist and her trademark red rose flower adorned her right ear. To the Queen's right shoulder, and the cause of Elliot's dejection, was the previously couch-sprawling comatose figure of Snow White, Krystina Letalis.

So she ran back to the Queen, loyal to the last… so much for Secarii –

"Our thanks for recovering our property Mr Blackstone," spoke the Queen, interrupting Elliot's train of thought.

"You are most welcome, your Majesty," replied Elliot as courteously as he could as he battled with his nerves. "Of course, part of the trouble, your Highness, was knowing where to look. We were led to believe it was not in fact not missing at all."

"Is that so."

"As such, your Highness, underwriters have seen fit to reject your insurance claim."

"Aerarius will be disappointed," the Queen lied, knowing full well that the royal accountant was dead. "And what, may we ask, was the reason for their decision.?"

"It may interest your Majesty to know that we have apprehended the six remaining members of the Vigilantag Seven." Elliot allowed his eyes to drift slowly to Snow White. The Secarius gave away nothing, even though they both knew she was responsible for Blöd's disappearance. She locked the attorney's stare and there was a momentary flash of recognition… the portraits that hung in Elliot's living room… Blöd's dying words. Krystina lowered her gaze to her feet as if saddened.

The Queen studied Elliot with interest. Was he bluffing?

"I have yet to question them myself, but what they have said thus far has been… interesting," Elliot continued.

While it might have been difficult for the Half-Angelic to read the Queen's mind, his heightened senses were responsive enough to pick up a shift in what the Monarch was feeling; a flicker of fear, then a slight disruption as if her disordered thoughts were rationalising upon a strategy… then nothing… coldness.

The Queen raised a gloved hand up to Snow White and beckoned her near with a curl of her forefinger. Krystina slowly stepped forward and bent low to hear what instructions the Queen wished to relay.

Snow White nodded her head, straightened up, and slowly marched to where Elliot was standing. The sound of her heels on the polished Palace marble eerily echoed through the throne room, like the mechanical movements of a clock-work time piece counting down towards Elliot's remaining time on the World-Tree.

Krystina lightly brushed Elliot's shoulder with her own as she came level. Then she stepped behind him and drew close until the attorney could feel the assassin's warm breath on the back of his neck.

Suddenly Elliot felt his left leg buckle and he fell to the ground. He stretched out his hands to stop his head from smashing into the floor that was rushing up to meet it. There was a sound like that of high-pitched violin string, the hum of which reverberated on the air. Then there was a sudden rush, a sharp breeze, then, where only moments before Elliot had felt the assassin's controlled exhalations upon his neck, he now felt the icy touch of folded steel. Krystina balanced the tip of her sword before the attorney's throat.

Back at Compenso a hysterical Abigail Hood broke down in tears.

"Killing me won't help anything," Elliot managed, straining to contain his pounding heart.

"That's what they all they say," the Queen replied coldly.

"Is that what Hansel said?"

"You should ask Miss Hood. Rose tells me you two have quite the history together. Childhood friends, how sweet." There was malice in her voice.

"Is it worth all the death?" Elliot asked, flicking his gaze towards the Carmen Speculum.

"More than you shall ever know!" the Queen roared. "Ah, my magic mirror," she continued in a quieter tone, like one of fond reflection, as she rose from her seat and approached the mirror's carved frame. "What this shall reveal is worth a thousand lives." The Queen passed her fingertips over the mirror, barely touching its polished surface. It was like she was trying to channel its power through the very core of her being, it was like she was trying to communicate with it… welcoming it home.

"Is anything worth a thousand lives?" Elliot replied, his voice breaking as he thought of Abigail's life.

The words jolted the Queen back to reality and her eyes flashed open. "Enough!" she barked, and then snapped her fingers.

Elliot felt the tip of Snow White's blade leave his neck. He could see Krystina's shadow cast over him… see her stance… see the sword raised above her shoulder.

"Wait!" Elliot called out as he saw the sword's shadow rush towards his neck. It stopped a hair's breadth from his throat.

The Queen turned to face the attorney. She approached him and bent low to his face. Elliot felt the soft silk of her gloved hand upon his cheek.

"I'm just trying to understand," Elliot managed, the tension tearing his heart asunder.

"We all are," the Queen whispered close to his ear. She then slowly pulled herself away and walked back to the mirror. She studied her reflection, the growing lines of age desperately trying to claw their way from the corners of her eyes, the rest of her face succumbing to the physical effects of worry… of restless nights. "You've never had children of your own have you," the Queen continued in a tone that was almost chatty, much removed from the rage of a moment ago.

Elliot shook his head gently, conscious that Snow White's blade was still near.

"I thought not… so young, like my son. You must be his age… still so young. You can't imagine what it must be like to think you might lose a first born."

"Like losing a childhood friend," Elliot ventured.

"Nothing of the sort!" The Queen's rage had returned. Then no sooner had it done so than she calmed again, even paused a moment to gently brush her Wolven pelt shawl. "We guess it must be our fault really, my fault… wrap them in wool we do. No, not our fault!" she corrected herself. "Arbor's fault, the World-Tree! To think it can take away my son!"

She turned back to Elliot, approached and took a knee beside him, caressed his face again as if it where the face of Prince Phelan. Then she continued in a tone much like that of a mother recounting a bedtime story to a sleepy child.

"You see, once upon a time, not so long ago, the Queen of Delator went to visit a Soothsayer… a Teller. And do you know what she said to me, do you?"

Elliot shook his head gently.

"That my son would die. That my sweet Prince Phelan would *die*." There was shock in her voice and an expression of miscomprehension dramatically drawn across her face. Then she shook her head and continued. "She saw it, saw his future… his death." The Queen peered into empty space, relived her meeting with the fortune-teller and how it made her feel. A tear welled up in the corner of her right eye then trickled down her cheek.

Elliot remained silent. He wanted to say something, to comfort the Queen, to show that he did understand the hurt. He found himself thinking back to when the Venator, Wilheim Tell, visited his parent's house and told him that Abigail's family had been killed.

"I had to know for myself, you see," the Monarch continued. "Had to know the truth."

"The mirror," Elliot whispered.

"The Carmen Speculum. He wouldn't let me have it of course, told me it was cursed. My husband wouldn't let me save our son. The wisdom of Kings!" she laughed, throwing her head back. Then the laughter petered out till it became a low drawn out sigh. "So I took it," the Queen added forcefully.

"You hired the Vigilantag Seven," said Elliot.

"Buffoons! I should have done it myself."

"Because Hansel saw them."

"What he was doing in the Palace in the first place I can only imagine. A secret visit with your Miss Hood no doubt. And to think those idiots thought they could threaten me! Me!"

"The gang was going to shop you to the Magistratum."

"I should have had them killed! But alas," the Queen sighed, "they had my mirror."

"So you had Hansel killed instead."

"He should have kept out of other people's affairs. To my surprise I learned that he was Hood's love interest. Our Meretrix and Secarius in training, Abigail Hood. Such a fortunate twist of fate."

"Abigail was being trained as an assassin?" Elliot asked in disbelief.

"Those previously traumatised often make the best killers," the Queen replied looking up at Snow White and giving her a knowing grin.

"But she would never – "

"Not at first. Not without some… some persuasion."

"You brainwashed her."

"I programmed her. And how joyous it was. Yes she had barriers, they always do. But in the end I brought out her… her *feral* side one might say."

"You used her experience with the Wolven," Elliot guessed.

"You are a clever boy," the Queen replied squeezing Elliot's chin between gloved thumb and forefinger. "Do you know what Wolven blood does if administered in small enough doses?"

Elliot shook his head slowly in order to keep the Queen talking, though in truth he did know.

"It gradually changes oneself. Makes own more suggestible. Gives one a killer's instinct. It's not like being bitten by a Wolven, no, no, quite different."

"But how?"

"How Abigail loved her apples. A drop of Wolven blood together with a potion of my own design insured the fruit's flesh, once consumed, would spread the Wolven virus into her veins like a – "

"Like a poison. And you knew eventually Hansel would confide in Abigail and then – "

"And that is when her programming would come into effect," the Queen added, clapping her hands together. "I know! I was surprised as you to learn how efficiently she took up her new assignment. Between me learning of the identity of the robbery witness, to learning that it was actually Hood's current lover, to getting her to kill him, all in the space of a few weeks. Quite remarkable."

Elliot allowed his head to sag. It was done.

"So now you know," the Queen concluded rising to her feet.

"Now we know," Elliot replied.

The Queen then looked to Snow White, nodded her head, and then turned her back on Elliot as she walked towards her throne.

Elliot turned his head briefly to the Carmen Speculum, gazed at his reflection, and closed his eyes.

*

Back at Compenso Judge Coerceo almost destroyed his gavel attempting to restore order to a court that had gone into a frenzy. Amidst the jeers and shouts and the incensed voices of those in passionate debate, the pyramid mirror, which had relayed the whole of the Queen's confession, sank silently beneath the court's floor.

As it disappeared from view, Abigail, screaming Elliot's name through a flood of tears, held out her hand in desperate hope that the attorney might step through the mirror and take it.

Elliot hoped that Vincent had, upon his signal, removed the mirror from sight. He hoped that Abigail would be spared the sight of his death.

He always imagined that Death would come swiftly, out of the blue, catching him unawares, like a sudden slap to the face that sobered one up enough to realise that time had been called. But it didn't, and the Half-Angelic attorney waited for what seem like an eternity for Snow White's sword to come down upon his neck.

It never did.

Instead, a bemused looking Queen watched curiously as her bodyguard and assassin cast her sword aside. As the blade clanged against the stone floor Elliot slowly drew open his eyes.

"By Secarii Law I hereby recognise that Elliot Blackstone is now my keeper," Krystina stated.

"Have you lost your mind Snow!" the Queen snapped. "Kill him."

The assassin shook her head defiantly.

"Sister?"

"Emilita, Blöd saved me from the Vigilantag… brought me to Elliot, entrusted Elliot with my care. When I took Blöd's life I didn't realise I was killing someone to whom I owed a life-debt. And so my life passed to Elliot." There was no panic in Krystina's voice, none of the desperation that comes from trying to make confused listeners understand. Instead she was composed and calm and terrifyingly lucid.

Emilita knew, as soon as her sister had stopped talking, that all of it was true. She had a choice to make now, for her life still belonged to the Queen. Would she deny a Monarch or kill her own sister.

The Queen watched, stunned, as Rose Red unclasped the brace of daggers from around her waist, allowing it to fall to the ground, before joining Snow White's side. The two former Royal assassins embraced each other then helped their new master, Elliot Blackstone, to his feet.

Elliot brushed himself down, ever the dramatist, and simply turned to leave, his newly acquired bodyguards stepping aside before following him.

"You forget your place!" screamed the Queen rising to her feet. "You forget who I am! You forget who had you trained!" She picked up Rose Red's abandoned daggers, unsheathed a claw handled one, and slowly stalked towards the departing lawyer.

She managed only a few paces before three loud knocks from behind the throne room's closed main double doors brought her to a halt. A moment later they silently swung open to reveal the King of Delator.

"What have you done?" he asked his Queen in a voice that had lost its regal authority and was hoarse and broken. He looked to his wife from across the throne room with bitter disappointment. Then anger. He stormed passed Elliot, Snow White and Rose Red without even acknowledging them. "Why?" he asked standing before his Queen.

"The mirror, my love, we can save – " she replied throwing her arm up and pointing towards the Carmen Speculum.

"He's already dead," the King managed, close to tears now.

"No, no… we can still see his future. There's time to – "

"He's gone. He was Hansel. You…"

The Queen's eyes glazed over. She looked lost then, as if she were mentally repeating her King's last statement over and over, confused as to why the words wouldn't register… how it seemed nonsensical.

"No, no… he…"

"What have done?" the King sobbed. "What have you done to our boy?"

Shock seized upon the Queen and she dropped the dagger she was clutching. Her hands went to her mouth and she shook her head furiously. Finally she broke down and slumped to the ground like a puppet having had its strings cut. Her shoulders began to shudder and gradually, silent at first as she looked up to her husband's face, her own face contorted with a woe that wouldn't get passed the lump in her throat, she began to weep.

The King backed away shaking his head and the Queen instinctively reached to grab his ankle, clinging on desperately as all hope and joy and love was being shredded away. Tried as she might to hold on, the King bent down and released the Queen's grip upon him. He backed away again but this time found no resistance. The Queen had curled up on the marbled floor, a clawed hand to her face, wailing uncontrollably.

By the time she recovered enough to glance up, she found that her King had left through the throne room side door and her bodyguards and Elliot were nowhere to be seen. She was alone… abandoned, left to her grief and the terrifying realisation that she was responsible for the death of her son.

As Elliot walked through the Palace on his way back to Compenso, escorted by Rose and Snow, he did so to the echoing howl of the Queen's heartrending cries.

31

The trial of Abigail Hood concluded within Judge Coerceo's closed chambers. Compenso had fallen into disarray and the Judge had no option but to pull both the Prosecution and Defence attorneys aside.

Fury, still left with the image of Elliot's imminent death, said little and her Angelic opponent would have otherwise embarked on a stinging indictment of the Defence's conduct during the trial had he not been uncharacteristically sedate himself. For all intents and purposes the trial was over. The fall of a Monarch and the fate of a Meretrix had become vaguely comparable, and Malaphar satisfied himself that at least one Human had suffered during the course of the proceedings.

The Judge however did not throw out the charges against Abigail Hood until he had voiced his own concerns, fuelled with the anger of having his courtroom reduced to a circus. His criticisms fell on Fury's deaf ears. She merely nodded automatically at those intervals when the Judge's ranting paused. She was preoccupied with the safety of her colleague and friend, and the criticisms of a Judge were little in comparison.

Elliot arrived outside the court alone, having discharged the assassins until such time when he might call upon their services, and just in time to see Abigail breathe free air upon the steps of the courthouse. Epona, Fury and Vincent followed close behind her.

Abigail, though free, carried herself as if she was one of the living dead, her shoulders dropped, her back bent and her head held low. She shuffled along whilst the rest of the Blackstone's Defence team watched her with a collected feeling of sadness.

It wasn't until she looked up and saw Elliot approaching that a surge of life changed her demeanour entirely. She bolted from Compenso's steps and flung her arms around the extremely weary but relatively relieved looking attorney. No slaps around the face this time, or beating fists upon his chest, which would have been due punishment for having again put his head quite literally on the line, just the vice like grip of Abigail's arms around his neck and the feel of her tears upon his cheek. Elliot held her tight, fearing that if he let her go all of time would unravel, that they might find themselves back at the Magistratum holding cells, or back in court, or even back at his parent's house all those ring-years ago.

They stayed like that for a long time, holding each other, and when Elliot finally looked up from Abigail's shoulder did he see the welcoming sight of his loyal Defence team; Epona punching the air with a clenched fist, Fury cross-armed and shaking her head in disbelief, a coy grin spread subtly upon her lips, and Vincent, who roguishly saluted him before raising a cupped hand to his lips.

Absolutely, Elliot thought. *Absolutely*.

*

In the weeks that followed much of Delator was still reeling from the impact of their Queen's implicit involvement in the death of Hansel, and many found their feelings torn between their sense of justice and the need for punishment and their loyalty to a Monarchy that had long nurtured the capital city and its inhabitants.

Those voices of dissension quickly faded, as the Palace released news of the Prince's death, and the anger towards a Queen was quickly replaced with the woeful mourning of Delator's favourite son. The Palace never released the true nature of Prince Phelan's death, for fear that it would bring about the end of the Monarchy altogether, and the official story was that he had perished whilst hunting Wolven.

Yet there were a suspicious few that doubted the validity of the story, and even whilst the Prince's funeral procession weaved through the city's crowd filled streets, those Delatorian conspiracy theorists still maintained, quite correctly, that Hansel and Prince Phelan were in fact the same person.

As for the Queen, she slowly withdrew from public life and even refused to attend the funeral of her son. Rumour had it that she locked herself away in the Prince's room at the Palace and became a recluse. In reality the King returned from burying his son to find that she had taken her own life, a half-eaten poisoned apple still gripped in her hand, the stain of dried tears upon her cold face.

The Queen never could come to terms with what she done. Death was the only release, the only way for her to see her son again.

The celebrations back at Blackstone's didn't begin until a number of days after the trial of Abigail Hood had ended. During that time Elliot had taken Abigail back to his parents home for a welcome respite. Elliot only returned to Tartarus after Abigail had reluctantly agreed to be placed under the care of Venator Wilhelm Tell, after he had made an impromptu visit to Elliot's parents to tell them all that without the Venator's help Abigail might never be fully free of the effects of the trace amounts of Wolven blood that still coursed through her veins.

"How's Abigail?" Epona asked as her mentor made his way to his desk.

"Well, relatively speaking. She's with the Venators," Elliot replied.

Fury and Vincent suddenly bundled past the office door. They were giggling and in cahoots about something particularly mischievous sounding. Elliot sensed a fondness between the Fire-Nymph and the Sandman that had flurried since the stress of Abigail's trial had passed.

"A two way mirror!" Vincent grinned. "So where is the real Carmen Speculum hey Elliot? You haven't been looking up the future have you?"

"We don't need a mirror for that Vince," Fury replied, "I foresee a great many drinks lined up at Brimstone's bar," she continued in a ghostly voice that brought a smile to Epona's face. "It's good to have you back Elliot you crazy lawyer you."

Then there were heavy footfalls and the three lawyers and the trainee promptly straightened themselves up and fixed their collars and ties. Asmodeus was approaching, his hands stuffed into his pockets.

He popped his head into Elliot's office and eyed the four colleagues with suspicion.

"Uncle," Elliot greeted.

"Elliot," Asmodeus replied. "Well, what are you all standing around for, there are a line of drinks at Brimstone's just begging to be drunk." And with that he continued on his way to the bar with a satisfied grin on his face. Vincent and Fury nodded approvingly and followed.

"Give me a ring-hour," Elliot called after them, "there's something I've got to do first."

"Suit yourself, we'll probably be there all day… and night…" replied Vincent as his voice trailed off down the corridor.

"So?" Elliot asked turning to Epona. "Coming?"

"Another adventure?" Epona replied. Elliot just tapped his nose conspiratorially, whipped his jacket back on, retrieved a twine bound parcel from his desk, and strolled out of his office.

Epona was far too curious not to follow.

*

"I want to tell you a tale," Elliot began, thirty minute-turns later, as he sat with Epona upon a stool in Briana Ce'aul's thatched hut, deep within the heart of Silva Tenebrae Forest. "But it doesn't end well I warn you."

"And I thought you were here for another reading. Remember what I told you the last time? So small were you back then," Briana replied.

"I remember."

To Epona's reckoning Briana must have been at least one hundred and fifty ring-years old, and the Mare'ess likened her appearance to those aged witches of folk tales of old, all hooked nosed and wrinkled.

"It is about a Teller," Elliot continued, "who long ago had a daughter. The daughter fell in love with a handsome young nobleman who was destined to become King of Delator… the current King's father in fact. Yet the love between him and the girl was forbidden, for she was the gypsy daughter of a travelling Teller and he was of Royalty."

Briana's grey eyes clouded over and she seemed saddened.

"The girl found that she could not live without the man's love, and in despair she took her own life. This greatly disturbed her mother the Teller, and she promised to take revenge upon the Royals for causing her daughter's death. She bound the girl's soul into a mirror and when the time came sold it to the son of the man who had seduced her daughter. This King bought the mirror in the hope that it would show him and his first wife a joyous future, for this is what the Teller had sold it to him as being capable of showing." Elliot paused briefly, allowing his words to sink into Briana's thoughts. "But instead the mirror showed nothing but death, driving the King's young Queen to kill herself, such was the malice of the mirror's spirit. Eventually it would cause the capture of a murderous band of Zwerg-Riese, whom had found false security in the mirror's dependability, and in turn it would bring about the death of a Prince, as a new Queen fought desperately to get hold of it. Do you know what the girl's name was Briana… the girl whose sole was bound into the mirror?"

"Carmen," the Teller whispered.

"I think she wants to be free." Elliot took the bound package from his satchel and passed it to the old Soothsayer. Briana tentatively unwrapped the parcel, carefully pulled at the knotted cord and separated the brown packaging paper. From within the parcel she pulled a silver lined hand mirror. In its centre she saw her daughter's kind and smiling face, exactly the way Briana had remembered her all those ring-years ago, unchanged by the passing of time. The Teller was overcome with emotion and burst into tears.

Epona wanted to comfort her but Elliot silently suggested they leave.

"Only you can break the spell Briana," Elliot concluded as he stepped out of the small hut with Epona.

The lawyers proceeded a few feet before the crying from within the Teller's hut ceased. It was replaced with a slow murmur, the ancient text of an arcane incantation. They heard the spell trail off till it became inaudible, before hearing the sudden sound of smashing glass.

Now it's over, Elliot thought to himself comfortingly as he and Epona passed through Silva-Tenebrae.

"I'm not the greatest fan of this forest you know," Epona said with a sigh.

"Agreed."

"Elliot, can I ask you a question?"

The Half-Angelic attorney looked through the forest's thick canopy and watched as the sky slowly turned to crimson as the sun receded. He thought of all that had happened during the past month, all the pain and the risk and the sadness, and how only now could the matter be considered closed and his documents in the case of Abigail Hood be safely filed away. He thought of how he wanted nothing more but to return to Brimstone's and sit round a booth with his colleagues and his uncle and laugh and begin the reminiscing and the story telling and the over exaggerations that would naturally flow from the same, accompanied with a full goblet of 'Merlot Diavolo'.

"Of course you can," Elliot smiled turning to Epona.

The young Centaur had come along in leaps and bounds since joining Blackstone's and Elliot felt a great sense of pride for the Mare'ess. He had asked a lot from Epona during the course of Abigail's trial, more than others might have otherwise accepted, and Epona had conducted herself admirably. Elliot looked forward to their next case together.

"Erm," Epona began half unsure, "why *is* your desk made out of a coffin?"

"Ah, well…"